HEADING

West

BY DORIS BETTS

SCRIBNER PAPERBACK FICTION
Published by Simon & Schuster

New York   London   Toronto   Sydney   Tokyo   Singapore

SCRIBNER PAPERBACK FICTION
Simon & Schuster Inc.
Rockefeller Center
1230 Avenue of the Americas
New York, NY 10020

First Scribner Paperback Fiction Edition 1995
Previously published by Alfred A. Knopf, Inc.

SCRIBNER PAPERBACK FICTION and design
are trademarks of Simon & Schuster Inc.

Designed by Irving Perkins Assoc.
Manufactured in the United States of America

1   3   5   7   9   10   8   6   4   2

Library of Congress Cataloging-in-Publication Data

Betts, Doris.
Heading West/Doris Betts.
p. cm.
I. Title.
PS3552.E84H4   1995
813' .54—dc20   95-8452
CIP

ISBN 0-684-80115-9

For Dennis G. Donovan
1932–1978
Professor of English
University of North Carolina
Chapel Hill, N.C.

PART

One

1

Every summer thousands of cars come rolling like shiny marbles through the ancient gneiss of the southern Appalachians and clot in many colors at overlooks and parking zones. At such stops, vacationing families pose year after year before the same rock slabs: they growing taller or older, the rock holding still.

The summer before this one, a man, his wife, and her sister had photographed themselves at Looking Glass Rock, by the Oconaluftee River, then with the old costumed Indian in Cherokee. In each place they had snapped two sets of pictures: first, Eddie Rayburn leaning into his wife, Faye, with a possessive smile, then one of Faye's sister alone with her teeth bared. The sister had wanted to take a Caribbean cruise by herself.

This August the threesome again drove west, the married couple paired in the front seat with the best view, the sister bouncing in back with food and luggage. She had still wanted to take a cruise. The sister's mind kept escaping Eddie's car. It floated down the Toe and Little Pigeon rivers and forgot the Rayburns forever. It ran away to the Indians. In Grenada it took up with gigolos.

"You couldn't drive a tank through those thickets!" Faye Rayburn exclaimed.

The sister's mind snaked downhill through laurel and rhododendron and emerged somewhere into a new and freer life.

"I'd hate to see my gas bill," Eddie grumbled. Nervously he kept checking that the yellow trailer was attached as they followed traffic west across the foothills of the Blue Ridge and Smoky mountains. Had the Rayburns or any of the other travelers paused for long outside their powerful cars, they might have learned what the Cherokee knew: not that they moved while the world was fixed in existence, but that the world moved with a roar and that in it they thinly, barely existed, perhaps as much as a snowflake standing in a fire. Nobody takes his week off from work, with pay, to find that out.

Especially Eddie Rayburn, the sister thought.

Winding switchbacks carried them past road markers that said WATCH FOR FALLING ROCK. The thought that these hills might be unstable also made Eddie nervous; the state of North Carolina, he felt, could *do* something about these avalanches if it set its mind to it. They were headed across the Blue Ridge to Fontana, planned to climb Mount Mitchell and even ride Tweetsie Railroad. Fake train robbers always attacked the fake railroad while passengers squealed. Mentally the sister galloped away with the gang and into a life of crime.

Miles north of their yellow camper, coming steadily south through Virginia, a lone man in a nondescript car had no plans except to see Miami. His own mind seldom left his body. Such concentration, he knew, made him superior.

Saturday the three vacationers blended with others, parked at rest areas, and ate Vienna sausages with bread and mayonnaise. The lone man drove Virginia back roads at night and ate in bad cafés. Dragging slowly over a great height, rain clouds dropped a thick curtain on the camper, later drizzled on the man's roof in Shenandoah.

Saturday night the yellow camper was in Price Memorial Park, where Eddie Rayburn complained that it was a waste of taxpayers' money to stock a lake with rainbow trout that wouldn't bite. By the shore the two sisters cooked hamburgers on a small grill. Eddie and Faye slept inside the camper and Faye said to him, "No. Not *here*. Not *now*."

Outside in a borrowed sleeping bag, the second woman thought: Anywhere; anytime. She watched a satellite slide through the black like a hot button.

Across Virginia, through the early dark, the other man continued to drive toward them.

The man liked to drive at night, where nothing was predictable, where a preoccupied cow could be discovered standing in the road, and dodged, where his headlights created Virginia in fragments as he passed.

What the man hated in the world, and could not name, was equilibrium. He had almost glimpsed its image once in a set of Rorschach cards with their black liquids dried into balanced forms and had blurted, "I am not like him!" He saw by the woman's face that he was making trouble for himself. Like whom? He had lied quickly, "Like those sissy dancers." Once he knew what she wanted he began to find trees with ink flowers, paired night cabbages and monkeys with black doorknobs in their heads; then, scraping bare his eleventh-grade education, had noted two beards like Shakespeare's and one dissected frog laid open like a pair of double doors. "Yes, doorknobs," he insisted, "to the back door." She was not satisfied with what he claimed to see. He did not stay long in that place and had few memories of it.

Now on a dark high road he drove deeper into the ripe summer. In one jacket pocket he carried a lot of money, in another the gun he never had to use. He did not intend to count the money until he got to Florida.

In Pulaski, he carried the heavy jacket over one arm into a grill that had a pool table in the back and an open jar of pickles waiting on every table. The ventilators must have been clogged with grease. He ordered barbecue and ate it mechanically.

He was tall with narrow eyes so embedded under sharp brows that they seemed slitted. As a boy, in the days when he was still able to confront mirrors, he had stood for hours waiting for his pimples to subside and concluded that this face, unlike his brother's, was built for silence. Now he avoided mirrors for fear his dead brother would look back at him, perhaps even speak.

When someone in the café asked for a match he shook his head, walked outside, and lit a cigarette, placing the filter neatly in the gap where one front tooth was broken. His movement revealed a tattoo on the forearm: a horseshoe, flower, several blue words. Nearby a theater had just opened its doors: *Dr. Zhivago.* A few couples straggled out of history and icy Russia toward the parking lot. The man ambled past the café.

A tall boy standing by his car saw the man coming and hurried across the street. Immediately the man spotted a long scratch the boy had drawn with a nail below the door handle. With a toothy smile on which his cigarette was impaled, he threw himself at the wheel and sped in a fast U-turn downhill. The boy trotted away on long legs. The man drove closer, jerked right, jumped the curb. He turned his headlights to bright. In the yellow blaze the boy's long astonished face snapped back over his shoulder; then he leaped between plate glass toward the locked door of a shop. The man nosed the car across the sidewalk to block him in. Behind them, the moviegoers at last had seen them, shouted, and begun to cluster. The man flicked his cigarette toward their voices. Plastered against the door, the boy had raised his thin right arm to throw an object he only dreamed of having, perhaps his discarded nail. So might a rooster threaten the ax with his wing. The man began tapping his horn as he hitched the car forward in matching jerks. In recoil the boy was swaying from the horn blasts against sheet glass. Now people came running down the sidewalk. With the heel of his hand the man bore down upon the horn and pinned the boy with its long scream. He threw suddenly into reverse. The boy, as if shot by the bang of the gear, winced and covered his face.

The man bounced his car backward into the gutter, shifted, roared down the street and away from Pulaski. Later, driving south with his window open, he often dropped his left fingers down the dark outside paint to feel the rough line in the metal. Sometimes he smiled.

The man spent Saturday night in a cheap motel. On the narrow mattress his lean body throbbed. He often feared he had cancer of the heart, which beat too heavily and made his bones vibrate like strings on a guitar. When his skin felt tight from excess blood and his bones were thrumming, it was as if his brother had filled him with the music of death.

From outside the room, yellow VACANCY light leaked onto his body. He curled up like a child and kinked his veins at knee and elbow, a trick learned from his brother. Feet and hands starved for blood and tingled; then numbness spread slowly inward and ate with sleep the body until only the central glowing coal was left to be restarted in daylight. The numb man slept without dreaming.

On Sunday, bored, he drove the Blue Ridge Parkway into North Carolina. Laurel and ferns came spilling downhill toward the highway. He bought a paper from a rack at the Sparta post office but found no mention of Friday's robbery. Because he read slowly, the search took a while.

Passersby, strolling to church, probably mistook him for a tourist. He was hard to describe, colorless, motionless. He had posed in the back row for institutional group photographs, staring hard at the lens; yet he could run his own finger across such pictures and almost miss his face. Once he had made a fine mug shot for the Baltimore police and had secretly wanted a print.

Though several passing men nodded, he noticed only that they were old and dressed in dark clothes too large, too long. Except as it might affect himself, he hardly noticed the existence of other people who, though located in the same world, passed him like birds or insects, doing whatever was natural for them to do. Half a dozen passed on the sidewalk now and were forgotten. When no one else walked by, the man counted almost eight hundred dollars and stuffed all but fifty into a paper bag under his front seat. Maybe he wouldn't like Florida?

He ate Sunday lunch in Little Switzerland. His waitress in the rustic inn was young and energetic; winters as a majorette she marched in Christmas parades. "We're always glad to have you northerners see our mountains," she prattled. He was not a northerner. She served small bowls of vegetables. "And the rain is over at last. One of the rangers claimed that the animals were lining up in the park two by two—you get it? For the new ark?"

Though the man said nothing, she chattered about a highway washout, the mineral show in Spruce Pine, the sourwood honey for sale down the road. The man thought briefly of taking her with him to Florida just to listen to her soft southern voice run on about nothing. Better than the radio.

"He'll show you his glass beehive, too!" she said with a giggle. It had been his experience that giggly women cried a lot. This one was also very young with breasts you could put a hand on but not under. He felt vaguely like masturbating if the time had been more convenient. His sexual desires, in any case, were not great. Sex, he had noticed, began in the body but somehow threw the mind skyward at the end. He preferred to be alone for that sensation; it simplified his reentry into flesh. I am not like my brother, he thought; appearances are deceiving.

While the dinner mint melted on his tongue the girl's face dissolved in his mind. From the cashier's counter he could no longer tell which waitress had served his table. He left no tip.

In the midafternoon, driving toward Asheville, he saw ahead the blinking blue light that meant police, so with a U-turn at Craggy Gardens he sped back the other way. Perhaps he should get off the main road until dark. He could have driven to Mount Mitchell Tower or blended with the crowd at the mineral museum but opted for distance and, at last, a rough unpaved road that promised picnic areas and Lake James at its far end.

Once off the manicured parkway he found the rocky road steep, curving, hemmed in by chokeberry and dog hobble. On one side lay Linville Gorge, twelve miles of wilderness where Marines practiced survival tactics and Boy Scouts sometimes died. He had never cared much for woods or mountains. Cursing, he bounced on the seat and fought the steep grade until he came finally to an empty parking area with three stone platforms built over the great ravine. Deep under clotted trees he parked, stood impassive in the cool shade. Everything smelled of black dirt and worms.

He walked down the huge granite stairs to sit on the stone wall of the overlook. Far below, the Linville River, brown with silt, ran between steep walls and hemlocks as blue green as the sea. Across the gorge were sheer gray cliffs with galax and myrtle clinging in the cracks. None of it interested him. He lay back on the stone, folding his jacket for a pillow. By accident the gun barrel rested in the groove behind his neck like an extended spine. He liked the danger and was soon asleep.

The clank of metal woke him. Eyes still closed, he listened to a vehicle straining up the bumpy road. A car with a yellow camper turned into the clearing. Instantly the man rolled and dropped silently several feet below the stone wall, dragging his jacket with him. He landed in forest duff littered with cigarette butts and foil. Sliding under thick laurel he began circling the overlook, seeking a spot where he could climb through forest and behind the newly arrived car. Above him its door slammed, another. Voices. A man, two women. One woman would have been plenty, he thought.

Rapidly he crawled through blueberry bushes so damp and limber that they bent without snapping. Old twigs crushed under him without a sound. His heart boomed like a cymbal.

He had arranged himself out of sight by the time Eddie and Faye Rayburn and the sister stood looking over the tangled gorge. In the late afternoon the view had gone gray; the damp air felt thick. The dark-haired woman laid her hand on the wall where the man had napped; he wondered if the stone might yet be warm. Her face was turned toward the river.

The woman with the fluffy light curls complained that you couldn't see the waterfall from here. "Eddie, is it too dark to take my picture? Look!" She posed sitting on the wall, bare knees high, bracing on her hands to show off her breasts and pale legs. In his crouch the watching man could not comfortably reach his penis. Never mind.

With the camera hung around his neck, Eddie took her picture.

"Get us together now!" The blonde leaped up and wrapped her arm around the waist of the other, taller woman. Even with the sky clouded and their faces indistinct, they looked like sisters. Something about that likelihood and their neat, symmetrical stance disturbed the watching man and raced his cancerous heart to the point of danger.

Eddie snapped that picture, too. "Don't you ever smile?" he asked the tall one.

She shrugged. "We ought to call home tonight to be sure they're all right."

"Worrywart," said Eddie. "You just like to talk long-distance."

Faye had lit a cigarette. "Think of the snakes down there," she said, leaning into space. The tall woman walked away and stood at the stone wall, back turned, as if to get a better view of the snakes. Faye said, "Come to think of it, you only telephone *me* when you don't want to see me. Like if you're getting ready to say no?"

"I rarely do," the sister said.

Perhaps Faye didn't hear. "I told you we should have taken that other trail, Eddie, to see Linville Falls."

"Tomorrow," Eddie said. "Besides, you can see a waterfall where we camp at Crabtree Meadows."

"It'll be dark by then. I'm getting a sandwich." She bounced uphill out of sight and slammed doors.

The watching man rested on both elbows while Eddie took a few aimless snapshots upriver and down. The man regretted his reflexive drop into underbrush. He could have passed them with a nod, been miles away by now.

"Bring me a ham, honey?"

No food was offered to the dark-haired woman. She had seated herself to one side atop the wall, legs dangling over the gorge. She wore long red pants with a white blouse. Taking off her sandals she braced both bare feet against the rock where her toes felt out the dents and crevices in the stone. She seemed to be locating them for her spring outward into space.

The blonde reappeared with Eddie's sandwich. Together they stood chewing, faces turned toward the far rim. "Rockefeller used to own all this." Eddie tossed a wad of waxed paper over the wall.

Screened by thickets, the man crawled a wide circle uphill until he could stand unseen among dense evergreens and slip through quietly toward his car. He sat on its rear bumper to pick twigs and pine needles off his clothes. The others, out of sight, were murmuring. He padded across the clearing and glanced inside their car, assigning the pink straw bag in the front seat to the blonde. He plucked a coil of rope from the floor of their back seat and slid it bracelet-style to his shoulder.

Standing by the door, he sucked a briar scratch on one thumb. Not much in that pocketbook but earrings and lipstick. Florida was hot in August. He would rather head west. He began to smile.

Lazily he moved to his own car and jackknifed himself through the driver's window to fetch his cap. He took from the jacket the gun he never had to use—unless you counted that faggot.

Not planning ahead was the man's specialty. There were planners enough: people on schedule, en route to work or to campsites, getting their eyeglasses changed by appointment, making their weekly bank deposits, unlocking doors on time. He knew their habits as a wolf learns where deer will likely graze or stop for water. Planners could be followed; they could be intercepted anywhere along the line of their intentions. Sometimes the man broke into the sequence for his own gain, to take possessions planners were too predictable to deserve, and sometimes—like now—he broke it for no reason but the pleasure of disturbance.

Hunched down, the man skirted the clearing until he could look between green branches toward the stone platform where the three stood in the fading light. Cooler air was stirring the leaves. He moved with it, brushing as the wind brushed, until he squatted within five feet of the first stone stair. Once Eddie looked straight at the bush behind which the man hunkered, but since Eddie only expected stems and dark leaves to be moving there, stems and leaves were what he saw.

"If Nancy plans to call home before Mama goes to bed, we ought to move on," said the fair woman. The taller one nodded. "It's clouding up anyway, Eddie."

"You can't tell bad weather from a plain twilight." They climbed the first tier of steps while Eddie snapped his camera inside a leather case. "The forecast was fair tonight and tomorrow." In Eddie's mind, a straight line ran uphill to the trailer, from Wiseman's View to the highway, and thence to the campsite he had already circled on a map. At the end of Eddie's vacation, straight as a bird could fly, lay certain rooms with symmetrical roses fading in the wallpaper; and through those well-known rooms he could anytime find his way to the toilet and back in the dark.

"It's not going to rain," Eddie said louder.

The man moved into their path.

2

When the man with the gun stepped out of a laurel thicket, she knew that part of her had been waiting for him ever since she memorized "The Highwayman." Beside her, Faye squeaked once.

The man said, "Easy and quiet now." A few strangled words poured out of Eddie's throat before the man told him to shut up. All three waited below his black revolver, poised on the rock stairs as if each had turned to matching granite—Eddie's fingertips testing the midair, Faye keeping her heart indoors with one flat palm.

The sister, silent in a different way, glanced at her bent right knee, lifted for a step it might never now complete. The gunman motioned her ahead of the others and the knee joint rolled in a movement newly precious and raised her to his level. He was taller. She was not curious about his face.

Faye choked out, "Don't you touch her."

He jerked the head she would not focus to see. "That your trailer?"

"Theirs," she said. A trace of bitterness? No one would notice.

To Eddie he said, "Hand her your keys." The flat leather case vibrated into her hand. The man said, "Let's all walk over there now."

Almost on tiptoe she, Faye, and Eddie climbed from the overlook at Wiseman's View, below which Linville Gorge wound away in a blackening tangle. She led them across the empty picnic ground to the yellow trailer. Cicadas and roosting birds chittered in the darkening brush.

"If it's money . . . " Eddie slid his hand slowly toward his hip, received a nod, handed over the wallet.

"Unlock the door," the man said. She did. He herded them into the trailer and crowded them between bunks; he tossed blankets, sleeping bags, and Eddie's new rucksacks to the ground. She had not noticed the rope coiled over his shoulder until he slid it down. His right arm was tattooed. As it passed in gestures back and forth before the small window, she could make out a thorny rose and one word: BOO.

He told her to tie Eddie's hands behind him. Faye began to cry.

Now Eddie talked in a rush: Don't hurt them; they would say nothing; take the car, everything; just leave them there; and so on. She tied Eddie with efficient knots, one of them a threat to his new digital watch. Once, she knew, the rope grated into his wrists and pinched skin. He had hairy wrists. When she had finished, the man briefly tested her work and claimed not only the watch but Eddie's Greenway High School ring.

Under his waving gun the two sisters were forced outside to wade through bundles and equipment he had heaved from the trailer. He can't rape two at once, she thought. Crying, Faye slumped against the steel wall like a set of wet clothes blown there by the wind. The man watched her, said "Waste of time," turned aside. "What's *your* name?"

Now she stared, not wanting her murderer to have no face. "Nancy Finch," she said, surprised by her everyday voice. "Nan." Nobody had ever called her Nan.

Faye moaned, "Don't tell him anything."

"My sister, Faye." She nodded toward the trailer door as she turned the lock. "Her husband, Eddie Rayburn." Throughout these absurd introductions she tried to keep her hand from trembling and to memorize the gunman in the fading light. About six feet. Late twenties, thin. A baseball cap, slick with wear and dirt, one-sided over pale hair—dark blond, she decided. The cap said PREAKNESS STAKES. Eye color? Uncertain. Between those hollows the bridge of his nose was unnaturally sharp. Narrow upper lip with peaks, then fullness, and the chin notched underneath. At the end of those details she was still not sure how he looked. She had been wrong about the tattoo. The only letters she could read now were B-O-R.

The man was memorizing her, too, but all he said was "Make her quit blubbering."

"Faye? You hear?" Her sister cried softer.

"Tie her at the steering wheel."

Gently Nancy helped her sister into the driver's seat, saying "Shhh, Shhh," while she bound both wrists to the wheel. As ordered, she tied Faye's ankles to brake and clutch. Nancy recognized this second rope as Eddie's. He had planned to teach the sisters how to climb on belay.

Not that I'll miss knowing that.

Later, she decided, Faye can bend her forehead to the horn if she ever thinks of it. Faye wasn't much of a thinker.

She had kept Faye's bonds looser but the man added slipknots. Afterward, almost absently, he pinched Faye's nipple, then prodded Nancy aside, slammed and locked the door. Half to himself he said, "I could push it all over the edge." He flattened his face on the windshield to show Faye a distorted smile. The gun drooped.

It was Nancy's first chance. With both hands she knocked off his cap, groped for hair, and banged his whole face hard against the glass. She ran for the road, shoulderblades cupped to receive a bullet. No, the man was running noisily after her, not stumbling in the growing dark, gaining so fast she could waste no motion to check behind. Before Nancy reached the road she began to feel light taps on her back where he touched her from time to time while keeping easily at her heels. Hopeless. Without even thinking it through she abruptly dropped to a squat to make him run over her. In the collision she grabbed for his gun before she went sprawling across leaves and gravel. The cool metal knocked her elbow going by in the dark air.

The next minute he had yanked Nancy to her feet and slapped her face on both sides. Her cheeks felt numbed. Her body began to shake. When he silently pointed her toward the cars and nudged her with his retrieved gun, she felt too weak to walk.

"Where were we?" the man said, pushing. "Oh, yes. Load the stuff in my car."

Nancy's numb face hurt now from far away or as if borrowed and unfamiliar. By armloads she carried the backpacks, the rolled tent, bags, white-gas stove, to the man's black car. She wrestled them into his back seat, memorizing the car's interior and upholstery, the pair of plastic boxing gloves that swung from the mirror. Above the back seat lay one of those black toy cats with a nodding head. Nancy, as if in a dream, suspected all was being invented one moment ahead, that even the door handle bloomed into reality just when her hand reached for it, that the toy cat sprang into existence, nodded, then disappeared when she looked away. He'll kill me, she was able to say in her dream. Admitting the worst calmed her.

From somewhere Faye seemed to be making a high mosquito noise. "You drive?" Nancy shook her head. "Better learn quick, then." He slung Eddie's key case into the evergreens and prodded her before him under the wheel.

He would not kill her then where Faye could watch through the bug-splashed windshield. Nothing of Nancy's life except a few tepid love affairs had taken place unseen by her family and she was almost glad to think she might die, at least, at a distance. She started the car and backed expertly between tree trunks. Its headlights lit a grotesque semicircle of Faye hugging the steering wheel, screaming now, her eyes swollen in her face. Faye would keep hollering to the owls without once thinking of the car horn.

Well, that's the family I got born in. Maybe I've done too much of Faye's thinking for her.

In the last year, Nancy's wish to be free of doing all the thinking for all her family had grown desperate. Some days their dependence ate her alive. No longer as choosy as she had been at twenty, she had stopped wishing for Prince Charming or miracles. She had prayed to be free of them on any terms.

Now as Nancy sucked on a bloody flap in her mouth she switched prayers: Just get me out of this, she broadcast to Heaven, and I won't complain again.

The man said, "Turn right here. It's a bad road."

This man is not what I meant, she prayed. Grimly she had to concentrate on turning narrow curves in low gear, beginning to hope that once she had transported him skillfully to the highway and God had made a few corrections, he would wave and drive away. Don't let him kill me! She would go home to Greenway then, committed to a lifetime of no complaints.

Like sparks, fireflies blew out of the forest, dulled briefly above the hood, then spattered on the glass. The man lit a cigarette. Her own were in her pocketbook, which she was surprised to find in her lap. They can identify the body, Nancy thought. Let me live on, Father.

He said, "I'd give you one but you might burn me."

"I wouldn't," she said, already wondering where to strike.

"I would if I was you." In the open window he draped his elbow, the pistol dangling inside the car. He rubbed his forehead and temple.

"You nearly hurt me back there," he said thoughtfully. He examined his left palm as if the skin smarted from the hardness of her face, then cupped his hand in the air between them. Nancy felt that her imaginary breast, or thigh, or more, was being tested in that hand. Don't let him rape me, either. The bumpy road was so narrow, meeting cars would need to give way, one of them backing steeply around switchbacks to pull off and let the other pass. Nancy drove downhill as fast as she dared over loose rock. She was willing for any hairpin turn to let go their tire treads and shrug them off the mountain. The man slouched beside her with his hand still floating did not care, even for the dusty skids that powdered the night air behind them, even when once he rose off the seat and his Preakness cap grazed the dome light.

She could hardly believe they were driving out of the Linville wilderness without another move or word from him. When he pointed, she took the turn. Don't let him hurt me at all, she prayed. At last while they were rolling along the Blue Ridge Parkway toward Little Switzerland his hand swayed, languid as a cobra; his fingers lifted one strand of her dark hair and dropped it. She resumed breathing. Each time the headlights showed picnic spots or scenic overlooks, Nancy expected them to stop. Surely here, at Greenknob or Chestoa, he would hurt her fully, then throw her into the valley like garbage. They drove on. The night rushed cool and damp through the moving car. With dread she finally asked why he had brought her.

"I was tired of driving." He braced the pistol between his knees, counted and pocketed bills from Eddie's wallet, tossed it on the dashboard. Then he rested the gun across one thigh, pointed at her. "You shouldn't have tried to hurt me. I might have left you there if you hadn't done that."

Her breath seemed more regular. Help me to handle this. She could tell little from his flat voice. Black leaves or lumpy stone slid by his window, black space by hers, as she said, "Some camper has found Faye by now."

"By morning maybe."

"Then what?"

"By morning you could be in Heaven."

"But if I'm not," she said after a quick breath, "what then?"

She sensed a long stare from those hooded eyes, color still unknown. "I was tired of driving. Now I'm tired of talking."

Nancy drove in silence, turning toward Asheville when he pointed, changing places with him without a sound while he hesitated at Interstate-40 and then, as if it made no difference, chose the westward lane. They meshed with a row of cars that, like a string of lights on a Christmas tree, rounded and climbed the Smokies and lit the Appalachians rising into Tennessee.

With the kidnapper driving, Nancy huddled against the car door and took inventory. Her body threatened again to quiver; no one had struck her since grammar school. She ate air slowly with her open mouth until she felt steadier.

Though forbidden to talk, she could still think. Eddie might have worked his knots loose by now, could be helping Faye walk that winding road to the highway. They had barely glimpsed the man's car. Faye's tears had certainly blurred his face.

Ideally, the man would be an escapee—from jail, an asylum—who had left a trail from gun to car to Nancy Finch. The color of his eyes might be printed on a thousand posters; Faye would then recognize his face hanging on the sheriff's wall in Mitchell County.

But the man could be what Nancy already feared, one who had not earned his pursuers yet, whose trail sprang out of nowhere at Wiseman's View, on impulse. Not for another week would his landlady report that kind of man missing, in his own car. Farm ponds on farms she had never heard of would be listlessly dragged for his body. While Nancy Finch disappeared on page one of the Asheville *Citizen-Times*, he would fade away low on page four in some West Virginia weekly.

"I don't know your name," Nancy said timidly.

"That's right." He had tucked the gun well out of her reach, between his legs in fact. Such overt phallicism made her fear he had no subconscious at all, but was as blatant in behavior as storms and floods. Jerking the wheel might wreck them, kill them both; she could not. She backed into the door handle and examined his profile, which vaguely suggested Lincoln's.

She wanted to ask, "Are you going to kill me?" but those words would deliver to him the initiative. She sensed that taking her had been his strong act of the night, that he—as much as she—now waited to see what would happen next.

Nancy closed her eyes and, by will, made her breath deeper, calmer. Would Eddie call home? No, because Mama might have a spell with nobody there but Beck, and the news could tip him into a seizure. For fifteen years her mother and brother had so steadily and so parasitically depended on Nancy that she could hardly imagine their helplessness if she died. Faye will have to look after them now, she thought; then, instantly, She'll hire somebody.

By feel she tested her jaw for bruises, cleaned grit from the scratches on one ankle. She could picture the Finch family distraught at her funeral, wearing wreaths as if they were leis. Then she imagined the closed coffin as empty, her body never found. Because? Because Nancy did not get murdered at all, merely raped! Merely? At that Nancy opened her eyes to steal a glance at the gunman's bony, nondescript profile. I could live through that.

And then vanish. Take my sore crotch and go.

As bluntness overrode her prayers, Nancy thought of how shocked Mama and Beck and Faye and Eddie would have been. To them she was Big Sister, Elder Daughter, Virgin Spinster. They knew the slots into which she fit: behind the desk at Stone County Library, in the alto row of the Presbyterian choir, looking moist at the washing machine or over a sickbed. But if it's a choice, Lord? I hope you don't still consider rape a fate worse then death? If I get a vote, that is, I think I could outlast the trauma.

The kidnapper said, "You gone to sleep?"

"At my own kidnapping? I'm saying my prayers." She was pleased at her word choice: *kidnapping*. Perhaps she could set the tone, the limitations.

"Better pray to me."

"All right. Don't hurt me."

"Don't make me," he answered.

She thought his flippant tone meant he had granted a stay of execution, so Nancy leaned back and once more went through relaxation exercises, in order to be alert and cool when her chance came to escape. The alpha rhythms finally began. Her feet and hands began to drift loose. She pictured Beck, the gray cat pliable in his lap, while he listened to television news of his sister's death. There went the alpha waves.

After melting more tension she was reaching alpha phase again when the slapped air from passing cars went away and the gunman turned off the highway, then onto a dirt road. Now? The tube of Nancy's throat went flat. Oh, she was not ready *now!*

"We sleep here," the man said, parking under dark trees.

"We, my foot!" She almost said "my ass" but that seemed imprudent. Pressing away she cried, "Don't touch me!"

"If I wanted to touch you I would. You coming outside?" When Nancy shook her head until her cheeks wobbled he dragged a blanket through the back window and propped himself against a pine trunk in front of the car. "You're being watched all the time even if I look asleep," he said. "Appearances are deceiving."

Of its own accord Nancy's hand flew left but he had taken the keys. Through the dark his voice drawled, "You'd run me down, wouldn't you?"

"Twice," she said, prudently or not. At a distance the bright eyes of cars and trucks still went by in a line. Nothing required that she follow *his* schedule for rape. For all she knew, he needed early morning and a full bladder. Even on the interstate cars would stop, she thought, for a woman waving both arms. She squeezed the cold door handle and waited for the moon to plunge into clouds. When she opened the door, the interior light would probably come on. Groping overhead, Nancy worked loose the plastic fixture, removed the tiny bulb, and thrust it behind the seat. From the highway she could ride with her rescuers straight to the police and with their help be home in time to eat with the others the third casserole she had frozen. Monday lunch—tuna. Scraps for Beck's cat. Or she could even keep riding west for a while with strangers. Others get amnesia under stress—why not me?

Forgive me, Father. But you know it's not an easy life.

With such uneven prayers and retractions she waited until the lump under the tree had softened and been motionless a long time, then she began slowly to depress the door handle. The latch had not yet clicked when the man said, "Don't try it."

She sagged limp across the steering wheel.

He coughed once. "Which are you—deaf or stupid?"

Not a sound, not a word, she decided. She didn't want him coming to the car.

"You keep on, I'll have to send you home to Jesus," he said lazily across the dark.

A new possibility occurred to Nancy and she made her voice a taunt. "With that unloaded gun?"

The dark shape straightened. Perhaps he aimed the gun.

"You could have shot me before but you didn't. I should have known it wasn't loaded then."

He had dropped the blanket without rising. Her hand was wrapped around the door handle again, the other fingers poised at a specific knob. With simultaneous motions she switched on the blinding headlights and shoved open the car door.

His shot crashed through the windshield on the passenger's side. Because by that time she had half convinced herself the gun was empty, Nancy dropped from shock and fell awkwardly half out the door onto her shoulder. She hung there, mesmerized by the large silver spider web that had sprung up in the safety glass above. She could hear herself moaning several times, "My God, my God!"

"You have wore out Him and me both," the man said. "Now go to sleep."

Drawn tight and small she dragged back across the seat and clumsily slammed the door. She lay rigid waiting for some farmer to investigate the noise and save her. She was still stiff and sleepless when the declining moon slid its light neatly through the glass bull's-eye and dappled the seat. Through that newly opened eye she felt pitilessly observed. Mouse and cat. Her prayers ran out.

She had not slept at all when thick clouds rolled out of North Carolina and sifted the morning through. With snapping movements the man refolded his blanket. Nancy sat up concealing the small pliers she had found in the glove compartment. She touched her thumb to the bullet hole in the center of the radiating cracks, announcing, "I would like to go home now."

He threw his blanket in the back. Sliding under the wheel he noticed and felt the empty dome socket. She saw for the first time that his eyes were yellow brown like a dog's. "Time Eddie brought us breakfast," he said.

"I need to go to the bathroom."

"What's that?"

She had to tell him twice. He looked disgusted. He stuck the key into the ignition and fingered its shape. "Squat by the car then." Nancy shook her head. "I can't see you except when you stand up; we ain't got all day."

Weakly she got out and closed her door, staring at his false Lincoln profile through the open window. He hates women, she thought.

"Right there, that's fine," he muttered.

Around them were only woods and fields. She scraped the elastic band and worked down her slacks, lowered herself so quickly she nearly fell backward in the dirt, and let the hot urine pour. She had palmed the pliers and now collected a firm stick as well, no help unless straight into an eyeball. As if to cover the sound, he ran the engine.

Nor would he look at her when at last they drove away and he asked, "How old are you?"

None of his business. "Thirty-four." She spread her right hand over her left fingers.

He grunted. "Are you afraid of me?"

"By now anybody would be afraid of you," she said with a nod at the shattered windshield.

"You were," he said, "but you're getting over it."

Was that good? Should she pretend insouciance? "I'm sure you'll let me go this morning."

At the yield sign he waited for a break in the I-40 traffic. "You teach school?"

Offended, she said no. Nancy Finch worked in the new Greenway branch of the county library, which had been set down—a box of steel and glass—in a residential block of tall Victorian houses. In that neighborhood, the modern building seemed like a cartridge dropped in a tray of earrings. The Finch family home, filigreed and slightly tarnished, was in the same block. "I'm a librarian," she said.

"All those books any help to you now?"

"Not yet." Her mind, in fact, was cluttered with Robin Hoods.

"No, you're not afraid. You're just working out ways to keep from getting hurt." He nodded. "Or to hurt me." Suddenly the car leaped to outrun a truck into the right lane. "I'm twenty-nine myself."

Her mouth sneered before she could stop it. "A professional kidnapper?"

He drove faster. For half an hour they were silent, even when he took at speed a curving downhill exit to a gasoline station with café attached, and braked there so abruptly that Nancy was thrown toward the shining bullethole. "I'm right behind you. And I'll do the ordering."

Smoothing wrinkles, she got out. The gun, she supposed, was in the jacket he carried. She hurried into the dim, artificially cool restaurant, curious to see how fresh it might look to her under these circumstances and who had materialized there to save her. A heavy woman dressed like a nurse dropped two plasticized menus on their table. She had acne. Nancy wondered what the cook had as she hid the pliers in her lap.

The man pushed back the menus. "Two orders—bacon, scrambled eggs well, coffee. No juice."

"And raisin toast," said Nancy. Condemned woman, hearty meal.

"We don't have raisin toast. Cinnamon?"

He was glaring. She said yes.

"Hash browns or grits?"

At the same instant he chose potatoes and she grits. Their stares locked, the waitress scribbling down their conflict as she walked away. Neither would break off staring first. Her voice squeaked when she found it. "I didn't have supper."

"Don't you lose track of the fix you're in," he finally said.

Since his teeth were clenched she could see where half an incisor was missing, and its edge stained. "They can eat what they want on Death Row," she said firmly. Something in his face told her this was the right move, this show of spunk. Jo March, not Beth or Meg or Amy. She slid the cheap vase with its cardboard daisy into his half of the table. He moved it to the wall as she asked, "Am I going to call you by an alias at least?"

He was, she saw clearly, a man no one would notice twice. The long thin face, the tooth, his narrow nose added up without distinguishing themselves in any way. Neither ugly nor handsome, he looked like a man who fixed refrigerators, carried mail, delivered milk; one would always be thinking about the letters or the milk instead of him. His quick smile surprised her now and, for a moment, brightened the yellow in his eyes. When Nancy saw that, by habit, he lifted only the right corner of his mouth and so hid the broken tooth, she was almost touched.

"Call me Dwight," he said through his crooked smile. Why anyone would pick that name she could not imagine. "Dwight Anderson." An insult, she decided, to some real Dwight Anderson. Quickly she looked about now to spot the F.B.I. agent who must be watching this fugitive and his spunky prisoner. No one. "It's about time we parted company, Dwight Anderson."

"You remind me of somebody."

Patiently she said, "Who?" The waitress brought coffee. "Is that why I'm here?"

He said, "I doubt it." Napkins and silver were put in place as if for any normal couple. When the waitress had gone he added, "I did it because I wanted to."

"That means nothing." Even with cream substitute and sugar her coffee tasted bitter.

"I'm not in the meaning business. You live with those Rayburns?"

"No. What'll you do if I scream right now?"

"You're not a screamer. Faye, now, she was a screamer."

And Faye always got what she wanted. Just Faye's luck to have wanted Eddie Rayburn; just mine to have wanted to leave home. Nancy made herself smile. "You're going to let me go sometime. I can tell you're basically a nice person," she lied.

"Well, it's not going to be in the middle of some café with two pay telephones," he said.

She noticed them in each back corner. "I could promise not to call anybody for an hour."

"You could promise eternal life." He yawned.

Religious lunatics were surely the worst. Breakfast came. Starved, she picked up bacon with her fingers and began to eat while she thought about her next line. "I can't believe you're planning to hurt me."

"I don't plan," he said. "Pass the pepper." He speckled his eggs so dark his taste buds must be deficient. "The one you remind me of, it's a man."

Nancy felt this information was meant to reassure her, perhaps to lessen the risk of sexual attack. There was too much fat in the bacon.

"In my family." Dwight Anderson watched her nibble out the lean streak, lay the pale greasy part aside. "You're hard as nails, you know that?"

Nancy had always feared such hardening would come to her. Lifetime victims, she had noticed, soon became skillful at the tyrannies of martyrdom. So his random shot made her say sullenly, "Precious little you know." As the jacket slid to Dwight's elbow she saw his full tattoo for the first time, definitely not what she had expected. A large blue and yellow horseshoe. Under its arch a blurred red rose with a red drop falling away from a sharp thorn on the stem. Spaced widely above, within, and then below the horseshoe were the three blue words: BORN TO BOOGIE. The legend was so harmless, so adolescent and outdated, as to make her kidnapping, his blows, especially the gunshot seem implausible. "Why the tattoo?"

"So if I turn up dead they'll know it's me."

"Fingerprints should be enough." With a thump his hidden gun hit the Formica's edge and she checked that her napkin covered the pliers. Perhaps because of the wavery rose with a thorn, which seemed plagiarized straight from Shelley, she said. "Maybe you're just a lousy shot. Maybe you've never even carried a gun before."

He looked humorless, insulted. Before he could comment the passing waitress recited, "Everything all right?" and went away before Nancy could decide about screaming.

"Lady, you are a roach to me. I keep you in a matchbox for a while or I step on you—what's the difference?"

"Very Kafka-esque," she managed to sneer, but all was wasted.

"The one you remind me of wasn't in my family. He scratched my car."

This made Nancy think of dropping her driver's license on the floor, her social security card at the next stop. A trail. Hansel and Gretel. She concentrated on the toast while choosing her next words. On the surface he seemed rational, with no plans, a man who might take the best that offered itself. Slowly she said, "I need to go home. My mother's almost an invalid. This is going to worry her." He ate peppered eggs as if deaf. "I look after her and my brother, too, who is also, uh, disabled. They can't get along more than a few days without me." Very deliberately Dwight held his cup aloft until the waitress brought more coffee. How much should she say? Suddenly Nancy's home life seemed unconvincing, especially her brother Beckham; they could have gotten along without her just fine, for all she knew. "I've done everything for them for years. "Fifteen, exactly. Her voice cracked when she said, "I'm not a roach to them!"

The way he spread strawberry jam across the toast distracted her, how he thinned it to pink film on each slice, carrying it neatly to the rim. "This was just a weekend vacation," she said, staring. "I asked Faye to stay home so I could take a cruise but she offered this instead with her and Eddie. We go through this every summer." On shipboard, Nancy had hoped to meet a man who would give her his full attention, would offer to take her away from all that; she had even prayed in the choirloft for such an encounter and promised no longer to be choosy about the man's habits, or income, or even intelligence. This man was God's answer? There were divine practical jokes John Calvin had never guessed.

Once all Dwight's toast was coated he began to eat each piece in three snappy bites. "You took a trip after all. Surprise."

Full, half-nauseated, she mumbled, "I can't eat these eggs." He did not chew his food enough. As a child she had been made to chew once for each permanent tooth due to arrive later in her gums. He had grown up with barbarians, ex-convicts. Rapidly becoming tearful she blurted, "When can I go home?"

"If you died, wouldn't those people get along anyway?"

Though Nancy had sometimes dramatically asked them that, the question chilled her. Both eyeballs dried cold. "What do you mean?"

"You ordered cinnamon toast; you eat it all."

He waited frowning while she forced a grainy bite of toast, then tamped down a throatful of eggs. "I don't want to die!" Things are bad at home, Lord, but not that bad. Dwight nodded and ate eggs. Her mouth was dry with crumbs. "Maybe I could help you, Mister— Anderson? If you're running from something, I could testify that you treated me well. No, no, I don't need to know what; that's your business." He was looking beyond her. "Am I a hostage because of . . . ?" Her voice dwindled but she tried again. "You'd never get much ransom money because they only draw social security." His toast was gone. "And Eddie's stingy."

The waitress laid down the check. "I need help!" Nancy wailed to her only to have the woman jerk a thumb toward the restroom while the man reached across and grabbed her arm. She had to release the pliers from that hand and the waitress was gone before they even hit the floor. Nancy wouldn't look at them as he led, almost dragged, her to the cashier and on into the car. He was angry. We must look married, Nancy thought. Without a word to her he bought gas.

Back on the highway Nancy said, "You could at least say where you're taking me."

"West. You ever been west?"

She pushed away thoughts of sunset, death. "I've never been anywhere."

"I was in Texas once." He folded a stick of gum three times and hid it in his jaw. "It's all sky; I didn't like it."

"Eddie wasn't carrying enough money to get us to Texas." Eddie had claimed they could afford no motels. For three days she had eaten little but sandwiches and canned fruit cocktail. "Make me two promises." No reaction. "I said, I want you to make me two promises."

"Wanting never hurt anybody," he finally answered.

"Promise not to hurt me in any way."

Chewing, he adjusted the rearview mirror and trembled the boxing gloves. "Like you and them pliers?"

She pressed on. "And I want you to decide when you'll let me go and say so." Perhaps the fuzzy head of the cat would affirm her arguments in his mirror. "That way, I can relax; I'll wait for it. I won't make trouble." She had never talked to a man so opaque; her words bounced off him as off a concrete wall. "If you'll do that, Mr. Anderson, I won't try to get away."

"Try if you want to. I ain't helpless."

She leaned forward. "You've got to sleep sometime." A mistake. "I mean, there are bound to be opportunities, and the longer you keep me like this, the more risk I'm willing to run." Stupid—that sounded like an invitation to shoot her now and save himself some trouble. "But if you're going to kill me anyway, I'd just as soon jump out of this car right here in Tennessee!" Nancy laid her hand on the door handle as he passed a car at speed, waved to the driver, went on waving as they swept by. The stranger waved back. "If I scream at every car we pass, somebody's bound to notice. We're probably on the radio news. "She had the feeling logic was wasted on him, like music on a deaf man.

He said lazily, "Alaska then."

"Alaska? That's north!"

As if working from a list he said, "Arizona. I'll turn you loose in Arizona."

Though she was certain he lied, her body softened with relief. Two days? She tightened again: two nights. Though he might be lying, so was she; she'd run first chance she got. "Is Arizona desert?"

He shrugged and showed a gray bulge of chewing gum behind his broken tooth. The meaningless bargain seemed to relax him, too, and they dropped to sixty mph and drifted into the right lane. "Turn on the radio if you want to hear about yourself so bad."

She heard guitars and fiddles. "Where are we now?" If they passed through Nashville, she could fall out the door at the first traffic light.

"A long way from Arizona."

Or she could jump the curb and drive through glass into a supermarket. "You want me to drive?" he said after dark.

Soon Nancy grew bored watching the grassy monotonous slopes alternate with stone walls engineers had hacked beside the highway. She hung one hand outside the window to feel the solid air grab hold, try to suck her fingers off, and throw them back forever into the landscape they were leaving. She flattened her hand into a blade and turned it like a scythe against the signs and tree trunks racing backward; behind the car she left a roadside sliced off ten feet above the blurred ground, symmetrical and green, strange as the Great Wall of China.

The game returned her to childhood and old trusts and hopes. "Talk to me," she said. Perhaps some recent tragedy had driven a quiet accountant into a life of crime. Dwight Anderson grunted and did not. "What kind of work do—did you do?"

"What I could get."

"For instance?"

His jaw worked on the gum. "Pump gas. Dig holes." He leaned back as if, relaxed, he might at last tell a secret. "Pulpwood."

"What's the best job you ever had?"

"Stealing. Short hours and high pay."

She could not tell which were his lies. "What's the worst?"

"Taxicab."

Quickly she asked. "Where was that?"

"Anywhere."

"Have you been in jail?"

"Sure."

Goodbye to the accountant. "What was that for?"

He spat his gum outside. "Breaking the law."

"You never finished high school, did you? You didn't know Alaska was north."

"Yes, I did." Something seemed to boil up inside his neck. "I know plenty."

She tested the advantage of angering him. "I can't believe that."

"I don't rise or fall on what you believe." The sentence bemused her. He added coldly, "Miss Librarian."

"You mentioned family before. Are your parents living? Do they know where you are?" She swung in the new direction. "Does your mother know what you're doing now?"

"Not unless she can think through water." His yellow eyes became dense as marbles. Nancy felt her own closed up whenever she looked through time rather than space. In the mirror she had tried to examine this blank departure, but her eyes would only gaze into themselves. She made her voice soft, sympathetic. "I'm sorry. What are you thinking now?"

"About my brother. He saw them last."

After waiting a long time she prodded. "Yes?"

"This was his car." He turned up the radio to end the risk of confidence.

"Well, he needs a new windshield now."

"That's not all he needs," Dwight said, "being dead."

Carefully Nancy said she was sorry to hear that. "What caused him to die?"

He sounded furious. "His heart stopped, what do you think? What are you talking about *him* for?"

"No reason," she said hurriedly, "none, no reason at all."

When he looked less tense she began thinking of Evaline Sample, home in Greenway, whose small nervous breakdowns had each been shocked back together by small jolts of electrotherapy. Awed tenth-grade girls had warned one another that spinsterhood had driven Evaline Sample crazy, that older women needed "sex juice" to stay normal.

Nowadays they plugged old maids into technology. When Evaline was again as sensible as a storage battery she would sit in the county library turning photographs into sketches for the Episcopal Craft Fair: the Hermitage, Belle Meade, Monticello, Duke Chapel, Mount Vernon. Every few years she returned to the state hospital for recharging and to have her prescription changed. Nancy had hung two of Evaline's spidery drawings in her upstairs bedroom, both of the Greenway Presbyterian Church. When Evaline turned to *National Geographic* for ideas, it was a bad sign; the milligram or the voltage count had dropped too low. She would begin to draw Mecca. Her circumcised minarets endorsed the tenth-grade view.

This man, Nancy decided, was crazier than Evaline; but how could she separate his average symptoms from dangerous symptoms? Laying fingertips on the window glass she absently chipped off tips of passing trees and chimneys while trying to recall everything she had ever read about mental illness. Between stamping books she had worked through Mesmer to Freud to Jung to Victor Frankl, and small help they proved now. Paranoid? Psychopath? Schizophrenic? Were his delusions of grandeur or persecution? Was it his father he hated— or—worse for her—some unknown mother whose traits she should not duplicate? Which would he murder—a slut or a lady? Had he not already called her hard as nails? Was this category good or bad? Nancy snuffed one cigarette and lit another.

"People shouldn't chain-smoke," he said severely.

She stabbed it instantly into the ashtray with an unsteady hand. No doubt his mother had smoked, had bought cigarettes when there was no milk in the house. In a flash she conjured up the brother, also an asthmatic sister coughing her lungs out in an apartment cloudy with nicotine. MOTHER, SON, DIE IN MYSTERIOUS BLAZE—SECOND SON MISSING, SISTER CRITICAL.

Dwight said, "I might as well go west by myself for all the company you are."

"You can let me out anywhere." She finally asked what he wanted her to talk about.

"Faye and old Eddie to start."

Easing against the door to watch his face she began slowly, waiting between each sentence to gauge his reaction. "Faye's my younger sister. Got married five years ago. She'd known Eddie for years." (Besides, Faye didn't want to get stuck, she thought, looking after Mama and Beck.) "Eddie's in the clothing store business with his father."

"Where is that?"

"Greenway, North Carolina," she said, and was sorry. "Well, not too *far* from there."

"He was dressed up."

"Always." She could shuffle like cards years of pictures of Eddie wearing different pastel cashmere sweaters. Camel's hair coats. Assorted tweeds. When Eddie drove Faye home from movies, they would park in the driveway. Nancy's high bed was by the window; her glance caught the lift of Faye's skirt as his hand went up. After that she could not help watching. Watched the night he took Faye's pale hand and rubbed it in his lap. It looked like a lazy bird, from two flights up, taking a dust bath. Other nights passed; clothes were loosened. Mostly he liked to finger her, sitting erect, watching almost coolly her closed eyes, waiting until Faye's blonde head rolled from side to side. Nancy would touch herself, watching; it must not feel the same. Once Eddie got out of the car and wiped himself with a hand-

kerchief and threw it away on the lawn—on the lawn! Nancy would-
n't pick it up in daylight and it lay in the grass till it rotted. Faye
learned to use both hands, two birds, an overpayment for his rapid
fingers. Carefully Eddie trained her. Soon, they would barely park below Nancy's window and the engine stop before Faye would be
crouched rear-up in the front seat with Eddie's hand slid around her
hip and out of sight, she with her face down in his opened clothes.
Bird to mammal. And Eddie never closed his eyes but sat with his
mouth half-open in a grin, counting the stars and the TV aerials and
using his hand to rock her steadily to him like a sweet machine. Surely
they knew Nancy watched? The next morning Faye would eat her
Cream of Wheat like everybody else.

About that time I took up with the coach, Nancy thought.

Into her silence Dwight Anderson said, "You don't like Eddie?"

"I don't need to, the way he likes himself." She had not meant to
snap, but it had just occurred to her that those scenes in the parked
car were far more vivid to her than to Faye and Eddie, that each one
had become part of her autobiography instead of theirs.

As usual, Nancy wanted to flee such knowledge into something
busy, to play cow poker or collect state license plates. Had Dwight
Anderson been a different man, they might have made palindromes.
Nancy decided her life could be summarized in two words: Unsatis-
factory Conditions, from which she was being abducted by an Unsat-
isfactory Kidnapper.

"What's so funny?"

"Nothing. It's hard to be Maid Marian with you."

"What else goes on in Greenway, North Carolina?"

"No, it's your turn." He did not answer, but turned off the radio so
her silence became silence in general. "I never expected to be bored at
my own kidnapping." Not looking at her he drove faster. "I can't talk
all the time, you know; when we get to Arizona I'll be . . ." Crazier
than you are? Let it go. "I'll be babbling about the weather. Let's look
for a hitchhiker." Still faster. The car was rocking.

"Shut your smart mouth." His words were low and threatening.
Nancy said she was sorry, just nervous; wouldn't anybody in her
shoes be nervous? Suddenly she visualized the calendar page for Au-

gust; Lord God, she was going to bleed between here and Arizona; what a great, evil private joke! And he, who had clearly been repulsed by her need to urinate—he might think blood was blood; he might choose to redden her thoroughly once Nature had made a start.

She mumbled, "How about sisters? Have you got any sisters?"

He said no, making it safe for Nancy to light another cigarette and suck on it hungrily. She could almost feel, radially from the lungs out, her circulatory system constrict. All points bulletin: Be on the lookout for a man, dementia praecox, and a woman, premenstrual tension. Approach with caution.

Nancy did not sleep, merely by habit pulled back into her skull with everything closed except her third, pineal eye. In this cave, as if in a private screening room, her private light shows often flickered through *Lorna Doone, Wuthering Heights;* books and applied daydreams of books had always kept her sane. But today she thought Heathcliff certifiable and felt half-deranged herself.

The car's abrupt swerve right made Nancy sit up as a sign flashed by—ISOLINE, TENNESSEE. She might have read the name off an eyedrop bottle. Uneasily she asked where they were going. He would not answer. "Arizona, you said!"

Past stores, houses, trailers, he turned onto a dusty road with vines and thistles growing down its banks. With tense glances, Nancy took note that his jacket was wadded against the door. They drove down a narrow track between young pines. "I had friends here," he said. Before a gray farmhouse he circled through an oak grove and parked, engine running. "Probably dead."

"It looks empty." She was afraid to leave the car. What kind of friends could this man have?

"Appearances are deceiving," he said, and blew the horn.

The house sat on high brick pillars with rusty objects thrown under the porch. Its long windows were closed; behind the glass hung thin cloth the color of dishrags. The screen door had stuck halfway open.

Dwight blew the horn a second time. As he waited his gaze would briefly snag on something out of place, perhaps absent, before moving on. He knew this house. "I'm not dead yet," he said to himself.

The oak grove suggested a rural homeplace whose back field had been turned into a housing development. "Come on." Dwight put the keys into his jacket and the jacket over his tattooed and bleeding rose. Outside, Nancy checked his license plate: Maryland. Rotten acorns snapped under her shoes as she followed onto the porch, then sat on the dirty banister while he scraped back the door and rattled the knob.

She said, "Nobody even put up the window screens this summer."

"He was in the hospital."

"Who?"

He grunted, trying to raise a locked window.

Tiptoeing across the porch, Nancy estimated from wires that every house back there had a telephone. Would he shoot now if she ran toward those lavender sheets hanging on the line? How quickly she could be home! Stay home. Mama and Beck; cortisone, Dilantin. She sat on that banister and swung up her leg but he grabbed the ankle and made her teeter there while he tapped his heavy pocket to break a pane and worked his fingers inside the jagged hole. "You keep on, you can be dead to match the others," he said, but he sounded bored. After he raised the window he jerked her ankle to bring her floundering to her feet beside him. "Like flies, the way people die around here," he said, and abruptly laughed *huh-huh* in a sharp dry way she found chilling. She was pushed ahead through the open window into an empty room with a sheet of plywood blocking the fireplace.

"Did you live here?" Her voice echoed. The wooden floor was painted red brown; dried blood, she thought, would hardly show. He drove her ahead into the next bare room with its blue linoleum runner tacked as a pathway from the front door. Here the sooty plywood had fallen from the fireplace; she saw long black strokes on the floor, smeared on the mottled green wall, even streaked in arcs overhead. Below the net curtains, torn and dirtied, lay dead chimney swallows too old and dry to smell. Feathers flew when Dwight kicked one. "Birds, too."

His recurring talk of death made Nancy doubly fearful. Down the linoleum path through a dim hall she hurried toward the back door that must be there, hurried too fast for him to get out and aim the gun. She would fly through the weeds and honeysuckle, screaming; the woman who owned those lavender sheets would hear. She ran ahead of him into the kitchen, across it—brass lock with its little knob. Greasy, wouldn't turn. Now. Yes!

But the damn door was bolted or maybe even nailed. He had known that, she supposed. Nancy held back the latch with both hands and shook, rattled the lower knob, and felt him watching her, confident. Suddenly his hand was laid across hers, too slowly, too lightly, the skin cool as leather. She jerked free of his touch, which returned to run down her inner arm. She cried. "Let me alone!"

Dwight shoved her past a porcelain sink against an oily wall. "Don't scream," he said, catching hold just under her jaw so the thumb and a finger ground into her vocal cords and hurt. She nodded, trying to edge along the slick wall. Softly he said, "A mighty short promise."

She was sorry they had ever left the car, sorry for how that thought must quiver on her face. Her fear seemed to excite him. "Maybe this is as far west as you need to go."

There was no weapon in the stripped kitchen. "You promised not to hurt me," she gasped.

"One broke promise breaks two."

Nancy looked eyes with him, willing him not to look down at her body. He did anyway. His left hand followed the look and closed on her breast like a dogbite. She kicked out and tried to scream, but the throat pressure forced a gurgle. Dwight Anderson was smiling.

Heavy footsteps.

Up the back stairs. He froze though she kept up her choked noises. The kitchen door moved in its frame, shook, and stopped. "Anybody home?" a man called. It was like a dream in which the dreamer is invisible and soundless. By then Dwight had pushed the gun, not into her stomach, but exactly onto her nipple. With their faces almost touching and Nancy gasping, they stared while the noises crossed wood, thumped down, and could be heard passing through dry grass under the window. Growling, "Shut up!" Dwight kept his head cocked outward to those waning sounds. When a car door slammed he ordered Nancy to hurry and keep her goddamned mouth shut and pushed her ahead through the hollow rooms.

He had returned the gun to his pocket before thrusting her aside and leaping off the porch to where a short man with a bright red suitcase leaned against the hood. He had a pale mustache and slightly wavy hair, blond going gray.

Nancy could not make out Dwight's low fierce question or the man's reply. When she reached the steps the stranger heard her thick breathing. "Did I scare you? I hope not."

Her voice must be bruised, unreliable. She kept walking until she managed to answer, "I've been scared worse."

As she drew closer he reached out. "Are you ill?"

"Not if she's careful," Dwight said.

The groping became a handshake. "Judge Harvey T. Jolley here. Just a transient, out studying the human condition."

Have I got a specimen for you! Nancy tried to make her restless fingers warn his hand. He was asking Dwight if a cat in the house had made the sound he heard, a tomcat, maybe, on the prowl? Dwight said yes, looking hard at Nancy.

"I'm afraid he thought I was stealing his car," said Jolley, looking apologetic. "But surely you two don't live here?"

"We're driving on." Dwight opened the passenger door and jerked his head at Nancy.

"Car's running a little hot," said Jolley with a pat on the hood.

"One reason I stopped." Dwight left the door open, walked unerringly to a yard faucet he found easily in the tall grass, knew already that a cut-off hose was attached to it, turned on water, and managed to lift the hood and unscrew the radiator cap—all without unpinning Nancy from his glare. His focus was so intense that the puzzled stranger also studied her, while Dwight stood behind wisps of steam with one hand poised in his jacket pocket and filled the radiator.

"I'd welcome a ride if you're headed toward the interstate."

Dwight shook his head but Nancy said fine while the stranger looked back and forth between them. "Uh, where did you say you were going?"

"Home," Nancy said, and at the same moment Dwight: "To hell, if we don't do better."

3

Judge Harvey T. Jolley had been feeling so sorry for himself that the choked caterwauling from the vacant house had played for some time like mood music before being actually heard and located. At last he thought of an abandoned and starving cat—the parallel to himself so perfect that he set off at once to release it into the fields and woods, where, like him, it could at least survive.

But in the front yard what looked abandoned was this dusty five-year-old car, probably stolen. Not that he cared anymore. He had grown lawless himself. When he spotted and retrieved a crushed paper bag under the driver's seat he was soon wrist-deep in currency. From such a tumble of bills, no one would miss the three twenties he slipped inside his pocket. With great deliberation, then, he banged the car door. Someone was running. He leaned on the car expecting teenagers—all boys except for one girl—to rush headlong out the front door. Whether he would rescue or fondle her the judge had not decided.

Instead a tall man folded himself through a window and made two hard jumps down the steps, yelling, "What in the hell are you doing?" His cowed wife was left on the porch.

As this was no pimpled youth, Jolley felt a little cowed himself. Tall bastard; looked mean. Low class. He explained that the car, at first, had seemed abandoned. He introduced himself. He smiled a lot and waggled both hands, the habits of a short man.

"Now that you know better than to straight-wire it, move on, old man; no trespassing." The angry man yanked open his car door and bent out of sight. "What do you mean—judge?"

"I mean I used to be." Thinking of the hidden money he said boldly, "I have crossed over to the other side." The approaching woman in red and white looked like all women who live full-time with drunks or brutes. The judge bowed and begged pardon for scaring her.

Soon he was trying to hitch a ride to the highway, while they were using him like a funnel to keep some quarrel flowing back and forth.

The woman had married beneath her. Slender, thirtyish, handsome—too wide a jawbone for prettiness. She kept sending him silent, incandescent messages, perhaps flirtations. The shoulder of her white blouse bore an oily stain. Filling the radiator, her husband said nobody that messed with his car would ever ride in it.

She answered, "Probably he's wanted for something, Dwight. I'd better go call police."

A southern voice, but with a twang, made her sound wry, perhaps sarcastic. Jolley said, "Go ahead. I've got identification."

The woman swung toward the small houses he had recently passed but the man told her to stay where she damn well was. "Or maybe he's a cop himself. Let's see it."

Jolley passed his billfold with social security card, driver's license, one gas credit card, a few dollar bills. Another card showed he had a bank account in Memphis. He carried the smelly checkbook in his shoe. Last February he had shed all but the big categories: citizen, taxpayer, driver. His only next of kin, Clara, had died then while driving well within the speed limit. By now he supposed some judge who still believed in law had decided the civil case.

The woman seemed to be alternately comparing Jolley with the billfold, the billfold with Jolley; no, perhaps she was drawing attention to the man's blue jacket hung over one arm? Slowly she circled one wrist with thumb and forefinger, let go, switched and circled the other wrist. Odd nervous habit, but Clara had sometimes, with quick strokes, smoothed all the hairs on her arm to lay them the same way. Now the woman backed against the gray oak as Joan must have stood when chained to the stake and she stayed that way until the tall man looked up.

Baffled, Jolley decided to keep talking. "I've been on the road since February," he said pleasantly, "which is when my old life ended. When I heard that cat, I thought—"

He was interrupted by the car door being slammed shut and opened again. "Get in, Nancy."

The woman stepped away from the tree. "Are you headed west?"

"No, he's not."

He thought of winter and California. "What a pleasant surprise! And I'll be glad to help drive." Since the man was shaking his head,

Jolley opened the back door and moved his suitcase onto the seat without facing him. "See you've got a tent here, and I'm carrying a book on campgrounds." Bending his head he got one foot inside.

In a level voice the woman said, "Wouldn't you rather have three, Dwight? In the car? In case?"

"It don't help that much." Hot as it was the man called Dwight put on the blue jacket and thrust both hands into its pockets.

The woman got between them. "I think if he came along," she said nervously, "we'd both find it easier to keep our promises. I know I would."

For no reason, the man threw back his head with a short bark of laughter. "Hard as nails," he whispered. He looked at her with brief admiration before he said, "I'm letting him out in Memphis—middle of town or middle of the road or middle of hell, it's all the same to me." From his jacket he handed Jolley the keys. "Move your suitcase up front," he said with the *huh-huh* laughter. "My wife and me, we'll ride in the back awhile. We haven't been married very long." He guided her in with a hard pat on the ass. The judge did not even pay much attention to the woman's flinch; he had seen female masochists before in the courtroom.

For a time nothing moved in the back but the nodding cat. When Jolley turned the mirror to catch the pale edge of the wife's face, she seemed to be staring through the sunburst dazzle of the broken windshield toward the spot where the road ran under the sky. He learned names: Dwight Anderson, Nancy; gave his again, explained that his wife had been killed in a wreck not far from here. They asked him nothing. "We hadn't been married very long either," he ventured. They did not even ask why a judge was out thumbing like some depression hobo. Dozens had complimented him with their interest since February and had given him the chance to explain his private depression. "I'm not over Clara's death yet," he said as usual. "It drove me forth to seek for reasons." No response. He did not mention that business with the bar association, Pharisees all, which would hit a man when he was already down. If Clara had lived, he would have fought the charges and still be on the bench. "I see you're from Maryland."

"He is." There was a muted scuffle in the back. In the mirror the woman's hair was flying; *huh-huh*, the husband laughed.

Distracted, the judge went into panic as a passing truck darkened the car and he jerked his body aside in a reflex developed since the wreck. Such a jerk somehow yanked Clara from under that other steering wheel which had snapped her spine. He leaned away, sweating, while the roar blocked and passed the car window.

"What in the hell you doing?"

He told Dwight, "A stretch." Nancy had seated herself on the edge and was half-hung into the front, combing her hair with spread fingers. She told the judge to stop if they came to a big drugstore so she could buy some things.

"What things?" said Dwight. "You are not on this trip to be an expense."

"A toothbrush. *Things*. I have some money."

"That so?"

She leaned even more toward the front. They were between Monterey and Cookeville. With one hand the judge unsnapped his suitcase latches and felt among the clothes for his campground magazine. She spread it atop his bag and hung over to read until Dwight goosed her somewhere and forced her into the back with him. The judge saw that she wore no wedding band.

He stopped at the first general store. Not only Nancy and Dwight but the car keys went inside, leaving him like a mistrusted flunky to have the tank filled on a credit card made out to J. D. Anderson. He said to the attendant, "Oh no, my name's Jolley. When he comes back my friend will sign the ticket."

"I know he will," said the man, scowling.

While Dwight finally signed, the judge helped Nancy lift her paper bag into the car; he saw a large blue Tampax box showing on top.

She said softly, "I'd prefer to sit with you awhile."

Jolley smiled as he transferred his suitcase. Though he had not married until quite late, he believed his long bachelorhood resulted from an excess of opportunities. He had always approached women as if to sell a Fuller brush, all courtliness and smooth patter. With a vengeful look at Dwight he helped Nancy into the front seat, trying some of it on her. "You women remind me of angels. The way you're always up in the air? Never have much to wear? The way you're always harping on something?" He laughed softly, giving her elbow a slight palm caress. "How about a Coca-Cola before we start on?" Nancy said no thanks. "What I miss most is the pleasure of looking after an appreciative woman," he said. He thought she answered, "Be careful of Dwight."

"Come back here where you belong," Dwight was saying as he got into the car.

"I need to give road directions," she said, retrieving the judge's campground book and beginning to read aloud. After five miles or so, they arrived at THE ARBORS: MOBILE PARK/OVERNIGHT FACILITIES. "You're the one said you wanted to get off the road early."

"And you're the one picked this dump," said Dwight. Old furrows still corrugated the field on which trailers, their wheels masked by pickets or sheets of plastic brick, were permanently parked. In their aluminum walls boxy air-conditioners dripped and whined. The trailers overlooked a pond that lay downhill like a large dusty water bead with campsites on the far side. After renting a space, Dwight drove to it on a road he invented between saplings and briars.

They were the only late-afternoon campers in a matrix of sites with separate spigots. As the Andersons tossed bundles to him, Jolley set them in a row, noting a bedroll with a name tag saying E. RAYBURN. He looked up from reading it into Nancy's fixed gaze and decided it was either her maiden name or the name of her real husband.

"What kind of judge were you?"

"Just a regular Tennessee judge."

"Retired?" Rather stiffly he answered that he was too young to retire. He helped Dwight set up the red tent, had to finish the job alone when Nancy wanted to walk down to the women's toilet and Dwight not only waited by its door but tried to see through its small window. It seemed clear, now, that Nancy's toothbrush was home in Mr. Rayburn's bathroom. The judge blew up his air mattress and, after a minute, hers.

When they came back, Nancy laid out food they had bought: bread, peanut butter, milk, three beers, a clump of browning bananas. "I feel like I'm still traveling with Eddie Rayburn," she said sarcastically, while the judge leaned forward to hear more. She took from the backpack Sierra cups and plastic knives. Judge Jolley's cup had the name FAYE printed on the bottom with nail polish—an abandoned daughter, perhaps.

"Clara and I regretted we had no children," he said as a test. The other two ate. "Are you moving out west or just on vacation?"

"We're going to Arizona," Nancy said. "Do you want us to call you Mr. Jolley?"

"Harvey. Or Judge."

"You're no judge," said Anderson. "I've seen my share."

"For years I held court in Somerville, Tennessee. I am widely known." As Nancy seemed especially interested he said into her dark eyes, "I'm sure you realize that it's not easy to pronounce sentence on your fellow man."

"Like rolling off a log," said Dwight, "for every judge I ever knew."

Almost purring, Nancy said, "Are you widely known by Tennessee law officers, for instance? Patrolmen and sheriff's deputies?"

He thought of last year's unpleasant newspaper publicity, even the editorials when he was acquitted of official misconduct in deciding cases out of court. Editors with a two-bit education from agricultural college had objected to his splitting of hairs between illegal misconduct and violation of judicial ethics, though any fool knew that the very business of law was to slice one atom of hair loose from its adjoining atom. "I ran a humane courtroom," he said now. Why, after all, should he not have the discretion to dismiss some tickets, or enter a Prayer for Judgment Continued that would not assess points against a driver's license? To Harvey Jolley, the distinction was as clear as when Jesus wrote in the sand without condemning an adulteress, yet drove the money changers out of the temple with a scourge! Relative seriousness.

"What kind of court?" asked Nancy.

"County. Fayette County."

Dwight blew a noise down his nostrils. "Dime store level," he said.

"Why did you leave?"

"After Clara was killed I couldn't function." Though he might have been removed from the bench in any case, a reprimand was more likely; and those troubles were minor when set beside his grief. "The meaning went out of my life," he said to Nancy, who would surely understand. "How could I think about justice then? That we live and die by accident was clear to me at last." So obviously did her gaze measure and analyze him that the judge decided she might be cold-hearted.

With that ugly laugh Dwight said, "If he's a real judge he can marry us for real." Nancy drew back.

Judge Jolley decided to say, "Look, I don't care if you're married or not. What business is that of mine?"

"Well, we're not. Do I look stupid enough to marry this man?"

"Watch out," said Dwight. "It's a deep pond." He did not seem to be teasing.

But Nancy slid closer to the judge's air mattress. "At first I didn't even take this western trip seriously, since it was so fortuitous." With an angry look at Anderson she spelled the word "fortuitous." He put on his jacket in the heat. Nancy said she had planned to veer off alone in Memphis or Little Rock, "and just go where I pleased after that." She had been in the car without ever being on Dwight's trip, she said sarcastically. "He's always thought he was taking me for a ride but I've taken him for one, you see?"

"You never fooled me for one minute," said Dwight, scowling.

"Now we've agreed to stay together as far as Arizona." As if to herself she said, "Otherwise I never will see the country." The judge asked why, but she only reached out with one hand and caught hold of air and released it. "Because. It's different with Dwight," she said, turning to him.

Politely Jolley also turned. Dwight had been thinking hard, said now with great care, "She had been sitting by herself too long reading these Kinsey books. Aha! You didn't think I knew that, did you? Doctor Kinsey."

Puzzled, the judge looked back and forth. Into the growing silence he said, "Dwight was the one who wanted to go west?"

"Florida," said Dwight. He was, the judge thought, an ugly man whose attitudes would have turned any woman cold.

"Either place suits me," he decided to say.

"Look at that windshield. And it's not even his car."

The judge agreed with Nancy that it was going to crack all the way across. Perhaps she meant the car was stolen? "Whose is it?"

"My brother's. I left him behind."

"You wouldn't take him along?" said Nancy, nodding. "Broke one of your own promises, did you?"

"She is the living expert on breaking promises. Yes, I did that."

None of the heavy atmosphere of concealment matched the words.

"In Isoline?" asked the judge.

"Close by." Dwight gave that barking laugh. "I left him outside the movies and took her instead."

Why these two should tell him anything, much less this set of lies, the judge could not understand, and confusion always made him nervous. Not lovers, they seemed more like business partners who had embezzled from the same till and would stay partners only until the booty was divided. He said vaguely, "The fair sex is always better company."

"But without the brother!" cried Nancy as if making a discovery. "Without him, we're short a driver and that's why we need you to go all the way to Arizona!"

"We don't need nobody," said Dwight. As he began, while pacing, to crumple his beer can in his fingers, Nancy reminded him again that three would be better than two. Perhaps they were real embezzlers with detectives in pursuit, the judge thought.

"Let the judge come," said Nancy firmly. "I won't make trouble if he comes."

Dwight laughed as he drew near, reached out, and laid the crushed beer can on her head. "Queen of the Road," he said. "You still think you've got something to bargain with." The aluminum crown slid off into her lap. "Look, I can give you this judge like . . . like I would give you a handicap in golf. But how well he gets along, that depends on you." He bent, put back the wad of metal on her dark hair. "Everything else depends on me."

"You have my agreement until Arizona."

"When it suits you I have your agreement."

"I have not gone deaf," the judge put in, "and if there's some un-pleasant undercurrent here, I might prefer not—" He stopped when Dwight's look passed over his head to the pond. On the far side a pickup was moving slowly along the shore with a man in the back spewing fog from a machine. "Insecticide?"

"Mosquitoes," said Dwight. The smell drifted to them across the water.

"He's driving them all to this side." Nancy crawled into the tent and set her sandals outside. Several poles of high lights went on across the lake, ringing the clearing from which gas drifted. As trailer doors opened, a dozen old men came out, then reached back; each took a pair of folded aluminum chairs. They carried these to the edge of the greasy cloud and laid them in the grass.

Nancy unzipped the tent to watch the men waiting there. "It's some kind of spectator sport?" she asked. "Watching the bugs die?"

Now sheets of plywood were unloaded from the truck and white-haired women gathered with the men outside the poison cloud. The man in the truck called to them to "wait a little bit!" One woman in the semicircle waved but whether across the water at them or at a nearby dizzy insect no one could tell. The plywood sheets, set across sawhorses, became a long table laid through thinning mist. When it was ready, the men carried chairs to it and helped with the unloading of a tall wire hourglass.

"It's bingo!" the judge said. "I'm good at bingo."

"If Dwight will give me a handicap," said Nancy crossly, "I just might play." She bent over to fasten her shoes. The woman scooping out corn kernels called them an invitation across the pond.

The judge extended his elbow just right for a lady's hand but Nancy walked past him and stood by the spigot, staring downhill.

Dwight said, "Don't you go over there with him."

"You coming, Judge?" She reached back for his sleeve and tugged him behind her. Even though the twilight was still hot and sticky, Dwight kept on his blue jacket and kept his hands in its pockets as he followed, kicking at stones. One of them struck the judge's leg but he assumed it was accidental.

4

The paired men and women at the bingo table looked like worn dolls who had been dressed and mishandled by malicious owners: the men wrapped in clothes which fatter men, taller men, should have been wearing; their swollen wives barely contained by flimsy and vivid garb best suited to adolescents. Giant climber roses grew on their breasts above lime green and fluorescent orange slacks. The husbands' starched collars were bent around loose necks like folded paper. To gaze down a row of these couples made the eye dilate and shrink: large-small; bright-drab; fat-thin.

The judge, who this year was more fearful than ever of old age, loneliness, and death, turned hastily to the bingo caller. He and Nancy bought four cards from a man named Yow, who owned the park. Dwight would not play but stood staring at the open box of money.

"What's the prize?" asked Jolley.

Yow spread his palm and apologized. "On Monday night there's no jackpot, just five dollars to any winner in the first fifty calls. If not, the five carries over to the second game and turns into ten, and then fifteen, and so on."

They found empty chairs by the only skinny woman, long-legged as an egret in the only pair of shorts, who said, "Where you from, honey?" to Nancy, but eyed the judge.

"Maryland," she said. Dwight stood behind her chair.

The woman introduced herself and her husband; so did the other couples until, in a mumble, a string of forgettable names had been offered halfway down the table and had dwindled away. They began to play bingo. The skinny woman talked constantly and was heeded by no one. As Dwight Anderson loomed over her shoulder she tipped back her head and said brightly, "How do you do?"

"I do what I please." Distracted, she fell a number behind.

After a dozen calls a man yelled, "Bingo!" and a summons went out for the floor woman, Mrs. Dover, who came forward to verify numbers and to start the prize hand-to-hand down the table. There were complaints that Mrs. Dover always won; no wonder she had gotten them started on this game in the first place; and now her friend was winning. The judge noticed Dwight move down the table near Mrs. Dover after he heard this talk. Immediately Nancy said with half her mouth, "We need to talk in private."

"I can see," said the judge, "that you have a lot to contend with."

"That's the story of my life," she said, but Dwight came back then.

The egret woman was still rattling on, trying to establish who they were and where they were going and exactly what relationship Nancy had with each man, but she got skimpy answers to her questions. Dwight said, "I hear that Dover woman won a hundred dollars last week."

"She used to play in New Jersey," said one player, and his wife added, "She cheats." Someone else said at night Mrs. Dover dealt a little blackjack in her trailer and one of the women said, "Not for you she doesn't." Dwight moved back toward Mrs. Dover's chair and studied her. The new bingo game began.

Between numbers Nancy scrabbled through her purse to find a checkbook imprinted—to the judge's surprise—with NANCY FINCH and a box number in a state too long to be Maryland. She broke into the skinny woman's monologue to ask if she would do her a favor: call Mrs. Leon Finch collect at this number printed right here, and explain that Nancy was fine.

The woman said suspiciously, "You can use the pay phone in the main office. Are you married?" she said, suddenly pouncing on the judge. He was caught off guard and said no, a widower.

"I can't get to the pay phone," Nancy said.

Meantime the woman's face was blooming while she showed broad rows of artificial teeth. "A widower! What a shame, a terrible shame! Mrs. Dover there, my dearest friend, has already lost her husband, too. You really must meet since you have so much in common—Mrs. Dover? Estelle?"

The floor woman, closely followed by Dwight, came toward them. She was heavy breasted. In her pink shift with black linen sleeves she looked like a giant robin. Nancy hid her checkbook in her purse. "The next game is blackout so let's just talk," said the egret woman.

"Estelle Dover, this is Nancy and this one—ha ha—does what he pleases; but *this* this man?"

"Judge Harvey T. Jolley," he said.

"*Judge* Jolley. He *lost* his wife, I understand. Estelle has made such a good adjustment for someone just born to be a wife and homebody."

"How long will you be here, Judge?"

The judge could not resist their attention. He rose and bowed. "Actually, I met my first wife while traveling," he said as he took Mrs. Dover's plump hand. "She was looking for a vacation and I was the last resort." He led the polite laughter, let his smile turn properly serious. "It's wonderful to have good friends after a loss, Mrs. Dover."

The woman pulled up a chair between him and Nancy, preventing for a while any private conversation. "Are you two related?" Mrs. Dover began, looking back and forth between him and Nancy. "No? No kin at all?" Like the light from a swung lantern an unpleasant thought passed behind her eyes.

He was so flattered that he leaned forward so he could be seen around the woman's ample bosom and sent Nancy a wink, but she was whispering an argument with Dwight. "How long have you been a widow?" he asked, remembering that Clara had often said he looked like Nelson Eddy.

To his horror Mrs. Dover began to give a full autobiography, beginning with her running away to the carnival with Alonzo Dover, who had taught the young innocent to gamble. He nodded thoughtfully. Years ago he had learned to let hours of boring testimony and jury speeches roar softly at a distance, like ocean surf. Her long story washed back and forth.

Nancy broke into it, "Did Dwight take the keys out of the car?"

"Surely he did," said the judge, nodding encouragement to Mrs. Dover's narrative. She had worked up to Alonzo Dover's army discharge. He saw Dwight talking to one of the men on the sidelines, who was pointing to a particular trailer. The judge thought about where he would begin when it was his turn to talk. With Clara? With the orphanage, probably. To be without parents on one end of your life and without a spouse on the other saddened almost everybody, and women especially.

"So we had our second honeymoon at the Grand Canyon," Mrs. Dover kept on, "and I'll never forget it. Have you been there?"

"Yes," he lied, hoping to stop her description.

"Then you know the full majesty." She began contrasting the North and South rims. With her hands she made copies of its layers of rock in midair. He saw that Nancy was now trying to lean behind the woman to say something to him and he tilted his chair.

"Dangerous," Nancy said, and something else.

"Unless you really want to play more bingo, why don't you come over to my trailer for a drink?" Mrs. Dover said.

"No, I really can't; we'll be leaving early for Arizona," said the judge. "What, Nancy?"

"Then you'll be visiting the Grand Canyon again yourself!"

Once more he leaned back and Nancy leaned back; she said, tensely, "Don't leave me alone with Dwight. I'll explain."

"These lovers' quarrels," said the egret woman, eavesdropping. "Do go with Estelle and see her slides of the Grand Canyon. She must have five hundred."

"I've been there twice," said the judge.

Nancy, on her feet, was rushing around Estelle Dover to his chair. "He's coming; now listen!" she hissed at his ear. "He kidnapped me, understand? Good. Act normal. We'll handle him." She bent down to pick up a bingo card that had fallen there, leaving the judge with his jaw muscles lax and Estelle Dover still saying, "But of course I meant for all three of you to come."

"We're invited out," Nancy said flatly as Dwight joined them. The judge gaped at the sinister face, the broken tooth, some bloodied tattoo showing under the jacket sleeve. He did not want to be mixed up in this.

"I'm sorry, I wish we could," he said to Mrs. Dover, though he could not take his eyes off Dwight Anderson. One of the bingo players suddenly said, "Judge Jolley? Are you from Tennessee? Didn't I read about you in the papers last winter?"

"Of course we can," Dwight said. "Yours is the trailer with the birdbath?"

"You're so famous," said Mrs. Dover as the judge now hurried her toward it. Nancy and Dwight followed while Mrs. Dover continued her travelogue. "The earth simply opens up there to the very depths," she was saying. "For the first time I understood what the Bible means by the bowels of the earth." She turned to the others so the judge risked a glance as well. Yes. Dwight had the face of psychopath. "When you're in Arizona," Mrs. Dover went on, "you do what Alonzo and I did—rent mules. They'll take you all the way to the bottom down a winding trail. I can't even describe it to you." She gave a sigh and a small nostalgic shiver that the judge could feel through their locked arms. "I played I was a cowboy all the way down to the Colorado River at the bottom."

At the judge's back came Nancy's low, wry voice. "What fun, I'll be Persephone."

In Estelle Dover's trailer, they sat as closely spaced as bonbons in a box while the air-conditioner blew back red ribbons and labored to swallow their body heat. The living room was crowded with china shoes, porcelain boots and slippers, ceramic footwear of all kinds. Most of it contained greenery; even the bronze baby shoes had African violets bulging forth. On the coffee table sat a full replica of the Old Woman, her shoe, and her excess children, with a snake plant pointing through her roof. "I have this green thumb," Estelle told the judge as she kept their arms locked and swung him across the room like a square dancer. "I wonder if you'd help me serve?"

He was trying to get closer to Nancy to ask questions but Dwight kept him blocked off.

"It's a quiet life," said Mrs. Dover to Nancy as the judge made drinks. "When I was your age Alonzo and I traveled all up and down the east coast. We ran a spindle and a carnival wheel and a flasher. Never a dull moment."

The judge brought drinks and tried to sit by Nancy with his but was now asked to help set up the screen and projector. Meantime Dwight slid to one side a potted rubber tree that was concealing a small iron safe in one corner. "I hear you win a lot right here in the trailer park," Dwight said, moving the pot back and forth on its casters.

"We can't stay long," said the judge, unrolling the screen. "They say that every picture of Grand Canyon looks like every other picture." He wondered if Dwight carried a gun.

"No picture does justice to the reality, that's for sure. Even your eyes are too small to drink it all in." Mrs. Dover centered a white rectangle on the screen. "Mr. Anderson, you want to get the light switch by the door?"

Dwight, near the door in any case, had been fiddling with its lock. When he snapped the room into darkness the judge felt his way toward Nancy and whispered, "Are you serious? Kidnapped?" She nodded. With a click the Grand Canyon sprang into Technicolor existence on the screen, a giant picture postcard.

"I'll confess I bought some of the best ones at park headquarters," Mrs. Dover said. "Now watch, I'm going to show Hopi Point at four different times of day." The cliffs brightened from dawn to sunny noon. "Nothing changes but the amount of light," she said, going to afternoon with its altered, deeper shadows.

"Just be aware," said Nancy, softly. With sunset the cliffs turned molten, the light spilling down their enormous stairs until swallowed by the abyss.

The judge sat back, wondering if the bar association would be impressed by a man his age who rescued a kidnap victim. He wondered if by habitual stupidity they would leap to the conclusion that he'd had some hand in the kidnapping. Dwight was out of sight behind the rubber tree.

Next came a view of Estelle Dover, younger, happier, astride a bony mule. "Alonzo took this picture just before we started down the trail from the South Rim. I couldn't work the camera, see, so he made nearly all our pictures and now I don't have but one or two of him on our last vacation. "She drew a long sniff. "When I see this I can remember how Alonzo stood there and snapped it but even in memory the camera blacks out half his face. Do you have that trouble about your late wife, Judge Jolley?"

"I carry her photograph," he said. No, he could never go back to Somerville. Some had testified that they paid him their traffic fines, then later read in the newspaper that charges had been dismissed. Why should they care? His way their fines really *bought* something. He whispered to Nancy, "When he's asleep?"

"Not often," she said. They both looked to where Dwight had wandered half-outside Mrs. Dover's front door. Its latch must be jammed. Because Dwight looked so dim in the faint glow from the projector Nancy had an idea. "Could I use your bathroom?" Estelle pointed to a folding door. "This next is at Phantom Ranch in the bottom of the canyon, where we spent the night. You're a mile into the bowels of the earth here . . . "

Nancy forced shut behind her the plastic door and stood in a tiny bedroom. She stepped aside to turn on the bathroom faucet, full, before tiptoeing to the telephone by Estelle Dover's narrow bed.

The receiver seemed to make a great noise coming off the hook and the buzz of the empty wire sounded like a burglar alarm. Seeing no telephone book, she dialed the operator and waited. The police could surely be here before Mrs. Dover had climbed her full mile to the earth's surface again and before Dwight's glass was empty.

But when the operator answered, Nancy replaced the receiver, herself surprised by the action. She paced the length of the room in four steps. Dwight Anderson had not really hurt her. And she did have an ally now. Not that Judge Jolley would be much help when the real clash came.

She slipped to the door and looked at the judge through the crack. He was smirking at Estelle Dover, an 1890s gallant, so all-inclusive with his tepid flirting that—except to old ladies—he must seem effeminate. Dwight, having finished his own drink, started on Mrs. Dover's.

Father, Nancy prayed halfheartedly, you have got the cast wrong. If Jolley was only the kidnapper! I could have smiled my way across the continent and gotten out in San Francisco with a wave of my handkerchief.

But Dwight? No. A nut. Besides, the Finches must be worried sick.

Sure now of what she must do, she rushed back and dialed her home number. She ran through her mind Dwight's license plate, which she had memorized in Isoline, while digits respun themselves through a computer far away and hundreds of relays began to lift across the miles. A xylophone played faintly in her ear, then the first ring.

She could imagine her family's anxiety. Waiting, Nancy yanked a

Kleenex from a box, then two. If Mama's knees were swollen she would be slow to reach the hall. Again the phone rang. Usually Nancy answered it. And the door. And Mama's bedside bell. Usually she answered the mail.

With long-distance pokes and pinches, Nancy now hurried anybody out of the parlor and across the faded rug toward the joy of her voice. Another ring. She counted voices from the next room, alert to Dwight's. He was not talking. Four rings! God! Maybe Estelle's toy sink was plugged and overflowing. Maybe worry had given Mama heart failure and even the undertaker had left.

I'll let it ring six; that's all. Her foot wandered against a bedroom shoe topped with browning chicken feathers. It wouldn't kill Beckham to put down that goddamned cat and come.

"Hello?"

She stopped shredding Kleenex. "What number is this?"

"Finch residence," the mysterious stranger said.

She could hear, then, the tall clock by the phone making the right flat tick and, in the distance, music for some 1930s movie wavering at the wrong speed. The voice had a Negro softness; after all these years had Eddie hired a maid?

She blurted, "Who is home looking at television?"

"They're all in the parlor," answered this jewel of a maid who had been hired so Faye could stay home in Eddie's bed and succor him. Oh Lord, thought Nancy, closing her eyes. Each to her own taste. Worse. "Who is this?"

"Whom were you calling?"

They had replaced Nancy with a grammarian, or perhaps the maid was an undercover F.B.I. agent. "Beckham Finch."

"Just a minute." It was safe to ask for Beckham, who seldom left the house lest he have a public seizure. He stayed home with Mama, who stayed home with arthritis. Nancy stayed home with everything, in case needed.

Now that her ear knew exactly the spot to which it was turned, she could easily hear the clock, could count the right number of footsteps to the parlor door, could hear the stranger's voice. More steps. The treasure of a maid said, "I wonder if you would like to call back."

"Do what? I suppose somebody's favorite program is on? Somebody's favorite program is always on! Isn't that it?" She was not sure whether her throat was filling up so she could cry or scream. Suddenly she realized that the running travelogue had stopped in the other room. "Tell them it's Tennessee and not to worry," she said in a rush, and hung up the phone before hurrying to the bathroom.

Since she had chosen to open the hot water faucet the cubicle now swam with steam. Twisting it shut, Nancy stared hard at her cloudy face in the wet mirror. It did not look like the face she was accustomed to finding in bathrooms. This one looked wild. It belonged to a woman who was no good at answering doors, telephones, bedside bells. With her torn Kleenex Nancy wiped the glass and cleared her features. Her skin looked coated with shellac. As she touched one cheek, the reflection of her glossy fingers leaped into the mirror image like a third hand.

Thoughtfully drying her hands, she tried out excuses for Mama and Beckham. Even terrified people had to spend time somehow, see TV, drink coffee. She decided in five more minutes she would telephone the nearest police, but first she walked into the living room just as the judge called out that she was in time to see Mrs. Dover read the tarot. Even Dwight was watching Estelle as she sat on the shag rug and dealt cards between the plants on her coffee table.

"Ask her if I'm due to take a trip." Nancy collected another drink in the kitchenette, stopping to examine carrot fern and seedlings that were trying to live in egg cartons on the windowsill. Just a few more minutes and she would call the police. She lifted a clump of soil from its cup; yes, already the thready roots were trying to live off cardboard. A maid! she thought, drank deeply. For a maid's salary I could have gone to the Leeward Islands.

In the living room Dwight bent to point to a particular card. Behind him the last photograph of cliffs and chasms still showed on the screen, all colors washed out now that the lamps were on. Maybe I'll see it, Nancy thought. The real canyon, not just its picture. I've read every travel book Stone County Library owns.

Her attention was caught by the judge's high, strained voice. "Of course not, calm down," he said to Dwight, who shook off his hand.

Below the two men Mrs. Dover was touching a central card, its colors like stained glass. From this distance, Nancy could not read which card it was.

"A stupid old lady who's asking for it!" Dwight shoved the judge. Whatever Mrs. Dover had foretold had made his upper teeth, even the broken one, clamp visibly over his lower lip as if he might bite himself. "Cheaters get cheated," he said. As Nancy hurried forward she could see the faint red notches where his teeth had pressed. In a slow, almost graceful swoop, Dwight's arm swung round and lifted Mrs. Dover's fingers high over her head.

She gasped and reached as if to rescue her wristwatch. The tight grip was frightening her. Hoarsely she said, "I say that only because we got the same answer twice, in pairs. Other readers might interpret the cards differently." Dwight left her arm standing up alone like a stake while he picked up a tarot card and tore it in half, then into smaller pieces. He ordered Nancy, "Get over here!" and added something strange to himself. "I'm not like him." Was that what he said? "You, too, Judge; move it."

The scene restored Mrs. Dover to carnival strength. "Who in the hell do you think you are? Here in my home like a son of a bitch?" She lifted the first china object that came to hand. "Goddamn right you're leaving!" The judge helped flutter down the quivering plant while Nancy, passing, breathed, "Thank you. Nice evening. Very much."

"You deserve what the cards say!" screeched Mrs. Dover to their backs. "It really means death, do you hear me? And I wish you a quick one!"

Nancy was being dragged away by one arm. "You put her up to that! Is that why you left the room?" She told Dwight no. "She'll be sorry, she asked for it." They floundered away from the trailer ankle-deep in damp ivy, past the birdbath with its terra-cotta shoe full of geraniums. "She'll pay."

"Stop it, Dwight!" Though the judge caught Dwight's sleeve, his gesture was as weak as his voice. "Let Nancy alone."

"I'm all right." She did not want to anger Dwight even more and kept in step with him across the clearing, around the pond's muddy edge. "The only place I went was the bathroom," she said. "I don't even know what Mrs. Dover read in your cards." Dwight's footprints oozed beside hers. "Why should you care what an old carnival fraud has to say?" Before she went too far, Nancy got a vision of Mrs. Dover, bound and gagged, stuffed into the trunk of Dwight's car. "It doesn't matter, though. You're too smart to be superstitious." The judge was breathing heavily behind them. "Let's forget all about Mrs. Dover."

"You try to leave me," he said, "before I'm ready and you'll really see something."

"All right." She had decided the heavy breaths were her own.

"I do the leaving. I've left them all."

"Yes," she said. They passed the Yows' trailer and entered the track his car had cut through the field. She could not help asking as they walked. "Which card did you tear? Was it the devil?" The judge warned her with a poke in the back.

"I always do the leaving."

But he seemed calmer. "We can even leave right now if you like," Nancy said. Dwight almost growled, "Not yet."

At their campsite, Nancy crawled into the tent and closed its flap. The two men, backs turned, sat silently on their air mattresses unlacing shoes. When Dwight pulled off his shirt the judge, more slowly, did the same. Each seemed to be guarding the other. Finally the judge crawled into Eddie's sleeping bag, from which, after humping and squirming, he sat up again with his removed trousers rolled into a pillow.

Dwight sat smoking, watching the last lights across the pond. Nancy grew sleepy while she waited for him to make some move. At last he rose, his back bare and silvered, to shake out his jacket. In the pale light he looked bird-chested. Occasionally he would touch his ribs as if he had indigestion on the left side.

For a long time she watched him, an odd statue, a Napoleon without a coat, holding one hand above his heart. Then the liquor did its work and she drifted into sleep in spite of herself. She was running down a street while fireworks or neon overhead gave off a rain of white, imitation stars. Dodging the hot shower between rows of closed brownstones, she bumped into a shabby Jewish peddler with a

beard—Joel, older. In the dream she knew he was Joel though the resemblance was not strong. The Joel-man was selling grapes to get rid
of them; his favorite part was the stem, he said, snapping one on his
sharp front teeth. She pushed by him, for she was in search of some
other fruit that grew at the end of the street. She ran on and the street
got longer. Ahead of her, doors began to open and old people carrying asbestos umbrellas stepped from stoop to gutter and walked
silently the other way. She recognized several men in the parade, former lovers grown old and cautious, but she could not go back for
them. The hail of fireworks ran off their parasols like mercury. When
this is over, the running Nancy thought, my skin will be burned. A
long way off grew the trees with something golden showing through
their leaves.

With a wrench she woke herself in the boxy tent, wondering if fireflies or a drizzle outside had set off the dream. Through the net she
spotted Dwight, now wearing his jacket, moving downhill toward the
pond. She had not been asleep long, then. Judge Jolley was snoring.
Near the water Dwight's shadow vanished; she thought it reappeared
beyond the bathhouse. "Judge?" He slept on. Dwight might be going
to the toilet. She tried to pick out Mrs. Dover's trailer in the dark and
keep watch over it.

Much later, she saw him return or else dreamed it. Certainly he
looked larger, heavier; the setting had subtly changed, but his bare
back was turned as it naturally would be and his skin shone as it
ought from the rain. Softly she called out, "Is that you?" And the
man, or Dwight, or Joel, or no one, said, "You know it's not."

It never is, she thought.

Sometime later, with a ripping noise, Dwight opened the tent above
her head. Blindly she slammed her pocketbook toward his face but he
blocked with a forearm. "Stop that. We're ready to leave, that's all."
Outside the judge was mumbling while stuffing his bag in its sack.

"It's not even daylight!" Nancy struggled out onto the wet grass.
"What's the big damn hurry?" The air mattresses were already flat
and folded.

Half-mocking, the judge said, "Dwight does the leaving." He
pulled his drawstring tight and shrugged.

"Don't make so much noise." Dwight slipped items quietly into the car trunk. "We can stop at a toilet someplace else."

"I want to stop now. I want to take a shower."

"People in hell want ice water. What's left besides the tent?"

Nancy pointed out that the night rain had left the tent fly wet. "It'll mildew if you pack it wet."

"Let old Eddie worry."

Nancy dragged her possessions out of the tent, the judge bending nearby to pull up stakes. When Dwight had squatted on the far side, the judge whispered, "If he's not armed, I can jump him."

"He's armed," she said.

"Oh."

By the time she picked out her eye corners and combed her hair, Dwight had wadded the rain fly into the trunk. He held open their car doors, with great quietness closed each one behind them.

In the instant while Dwight was approaching the car Judge Jolley asked, "What do you want me to do?"

Nancy shook her head. As they drove slowly around the pond, she leaned tensely forward to retrace the path Dwight might have taken in the night. People were still asleep. They passed the ARBORS sign and were down the asphalt road a mile before Dwight turned on the headlights.

Nancy said, "I thought you paid for the campsite. Then why do I feel like an escaping thief?" She got a good look at Dwight's uneven teeth bared in a grin. "What's so funny, Dwight? Dwight?" She grabbed his shoulder. "Is Mrs. Dover all right?"

"Sleeping like a baby."

"Then what is it?"

The tires sang on the interstate. "I borrowed us some of her bingo money, that's all. The game's fixed. She keeps a special card and Yow knows the numbers. They split the take."

The judge said, "It was simple revenge because you didn't like the way she read the cards. Miss Finch and I both want out in the next town, do you hear me? We are not thieves. We don't want to be accessories."

But Nancy had begun to laugh. "We can just sit here and listen for the siren, Judge Jolley. I give him half an hour. Mr. Yow won't have any trouble describing this car. Probably he writes down license numbers."

"Maybe so," said Dwight. He didn't sound worried enough. "Bingo for money, the way they run it, isn't legal in Tennessee—is it, Judge Jolley? Mrs. Dover won't call anybody."

When she sought his face, the judge nodded.

"Not that he's the living legal expert," said Dwight. "Some of those men remembered you, Judge. Didn't you get disbarred?"

"I did not," said the judge. "Some matters about my court are being verified, that's all."

"He took bribes," said Dwight. "People think you're in Mexico, you know that?"

"I have not been hiding. Would I be in Isoline if I were hiding? No, I've been thumbing around the state, that's all, trying to regain my balance. I am not, Nancy, wanted by the law."

"Not yet, because the case isn't settled yet," said Dwight Anderson.

"I gave Clara the car she was killed in," said the judge. "I taught her how to drive it so I knew she wasn't very good. She had persuaded me to let her drive not thirty minutes before the accident, Nancy."

She did not know what to say but Dwight did. "Takes a lot of traffic fines to pay cash for a new car, don't it, Judge?"

5

For Nancy, even in a town like Greenway, there had been men; Joel Epstein was only the most recent.

Riding west, Nancy closed her eyes to revisit Joel in last night's dream. Manischewitz grapes, no doubt. His wife must still be eating their fruit and he the stems, while Nancy got neither. Dreams are very economical.

Before Joel, a high school coach who should have played pro ball, should have been asked back to his old college where he had starred, should have married a blonde from Kansas instead of the redhead from Ocracoke. What had attracted her? William's size or the scale of his dissatisfactions against which to measure her own? When he moved on to a larger school with a winning team, they ended friends.

Before him, a banker from an old Greenway family and a bachelor forever. Something about his avid courtship and tepid consummations reminded her of Judge Jolley. With Patrick she had made love only rarely, on a water bed she mistrusted, where she found he did not really desire her much but said he did from good manners. At local dances, restaurants, and high school games, where she had begun to study the coach's body, Patrick spoke ardently, but once actually on a mattress he became fearful of "not satisfying" her. He talked, kept talking, asked questions; he tried out all the variations he understood women wanted, with inquiry. Did she like this? That? The other? Why weren't her nipples hard?

"Soft nipples, hard heart," she said once, but Patrick could not joke at such moments. His steady assessment of her symptoms made Nancy feel like a patient doing exercises for a cardiogram. Nowadays they only attended banquets or movies though he still spoke passionately to her at odd and public times, and often he spoke passionately *about* her, making others envy their wild offstage lovemaking. Eddie had wanted to invite Patrick on their mountain trip. "Us old married people will mind our own business after dark," he had offered with a wink.

And before Patrick—yes, there came the kink in her breath. Before them all, Oliver Newton. A preacher, of all things, staunch Presbyterian at that, a man who never once laid a hand on her—though both had wanted hands to be laid. Nancy was twenty-one then. That was the last time, she thought now in the moving car, that by doing nothing I did something right.

"You asleep?" the judge asked from far away. "The prisoners have been offered breakfast."

Yawning, she sat up as Dwight parked at DAVY JONES LOCKER. She followed the judge into a restaurant whose walls were covered by giant mounted indigo fish, their artificial mouths gaping as if to scream through imagined water. "You were smiling in your sleep," said the judge, holding back fishnet curtains with papier-mâché starfish. Dwight pushed her into a booth under a red ceramic anchor with fluorescent barnacles crusting its prongs.

"This is a better dream than the one I was having." From her cardboard yacht she ordered Seafarer's Scrambled Eggs with Scurvy Cure Juice and Neptune's Toast. "When we get to the Arizona desert, I suppose we'll be eating in fake igloos."

"*I'll* be eating," Dwight said. "I don't want you to have to eat off this tainted money from Eddie or Mrs. Dover."

"Who's Eddie?" Neither answered or noticed the judge's growing horror as he decided Eddie was the name of some dead body left behind at the kidnap site. "Beyond belief," the judge began to whisper, flattening his body against the wall. "Simply beyond belief."

"Did you go inside that woman's trailer?" Nancy asked.

"What did you think—that I siphoned the money out a window?"

"Then I'm sure police are on the way. Bingo is small stuff compared with burglary. Let's relax and enjoy ourselves, Judge Jolley, until they come."

"Actually," said the judge, "I've been thinking about changing to Louisiana. If I went south from Memphis, I could see the orphanage I was raised in."

"What? And leave me?" Nancy tried to control her indignation. So far, Dwight thought the judge knew about theft but not about kidnapping.

"When I say so," said Dwight as the juice and coffee came.

"Beyond belief," said the judge. And louder, "I guess Dwight does *all* the leaving."

"I'd like to wash my hands." After a pause Dwight let her out of the booth and watched her enter the room marked HEAD with its female silhouette. Inside was a lounge with tanks of bright tropical fish, and—to her surprise—a pay telephone.

Quickly she washed, scrubbing her body and crotch with paper towels that peeled into bits and would probably cause cervical cancer. She felt her clothes had grit and sweat in every thread.

Then with a handful of change she hurried back to call Greenway again. It was just past five a.m.; the hall clock would have finished its chime, or was she in a different time zone? To think of Mama and Beck asleep in their beds while the telephone rang excited her. When words were mumbled far away she let fall a clangor of coins. It was Faye. "Hello?"

Watching the door Nancy whispered, "You got out of the gorge all right?"

"Nancy? Nancy, is it you?" Faye, too, was whispering. "My God, are you all right?" It was just like Faye to babble so a kidnap victim couldn't get in a word. "Did you call last night or was that a practical joke?"

"Hush, Faye. I'm in Tennessee, right off I-Forty." The opening door cut short her words. She almost had the phone on the hook before she saw it was only a waitress, not Dwight Anderson, and too hard she slammed the receiver against her ear. "Thought it was him. Heading west."

"Is he there? Are you hurt? Have you called police?"

"I will. Listen, was that a maid last night?"

"You can't imagine what it's been like here."

"There? What about where I am?" As the waitress carried out paper towels, the door hung open long enough to let Nancy's rising voice escape. Dwight was looking from the booth though she felt sure the telephone was blocked from view. In her ear Faye began screaming for Eddie to get downstairs this very minute! "Send help," said Nancy, "he's a loony," as she saw Dwight rise from the booth. The door closed to shut him from sight but she hung up and hurried away, partly because she had not been able to hear the clock that had been ticking in the Finch hall the night before, that had been ticking for years and should have been at Faye's elbow ticking now. Nancy had always forced herself to sleep against its hated knock and gong, which the others found soothing. Now, for Faye, they had stopped the pendulum.

Outside the door she almost ran into Dwight. "I got to wondering if there was a back window."

"No," she said. "I looked." She now snapped a glance beyond to see if the judge had made it to the manager's office yet but, no, he was pressed into one corner of the booth muttering. His fear, Faye's voice, the clock, all set her mind afire with anger, one thought igniting the next, like pine cones catching the blaze. As always, she saw, everything depended on her alone, including her escape. She shook loose from Dwight's hand. The judge was terrified; the Finches were incompetent! Maybe she'd redefine escape. Maybe she'd never go back!

Nancy almost threw herself into the booth and began eating like someone who needs to build up strength.

Dwight said, "Something you told the judge has confused him. He's not sure you're here of your own free will. Pass the pepper." Stupid old man. "Well, I am," she said angrily.

"She stays because of my tattoo." Dwight leered. "My other tattoo."

Nancy thought: Faye is sleeping in my room, where the letters are, the photographs not only of Oliver Newton but one of the naked coach doing a headstand with everything hanging the wrong way. She is reading my journal.

"I don't understand," said the judge.

"It was Nancy's little joke."

"Even if that were true, what about Mrs. Dover's bingo winnings?" asked the judge.

"That one's my little joke."

"You don't seem frightened now." He leaned forward. "Nancy?"

"I'm fine, I can handle everything."

Unconvinced, the judge forked up his food while at last he began slyly to examine the restaurant for assistance. In another minute, Nancy saw, he might decide to sound an alarm whereupon Dwight would shoot through him just as if he were a windshield. In fact, Dwight was watching the same clues in the judge's movements; they caused a brief, uncharacteristic vitality to flare in his yellow eyes. She felt Dwight barely existed between such crisis moments and she tried to conceive the torpor of a stone while it waits centuries for someone to find and throw it.

As Dwight would say, I'm the living expert on torpor. She caught the judge's hand. "I don't even want to go home," she said, too loud. "After we get to Arizona, I plan to go someplace else. So don't you run any risk."

"Let him try, see how far he gets," said Dwight.

The judge squeezed her fingers but his face looked not reassuring but relieved. "I won't let him harm you," he said *Huh-huh,* laughed Dwight in contempt. "Why does he want us with him?"

"He doesn't know; it's probably repressed."

Dwight said he knew everything he needed to know.

"Then why?" Nancy asked.

"Right now I don't want either one of you staying behind to tell about me" was all he said.

"I believe him," said Nancy to the judge after they had eaten awhile in silence. "I believe that to be senseless is normal for Dwight." Dwight told her to shut up. "He's got no motive, no goal or cause. We or any other two people in the world could be sitting here. It makes me feel—" She jerked when Dwight pinched her arm and held on with a fingernail. Coffee sheeted over her cup and across the table. Nancy waited motionless until he let go, then she reached for a napkin and wiped the table. "It makes me feel trivial, like spilled coffee, but he's wrong. I won't be reduced like that."

"This is beyond belief!" The judge tried awkwardly to stand in the booth. There was no one to summon now except teenage waitresses and two fat women.

"He happens to be a big nuisance on *my* trip west," Nancy said.

Huh-huh, Dwight laughed, and said after a few minutes' thought, "You ever noticed how a mouse entertains a cat? He can eat it just any time." When the others had finished he picked up the bill and read the price of each breakfast.

"Don't pay a cent," Nancy hissed to the judge.

"Mrs. Dover's buying; you saw how she liked the judge's style." Dwight added that it was time to go, starting to rain again. He held Nancy's wrist while the cashier made change. Outside he said, "You just keep track of how things are. I can throw you out to a crowd of drunk hitchhikers. I can leave you without a penny in places you wouldn't want to go to rich." Yet he seemed to enjoy her rebellion and was whistling through the space in his front teeth as they came to the car. "You want to drive *your* car on *your* trip west? Get in, Judge, that man ain't got time to listen to your sad story. Don't even speak to him. That's right."

She took the keys. "The truth is," said Dwight, "without me you got no place to go, either one of you. This is the only man," he said with a jerk of his thumb toward the judge, "I ever heard of that hitch-hiked in circles. He's been on the road since February and how far away you think he got from Somerville?"

"Stay out of my private life," the judge said, but Nancy saw his fingers trembling.

Long before Memphis the thin gusty rain settled into a thick roar that overran the track of the windshield wiper. In the downpour Nancy had to embrace the wheel to see the road, or lean out the side where long slices of water were thrown up by their tires.

In the passenger seat, the judge—who had been quiet for a long time—said, "Don't sit that way. I used to tell Clara if she took a deep breath the horn would blow. That's how she was driving when she died."

Leaning back, Nancy watched their headlights play on the streaky wall of rain. When a swaying lump materialized through it as an auto trunk, she jerked aside so fast the rear end hydroplaned before catching the road's surface. For a few extra seconds Nancy continued to float sideways inside her skin.

"See?" said the judge with a slight waver. "It's easy to die. You or somebody else forgets to fight it for one second—that's all you need."

Dwight said from the back, "I notice you lived through this famous wreck."

"In a way I outlived it." After a lightning flash he braced for the metallic crack of thunder. "How slick are these tires? Let's pull over till after the storm."

"I'd like to pull into a motel and get a hot shower."

"Keep driving," Dwight said to Nancy, "and if you need to wash just stick different parts outside."

The lightning began to break more frequently. It did not seem to radiate from the sky but to burst about them at ground level from the heart of every object. The judge twitched a brief smile. "Am I the Jonah?"

Though Dwight had pulled his cap onto most of his face, she could see his lips moving in the mirror. "Should have thrown you overboard in Isoline," he said.

As she drove through the storm, she tried to picture Dwight Anderson as an open-faced boy in some Lutheran Sunday school listening to Bible stories on a flannel board. No, she decided, Catholic. Catholic lapses were the more spectacular. The end of her own prayers, she realized, was a sure sign she was taking charge herself. When Dwight had again been quiet for a while the judge mouthed an elaborate whisper. "We must plan how to reach the police."

"I've reached them," she said—if Faye had conveyed their location. The thought that rescuers might arrive any minute was not as pleasing as it should have been. She rubbed the arm that bore the dents of Dwight's fingernails. Pinches, yes; but for some reason of his own he would not kill her; she could keep him from killing the judge, too. At least, she thought wistfully, for one more day—long enough to cross into Texas and see one mesa and a gulch. She hated to be shipped home to Greenway with western memories as secondhand as Mrs. Dover's slides.

The judge asked how; she said softly that she had been in touch with her home by telephone twice. True, so far as it went. "But I don't think he'll harm us as long as we don't run from him. He'd put a bullet in your back or mine."

"Or in our faces, for that matter."

"He doesn't seem like a killer to me, too third-rate, small-time. One reason I feel so trivialized is that as villains go Dwight is small potatoes."

The judge flapped one open hand outward before whispering back, "In every murder case I ever heard there were no grand-scale villains. Killing is always a failure of the imagination; people can be tenth-rate and do it."

"But he lacks energy."

"I can be just as dead from a lazy man's pistol as—" He broke off when Dwight stirred in the back.

More lightning flashed. "Your last hitched ride must have been a lot less interesting."

"The prospect of my own death is not, to me, merely *interesting*." He helped find some paper to wipe moisture off the windshield. "Though it would put an end to the grieving over Clara," he said, letting out a long breath. "I should have died when she did."

"Why didn't you kill yourself, then?"

Aghast, then offended, the judge said, "Maybe I will, maybe I will yet!"

"If you really want to die, Dwight's the man you're looking for."

"*Should* have died, I said. I didn't say I *wanted* to die. I'm a Christian, anyway, and I consider the power of life and death to be in God's hands!"

"You're a Christian?"

"What does that tone mean?"

"Just surprise. Or do you mean a churchgoer?"

Before Jolley could object Dwight sat up, spat into the rain, and instructed Nancy to come into the back seat now. They were in the outskirts of Memphis. "We'll change places while the judge earns his keep and gets us to the bridge the fastest way."

She parked on the highway shoulder and they crawled over the seat back in a tangle. Nancy, midway, reached out on the off-chance of finding Dwight's gun in the nearer pocket. By error her hand grazed his thigh. As if seared he fell away, turned back to frown at her.

She blurted, "I'm sorry I touched you!" and snatched off the floor of the back seat a Memphis paper she had not seen Dwight buy. They drove on, Dwight still studying her thoughtfully from time to time. Nancy, flipping through Tennessee versions of rape, strangling, and burglary, had to bite back a gasp when her own name flew to her eye out of a column called "Highway Patrol Radio":

CONTINUING ALERT: Black car, possible Ford/Chevrolet, possible 1960–70 model, carrying Nancy Finch, 34, librarian, Greenway, N.C., with unidentified male Caucasian kidnapper, 35–40, described as 6 ft., 4 in., 200 lb., unshaven, black hair, black eyes, leather jacket, possible vertical scar beside left eye, husky voiced, muscular, may be trained weight lifter, believed under drug influence, definitely armed and dangerous; car may contain stolen vacation clothes and camping equipment bearing ER, FR, or Rayburn nametags, believed to be traveling west on I-40. Victim is medium height, medium weight, dark brown eyes and hair, no identifying marks, last wearing blue dress, bites fingernails. Abducted late Sunday, Linville Gorge, N.C. Rangers and National Guardsmen are leading mountain search.

After gaping over this Goliath who had outfought and tied up gallant Eddie Rayburn, Nancy repeated aloud, "Bites fingernails!" In the thunder nobody heard. Once more she read about colorless Nancy Finch, who had vanished wearing a dress she did not even own. *Bites fingernails!* She stared over Dwight's shoulder where Memphis was fragmented and shiny through the broken windshield. She ran one finger over the long scar at her elbow, earned one winter day when Beckham had fallen in convulsion and she—trying to catch him—had put her elbow through the back door pane. There was a mole just under her right breast; Joel had lifted slightly to find it in the crease. Her eyes, more hazel than brown, had in both inside corners a shallow crater where she had picked out a chickenpox scab.

The judge, who had missed a turn, shouted to pedestrians under an awning.

She had quit biting her fingernails for her twenty-sixth birthday, over champagne at Patrick's.

The same gray hotel with its splotches of wet pigeons went by her window three times before they found the right road. In front the judge said sharply, "You're right, Nancy, here they are! How do you want to handle it?"

Dwight crouched near the wet windshield, his Preakness cap in one hand as traffic slowed, their car pinned tightly between bumpers. When she rolled down the window Nancy could see through the rain a roadblock where the bridge crossed the Mississippi. Two patrolmen in yellow slickers were checking driver's licenses looking for a woman in a blue dress riding alongside Samson.

"I'll do the handling. Got a license?" While the judge found his, Dwight slid a card from his billfold and with its corner began raking straight lines down the condensation on the glass. "Let's turn around."

"I'm blocked. Nancy?"

"Play it by ear," she said, dropping the newspaper to the floor.

The judge edged them forward. "What does that mean? This is beyond belief!" After Dwight hung his jacket over the seat with the fatter pocket near his hand, he nudged Judge Jolley with the hidden gun.

"You were right," he said lazily to Nancy. "Three is better than two."

The judge asked hoarsely, "What about car registration?"

"I hope not," Dwight said.

Though she squinted as Dwight scraped his license up and down she could not read the name. "If I had a blue dress I'd put it on."

"I read it," Dwight said.

Now a patrolman at the window said, "Take it out of the wallet, please. Oh yes." Dwight began running his jacket zipper up and down, up and down. "I know you; not you, sir. Over in Somerville?"

"Me?" said the judge.

"It's a good thing you're not speeding." The officer leaned forward and made an ostentatious show of smelling the judge's breath. "I ought to search this car."

"Do that, do that!" cried the judge with a whirl of his head to Nancy.

The yellow hood came in out of the rain while the man looked over both passengers. As if of its own will, Nancy's hand with its long fingernails came forward and spread itself on the seatback in plain view.

"What you up to these days, Mister Jolley?"

"I'm still a judge!"

"Not to me." He called to his companion. "Remember Harvey Jolley, judge over in Fayette County? He's leaving the state!"

"Rush him along," said the other patrolman.

After a tip of his slicker hat, the patrolman waved them into a slow procession over the wide, rusty river. The judge said, "You can still get out and run back, Nancy."

"No, she can't." Dwight had kept his jacket close to Judge Jolley's ribs and he now ground the hidden gun barrel deeper.

"I meant to tell them." Nancy craned her neck to look back. Their path was crossing over that of a southbound barge hauling timber. "It happened so fast." The lost moment and now the river boundary seemed to mark a dividing point between this part of her life and the next. She stared ahead through the misty rain trying to see the country's second, western half. Though the drizzle seemed to disappear below the bridge without reaching the river, the loaded logs gleamed dark. The car passed into West Memphis and traffic thinned out.

"Would he shoot this gun or not?"

Nancy said that's how the hole got in the windshield. What she had done, not done, was irrevocable. She had committed herself to everything she had heretofore told Dwight only to goad him; she had made the trip hers.

"I shot a man not long ago," said Dwight, "but he wasn't a real man; appearances are deceiving. Sun's coming out."

She did not know whether to believe him or not. Too late. All because of a maid and a stopped clock and that blue dress.

"He was degenerate," Dwight said.

As if now all three were committed they pulled away into the car's corners and said no more. For miles Nancy stared at the rising basin country as it brightened and steamed in the emerging sun. Unable to remember such a glistening green in nature, she snatched off her sunglasses to double-check.

"Ain't the judge quiet? Who would have thought he was so famous!" Dwight said at one point. "*Huh-huh*, Judge!"

In contrast with this gleaming vegetation, Mrs. Dover's western photographs had shown no tender green, no leaf, no grass. If they drove until the southwest turned to stone, Nancy would have her chance to see muted reds and blending golds in the layered cliffs, the color of light on implacable stone. A place like Grand Canyon, she thought, would give Sisyphus bad dreams.

6

The worst—that's all anybody ever remembers! What if I'd grabbed Dwight's gun and been shot and died? Driving, Judge Jolley snapped his head forward as he mentally recognized and read to himself the headline: CROOKED JUDGE KILLED AT ROADBLOCK.

The trouble with moral bookkeeping was that the older you got and the thicker your ledgers became, the less was publicly known until finally you would outlive the last man to whom you had done a kindness but be outlived by whatever failures were on the record. This outcome was precisely what had kept pulling him back to church with a recurring hope of eventual, overriding, omnipotent justice. To be written up with meticulous care in the Book of Life was religion's most appealing metaphor.

Because the other two fell silent as they drove out of the rain and stayed silent across almost half of Arkansas, he had plenty of time to balance his own accounts. The environment finally got lucky, but God knows what the genes were like. I may be inherent trash, I may have done wonders of triumph uphill against all likelihood—God only knows. He kept inserting this last thought into his memories like a rhythmic motif, for it comforted him. God only knows.

His name—all three names—his home, and his profession had come by accident. As a very small boy he had lived with migrants, though he barely recalled a woman's red chapped hands holding a metal hoop; fruit that passed through the ring was too small to pick and whatever stuck was large enough for the basket—peaches, he supposed now. She abandoned him as a four-year-old in Louisiana near the old Harvey canal, along with a note saying that since she expected a child of her own she could not care for this foundling. A bachelor who shrimped and trapped kept him for several months and named him Harvey but after a bad season turned him over to the Methodist orphanage in Ruston. There he was called Harvey Trace, because there wasn't a single one of either parent.

His schooling was supervised by the Reverend Easterling, a skinny zealot whose tension between God's will and God's grace had electrified his very bones. For all his pupils, whether they studied the alphabet or the multiplication tables, Easterling strung a long singing wire between perfection and imperfection. Emphasizing that at every moment they would be free to choose or reject God's gift, whatever its disguises, he set before them a long sequence of either/or choices, vibrating ahead across time toward a death that would find the word Yes or No upon their cooling lips.

In this atmosphere, which magnified his smallest action into a deed that elated or grieved his Maker, Harvey Trace learned to read and cipher. Because he was making a temple of his life he soon became an excellent student. He obeyed Mr. Easterling and set aside a time tithe, 10 percent, during which he would meditate or search scripture or pray.

Though he tried for over two hours daily, he could not repent of his dislike of the orphanage or learn to enjoy cornmeal mush, peas, hard beds, thin blankets, honest labor. He offered up his skill at long division for whatever use the Lord might make of it, and praised the good motives of farmers and their weary wives who came shopping for sons and passed him by for taller and heavier boys. Doggedly he thanked God for Mr. Easterling, who followed the model and loved whom he chastened.

Like the others, he searched the Bible for life verses, each one beginning with the initial of his names. He would grave these mottos upon the doorposts of his heart as soon as he was satisfied he had chosen the *right* ones. As usual he had the freedom to choose or reject the right ones; if he settled for second best, God would be grieved. The new surname, Trace, was the harder since verses beginning with "the" abounded on every page of both Testaments. He kept changing his selection.

At eleven, unjustly whipped for another's lie, Harvey made his last sweep of the T-verses and knew by the flushed tingling of his skin which instruction God had meant all along, in Matthew 20. Next morning he ran away from the orphanage and before sleeping in the woods after meals of stolen melons and tomatoes, he would recite his special verses:

> HAPPY is the man that findeth wisdom, and the man
> that getteth understanding. (Proverbs 3:13)

> TAKE that thine is, and go thy way: I will give unto
> this last, even as unto thee. (Matthew 20:14)

He was not sure what he would be given. As he ran east, Harvey Trace so much resembled a boy headed down the road on an errand that people waved and passed on. He lived off gardens and orchards. As they drifted home at dusk, sometimes cows would be surprised by him and would hold still for a short milking before they remembered the feel of other hands and kicked free. Bitten by a farmer's dog, he waited two days by a stream for hydrophobia and promised to go back to Ruston if God would spare him. God spared him with only a mild bloat from living off water and blackberries—a sign that he read like the sparing of Isaac. He moved on around Monroe and its gas fields, happy, and walked the railroad downhill through lowland cotton and sweet potato fields from Delhi to Tallulah, by Roundaway Bayou and over swamp.

He had been terrified of crossing the Mississippi then, too, but after two days' planning he hung himself like a bat against a boxcar ladder and rode across the clanking trestle in the dark. Midway, his legs began to tremble. He had to work off his belt and buckle himself to the rungs like a window washer. In the freight yards he was the first thing noticed and unloaded, but he broke loose and ran up the railroad tracks from Vicksburg, finally caught on to another freight, and had to steal food again in Memphis. "Take that thine is, and go thy way."

He had begun by then to try matching his face to those of older men, for he was convinced that blood would identify itself. In the farmland east he paused to watch strangers plow in case some reflex should tell them both to meet. Even if he should pass his nameless father's tomb, he believed, his heart would jerk downward like a dowser's wand.

In the rain near Somerville he caught cold and climbed into a man's corncrib. He was feverish. Next morning the tenant wrapped him in a quilt and carried him by wagon to the home of Robert C. Jolley, landowner, part-time lawyer, embittered Catholic, who had lost a son in Woodrow Wilson's war. This boy had the wrong face, yet Jolley and his wife snatched him from their tenant's arms. In a month, when Harvey told them the truth, they made the adoption legal.

To please his new father he agreed to read law when he was older. At thirteen he chose the new verse to fit his third name. Robert Jolley said that, as a matter of fact, a man named Tolstoy had read that verse incorrectly. "Judge not that ye be not judged" meant only that criticism of self and others must be made with equal stringency. "In those terms," he said with a look at the first son's photograph, "God's welcome to judge us if He's got the nerve."

When Harvey Jolley became a county judge and uncomfortably

fulfilled his last verse, it was like having Mr. Easterling's yes-or-no enacted constantly. He often underwent weeks of confusion during which every defendant or none seemed really guilty; when the pendulum swung and he judged himself, his verdicts were harsh. Though neighbors seemed embarrassed, he would rush forward at revivals for different denominations to be once more "saved" alongside everyday farmers; thereafter he could tell for a while who the criminals were. He had been between baptisms when his courtroom filled up with relative innocents whose cases he decided to handle privately. From him they got clean records, slightly reduced fines, and sincere forgiveness—the last not usually available in a routine trial.

His marriage was brief and ardent. As a widower he then understood fully the despair of Robert Jolley into which he had wandered as a boy, and he waited a month for some accidental surcease to relieve his own. No child or woman came; instead, the county clerk launched an investigation into the finances of his court. After his physical injuries healed he might have recovered from his guilt over Clara's death if not for the self-righteousness of his accusers. They made no allowances for his grief. In such extremity, how could he remember where the money went—such as it was? Dribbled away like most money, he supposed. Had his motive been greed, wouldn't he have levied at the fur coat and limousine level?

At this point in the judge's regular life audit, and long before he could leap forward to evaluate the mess in which he now found himself, Dwight Anderson took the wheel and drove them through Arkansas cotton country and over the ridge. They crossed the level farmlands and pastures of the Arkansas River Valley and by late Tuesday afternoon were in Little Rock. Nancy was driving when they entered Texarkana, with its imaginary dividing mark down St. Line Avenue and its court building, which—said the judge—had doors that opened into either state and might have been designed with him in mind.

The motel lobby had mirrors glued to the wall in longitudinal strips. To see a dozen pictures of his own fatigue and rumpled clothes made the judge feel broken into a series of weakened copies. Even

Dwight recoiled at sight of the mirrors, as though expecting the crowd of replicas to attack.

"No," he said. "No, back outside; this won't do. Let's go."

He made them get into the car again and find another motel. This time he didn't like its name, Double Value Lodge. "It's bad luck," he said. "I knew we should have gone straight across Oklahoma."

Though Nancy did not understand his nervousness, she decided to use it as a weakness, so edging to the clerk's desk she said quickly, "A double and a single, please," and lifted the pen to sign.

"No." Dwight took it from her. He wrote *Dwight Appleson,* perhaps because his right hand quivered. "One room, double beds."

"I can pay for my own!"

"You can do what you're told."

Nancy saw that nowhere in America was there a bellboy or waitress or gas attendant who could distinguish abduction from marriage or cared to try. This bored man handed them a key and went back to his magazine.

The judge whispered, "I'll look after you."

She supposed he was better than nothing. They left the clerk still reading *Startling True Detective* in lieu of solving the crime at hand, and climbed the concrete stairs to the cinder-block rooms that lay behind the building's brick facade.

As soon as Dwight unlocked the door he began to pace and growl. "I can't trust you for a minute, can I? Let me take one nap and you get him off I-Forty where you want to go!"

"What's that? You were the one in a hurry to get to Texas, you said. Besides, I didn't believe you were sleeping."

He said to the judge, "Didn't I tell you to go straight across Oklahoma to Amarillo?"

"No." The judge backed to the bed and sat on its yellow coverlet. "No, you didn't."

Dwight looked back and forth at their faces, while he stood by the door and snapped the light switch steadily on and off with the scythe edge of his hand. He had not shaved for days and as the blood poured into his face his jaw turned black from it. "She was giving orders right away, admit it; she is the living expert on giving orders."

The judge felt half like a bulb himself and from fear said, "I'm not the one who drove into Texarkana!"

"I know you're not." Snap and click, dark and light. "She did it."

Nancy said suddenly, "Why do you avoid using my name?"

"It's so damn ugly." Dwight snapped the room dim again and went into the toilet leaving the door open, where he peed straight into the water as loud as a horse.

The judge must have caught Nancy's look accusing him of betrayal, for he began talking very fast. "If we'd gone the other way we'd still be in the middle of Oklahoma with those little oil wells, on and on; you know, the ones that dip down like the plastic ducks. Toy ducks? With toy water buckets? So we're in Texas sooner, what's so bad about that?"

Dwight came out zipping and as he passed the bed he flicked the back of his fingers into the judge's belt buckle. "You got one gut," he said, "like any other worm."

Truth made the judge bend double as years of memories slammed into his middle: the insult not answered, a blow never returned, a hundred canceled fights in the orphanage. The night before he ran away from Ruston he had promised to fight the true culprit for revenge. Once, after a spring tent meeting in Somerville he had tried to talk out his fears with the preacher, saying, "The one in the whole New Testament I understand best is Simon Peter," only to get back temper, righteous rage, the ear of Malchus, and the understandable temptation of a courtroom judge to usurp the vengeance of God.

Embarrassed for him Nancy said, "Does that bathroom lock? I want to take a bath."

"Wash with me, then." Dwight toed off his shoes, threw his shirt into the cardboard box that contained his possessions. Yes, he was bird-chested and there were bruises of different ages on his left ribs— some blue, some dimmer, some with a yellow aura. She turned her back but the bathroom door banged behind him. Outside the wide window a long twilight was spreading.

"He's crazy," said the judge, reaching for the telephone.

"Don't. He's listening inside the door."

Dwight barked laughter; then faucets roared and after a while the doorframe leaked steam.

The judge spread his swollen fingers. "I should be soaking my arthritis."

"Don't leave me alone with him." Nancy had knelt to rummage through Dwight's pasteboard box, which said SMIRNOFF'S VODKA on the side. She took out jeans rolled into cylinders, then toothbrush and wrapped bar of soap, toothpaste still in the box, a comb sealed in cellophane, razor and blades in their sales case. Only the socks were old and rolled into faded black biscuits—a man who owned all-black socks would always have a pair. In silence she handed the judge a sheet of paper from the bottom, certificate of title for one acre of property on the moon made out to Dwight Anderson. Such documents, part souvenir, mostly scam, had been sold just after the first American space walk. Dwight's acre was located in Sinus Aestuum south of Eratosthenes crater, the location pinpointed by degrees of longitude and latitude from a standard lunar map. She said softly, "There's liquor in here, too."

"He'll be a bad drunk," the judge said. He tiptoed over to ask in her ear if in her phone calls she had pinpointed their location. "Then why did you get us off I-Forty?"

"Being with a crazy man is contagious."

He slid the phone off its hook and dialed the desk operator. The line was busy. Pointing in mime he tried to get Nancy to find the telephone book, but someone had stolen it from the room.

Dwight came out of the bathroom damp and naked, looking straight at Nancy. She saw he was large and uncircumcised with a navel that grew out instead of in, like a wrinkled cyst, before she whirled to the window again and he put on a towel with one *huh-huh* laugh. He threw the judge the bottle from the box. "Make me a drink. Make her one."

The judge fixed them in sanitized glasses from the washstand and took back the one Nancy would not drink. She had pressed her forehead against the picture window, thinking it didn't look western out there at all but like any street in any city anywhere. Dwight was getting the bedspread wet as he sat there with the judge's travel guide open on his hairy legs and used a motel pen to trail their immediate future under the northeastern boundary of Texas—through Paris,

Sherman, Wichita Falls, Vernon, Childress, and on in a blue line to Amarillo, which centered the square block on the state's high left side. "We go this way, not where she says."

The judge nodded to placate him. "Eighty-two, then two eighty-seven in Wichita Falls; I've got it. Is it time to reset my watch?"

"I didn't know you had a watch." Dwight reached out and stripped it off the judge's arm.

Without turning, Nancy said, "Give it back, Dwight."

To everybody's surprise he did. "You like watches? I'll get you one," he told her as he stepped into his jeans. "I'm not going to shave in that bad mirror." They watched him sit back on the damp bed with his revolver, drinking, and after a while empty five bullets on the spread and begin turning the cylinder. The judge went into the bathroom to sponge off at least.

"Hurry up in case I want to go someplace," Dwight called. "You got to go too. You're my hostage. She was my hostage but now you're my hostage to keep the hostage in line—how you like that?" He spun, lifted the revolver at Nancy.

Quickly she asked, "What is it about mirrors?"

"You ever met a lesbian? Female queer? Whatever you call it?"

"I don't know—I never asked."

He clicked the gun and sent her in a dive behind a Danish chair. The sight gave him the first hearty laughter, fuller than barking, she had heard yet. "There's not!" he gasped, laughing. "There's not"—laughing—"but five"—coughing—"bullets in the first place!"

She sat on the rug greatly tempted to cry. As soon as the judge came out to see what had sent Dwight into a fit, she snatched up every bag and case she and Faye had packed; and lugged, pulled, kicked these into the bathroom, slamming the door, finding a lock, stacking everything against it. Of course there was no window.

Sniffling, she sat on the commode lid but could not summon enough tears to warrant the effort. Her body was so tense she felt sparks snap when she bent a joint, and her stomach had started to ache. On the tile she poured out her pocketbook to check that the four hundred dollars she had withdrawn from savings before the trip, as if psychic, were still zippered there. Quickly she parceled bills into aspirin boxes and a compact; she even rolled a fifty inside a Tampax tube. Next she unbuckled Faye's backpack. Nancy had been told to bring old clothes. She held up for size the pink shorts with price tag still attached, a peach nightgown, imported shoes. The jewelry was too colorful and glassy—Faye had always passed along grocery aisles like a loose chandelier. She's shopping for Mama now, thought Nancy as she draped herself in beads and chains and took a look in the mirror.

She left on one necklace while filling the tub for the pleasure of its cool touch after she had stepped into the hot water and lain down to dream. The unexpected ease and languor, no matter what might be happening in the other room, were like those early mornings at home when Nancy would let her mind walk briskly down the block to work while her body fought the need to wake and get out of bed; it went walking across Texas now from such training. Sent home to Greenway, her astral corpus walked along Crosby Avenue down the slope where sweetgums had cracked the sidewalk and sent up shoots on the far side. She set an ectoplasmic foot on initials some long dead child had fingered there in wet cement as she passed the car of the newcomer who, in 1960, had circulated a petition to rename the old street for a Hollywood singer; Mama had never resigned herself to saying Crosby instead of Boykin. The newcomer's radio went on at eleven p.m. and played until two. Like her values, the music came from Cincinnati.

Now the turn into the Finch yard, over the concrete stepping stones, the front porch, tapping down the dark lemon-oil hall where the clock had been stopped because Nancy was gone, all the way through the back passage to the kitchen. It had once been a separate cookhouse.

Why, there was her brother, Beckham, alone at the table! Perhaps the power was off or the picture tube broken. He looked sad. Yes, he would be missing her. Millions of people in the world, Nancy thought, and here is the only one who reliably loves me—a young man of slightly subnormal intelligence who sometimes has fits.

At that her invisible ghost in the visualized doorway began actually to cry, perhaps from shame.

"Nancy? What's the matter?"

She knew then she had gone into a replay scene, that she had walked across not only space but time and was twenty-one standing in that kitchen doorway with tears still wet after all those years. She said, "The Newtons are moving to another church. Oliver's leaving. He's all that has kept me going."

"A bigger church? Isn't that good for them?"

"I've lost all my faith," she said dramatically. "Not now, I mean, but years ago; I've only been pretending. What is wrong with the church that nobody gets past thirteen anymore still believing in what it says? Even somebody that needs to. I am asking you, Beckham, you of all people, because you won't remember half of this."

He moved uneasily. "You must say more prayers."

"How old-fashioned it sounds—losing faith—now that everything's no-deposit, no-return, and all these empty containers are piling up. But I've had that to talk over with Oliver Newton."

"Good," Beckham said. "He's a good man."

"I am not making sense."

"Sit down. You want some milk?"

"I'm sure he's been looking for another church, Beckham, just to get away from trying to explain Anselm to me. It's a poor substitute. Anselm never knew he'd be used like a cold shower, did he?" She sniffled. "Beckham, I can't stay here."

He put the milk back. "I'll go with you."

He would, too. And Mrs. Newton would go with her husband. Some futures seem fixed, as Kant waits for Anselm down the years. If my father had only lived, thought Nancy, he would be here and I could go. Maybe he foresaw. I could go anyway. No, I don't believe in the Creed but I'm stuck with the code of behavior. Empty, empty.

She cried more. Beckham sat down saying, "The new preacher will probably be good."

"I hope he's old, old, old!"

"They have more experience."

Angry, she said as if accusing him, "I just want to be happy. I want to have my life back!" She liked the second sentence so well she began saying it over and over, producing more tears. "I want my life back."

"Should I call Mama?" Beckham, not knowing what to do, pushed the fruit bowl toward her, kept touching her arm, looking past her toward the stairs. At last he bent under the kitchen table and picked up Esau, the Persian cat she had given him.

"You can have him forever," Beckham said. "What else?"

No wonder the moment wrenched her. As it had wiped out self-pity then, it returned her to Texarkana now. In the high, hot bathwater she let her feet float like boiled meat to the surface. No wonder they soaked lunatics, a pity someone had not scalded Dwight to death in a state institution long ago. The Baptists should have used this long steeping. She had seen her girlfriends shiver under wet white dresses pasted to their early nipples. A little warm hydrotherapy and the Baptists could have dissolved puberty and simmered girls straight into the mission field, maybe even a boy or two. Nancy had been sprinkled on her baby scalp, the Presbyterians being at once stingy and premature in what they gave and demanded.

Through the bathroom door the judge called, "We're going after ice."

"And another bottle." She heard Dwight slide a chair under the bathroom knob before the room door slammed. Nancy finished shaving her legs higher than ever before and when she stepped out, waterlogged as a teabag, she had to catch hold of the towel rack from dizziness. At the mirror she rubbed in Faye's Protein Cream with additives of vitamin E. Should a fly light on one cheek he would be glued down forever. She tried the door, got it back far enough to reach the bottom chair leg and dislodge it. With a towel she hurried into the bedroom, half wrapping and half drying. She was seated on the bed with the telephone at her ear and scrubbing between her legs before she discovered the cause of her stomach cramps. Since she could seldom remember her lunar calendar to the day, she was always going anew into menarche, surprised by its advent. "Never mind," she said to the desk operator, hung up, and went back to the bathroom.

Hell. Inserting the tampon she thought of centuries of women and the inconvenience of crossing the Sinai wilderness or the Rocky Mountains while constantly boiling rags. At last wearing Faye's lace underwear and her unbuttoned dress, she moved the chair and jammed it under the hall door before returning to the telephone. But the Georgia number did not answer—it rarely did. Subconsciously she might be calling at hours when Oliver was unlikely to be working in his church office but rather was visiting the sick, holding services, home for meals. They had given up the early frequent correspondence, her letters brimming with Tillich and Niebuhr and Karl Barth. For him she had scooped up evidence of believers and converts. Did he know of Flannery O'Connor, C. S. Lewis, G. K. Chesterton, Graham Greene? How much had he read W. H. Auden, Robert Penn Warren on Original Sin? John Updike? Her hobby for the first year or so had been searching the library shelves for safe subjects for her letters. Only once, in Greenway Presbyterian Church itself, had she ever said, "I'm in love with you."

Sweeping his hand he said, "This."

No one could love so much dark furniture and narrow windows— even the architecture, stern. "You think I'm one of those pious women with her emotions cross-wired, but, Oliver Newton, I have always known the difference."

She went back to the telephone intending to call the police immediately—well, as soon as she called Joel Epstein in Detroit. Nothing. It was insane to postpone calling for help. Insane. She thought about the only other crazy person she knew besides Dwight and, on impulse, dialed one other number from memory. This call went through while she sent her astral self far away to watch the telephone lifted on a well-known desk.

"Stone County Library, Greenway Branch." She recognized Miss Boykin's whisper, always respectful of the scholarship which might someday occur nearby. Miss Boykin was sixty-six but the county commissioners could not retire her because she was a fixture in the town. They called her that—a fixture—like a lamp whose cord had rooted itself through the floor. "Stone County Library?"

Nancy asked to speak to Evaline Sample.

"I don't think—yes, she is. Just a minute." The phone, Nancy knew, had clicked down precisely beside a sunken row of overdue cards, near the seasonal flowers contributed weekly by one of the garden clubs. Miss Boykin, who did not know her voice *could* be raised, would tiptoe from behind the desk to Periodicals. Usually Evaline worked in a corner there on a slanted table built to hold open copies of magazines the size of *Life*. Perhaps because of its slope, her drawings were often fat and free on top, crabbed at the base, as if a wind might dislodge a famous roof while an earthquake could not touch the crosshatching of the lower stairs. On bad days, Evaline's charcoal ran off the page and nicked a black sunburst margin into the wood. She chewed her tongue gently while she drew. During an afternoon her forehead would darken from smudges caused by pushing back her gray bangs, until late in the day her narrow face often seemed bruised from recent beatings. She would then go out at dusk, down the wide front steps like one of Browning's poised chimney sweeps, to a fall predicted by her face. She *did* fall once, but lightly, and regained her feet before anyone could help.

Miss Boykin's steps had faded and Nancy's ear filled up with silence. She realized she did not know what she had meant to say to Evaline, if anything.

Miss Boykin's whisper: "She's coming."

Evaline never hurried. In her world, Nancy suspected, there might be no time at all; Evaline had to relearn its one-way movement as proof that each shock treatment had worked. Like Beckham, she moved in a drowsy, medicated world. The library's cement steps may have felt soft as butter when she fell. Once Evaline had wandered into the workroom and gone to sleep on a table; Miss Boykin feared she had been eating paste or drinking mimeograph fluid, when actually she had only dozed off from the effort of copying the cathedral at Chartres. When Evaline became Gothic, buttresses were apt, in truth, to fly.

"Here I am," said Evaline in her ear.

If a rag doll could speak, its voice would sound like that. "Is this Miss Evaline Sample, artist?"

Into the cotton batting the idea went. "Hello?"

Nancy could hardly believe her own next words. "Evaline Sample? This is the Angel of God."

Doubtfully Evaline said again, "Hello?"

She saw that in spite of lunacy, Evaline was as innocent as Eve before the Fall and everything else happened in consequence of that thought.

Nancy coughed before improvising. "What are you doing in that place with your light hidden under a bushel? I have been watching you and you have a definite gift." Although it was not much of a gift, really. Well, how much talent was required? Did not a drawing equal a sparrow's fall? "The time has come, Evaline, for you to make something beautiful, or at least complex." Nancy hesitated and added, "Complicated." Then she thought of Evaline's meticulous work on the Renaissance front of Amiens and how the Paris Opera House had put her away for several months. "You must take charge of your own life and complete a work which no one else could do," she amended.

Evaline said nothing, perhaps rolling her eyes toward the watchful Miss Boykin, who was honor bound to call the doctor if Evaline ever grew agitated during library hours.

I'll get her committed again if I'm not careful. Nancy said sharply, "First of all, never tell anyone about this call. Evaline?"

"All right."

She was not sure if the voice had turned nervous or just secretive. "Keep your hands away from your hair," she said tensely. Everyone knew when Evaline began tugging her hair that her scalp was crawling with whatever crawled there that could never be permanently crisped away. "You must promise not to tell anyone and not to pull your hair." Oh, this was wrong; Evaline knew herself she could not keep promises. "You must tell Miss Boykin that this was someone ordering a picture. That's the truth; we never ask anyone to lie." We? Meaning God and I? "Evaline, you are entitled to freedom and happiness."

After a pause Evaline asked, "What kind of a picture?"

Good. Miss Boykin was probably back sorting cards. With relief Nancy closed her eyes saying vaguely, "You must start using colors, not just charcoal, not just India ink." A quotation swam up from somewhere. "What art says to us is that we must change our lives." Us! Not only had God turned plural; He had been demoted to objective case!

"I don't use colors."

"Until now," snapped Nancy, "until *now*." She could see the library as clearly as if her astral body were there with Evaline, as if she were lying in the Finch house willing herself out from under covers to fulfill duties by surrogate. As a child she had often sent her projected self in dreams to the bathroom while her body wet the bed. She said, "Your life is opening up, Evaline. Now I want you to read some books." She gave directions, citing numbers off the spines of remembered volumes while Evaline wrote them down. "Yes," Nancy said, hearing her words read back. "Good. Are you touching your hair?"

"Just once."

Nancy said firmly, "That was the last time. Now. Almost in the middle of that row is a big green book. Bosch. Hieronymus Bosch."

"Spell it," said Evaline.

She did, distressed to hear Evaline repeat each letter. That would lift Miss Boykin's curious head! In Nancy's mind the book opened, first onto the color plates of the Seven Deadly Sins that Philip II had ordered, a sight that made her say, "Think of this new work as a commission," as she paged mentally beyond the glutton who slobbered at the pitcher's mouth, past the marriage at Cana. She had arrived at the Creation triptych and its garden of earthly delights, letting the whole burst full and multicolored in her mind. "No, no!" she said quickly. "Not the green book after all, never mind that one." Evaline said she had no eraser. "Scratch it out." Panicky, Nancy could remember no other titles on that shelf of art history except the *Collected Masterworks,* which had to be there. She began babbling about it. "Now God and I do not need any more Bible pictures; skip those first chapters," she advised. "Let the madonnas go, and the saints, and the horses and farmers. People use tractors now."

"Tractors?"

"Scratch that out. And that light and shadow, skip the French, you must build on your own skill of drawing lines; you must use what you know . . . must turn . . ."—she had it—"turn to Morris Graves, look at his picture, that *Little Known Bird of the Inner Eye.* Have you got that?"

Evaline repeated "Bird" and "Eye."

"Just look at it, Evaline. Let that bird look at you. You have to freshen your eye for whatever you know best."

"Spell Graves," said Evaline. Nancy spelled it. "I don't do birds."

How would God's angel respond at such a time? In the Old Testament, He was blunt with His temper; by the New, He had grown older and more subtle, more palatable, in fact. Either He and His messengers had lost arrogance or they had learned the market better; Nancy had never been sure which. Nowadays, surely, He would whisper something mysterious on which a baffled hearer could elaborate later in his own way. "Buy oils, a palette, learn to mix," said Nancy. Mundane! Mundane! "And paint; this is going to take a long time, Evaline. Don't get discouraged, paint faces, no, not faces, but paint what is in them, no, not those lies." Nancy herself was looking inward at her memory of Graves' bird, at those bulbous eyes on the sides of its head, so widely spaced that a viewer inadvertently would stare between them and pierce the pineal gland with his gaze. "You must paint what you know best. Paint electricity."

"Do what?"

"You heard me," Nancy said with godlike disregard, and hung up the receiver.

The weight of the telephone on her stomach had worsened the cramps. She rolled over, contrite. Evaline's mind was literal, literal; she would be out in the pastures tomorrow sketching power lines and steel towers, drawing Shazam-sized streaks of lightning over the slope of Hoover Dam, each jagged ray as daffodil yellow as the bedspread on which Nancy lay. Because of this impetuous foolish call someone would notify Evaline's doctor and he, again, would ship her to Morganton or Raleigh and insist that the Angel of God inside her head be safely electrocuted before giving worse advice.

It was taking the men a long time; maybe Dwight had gone all the way to the still for whiskey. Leaving her alone was his test and she was passing it—but why? She lay with one hand on the telephone and waited. Once Oliver Newton had telephoned her. His wife had breast cancer—he was in despair. By then they had two sons, whom Nancy had never seen.

She had heard herself being tactless and selfish. "And you're calling *me?* About *that?*"

"There's nobody else."

Except Jesus and all His angels. "I'm sorry, Oliver. I was just surprised. What can I do?"

"Pray for us."

Unless Sylvia died Oliver would never be available; therefore, Nancy did not trust her prayers to be scrupulous. "Right now you should be talking to her, not to me."

"I know you pray, Nancy. Remember us."

"I pray, but from habit. It helps me think things through." They talked of the coming radical mastectomy. After a while she asked if he had read Walker Percy or Charles Williams. Simone Weil? Gabriel Marcel?

"Yes," he said wearily.

Those days at the library desk she was working through Saul Bellow anyway. And Sylvia Newton had lived. By now their sons were nine and ten years old, while she, Nancy, kept on menstruating for nothing.

A blast from the telephone still resting on her stomach almost gave her heart failure. Dwight's voice said, "I can see you."

"What do you mean?" She sat up to button Faye's dress.

"I'm across the street, upstairs."

She stepped toward the window, yes, he was behind glass at an upstairs shop. "What are you doing there?"

"Waiting for squad cars just in case. There'll be one less judge in the world if you've called them."

"I called a friend, not police." If he had asked her *why* she would have been unable to answer, so she plunged after his hidden motives instead of her own. "You wanted me to, didn't you? You want to be caught, maybe shot down; maybe you're using me to get killed with— is that it?" He hung up.

In a few minutes they were back carrying bourbon and a bag of cold cheeseburgers. The judge, who looked thoroughly frightened, could not finish eating his.

"You've decided to quit trying to run," Dwight told her.

She thought she was just beginning to run—away from Miss Boykin, Evaline Sample, from turning into the old women they had become. "I'm just keeping my promise about Arizona." Dwight's second drink made her uneasy and the nervous judge was having his third. She put out her glass to lower the supply.

As he poured it, his broken tooth came into view. "You been good too long, that's it."

"I've not been good." She said sharply to the judge, "Let's both stay sober."

The other two did. Nancy walked up and down, drinking and murmuring about Mama at two hundred pounds, whose rheumatoid arthritis came and went. Gold salts, copper bracelets, cortisone, paraffin baths. She thought out loud about the exercises and massage, that enormous corset which had to be laced for her. And unlaced. And laundered. The knees that would sometimes reach the size of cantaloupes.

The judge said, "Don't you have a brother? Can he help?"

She told him how she had come home from sophomore year at Chapel Hill so Beckham could work; she had been waiting tables there, using Escheats scholarship money, taking out loans, living off navy beans and bread with peanut butter.

"At night he could still help," the judge offered. Dwight looked half-asleep.

An English major, reading Pope, stuck at the eighteenth century on her long backward trip through literature. Had to read Shakespeare afterward, clumsily, alone. In a year or two, when Mama's medical bills were paid, she had planned to go back to school.

"Waste of time," Dwight muttered.

Then she told how Beckham himself had changed—though he had never been a mental giant and his best job was loading bricks. He'd be talking and then freeze midsentence, walking and wait with his foot in air. She told of the doctors, the trips to Baptist hospital in Winston-Salem. Encephalograms. They were diagnosed as focal seizures, not grand mal, caused by a lesion in his right temporal lobe. Probably he had been born with it; maybe Nancy also had one, larger and ripening, still asleep. Later his seizures had worsened and were full-scale now.

"You think *you* got a brother!" Dwight suddenly crossed the room and stood in the bathroom doorway, where he smote his left chest with one fist. She saw what had caused his bruises. "Don't talk brother to me!" he yelled, slamming the door.

Beck was not strong, she explained aside to the judge, not strong of will—well, he was lazy, really. So much had he hated loading bricks that for a long time Nancy had half believed he had subconsciously activated his illness, had mysteriously known that a break in his cortex could be turned into a loophole, had been able to tear it open like an old scab. She nodded as the judge eased to the telephone, finger to his lips.

When Dwight came back into the room, Judge Jolley dropped the telephone receiver as if it were hot, so Dwight took the phone, put it under a pillow, and put his head on that pillow.

"She was telling me more about Beckham," said the judge with a nervous cough.

"Jesus, I hope not," Dwight said.

Beckham now did very little except watch television, look after his cat, and enter contests. He was not, had never been intelligent, and had failed two high school grades without graduating even in the vocational track, but he was a sweet person.

"My brother was sick a lot, too, but he's dead," Dwight said. "You can catch cancer, did you know that?" The judge said no.

Sweet. Beckham apologized for asking favors. You could no more fight with him than with a featherbed and it shamed you to be tired and cross when the high point in his day was a fact he had known on a quiz show and could win no prize for knowing.

"I don't want to hear about him," said Dwight. His face had grown dark red, doubtless from continuing to rap himself over the heart with the butt of his gun. "You're not like him!" he shouted.

The air suddenly sang with danger; its heat evaporated every drop of alcohol Nancy had taken in. Dwight said, "You can sleep with me."

She could hardly get the word out, "No."

"I won't sleep with any man!"

It seemed to Nancy later that he did not sleep at all. In the dark room she flickered in and out of wakefulness; sometimes in the other bed Dwight's open eyes picked up a faint glow of city light. He was watching her. The judge, propped miserably in two Danish chairs, shifted and snored. Nobody had undressed. It seemed to take twice as long as usual for the morning light to rise out of the Atlantic and come slowly westward to where they were waiting.

Next morning Dwight said they would stay in Texarkana another day because he had business to attend to and the judge would go with him and be his number-two hostage. "If you don't want him hurt you stay right here."

Deciding it was actually another *night* he wanted to spend there, Nancy had the intuition that she was closer than before to understanding him, that he wanted to keep Jolley with them as much as she did because that way he could always be near sexual assault without having to act. "I won't call police. But when I cross that Arizona state line I'm going to run like a rabbit."

"Rabbits get shot," he said.

Plaintively the judge said he didn't want to go out into the city with Dwight again. Dwight stole things. "Maybe people have made accusations against me in Tennessee but that was nothing like this. He is trapping me into being an accessory!"

"Come on, Judge."

In the doorway the judge said, "And nobody notices a thing. I must look terrified; nobody notices. Dwight picks up whatever he likes; nobody sees him. I know what they mean about robbing you blind."

The door had barely closed before Nancy was out of bed and yanking off Faye's dress. She changed into a flowered one while looking up an address in the yellow pages, combed her hair while calling a cab, put in a fresh Tampax and briefly considered dropping the used one inside Dwight's cardboard box. No joke was worth getting shot.

The cab carried her to a low imitation-adobe building filled with women whose faces looked half Japanese. Giving her name as Celeste Victor, she waited in line until the nurse finally took her into a small examining room.

The young doctor hardly noticed her nervousness, being more irritated to find she was menstruating. When Nancy explained that she had to take off from work on the office schedule, not her lunar one, he did a quick gloved pelvic examination with distaste. During the probe he looked beyond her and read his own diploma off the wall.

While he took cervical smears the bored nurse filled out the government clinic form by reading questions to her. Nancy gave her communicable diseases and uterine history. All the time the doctor was diddling her cervix back and forth so evenly that she thought of the nodding cat in Dwight's back seat. Her blood pressure stopped the doctor's instrument at the proper numbers. No, regular; and the cramps minor, she said, and, yes, she'd be back for follow-up or side effects. "If," said the doctor sarcastically, "you can get off work midcycle?"

Nancy snatched the prescription he wrote, asking "What time is it?" She'd be back in the Double Value Lodge long before Dwight and the judge; perhaps they were in jail by now. Her cab waited outside the nearest pharmacy while she bought a six-month supply of contraceptive pills that looked like orange-flavored children's aspirin and came in a white compact with holes in the bottom. They would last into the new year, she thought.

As if he knew what she had bought, the cab driver flirted. Nancy was preoccupied with the small brochure. Norethynodrel, 2.5 mg., mestranol, 0.1 mg., she read. That's all it took. Because of the rider the battle was lost, and all for the want of a horseshoe nail.

On the sidewalks women and children became transparent; all she could see in the passing crowd were men, men, men—their faces more blood-congested or windburned than she was used to. Too often she had confused attraction with altruism—no more, no more. Let all the needy boys pass by.

She thought about tearing off the Enovid cover from its folder and scrawling through the brand name, "Better late than never," and mailing it anonymously to Joel Epstein's home. His Detroit address she knew well—from two years of mailing nothing to it. Or she might write in the margins to Oliver, "How about Maritain?" Anyway, just in case she had misjudged Dwight and he summoned sexual energy after all, rape would have shorter consequences than pregnancy.

Now she was willing to wait in the motel. If they did not come back she would break into Dwight's car, steal everything, and go seeking her own west. If he did, she would take her turn sleeping in the Danish chairs and continue to outwit him as far as Arizona and freedom.

In the motel newsstand she had to buy travel guidebooks on the southwest by prying cash out of an empty perfume bottle. She wanted to be able to distinguish saguaro from senita cactus, identify the chollas, the pears and barrels and hedgehogs and pincushions. Had she not, the first year after leaving college, determined to read the *Britannica?* And made it to K?

During the long afternoon she read how desert thorny plants could withstand two years of drought, how cattlemen would burn off the hard-won spines of the prickly pear so their herds could eat. She was training herself to live there.

But the wakeful night keeping guard over herself made Nancy reread and yawn and wander. When the men finally came back she was sleeping and sprang from some vague dream about tents and nomads into the reality of fear because Dwight's hand was holding her chin.

"I called, where were you?"

"Drugstore."

He didn't believe her. After accusations he said, "Then show me what you bought."

"There's the bag." Thank God she had kept it, the pharmacy name clearly printed on the side. He asked where else she had been, where had these books come from? "Downstairs, go look on the rack yourself."

While the judge, white faced and looking sick, lay across one bed, Dwight prowled the room and studied the parking lot from several angles until he was satisfied the police were not hiding there. Worse, he was pleased. "You like me, don't you?"

"Not one damn bit."

Eyes closed, the judge said, "I might be having a stroke."

"Well, do it after we eat. My brother claimed women would never trust me."

Nancy said she could see why. "Are you dizzy? Having any pain?"

"In *my* neck," Dwight said.

"I feel sick all over. At heart, sick at heart."

Dwight began talking incoherently about *real* heart attacks, the kind where the heart attacked you by making its cells malignant. Listening to him explain and watching him mold with both hands in air a kind of pulsating hungry vacuum, she imagined his heart like a black hole in inner space that would someday suck him wrong side out. "That's not what you've got, Judge," he ended, "so come on and eat where I can watch you—downstairs."

"I'll sit with you and have a salad." The judge sounded as polite as if dining out with kin.

On the stairs she asked what they had done all day, but the judge would only shake his head and say mournfully that now he was worse than an accessory. "I'm an accomplice. I hope I'm not having a stroke. Because of guilt."

Nancy did not want their dinner to be pleasant and friendly. For the first time Dwight looked as if he would have liked to make conversation had he only known how, so she refused to answer anything he said but ate doggedly, looking past him at every other man in the restaurant.

He would say, "My mother trusted me, and Grandmaw, for instance." But she did not comment.

"And I bet they're both dead," murmured the judge. Dwight looked surprised as if he had just remembered that indeed they were.

Nancy's only talk at supper was to ask what Mrs. Dover had seen in Dwight's tarot cards.

"I forget."

"You had a bad set all the way around. The central one was La Maison de Dieu—you don't know tarot, Nancy? It's a house with a thunderbolt signifying some catastrophe. She only read the death and destruction she said she saw."

Nancy slipped up and remarked, "One more woman who didn't trust you, Dwight."

But he was sullen now.

"He didn't draw the Priest with its number thirteen; I think that's the true death card, but he did have the man that hangs by one leg and the last judgment and I forget what all," said the judge.

"So that's the one you tore up."

"There's not any last judgment."

"That wasn't the one anyway, Dwight, it was the hanging man you tore."

"Big Mouth is feeling well enough to talk too much. Keep on, I'll *give* you a stroke."

They went back to saying nothing. That night because the judge looked both exhausted and ashamed, Nancy insisted that he take the bed and let her roll up in a blanket across the two chairs.

"You don't have to sleep by yourself the hard way," Dwight said this through the dark to her long after she thought he had gone to sleep. "I've got room."

The offer made Nancy jump. She pretended not to hear. He did not try again. Maybe an hour later he said in his sleep, "I'm the healthy one. He's not like me."

Thursday morning they got under way sluggishly in the heat. Dwight could barely bend the dark crown of his new Stetson low enough to enter the car. He discarded his Preakness cap under the motel shrubbery.

"It's down to your eyebrows," Nancy said, turning the rearview mirror so he could see for himself how he resembled a capped bottle.

Without looking he readjusted the brim. "You want your present?"

She shot a look at the judge, who was already in the back seat. "What is it?" Muttering about Greek horses bearing gifts being looked in the mouth the judge fanned himself with a Texas map on which their planned route was marked. He kept glancing around nervously. Having seen Nancy's long-distance charge on the motel bill he now believed a policeman was hidden behind every pyracantha.

"Yes or no?" To her nod Dwight handed over a ladies' wristwatch with a stretch band and diamonds studded where the hours were. He dumped the shining gold wad into her palm and started the car.

"You stole it! And you made the judge help."

Dwight mixed them into busy traffic. "You don't want it, just throw it in the street. Like this one better?" He pulled a more modest watch from his pocket.

"I don't want to wear a stolen watch!" Without a wasted motion he tossed the second one out the car window and drove on.

"Put the damned thing on, collect state's evidence," said Judge Jol-ley. "Somebody's got to be around to testify I was under duress."

Dwight drove fast across Texarkana, which whirled about them like a moving Rube Goldberg machine. Nancy put on her sunglasses, which had cracked when she struck at Dwight in the tent; once past the last checkered water tanks on the highway she began blinking at how the glasses made the top of pines bounce loose from their trunks. Grit had worked itself between the halves of the broken lens and sparkled there, making her feel one eye had been lightly slashed. Not wearing them brought glare banging off other car windows. Grouchy, she put them on again. Miss Nancy Finch of Gaza, North Carolina, taking the Grand Western Tour, when last seen was getting a headache from a mixture of eyestrain plus periodic female edema.

It took over six hours to reach Wichita Falls, during which Nancy suggested sourly that next time the two men were stealing something they might look for an air-conditioned car. She had cramps. The judge drove until Sherman, where Dwight said, "You must of took driving lessons from the snails," and claimed the wheel again.

By midafternoon and near Childress, Nancy was driving them across land that began changing. Though she felt hotter, her sweat was sucked off by drier air that also blew through blunt grasses which looked mowed. Only by the greater gas pressure needed to maintain speed could she tell the highway slanted uphill. When she slipped off her cracked glasses to check the color ebbing from the wide plains, the dirt had turned gray.

"What time you got?" Dwight said beside her with heavy empha-sis. She looked at the blinding new watch to tell him. There is a mo-ment in every day, she thought, the Devil cannot find. Blake? Why didn't I read criminology?

Ditches appeared by the highway, then deepened and were gouged into small canyons with walls showing ocher and tan. Nancy began to feel excitement when she spotted the first graceful cottonwoods. "We're in the west! Stay awake!" She nudged Dwight, who lifted the black hat, looked once, and dozed again.

The judge said this visible change ran in a rough line along the meridian where lay the border of Oklahoma and the Texas Panhandle, that here the amount of rainfall dropped and as a consequence eroded fiercely whatever it fell upon. She snatched off the glasses, not wanting even the bright low sun to be modified.

That evening the judge was driving toward Amarillo past neon signs boasting many hotels. Dwight insisted on a campground east of town where he ordered Nancy to carry everybody's dirty clothes to the laundromat. His voice set off echoes. Time for my medicine, Nancy. Bring me a glass of tea. Is breakfast ready yet? Did you feed Esau? Help me upstairs. Familiarity made her cry out, "Stop ordering me around!" She snatched off and held out the wristwatch. With an elbow Dwight fended it off.

The judge, waiting by the car, called, "Hang on to that, Nancy! Dwight says he'll testify I've been traveling with him all summer long. He'll blame months of crimes on me, maybe assault, maybe even murder!"

"She's turning into *your* hostage, ain't she, Judge?"

Again Nancy tried pushing the wristwatch into his hand. It slid across his knuckles and along the tattoo before falling into sand between their feet.

"I don't mind washing the clothes," offered the judge.

She snatched the bundle and stalked toward the low building, leaving Dwight to find the watch. The evening sky seemed heavy, uneasy. Nancy could see a full horizontal purpling storm with long dark streaks latching one boiling cloud to earth. Half a world wide, it seemed, and she underneath—infinitesimal. Suddenly the near edge of turbulence flapped the air nearby and for the length of her walk scant drops of rain were slung in her face like sand before the threat blew past to join itself to the dark rolling far away.

She moved by reflex to the laundromat's pay phone but it was out of order. When she had started the washer, Nancy came outside again to see the great roof that the car's roof had all day closed away from her. On the hill, the judge and Dwight and the blowing red tent were tiny. She seemed for the first time to stand on the edge of a west she had only seen in pictures.

The judge almost whined when she came to the car. "They'll believe him, Nancy. People believe only the worst."

Unerringly she circled the car and bent to pick up the glittering watch and slide it on her arm. Stolen time ticked against her pulse.

Before Dwight could reach them the judge whispered, "You called home from the motel?"

"Yes." She wondered what lightning bolts Evaline was painting now, and as the judge went off, smiling with relief, she gazed west at the electric blaze of Amarillo, a challenge for any palette. Beyond, all the buttes and mesas and chasms stretched, then the crazed rocky land as it broke toward the deepest gorge of the Grand Canyon.

In Nancy's mind, though, these were still mere photographs, two of which were suddenly dealt out and played in her mind like a tarot pattern—she on a rock wall above the muddy Linville, hungry for change, and Mrs. Dover posed on the South Rim above the Colorado, mounted on a beast she hoped was kin to Balaam's ass.

PART

2

7

Texas, halfway between Atlantic and Pacific and bordering a foreign country, slants southeast from mountains. As their moving car climbed the Great Plains, opposing Texas rivers drained downhill from the fall line. Their car seemed to go forward while Texas rolled back.

Beyond Amarillo in the hot Panhandle they could see isolated buttes, then indistinct mesas that proved an hour or more into their futures. Details of these mesas came so gradually into focus that Nancy melted through one view to the next until a dark edge in the distance turned into a massive cap of sandstone while a speckle of shadow became dark blotches of juniper with roots nailed into rock. Nancy felt less aware of movement than of earth's growing visibility. Then the hills vanished and left them on the high flat land where horsemen had once marked trails by driving stakes into level sand.

Once when Dwight was driver, their car swept by a long green busload of singing voices at such speed that words painted on one side could not be read nor musical phrases understood. Later, the judge driving more slowly, they saw the church bus lumber evenly alongside to pass. The sentence lettered on its flank, which Nancy reassembled backward, said, "Believe that God loves you in a way that you cannot imagine." The passengers were singing "Have Thine Own Way," as they rode by. Through the long row of windows, one dusty evangelist after the other looked down and smiled at Nancy above his assigned word in the verse: *Potter* on the front seats, *Clay* at the rear. Feeling suddenly old and tarnished, she said to the judge, "What kind of Christian are you?"

I've been saved so often it's more like being pawned. I can't . . . I can't sustain? The feeling evaporates."

"In my church you only get saved once, at about twelve, just before puberty can cloud the issues, and then you're expected to develop the feelings, not to sustain them. It's like falling in love and then getting married." Privately, she had thought Oliver Newton's metaphor cruel at the time, though she recited it smoothly now. "To expect constant novelty is to be what one preacher called spiritually promiscuous."

"So you're a Christian, too! People would rather admit to being bisexual nowadays."

"Not really, though I still say prayers. They seem to help."

"Maybe they're answered."

She turned to frown at Dwight, saying, "That's the risk you run." Outside, even dry mesquite had matched itself to dry soil, the chief contrasts of color or shape being reserved to the land alone. If there were native animals all had vanished by being imbedded in the countryside, like stones.

"Since Clara died I can't pray. I shouldn't have let her drive." He smacked the steering wheel with one flat hand and said very rapidly, "She made me mad, that's why I let her. She had a high voice. C-sharp. I would have given anything to make it stop for a few miles."

They rode for a long time just behind the bus exhaust until both grew tired of responding to waved hands behind that glass and neither could believe how many verses were needed to notch the altos and Jacob upward. When the bus turned down a mere track toward someplace she could not see, Nancy rolled down the window and pushed her face into the hot wind to hear as long as possible their rather doleful "higher, higher" as it faded away evenly between the two vehicles, thinned, and then broke.

The Christians had put Dwight to sleep. His first soft snore made Nancy turn. His hat was tipped across the top half of his face. Perhaps his mind was as bare as this place, and his few thoughts, to survive at all, had turned the color of sand. "His gun," she whispered, "is still in his hand."

The judge nodded, driving. "I think he killed his brother with it."

She made a louder test. "He doesn't care about his heat; he could sleep in hell." Seeing that he did not move and that his wallet had worked off his hip and hung away from his left pocket, she rose on her knees and said louder, "That son of a bitch Dwight sleeps in hell all the time!" Nothing. She touched the judge for caution, rose taller, swooped one hand and dropped the billfold beside her in the front seat. Dwight had not moved.

Before trying for the gun, she eased the wallet onto her lap and hid it under a fold of Faye's skirt. "Oh," the judge was moaning. "Oh, oh." By feel Nancy opened the wallet, turned past limp plastic flaps, then fingered a stiff one while the judge adjusted the mirror to center Dwight in its frame. She folded back her hem.

She was looking at an old photograph of two browning boys the same size, maybe ten years old, both in overalls. Between them a fish hung head down. The boy on the right, who seemed bulkier and more distinct as if nearer the camera, held the fish's tail. The second boy's fingertips rested near a fin. They were brothers, of course. Their faces? Nancy slapped her skirt over them. Twins. Sharp-featured, skinny, brown-haired, country-boy twins. Identical, though the boy on the right looked somehow like the original and the other like his duplicate.

Softly the judge said, "What?" and more sharply, "What is it?"

Nancy shook her head as she checked Dwight's angled face in the mirror and let her fingers rub the photograph out of sight. Suddenly Dwight said from the back, "Where are we now?"

Spinning, she knocked off the wallet and stamped her shoe upon it. His hat was still down. The judge said quickly, "Between Vega and Adrian." Though he had probably invented the names, she saw that Dwight seemed satisfied.

"Go back to sleep," she said, almost ordered. From the back came noises of resettling that made Dwight's reflection drop out of the mirror until the judge tipped its face lower without finding him. The judge then gestured with his thumb for Nancy to replace the wallet. She snapped her head: no. He made his eyes bulbous and thumbed backward again. Nancy only pressed her shoe flatter to the billfold on the floor.

They mimed this impasse several times and, to Nancy's surprise, shot through the raw settlement of Adrian. Bending slowly, she lifted the wallet and laid it gently between them and tapped the boys' photograph. The judge slowed the car to glance down, looked at it again. With whooshes of hot air, a car went by them into Texas.

Nancy drank from one of their plastic bottles while keeping an eye on Dwight. Was he the boy who had the firmer hold on the fish? No. His brother's car? His brother's fish.

While Jolley fiddled with the mirror she tried to decide if the tree was the oak in that yard in Isoline. And was the more vivid boy really dead? "I am the healthy one," Dwight had boasted in his sleep. In one way both boys were dead, she thought, and so were two chubby girls named Nancy and Faye in the photograph albums stored for years on the shelf behind Beckham's chair.

The judge cocked an eyebrow, meaning again that she should return the wallet.

But Nancy turned its next empty glassine envelope and the next until she came to a driver's license. She would have thought it stolen had not the small i.d. photo showed Dwight's adult and nondescript face. The small print on the card was hard to read.

Melrose Lee Shelton. Melrose? Nancy flipped to the first picture to see if two matching names might be written on the back but it was blank. The license had expired three years ago. The address was in Roanoke, Virginia.

The judge was shaking her arm. She jerked loose and hurried through a thickness of bills, eight credit cards with various names, none of them issued to Dwight Anderson. She stuffed everything back inside the leather, which suddenly smelled disagreeable. Had the cards been in any order? Her fingers felt watery. She almost threw the wallet into the back, where it slapped the seat too loud and too far away from Dwight's pocket. She rose on her knees either to relocate it or to make a try for his pistol.

. "What is it?" said Dwight, eyes still closed.

"You're going to mash your hat." He located it by feel and tossed it under the back window with the other souvenirs.

She sank into her seat but watched him. Melrose, she mouthed silently. Wake the hell up, Melrose. The car jerked when the judge took his shoe off the accelerator and nicked her ankle.

Near Glenrio, just before the New Mexico border, Jolley pulled onto the shoulder to trade driving with Dwight. Before climbing into the back seat he said at the door, "That your wallet, Dwight?"

The man slapped his buttocks. "Yeah. Hand me my hat, too." He slid into the front beside Nancy, yawning, and settled the hat low on his sweaty forehead. Suddenly he growled, "What are you staring at?"

"Not much." She had not realized she was staring, trying to bring together this puffy, sleepy face with both a dim boy's face and a different name. I know you, Rumpelstiltskin.

Dwight kept the car idling by the road while he nodded the black hat brim at the wide sun-washed land on either side. He said softly, "You plan to run, run now."

"Tucumcari comes next." She saw him glance at the watch on her arm as if, like a dog collar, it marked her for an owner. "In Arizona I am giving this watch back." He said no. "You have to take it back."

"I don't have to do anything but die."

"Like your brother?" He pulled onto the asphalt with the tires flinging back sand. Still the dry land rose gradually, though the buttes had moved south of the road and far away. Only rarely did these high plains throw up a distant hill with its peak axed off, still red. "What I needed you to steal was a pair of new sunglasses," she said. "Is your brother about your age?"

"What makes you ask that?" He drove left-handed, his other fingers probing and poking his left ribs. "Shit." She, too, saw a wisp of steam leaking from under the hood and immediately eaten by the desert air. "Where's the water bottles?"

"On the floor, but there's a service station. Dwight has good luck," said the judge. "There's no justice."

The overheated car crept to the only building visible for miles with its modernized adobe coating thinly smeared over brick and now coming off in chunks of dissatisfied chemicals. When Nancy stepped out of the car, her lungs fed on nothing but light. She had to stop and breathe deep while she looked deep to take in the world's lighted curve matched so enormously to the shape of her eye, to her dry eye socket. They crossed oily sand and sunken bottlecaps to the door of "Tim's," where a sleeping cat had elongated its body to fit inside a strip of shade.

Inside, a man was scraping his boot sole on newspaper. "Be just a minute—cat shit," he said. "Biggest sandbox in the world but she won't dig, just dusts it a little." He was perched on a greasy table with dark metal objects piled everywhere and overhead wrenches and belts and filters and crowbars—Nancy edged toward a crowbar—swinging from wires. In the kitchenette behind a plywood wall, a woman made sandwiches for sale.

While Dwight talked about the radiator, Nancy ordered an egg salad from the woman, whose huge wet eyes were as black as the hair pulled back like a scarf from her face and whose mouth looked soft and fruity. As she worked, she looked past Nancy at Tim with his messy shoe, a look so full of delight that Nancy felt its heatwave pass her earlobe. All *she* could see was a rangy spindle-shanked man with a blond mustache that might feel in the dark like a second tickle mouth. She felt jealous. She wanted to call up Sigma Nu in Chapel Hill and ask if they had a current telephone number for Warren Claver, Jr.—a fool, but at twenty his tongue had been like the bloom on a trumpet vine. Instead she went into the tiny bathroom, teeth locked, and changed her Tampax. She came back with her hands smelling of soap and carried her sandwich to the only booth, where the judge was eating potato chips. He looked despairing. "I'll never go home," he said. "Not now."

"That's how I feel."

"I wanted you to keep the watch but you don't have to wear it. Want some?" He heaved a dramatic breath. "Remember I told you I was on the road looking for reasons? For Clara, yes, but other things. I never once came up with a reason while I was thumbling around feeling sorry for myself. But I see some now. Because of this pressure, I guess."

Trying to translate, Nancy said, "Reasons for what?"

His laugh sounded tenor, near-hysterical. "You know how opposites attract? I didn't have much money but Clara did."

Nancy said he was just succumbing to the current disease, counting only his worst motives. "I'm sure you loved Clara, too. You didn't marry her just for her money."

"Just? I never got a cent. She left it to the D.A.R."

Dwight came in drinking a Coke, examining the pretty cook. "Leak in the radiator," he said. "Could be a hole, could be clogged. Scalded the guy's elbow when he unscrewed the cap." He laughed *huh.* "You should of seen that cat take off." He studied the cook's curved back as if he were curious about a garment that might be his size and Nancy could see one trouser pocket crawling as his hand inside it groped. Maybe he planned to exchange women here and not just radiators.

Carrying a stack of butter patties, the cook went out front and could be heard speaking softly as she treated the burn. "If he can't fix it, we'll thumb. The car's not worth a new one," Dwight said, following.

Nancy grew alert at the possibility of being left here, or of trying to warn strangers. "Anything people steal is not worth much," said the judge primly. Dwight said the judge ought to know and disappeared.

The judge whispered, "If I jump him, Nancy, and right away you do the same, it'll be all right, I'm sure of it. Two against one."

Long ago she had thought of attacking Dwight and relying on the judge to follow suit. She was uncertain how delayed his reaction would be, felt he would hesitate just long enough for Dwight to overpower and use her as a shield. "Let's pick a better time and try not to involve others. The gun's inside his shirt now; did you notice?" He had not. Still she thought of standing by the door with that crowbar and cracking Dwight's skull when he next came indoors; she even stood there awhile hefting her tool, and waited. He did not come back and when she almost brained the cook the woman drew away with a gasp, hurrying back to pet the cat and nervously watch the door.

After a while Nancy replaced the crowbar and stepped out the other door to see whether any refuge might be in sight. Downhill was a steep-sided ditch, perhaps flashflooded in certain seasons. Several old cars also not worth repair had been pushed in against erosion, and one, fallen on its side, looked like the head of a giant dog with a sand drift built up between eye and nose.

She walked toward it through thick sun. Pure contrast made her remember the creek in her grandfather's pasture, the step log he had hacked level on one side and laid down for a footbridge. She thought of the mica glitter stones she had waded below to collect. All that scene cool, rich, green—a color print. All of this sharp, bright, bare—a photographic negative.

Downhill the grass tufts rose on lumps of pale soil; Nancy saw how the wind cleaned as close to the root as it could. Down the dry stream bed water had left its delicate trail. With one foot she gingerly tested the side of the junked car, stepped there, sensed the scrape of sand for friction. She stepped noisily onto the car's body and walked by its side door handles. The hulk shifted below; she jumped for the far bank. Heat from dark metal had come through her shoe soles.

One day, tiring of her fear, her grandfather had left her on the far side of his bridge, crossed quickly, and held out both broad hands. "You're too old to be carried." Nancy wouldn't come. Instead, she decided to climb down and wade the stream safely and crawl up the other embankment to him. As she started down the clay slope, he threw a small rock which stung her ribs. Again she moved, and he struck her with stones. He sat down to wait, a big man in overalls with a face time had slashed instead of wrinkled. When she called, he said nothing. If she cried, he lit up his pipe. She danced around on the far bank and begged for help. Finally, screaming, she began to throw stones back. He moved beyond her range, waited. A long time passed before he started down the path home without her. She crossed the bridge alone and went to his house another way, skulking from bush to bush. She would not come in to supper that night. They never spoke of it.

Nancy thought of him now as the only person from her childhood who had cared enough about her to teach her anything difficult.

She dropped cross-legged onto the hot sand and wondered how Beck and Mama and Faye were feeling while they did the difficult for themselves. On her forearms, sweat she could not remember feeling had dried to salty talcum in the hot air; she tested its brine on her tongue. Then she closed her eyes, lifting her face to thick yellow heat, and turned both palms upward. So long as she was in the sunny west, she wanted a tan so rich it would coat even the ventral portion of her arms and darken the tender veiny fold inside her elbow.

8

Behind the city's high-rise buildings, the Sandia Mountains lifted through rosy gray and into dark blue. The driver, Judge Jolley, watched their colors crowd the mirror. Half out a rear window, Nancy was looking back at the rugged slopes. "How high have we come now?" She inhaled freely. "Can't you tell the difference in the air?"

"Yeah, I smell Albuquerque." Dwight told the judge to go north here. "Your book says we can camp near Bernalillo." He pronounced it to rhyme with armadillo.

To catch Nancy's attention the judge said loudly, "Arizona isn't north. Colorado's north."

Dwight twisted to look at Nancy's dark flow of hair as she still leaned toward the mountains. He said to her back, "We're going approximately to Arizona. I never said in a beeline."

She faced him calmly. "Naturally you'd travel like a sidewinder, but I don't care. I'm seeing the west at last."

To Judge Jolley "west" did not mean romantic frontier but hinted at perishing, pointed to sunsets and evening stars. Thanatopsis. Everyone but social workers knew the golden years were yellowed only from that ripeness just before rot. Clara had gone alone to the Ultimate West.

Like a jill-in-the-box Clara popped to life inside his head, looking furious, saying again in C-sharp how well her first husband had always treated her. No offense, Clara! Deeply offended, she descended into the halls of death again. Lately she had come out less often.

Sometimes he had to raise her by prompting with her photographs; sometimes the ghost face matched and re-created his grief all over again; lately it had been melting and re-forming on its own. Once her features had flowed into those of Annette Jolley, who said, "Son, I forgive you." He did not feel forgiven thereby. A few times Clara had dissolved into the way Nancy would look in ten more years.

For no reason the judge decided to tell Nancy how well she was looking today. Perhaps she did not hear him. He was driving on toward Alameda, an extended business suburb, when something unnaturally sweet in Nancy's tone alerted him.

"You feeling like yourself today?" she purred from the back seat. "Dwight?" Her pause and tone italicized the name and made it an alias.

"Who else?" said Dwight without turning.

"That's right, you have trouble with any empathy, don't you? Dwight?" She waited. "It's a perfectly good word for anybody who finished high school, isn't it? Empathy. Dwight?"

Roadside stands and gas stations went by. Just as the judge had begun to relax she said, "I thought maybe you were feeling like your brother today, Dwight?" Silence. "Would your brother have liked these mountains? I bet he liked cities better. Dwight?"

"He never saw any cities," Dwight finally said.

Now Judge Jolley could almost visualize the set of questions tried out in Nancy's mind, a wheel of combinations considered while her options turned slowly by. "I'll bet he looked like you. Dwight."

Though he had braced himself, the judge's head flew around and he flared her a look of warning. Next she chose to ask, "Why did he miss seeing cities? Dwight?"

No clues showed in Dwight's face. He rode with one elbow out the front window, watching the buildings pass. Almost dreamily he said into the airstream, "Marvin died young."

The judge allowed his breath to come and go very lightly as he waited.

Nancy was almost whispering. "And how did Marvin die? Dwight?"

"Drown-ded."

The word came so easily and soon that the judge briefly forgot to take in oxygen and almost gasped. To avoid looking at either passenger he glanced toward the Rio Grande paralleling the highway. Its slow southward flow might have prodded Dwight's memory or even suggested a lie. "All three drown-ded," Dwight said. The judge tried to hold their speed steady and smooth as they passed small houses, gardens, and a distant field of sorghum.

Behind him Nancy said casually, "Losing your family must have been hard on you. Dwight." Silence. "Being there and all?"

"Wasn't a thing I could do." Dwight lit a cigarette. "We were both just boys."

The boys he had seen in the picture! Fishing in the very water where one was to die! Three? Why had Dwight said three? The judge checked the speedometer and looked nervously ahead to avoid bumps or sudden movements. He could smell smoke from the back—Nancy matching Dwight's cigarette, holding a magical balance herself. "In the river?" she cooed.

"At the quarry," Dwight answered.

I'm going to cough. So hard did the judge swallow that a solid ball of air rolled down his throat and carried the cough with it.

"Just ask Marvin and he'd tell you he was the best swimmer. He always made me watch from the bank because he wanted somebody to clap." Dwight had eased out both legs; perhaps he was sitting again at the base of some long-ago summer tree. *Marvin.*

"His mama spoiled him," Dwight said to nobody.

Nancy kept on. "You were both swimming in the quarry?"

"He was. When he started hollering, what could I do?" Was Dwight's mouth in a smile? "By the time I climbed down the rocks, he had gone under the last time. The nearest house was two miles."

His words were so slow, so wide apart, that he seemed to be reciting and the judge had ample time to turn them into pictures. He saw first a skinny, yellow-eyed boy rise languidly from his seat against a tree trunk, walk slowly to the rock quarry's edge. It was twenty, forty more feet down to the water in which whiteness was thrashing. The boy watched. White arms. Strangled noises. The boy in jeans started slowly, almost lazily, down the rock cliff along a slick path both boys had carved into its surface and smoothed with their tough bare feet. They had been swimming and fishing here for—years? The mother, Mrs. Shelton, had—abandoned them? Miss Shelton, maybe. Now the descending boy was careful to keep a good handhold on rocks or the roots of bushes. Below, more gurgled calls. Then, nothing. Now the boy had climbed down all the way and stood alone on the flat rock from which they usually dived into the dark water. He counted bubbles still breaking through the surface from the spot where Marvin had gone underwater to be with the biggest uncaught fishes in the pond. When the last air broke its membrane, when the last ripple had waned softly against the rock, the smaller twin lifted both hands and clapped them. One. Two. Three. Maybe he said *huh-huh*. He then hung on to an alder and lowered himself into the cold water till all his clothes were wet. He ducked his head once below the surface. Grunting, he climbed heavily out and started with care up the steep path. Halfway he reached aside under a clump of moss and smeared mud down the middle of his forehead. Once on level ground, he set out at an easy trot through the woods, tearing one wet cuff of his shirt sleeve with his teeth. When he could see the neighbors' house, he rasped his chin with a small stone, checked to make certain he had drawn blood, threw the rock behind, and burst at full running speed across somebody's yellowing rye field. Under the persimmon tree by the barn he began to roar for help, and by the time the housewife had come to her back porch, the surviving brother was hoarse and panting.

I bet that's as much excitement as Dwight ever showed anybody in his life.

"Jesus Christ, you'll kill us yet!" said Dwight, grabbing the wheel. The car had slipped off the highway shoulder. Judge Jolley clamped both wrist joints and turned them sharply left. Nobody could prove anything, he was thinking. Suddenly every manslaughter case he had ever heard in court seemed like a lie.

Dwight said calmly to Nancy, "Marvin just dived from too high. Hit his head."

The judge swallowed. "So whose car am I driving?"

"Mine—what difference does it make?" Dwight snapped on the car radio. "Don't think I'd waste the truth on you. I never even had a brother." Music blared. The judge drove while shaking his head to keep Nancy from asking about the photograph or driver's license.

She said, "I think you do have a brother. You always wanted to be like him."

No one expected him suddenly to lunge toward her, slapping air. If the blows missed it was only because by luck she was out of reach. The car rocked as the judge lost and regained his grip on the wheel.

From the far corner Nancy whispered, "All right, I know where it hurts now."

"Nothing, you know nothing."

"You want to wreck us?" The judge's hands were trembling.

In silence they camped above Bernalillo near the site of Jemez Canyon Dam, within earshot of a troop of Cub Scouts and scoutmasters. The shouting boys spread themselves down a slope and sliced the twilight air with orange plastic Frisbees. Nancy could see below their flights a man and woman tending a fire near the darkening spruces or firs. She looked at the feathery branches wondering why she had taught herself poetry meter instead of the difference between lodgepoles and white pines. All her life she had leveled out the world's conifers into Christmas trees or not, because she had wanted her days to pass like the pages of books.

"That was beyond belief!" the judge whispered as he hammered home the last tent peg. "Where is he now?"

"Edge of the woods. He killed his brother, didn't he?" She was unpacking food.

"Sure. That's who accuses him in the mirrors."

"All the more reason to humor him right now. In Arizona we'll make a plan; we'll split, you'll go straight to police—" The judge interrupted to ask where *she* would go. "Where they are," Nancy said with a wave toward the man and woman embracing by the fire.

The judge stared at the Frisbee game, puzzled. Nancy got out Eddie's white-gas stove. "I want hot soup. You know anything about these?" He didn't. Dwight had disappeared into the woods to find a toilet, she supposed. Actually he had left camp twice, the first time hiding among those nameless needled trees until she sidled toward the scout counselors. Then from the forest his voice called, "NAN-cee!" and the woods seemed to laugh a mocking *huh-huh* when she instantly dropped flat to the ground like an infantryman. Nobody else in the campground paid the least attention.

Nancy warmed the small fuel tank in her hand. There were no instructions on the metal casing. She pumped the small plunger, then fiddled with the key in both directions. "Got a match, Judge?"

In no time the entire burner unit blazed up and, by reflex, she threw the stove away. The judge kicked it back from the tent so the fire went out. Nancy sat on the ground and blew forth an angry breath; she was hot, tired, menstrual; a murderer might shoot; the damned stove was dangerous; and she didn't know how to dispose of a Tampax in a place with no garbage cans. She couldn't remember if wolves, sharks, or both were drawn by the odor of blood, nor whether any wolves were left in the whole damned state of New Mexico.

She told the judge grimly, "Once more." This time she turned down the vapor until flame roared into a blue circle, then slid the unit inside its metal windscreen. The low moan of burning fuel seemed beautiful, like anything achieved by trial and error, though the unimpressed judge had already begun collecting firewood. "I'll add a can of chicken to chicken-and-rice soup, o.k.?"

"What if he's not a mean drunk but a sleepy drunk?" From the grocery box the judge lifted Dwight's bourbon. "Want to try that?"

"I'm the one who can't hold liquor and if I ever got really drunk he'd make a pass." She battered the can opener home with a rock and worked around the rim in uneven chops.

While the judge poured bourbon into a plastic cup she set the soup pot on the flame and hammered the opener into the can of chicken meat, the diamond watch shimmering unnaturally on her aching wrist. An undetermined amount of sand fell off the rock into the food—she didn't care. "I feel him watching us right now; not listening, he doesn't care what we think or say. Just watching what we do." She upended meat into the yellow soup and stirred with a knife—it began to smell wonderful. At home she couldn't stand it.

The judge pivoted toward the shadowy forest. "I thought he was going to strangle you in the car."

"It's his brother, me and that brother. Some sick connection."

"I've known some women to be attracted to men like Dwight."

"My problem has been more the wish to do good in the sack, but you wait! Next time I'll pick a man for no reason at all, somebody disposable the next day. It'll be like trying out a bicycle. I plan to try out plenty of bicycles between now and the time some man wants to do good to *me*."

"That's not hard to want," the judge said. "You're attractive and you're intelligent."

"But a fool." The coffee boiled over and sizzled on the fire and was switched again with the thickening soup. "Maybe I will try some bourbon in my coffee." Dwight did not come back. The man and woman in the next camp were mouthing each other's neck.

They had finished half the soup before Dwight reappeared. By then Nancy felt like the last coal in a fireplace, especially rotund and heated, smooth enough to roll downhill if nudged, and spark on the way. Dwight and the judge sat on either side, each of them cooler, more lifeless than she. Her sunburn was hot; hot soup, hot coffee, hot liquor glowed inside. It was dark now and the scouts giggled distantly inside their square tent. At the downhill camp, the unknown man and woman leaned close in firelight, too well fed on each other to need supper. Nancy lifted a cup of straight bourbon saying, "The hell with Martin Buber and Nels Ferré."

"Suits me," said the judge. Sure enough, Dwight began to look lustful. She slid off his watch and hung it on the tentpole. When she turned off the stove and the judge lit his firewood, she almost seemed to be nesting in its blazing twigs. "Don't fall in," warned the judge.

Though the campfire was hypnotizing, it was equally good to look away from flame and let the pale stars arrange themselves hastily overhead where each was supposed to be. In a few minutes, Nancy thought, shifting back and forth from fire to star to fire to starfire, I'll forget who I really am.

"Sit by me," Dwight said.

No, he's the first thing I'll forget. Nancy yearned toward that amnesia. They'll wake me up here, tomorrow, and I'll be a woman from Sandia Pueblo with no relatives. Speaking in Tigua. I can start over with a clear conscience. She closed her eyes, drinking, dreaming, leaning toward some central heat through which she sensed safe passageway. On its other side, she thought, when I've come through— Dwight broke in. "Sit here, I said."

She could have cried. His pull on her arm made everything vanish. She was left on this side of metamorphosis, shaking off his too-real hand, everything too real all at once, including her knot of a bladder and a sense of seepage into her underwear. I'll burn the Tampax, wolves or not, she thought. It disgusted her to come instantly out of a firelit dream and be able to think that. Holding her full cup she wavered to her feet. "Where is it?"

"I'll get it; what?" said the judge.

"The toilet? Follow that path." Dwight pointed below the young couple's campsite.

Despite dizziness, she sorted from her pack a washcloth, toothbrush, and tampon and with dignity put these inside her pocketbook, which must never be left where Dwight/Melrose could steal her $400 savings. Hugging it to her chest, Nancy walked off the island of their firelight, stumbled on rocks, hit at last the golden island of firelight radiating from the lovers' camp. There she stopped to sip deeply from her metal cup. The man and woman had turned their reddish faces toward her. Nancy called, "Everybody ought to be happy!"

"Hello, yourself!" They smiled, the woman waving. To Nancy it seemed that half the man's arm had disappeared up his companion's shirt, that he was fondling her far breast. Farther? She stopped walking to think about which, even touched her own. Dwight called, "Straight ahead." She wondered why he struck himself there.

She walked precisely around a wavering ring of light like a moth on a lampshade. As she moved, the two campers rotated their heads like owls to watch. Had she known them better, Nancy would have explained the difference between owls and phoenixes. She was still following the wheel of light when tree branches struck her face. With great confidence, as if lifting a curtain to a tester bed, Nancy lifted this greenery aside and stepped into the full smell of cedar or pine or spruce, or something.

Ahead was all darkness. Turning back to part the crisp needles she peered out. Home base, campfire. With her cup rim she sighted to the red tent and dropped a mental plumb line to where the stolen watch was shining on the pole. Splendid. She swallowed warm bourbon, turned gracefully, and walked into a tree.

Yes, from the feel, a tree. Call it a ponderosa nicely lined up with her tent—she'd remember that. Nancy scraped around its trunk while her sandals felt for a path that was not there, only sand with slick litter on top. He'd lie to me. She stood still. I want my eye pupils to bloom like roses, she ordered; in the increased dark they did. She could see straggly bushes, occasional trees, and lumps that must be rock. She felt wise to impose this order by mere clues of light and shadow. One hand free? She slid the loop of her purse up, spread the fingers of that hand, and laid on the first dim rock a set of five cool responses. Rock, sure enough. For the first time she thought of rattlesnakes and jerked back. No sudden movements. She waited, but no viper followed its heat sensors to her toes. When she walked on, her palm identified the next low shape as a bush with prickles everywhere, but she could still see no path and no outhouse. Though the firelight had dropped below the hill's curve she was not worried. A straight line can always be retraced.

Soon the landscape had tired of making bushes and was making boulders, most of them the wrong shape, and she felt there were noises coming behind her. Nancy banged her pocketbook until a rock seemed snakefree enough to stand on and look back. Still no firelight, no pursuer, but fires must be burning back there in the straight line to her tent.

She swayed to catch balance; her body remembered the movement. Her father's open coffin had been set on such a high dais that Mama had brought her and Beckham a wide chair to stand on. It was not wide enough for both so she had been bumped into the cloying wreaths and given credit for tears of sorrow, though neither child had known much of the dead man who had always been riding off on trains anyway. Another time, yes, on an overturned oil drum to watch the Christmas parade. Its best floats passed before she climbed up; the rest were no more than a snake tail turning after. The podium had wobbled when she helped narrate, in fifth grade, the drama of the

Pied Piper. Once, too, when the big school joke had been that a girl needed a ladder to kiss the basketball center, she, Nancy Finch, had proved in public that an overturned waste can would do as well. I was an exhibitionist but I couldn't keep anybody looking long enough.

She drank and climbed off the rock. Walking, she broke suddenly into light as though the stars here were fixed to a lower ledge of sky. Through fewer thorns, more rocks, she picked her way and cried, "Oh!" when she found herself at the edge of a small canyon. In it a narrow streak of silver broke into foamy cataracts, calmed, and broke again. Behind her, bushes were definitely thrashing. If it's a unicorn, I'm going to lie, she thought. The sounds veered off. She turned to the distant Rio Grande Valley, which held the lone lights of houses and the clustered ones of communities. That farthest subterranean glow must come from Albuquerque's bars and theater marquees. She thought, maybe said aloud, None of us knows the other's here.

Nancy finished the bourbon, banged the tin cup against the stone she was sitting on. She took out toothbrush and facecloth and looked at the stream far below. Oh well.

Squatting in the sand, she remembered her mother instructing her and Faye in movie toilets about how to drape the commode seat with tissue, then urinate by sliding the crotch of their panties to one side. "Let nothing touch you!" her mother had said, whether against V.D. or all future arousal, who could tell? The old skill helped Nancy make with urine a wet navel in a damp circle of sand and she could remove and replace Tampax without disrobing. A little thumb-forefinger opposition, Brother Darwin. Noli me tangere. She buried paper tube and bloodied cotton. Anything that can make babies is biodegradable.

Including me. Without having made a baby or anything else to speak of.

The soup must have been overtaking liquor in her bloodstream, since her thoughts were doubling now: self-pity with dislike of self-pity, cuteness along with embarrassment. She sat cross-legged on the rock. Once the last overlay of coffee had restored her inhibitions she would march straight back to camp: rocks, thornbush, tree, fire circle, tent. Meantime, she decided to indulge in a fantasy about being delivered to strangers who had won her by lottery. Those sexual fantasies which canceled out all question of volition usually worked best for her; yes, she'd read the books analyzing that. The nameless stranger had two henchmen, George and Frank. "That's right, George, lift her leg wider. Now get the skirt up, Frank." Neither Mama nor the church elders could hardly blame a helpless wench in some circumstances. "God Almighty," George breathed huskily.

Little else had happened in her fantasy and Nancy was not even tempted to touch herself yet when a stranger *did* loom up on the canyon's rim with a red cigarette tip where his face should have been. Nancy willed herself into a geological formation.

By the ravine the shape was outlined by light into a tall man under a huge hat. Dwight or the phantom of Dwight. The pun made her want to smite her forehead as Dwight smote his own chest. I may give up reading.

Perhaps Nancy's imagination had materialized him here with his Stetson boiling with thoughts of rape she had broadcast unawares. She hugged her knees tightly together and turned into Niobe.

With his edges ashine, the phantom paced the rim talking to himself. Nancy could hear only a muddle. "Better than what you do . . . she's the proof that I'm not . . . appearances . . . better than them . . . by myself . . . better than he is." His dark back turned to her was flat as a shadow on starry wallpaper, then it folded. He had picked up and thrown a stone toward the far stream, maybe across time and a continent to fall into Marvin's water.

She knew Melrose Lee Shelton was silhouetted there. Nancy tucked all parts of herself inward and smooth lest she slide into existence in Melrose's world. If her cup or pocketbook made a clatter it would uncoil her whole body into view. From his profile she saw the hot end of his cigarette float off, return below his nose and flare. Was he looking for her? For anything? She could not guess the content of that phosphorescent head. Nothing had trained her to judge solely by results rather than by intentions, yet any attempt to understand Melrose's motives made her blood run backward.

Dwight/Melrose was sitting on his own rock to finish the cigarette.

Nancy began to itch in odd places. How long could she hold still? Her arches kept tingling. With his usual disregard of consequences—forest fire, anything—Dwight sent his spent cigarette flying at last over the ravine and said again, "Better than what he does." A wind made him catch hold of his hat. Nancy had a quick image of some downwind animal far away, lifting its dark nostrils to the flood of their mixed scent; then the air quieted.

Now what was Dwight doing? He had braced both shoes on the sand and his hands were wrestling in his lap. Three hands. Three *hands?* With his head thrown back, the moonlight got under the hat brim and whitened his empty face. I don't want to see him do that. Her body leaned forward in perfect balance anyway.

He worked slowly at first, as though smoothing a glove down a giant finger.

Though Nancy knew how it felt to make love to her own hand, she had never been outside that act as a spectator. Nothing in her hand understood the movements of his; her genitals could not recall what his must be feeling now. Even without the wind she felt chilled.

In distance and dim light, the stylized figure stiffened at last on the rock. The shuttle paused. If there was any human noise Nancy could not hear it. Only the hat rolled off and dropped without a sound and spun once like a bent coin before settling.

She had no breath.

After what seemed a long time Dwight's breath must have returned. He stood with his back to her, looking down, his elbows active. He shook one foot. Then he scooped up the fallen hat and pivoted while his gaze swept around like a lighthouse beam. She was part of the space it automatically passed over. He stretched widely, put on his hat, and walked away.

Nancy was shivering. What she thought, first, was that she had never seen anything more lonely; then, no, sublonely, that the word had acquired no meaning here yet. Then she was defensive: It's not the same with me. Last she felt soiled, as if she had in some secret place been spattered by his sperm.

9

Friday afternoon their car was climbing a highway between tan cliffs past mesh fencing posted KEEP OFF! DANGER! U.S. GOVERNMENT!

Not far from these exploded tufa cliffs, on a ranch astride the old Jornado del Muerto, an atomic blast in July 1945 had caused a security guard at Los Alamos to cry out, "Jesus Christ! It's got away from the longhairs!"

Such neat foreshadowing must be myth, not history, though the local history already sounded to Nancy like myth. A century ago the old Spanish trail swung with the Rio Grande on an arc west; impatient pioneers who turned their wagons off at Robello could struggle the straight but dangerous shortcut north and rejoin the safer route ninety miles away at Frey Cristobel. Many died on this arduous shortcut, the same Jornado del Muerto where the bomb to shorten World War II was tested.

Nancy read aloud these facts and fictions from her travel guide.

"I don't like to be read to," Dwight complained. "It stops me from thinking."

"What in the world do you think? I'm serious, tell me," the judge said.

Barely listening, Nancy read on, thinking the Author of Reality had a secret taste for melodrama. And now Los Alamos, a company town spread on a 7000-foot mesa with suburbs and shops, displayed in its town museum the ballistic cases of Little Boy and Fat Man, the named bombs that hit Hiroshima and Nagasaki on August 6 and 9 to shortcut peace.

"Why not?" said Dwight. "It ended the war." They drove past more NO TRESPASSING signs headed south to Bandelier National Monument and Frijoles Canyon. "They had Japs to spare."

"Frijoles! Bombs and beans!" Nancy shook her head.

Dwight told the judge, "I think about the things I want. That's just one example." He poked Nancy when she began reading again, so in silence she read that Adolph Bandelier, a Swiss-American, had studied the prehistoric ruins here in the late 1800s and written a novel called *The Delight Makers*. Dwight said, "Money? And women. I think about steak." He saw that Nancy's eye was fixed on the page and poked her again. "Even Miss Librarian here would come live in a big rich house."

The Pajarito Plateau had been formed from consolidated volcanic ash, the soft tuff since carved by weather into torsos and broken towers. Here the Keres Indians had gouged out their honeycomb homes in the soft pink cliffs along the gorge dug by the Rito de los Frijoles as it poured from the Jemez mountains and dropped by two waterfalls into the Rio Grande.

Dwight said angrily, "We could put a truckload of books in it." He snatched the travel guide from Nancy and flung it over his shoulder into the back seat, then drove faster between the irregular flesh-colored cliffs that might be radioactive.

Nancy was feeling too dreamlike from the setting even to argue with him. From pocks and pores the swallows and hawks flew in and out the canyon walls near the cliff dwellers, and still flew. Sometimes the wind made a long whistle-flute from an acre of their empty nests.

From the back the judge chided, "Women want more than money. They like to be appreciated for themselves. They prefer companionship and taste and other gifts of maturity."

"Maybe in the dark ages." Nancy was puzzled when Dwight added, "There's too many faggots now."

So soft was the spongy-looking tuff that barefoot tribes who vanished before Coronado had worn their curving trails twelve inches deep. These ruts led to walls of fierce petroglyphs or just to a view of the Sangre de Cristo mountains. Somewhere in this porous landscape were two crouched mountain pumas carved life-sized from lava to guard reentry to the "down below" world from which southwestern Indians first crawled on their pilgrimage to light.

"That's why Rome fell, from the faggots," Dwight announced.

The car's shadow poured now along the walls beside them as they crossed the last slope posted by the Atomic Energy Commission and turned downhill into an oasis with a wooden bridge crossing a stream. Unexpected trees with their burst of dark green made Nancy pull off her cracked sunglasses—all was greener still.

They parked at a stone lodge with a shaded patio where blackbirds were eating corn from trays nailed to a cottonwood. Dwight muttered that those crazy mountains looked like foam rubber. He sent the judge inside to get them a campsite, reminding him again about hostages for hostages.

While they waited Nancy said, "You never really look at the world; you don't know how."

"If it wasn't for me you wouldn't be looking at this part of it." He moved as if to touch her but only held his new watch by hers. "I'm ready to leave the old judge."

"I'm not," she said. "And this is not Arizona." All she knew to do was to treat that stupid promise like a serious vow. He switched on the ignition. "He'll have no choice but to tell the rangers everything if you drive off," she warned. He kept the engine running until Judge Jolley came out carrying directions to a campground on a higher mesa.

As they unloaded there under the pines Dwight whispered to her once, "I could leave you and you'd wait where you were left." He set down the tent roll and paused, but Nancy did not answer. "You'd wait."

"No." She shivered. Families were camped on all sides, people trekking past to a nearby toilet. The crowds made it safe to say, "I'd run like hell."

"You lie." Next time Dwight passed he ran one finger down her spine so fast and sharp it could have filleted a fish. Nancy leaped away and made a threatening show of picking up a large pale stone. Overhead flew her hand, surprised that the weight was so disproportionate to size. Even her thumbnail could scratch the tufa surface.

Still she brandished the featherweight stone overhead. The judge snatched up a tent pole that was not much heavier. "Go ahead," Dwight told her with a sneer. "Throw the fucking thing."

She dropped it on the weathered table. Might as well beat him with a tulip.

But he was as angry as if she had hit him. "Drop it!" he ordered the judge, who sent the tent pole clanging. "I'm sick of you. Both. I never needed this trouble in the first place." They stood without moving while children ran past. "One more time," Dwight said, his broken tooth in grim view. "We leave the judge here and go to California."

Well, let it happen. "I'd bust first," she said with a shake of her head. She recoiled as Dwight reached swiftly and stripped the diamond watch off her arm.

"Sit down." He pushed the judge beside her at the picnic table with her crumbling rock in its center. "Let's talk over what you *don't* want to do. You don't want to worry any of these people on their vacations, do you? You don't want to bother any ranger." With a hitch of the belt he moved his gun into view. "Do you?" Dumbly they shook their heads. "No, you want to wait right here twenty-four hours without a fucking word to anybody. By then I'll be out of Los Alamos in a different car. You got it?"

"Fine," Nancy lied. "Just go."

"If you want my word, you have it."

"A judge's word ain't worth shit." Dwight leaned to probe with a forefinger the spot between Nancy's eyebrows. "Hers ain't either, but let's say she don't. I've got old Eddie's billfold. I can find any southern hick town anytime."

The judge spluttered. "You'll be behind bars, Dwight Anderson! You've carried her over state lines, you know!"

Still he kept boring the message through her brow. "Or I can send somebody. Somebody to see your fat mama? Give your sick brother the cure?" His fingernail began to reach raw skin. "Hump old Faye? You notice I ain't even *down* to you yet."

"Twenty-four hours," she said. But as soon as he turned, her fear evaporated and her thoughts flew up like a quail covey. New social security number. Denver, El Paso, Santa Fe. Celeste Victor might marry a rodeo king. Peroxide, a permanent. Mexico. Berlitz Spanish.

"If I was you," Dwight began, then stopped. He adjusted his western hat while the judge screeched, "You're not, you never will be!"

"*Her.*" Dwight slid into the car and drove past a number of fathers who mechanically touched their baseball caps.

"It's too easy," breathed Nancy. She watched him out of sight.

"He's not gone, he'll be back for me, there's something he wants that I don't understand." With her lightweight tuff she chalked a long line across the table, then paralleled it.

The judge was talking fast. "Leave everything where it is and come on. How far is that lodge? I'll get us a ride; he won't even get out of the park. Excuse me, sir?" One of the fathers stopped.

In a dull voice she reminded him of the twenty-four hours, of Mama, Beckham, Faye.

Empty threat, he said, empty. "Could you ride us to the lodge, sir? What is it, two miles?" The man said he was sorry but his wife had the car. "Or if you don't want to involve these people, all right, we'll walk." On the campground map he tapped the location of headquarters. "They'll try him in North Carolina and he'll be under the jail till he's an old man, believe me, Nancy."

A dark car came into view. The judge dropped his map. They watched Dwight drive directly toward them and pass at five miles per hour without turning his head, collecting more salutes from nearby campers.

"He's been in jail before but he's out now. You'd better help me decide how to spend those twenty-four hours."

"You think that'll make any difference to a crazy man? If we send him to jail, he won't care if it's five years from now. Did I say where my home was in front of him? I did, didn't I? Somerville? He knows it!"

She was spreading the area maps. "We could just walk into the back country and hide until Saturday afternoon. Nothing too strenuous or isolated." Her finger crossed Alamo and Capulin canyons.

"Let's wait near all these people at least." The judge decided if he could once get her to headquarters he would persuade her just to wait there, watching the rangers' clock until time to tell. After some argument they began dragging possessions down the Frey trail. Struck breathless by the altitude, the judge wheezed behind under Eddie's backpack. He expected to die of a burst heart between the mesa and the patio where he had seen the tame crow eating corn and was grateful when teenagers, gauging their predicament, offered to help. Nancy was already inside when at last he came puffing onto the patio and dropped onto a bench made from half a tree trunk. "You can see?" he puffed when she came out of the snack bar. "In the wilderness? I could never!"

"Horses, we'll rent horses. That would give us an advantage in case he comes back."

"Why would he come back? If we've told, he'd walk right into a trap."

"I don't know, there's no sense to Dwight."

"I've not been on a horse in years."

"Think of all your years in court. I'm counting up mine in the library."

Something in her phrasing made the judge hope he had suddenly become what Dwight aspired to be—a close companion on Nancy's flight to whatever happiness she had dreamed up. Like most women she looked prettier when coaxing. "All right, I'll go. And afterward?"

"Anywhere but home," she said. "Maybe a new life, who knows? Maybe Dwight did me a favor."

He gave a warning. "Once we talk to the rangers tomorrow, you won't feel as free as you're feeling now. There'll be police, questions, reporters, even pictures. Your family will be on the telephone or maybe some will even fly out here. It won't be easy just to keep moving away from home."

"I never thought of that," she said. She didn't talk much at lunch or while leading him to the corral. Never had he seen a horse so big as the chestnut a boy led toward him, seventeen hands at least, with a disagreeable blood vein that bulged downward to one black nostril and undulated with every whuffle. Nancy's mount, white dappled with liver spots, looked leprous.

He tried patting the chestnut stiffly, his hand like a spatula. Rigid, he waited while their packs were lashed behind each saddle, Nancy and the boy chattering like fellow professionals. She caught her reins, grabbed mane and cantle, and swung into her saddle. "Judge?"

"Need any help, sir?"

"I hope not." The judge was thinking: left foot, left foot. He held on to everything projecting from flesh or leather, hoisted himself halfway up, and then subsided.

The boy said gravely, "Stand a little closer to the horse." Again he sprang; his right shoe struck the horse's left haunch and it moved aside from under him. Like a monkey he hung sideways, hugging the animal with every limb until somehow he heaved his body higher, crested, and began to slide down the other side.

"Whoa!" The boy steadied him into his saddle and shortened stirrups. The judge counted all the irritable twitches traveling here and there below the horse's hide. The surface was restless as pudding cooking in a pot. He checked the great distance to earth. Also, the horse was too broad and every tendon in his leg was under strain.

The smiling boy said, "Gentle as your mother," and slapped both mounts to send them lurching out the gate. The judge was recalling that his mother may have been a termagant.

"Ride looser," Nancy suggested as they entered shade. His mouth was full of slapping leaves. Now he jerked away from the bridge rail against which this animal might pop his kneecap. "Heels down and relax," Nancy said. "Nobody can ride standing *up*." When by willpower he had unlocked his joints she said he was slouching. They rode beyond the Rito de los Frijoles and turned toward the waterfalls. If he ever slackened pull, his horse would move past Nancy's leprous one as if they were in a race.

Too tight, too loose, too high. Not until they had climbed out of the greenest part of the canyon did the judge feel easy enough to ask the horses' names.

"Yours is Clancy. Mine's Mike."

"Geldings, I hope?"

To their left, the stream had dropped lower; the riders could already look down on the tops of willows and bushes. Beyond rose the porous walls of Frijoles Canyon dotted with irregular cavities. Nancy rose in her stirrups when they saw the first high stone room tucked in an overhang.

"You can't reach it from here," he said quickly. "If you want to see the dwellings, you take a guided tour with the ranger."

Nancy said she'd already had too much guidance. They rode beside the river, dipping into forest glades and then stretches of sunlight. At each rustic bridge Clancy would drive straight to the bank to drink and tilt the judge dangerously forward. Clara had claimed to be a life member of a hunt club in Alabama, still able to ride to hounds every season. She lied, thought the judge, hanging on. Every charitable thought was leaving him. He thought of the undertaker whispering, "I know what you're feeling. You keep asking how you can live without her." And he had thought but did not say: Cheaper.

They came to a shallow crossing behind a natural dam of stones. A large bearded man and a boy were soaking their feet in the pool. The judge had seen this man reading in the lodge while his son was in the parking lot leaping from one auto bumper to another.

Smiling, the man stood in the water, his eyes on Nancy and on the shorts she said were Faye's. "Son, I wish we'd tried what these people have tried," he said, giving her a slight bow. He looked like a fullback; the baldness must be premature. The judge rode between them, splashing.

The man watched Nancy's legs while she dismounted to let Mike drink downstream from the boy, about twelve, who sloshed toward the uneasy horse. The boy's T-shirt was printed with a giant beer bottle and a popular starlet languishing inside, naked except for well-located foam.

Without turning, the large man said, "Help you down, sir?" The judge, who was not *that* much older, told Nancy they ought to get farther from the lodge before resting. By then the boy was trying to pet the horse and the father was introducing himself. "My name is J. Waldo Foster and this is my son, Benjy." He held Nancy's hand too long, the judge saw. He was biased against men who parted their names on the side like that.

"Your wife with you, Mr. Foster?" he asked.

"Doctor. I practice in Sacramento." Benjy said his mother was in Los Angeles, where *he* lived. While the weekend father stroked the horse, Nancy introduced herself and Jolley. "I do the father-and-son bit with Benjy as much as possible," said the man.

After his title had been given, Jolley said he used to do the judge-and-jury bit. Like a child herself, Nancy seemed to have forgotten Dwight as she splashed with Benjy. "We'd better go along before Dwight comes," said the judge with careful enunciation, and to hurry her he urged Clancy through the pool and downtrail. Waiting in the

cool shade had stiffened his muscles. The sooner they reached Capulin Canyon the sooner he could see if his knees, under stress, would
fold in the wrong direction.

Nancy did not catch up until they reined in, silently, to look at Upper Falls, where the river dropped eighty feet down two tiers of a lava
cleft. The bouncing judge hardly noticed the second, smaller fall. By
then his energies were bent on an inner recitation that Nature would
send nothing a man cannot bear, paraphrased from Aurelius, unconvincing to his sore body. When finally they turned into Capulin, four
miles remained to base camp; he expected his spine to be ground to a
nub in that distance.

"Forget regulations; let's camp in the first cliff dwelling we see. You
shouldn't have wasted so much time with that doctor fellow." Soon
after, Nancy pointed out and led the way up the trail to Painted Cave.

Eating sandwiches, they watched the canyon fill with darkness. "I
wonder what Dwight is doing now," she said.

The judge, who hurt everywhere, said he didn't give a damn what
Dwight was doing. "I hope he's being hit by a train."

"He can still show up one day in Somerville or Greenway for no
good reason but the impulse. I hope I'm not there."

"Ummmn." If man were a "little soul, dragging a corpse behind,"
his present corpse was so full of pain and edema that it had fallen
upon his spirit like an avalanche. He no longer believed that Aurelius
by the Danube had ever tested his stoicism against such a range of
physical anguish. "Someday he'll die in a jail we never hear about under another name, but between now and then he'll enter the lives of
other strangers and make a pattern of trouble and go out again."

"As monotonous as wallpaper," she said gloomily.

He thought nothing would ever taste as good as this lukewarm
crushed sandwich and began to feel better. "I'd like you to understand what happened back in Somerville," he began. "No doubt
Clara was used to a high standard of living. I used to say—*heh-heh*—
that she kept breaking things, mostly twenty-dollar bills; now that's
no excuse! I know that! But you must understand right away that at
heart I'm not the kind of man who—"

"What's that?"

"What? That? One of the horses moving."

"I thought it was him."

The judge compressed his lips and looked into the shallow cave, where the smooth back wall and its fifty feet of drawings were getting dimmer as the sun went down.

"I suppose Dwight is sick. What sickness is it?"

It was too soon. He must not push her. He said he didn't believe in those books that announced new names for human frailties. With a sigh Nancy said, "I know that book, too. *The Myth of Mental Illness,* Szasz. That's what I've got between my ears: one big card catalogue."

For a minute the rustling of the horses while they fed by Capulin Creek sounded to him, too, like Dwight Anderson slipping through underbrush. He would always be looking for Dwight Andersons now. Nancy was back examining the cave drawings, later ones superimposed over faded black stars and red snakes, a mission church complete with cross intruding on the rim of a sunburst. "In the end," she said, "there was something about me he wanted. I don't like that."

Leaning into the grainy wall the judge said, "I've seen it in court before. Someone like you always wants to ascribe to someone like him dimensions that aren't there. You give credit for losses he never felt." He thought of all the softhearted schoolteachers who had been in and out of his witness box offering sad excuses for a defendant who warranted them no more than a copperhead. This expenditure of pity upon pitiless had always seemed to Harvey Jolley a perversion, as sentimentality is the perversion of love.

"You think he's not like us," Nancy said. "I think he is."

"He's gone, that's all I care about, and don't flatter yourself that he remembers us at all. He was just moving, the way a shark moves toward sound or a snake to heat. We were a temporary noise. Hand me that air mattress." He inflated hers semisoft, though the cave was little more than a scoop behind a ledge off which any sleeper might roll and fall among yucca and stones. "We should talk over our meetings with police. I want those patrolmen at the bridge to be reprimanded for their attitude. And don't forget to tell them that Dwight forced me to help steal; that's important."

"And then home."

"You once said you weren't going home."

"I'd feel guilty just to keep running."

"What if you took a job out here? Sent money home?" He gave her a sly look. "You might meet someone you would want to marry."

She said to herself, "Happily ever after."

"On my way home," he said with sudden inspiration, "I might visit the orphanage I was raised in. I could adopt a boy myself. I'm not old, you know, I could marry again and adopt a son. Or even marry a woman young enough to have a son."

"More obligations and duties, no thanks."

He said stiffly, "I wasn't proposing."

With a laugh Nancy said, "And I wasn't declining! I was just thinking out loud in generalities. Yet I'd like to be married someday. It's funny how I still believe in commitments. Selfishness destroys—that's true. Yet I've been living a home life that must have looked unselfish to others—and I hated it."

"It wasn't unselfish if you were primarily thinking of your own reactions."

"I was no saint. A wife doesn't have to be, either."

"Clara wasn't," he blurted. "One reason we never had a real fight was that she outweighed me." Immediately the judge laughed so she would think he was joking. He went on laughing until she submitted a dry chuckle herself.

"But you miss your wife."

"Of course," he said, instead of saying not lately. It was nearly dark, and Nancy's face grew silvered, more beautiful. Trying not to grunt with pain the judge scooted his air mattress closer to hers as she sat down. "You'd be a wonderful wife."

Impatiently she said, "I wouldn't and that's the whole point—wonder isn't required! Marriage is such a mortal institution. If everybody didn't realize how fallible and weak we are there'd be no need for that high-flown ceremony full of those impossible promises."

It annoyed him to be made to feel naive by a woman so much younger. "If you're looking for somebody fallible, that J. Waldo with one ruined marriage behind him already should be about right."

"Who? That doctor, you mean?" She might have been smiling as she muttered to herself "Bicycles." Then she tested a small flashlight from her pack, the bottom of Capulin Canyon having turned black by now. "Be back in a minute."

It must have been the sight of Nancy planning to carry her pocketbook downhill that made the judge so angry. "I'm not Dwight Anderson, you know. I don't steal ladies' purses on my own time!"

At his tone she marched back, slapped the bag onto the tufa floor, and held it in a quivering circle of light. In silence she jerked from inside a flat blue box and waved it in a fast circle around the tip of his nose; through a cross-eyed blur the words "feminine hygiene" floated upward into his understanding. She then left the purse and took only the package down the footholds hacked into the cliff. He could see her yellow disk of light move through pinyons and pause while she said something irritable to the tethered horses. It went under a speckle of leaves and then out.

The judge surrendered to private embarrassments. Clara had been past all that, and was nearly past sex as well. He got into his sleeping bag and stretched out with a groan, his backbone like a heated rod. Soon Nancy climbed the crude steps and light broke over the edge. She stepped over the mummy bag as if over a giant larva, making him thrash around from insult.

She sat on the edge of the stone shelf dangling her legs. "It was stupid of us not even to get a knife or a weapon of some kind in case he does come back."

"You're right." He could not reach the zipper.

"Dwight's all we had to talk about, isn't he?"

He got one arm out and floundered into a sitting position. "That's not true!" He began proffering a list of facts. "I have a house on two hundred fifty acres and some Angus cattle and I've been to New York eight times—you can have it except for the plays. War novels are my favorite reading, Winslow Homer my painter. I thought Jennifer Jones a beautiful actress—you're a little like her—but I quit going to movies when they got self-conscious and depressing. I like TV sports. We need to balance the national budget and not meddle in Africa." Deep breath. "I was a foundling. I collect coins and old farm tools like corn shellers and those apple peelers where you turn this handle . . ." In midair he was demonstrating.

"I'm sorry," she said quickly.

"It's all right; there's no hurry," he said, and dropped his hand. "Don't dignify Dwight Anderson too much by your attention, that's all. And think about something, Nancy, think about a real vacation. We could go to Mesa Verde—it's got more cliff dwellings than this place: and the Grand Canyon, and maybe Carlsbad Caverns."

"It would be a shame to be this close and not see Grand Canyon."

"Think about it. By Monday police will be through questioning us."

She went to sleep thinking about the light and color and magnitude of the canyon barely suggested by Mrs. Dover's slides, and tried to transpose this scenery to that scale. Morning light striking the opposite wall woke them early. The judge's legs felt like the spread blades of giant shears as he tottered to saddle the animal that had maimed him. "Ho. Easy."

The horses behaved as if they had never seen him and reared away with a show of yellow teeth. It was a long time before he could saddle them and tighten cinches. From the way Nancy mounted and from the winces playing on her slightly swollen face he saw she also must be stiff and sore.

"I've stayed home the last fifteen years!" she declared. "They don't seem to be suffering while I'm gone."

"You might like to see the Rocky Mountains," he said in a mild voice, trying to remember the balance in his Memphis bank account. Over the river flycatchers were cleaning gnats from the air while the sound of their hoofbeats drove a flight of swallows unevenly along the sheer right wall. Every movement of the horse was painful. "If you're holding to the twenty-four hours, let's slow down."

"It's ten miles to headquarters." But she pulled her horse into an easy lope across a plateau to a walled enclosure where the stone lions had been carved. Her shoulders slumped as she looked down on the effigies. Both must have been very old, for erosion had worn away detail until the mountain cats seemed less crouched than puddled. Though his thighs were on fire the judge tried to sound like a cheerful traveling companion you would enjoy on a long tour: "Must be six feet long." She shrugged. "I wonder what they used to carve the lava with?"

She snapped, "Their left feet, it looks like." Somebody laughed, and he saw J. Waldo Foster coming from the nearby pueblo ruins.

"You mustn't expect too much. Benjy wants to know why we're not at Disneyland."

"Why aren't you?" said the judge, unheard. Nancy got down and went off to look at an altar, leaving him with two sets of reins. It wouldn't be long until—yes, here came that unpleasant Foster boy in a T-shirt that said REAGAN SUCKS. Benjy rubbed Mike's nose and tried to slide a finger into the dark nostril.

"Stop that!" The horse snorted away.

"What's his name? Can I ride? Daddy said you'd ride me. She said so, too."

"No doubt. No. And don't poke his eye."

"Can he see where he's going without any white part?"

"Put a fool on his back and he doesn't *care* where he's going. You mess with his tail and he'll kick."

"I'm just getting this briar loose." The horse kicked and missed, dragging the judge in a jerky half-circle.

"Listen, Benjy, you reach under *there* and I'm going to *let* him kick you." They locked stares, the boy with one hand poised near the horse's sheath. "I'm going to *suggest* it."

"O.k. She says you're her uncle."

She does, does she?"

Benjy began running at speed around the two skittish horses. "I've got a swimming pool. My mama and I swim without clothes. I've got a color TV in my own room."

The judge wondered if his list had sounded like that to Nancy. He decided to lead Mike and Clancy downhill into shade and set off at once. When the horses crossed unexpectedly into his racecourse, Benjy fell against stones screaming, "My leg! My leg!"

"Watch where you're going."

He was up instantly. "That didn't hurt. Do these horses swim?"

"The creek is too shallow."

"Yeah, but can they? They're pretty old horses, aren't they?" He ran ahead shouting "Glue!" and "Dogfood!" several times.

As cooler air blew off the water Clancy and Mike began nudging past the judge's shoulders. Fearful of being suspended and crushed between their bulk the judge dug in his heels and slid.

"Let me ride the oldest. Stop, you!" Benjy grabbed the nearest tail. The judge continued to skid, calling, "Get out of the way! Let go!" They half fell under the trees, where both geldings became sedate and paced calmly to the creek's edge. With much struggle, the judge finally got them snapped on to crossties between cottonwoods. His hands were shaking.

With the sun higher, campers were crossing the canyon, some carrying transistor radios. On a still surface of a pool, the judge found his wavy face—red, ruined. Every rock Benjy threw into the water worried the horses.

"Sit down. I saw a fish."

"They don't have fish in here." With a dead limb, the boy swatted the surface to prove it.

The judge wiped water off his jaw. "Sit down anyway." In silence he watched two backpackers pass, the woman calling, "What a cute little boy!"

Benjy piled duff in one palm and blew it toward the judge's face.

The judge said, "Why aren't you in school?"

"It's holiday. I go to a Catholic school."

"It's not doing you much good." Annette Jolley had clung to her Catholicism long after her adopted son became known as a faucet Baptist any evangelist could turn. She never preached to him except by example and in silence. The silence would roar in his head when he was attending some Baptist ice cream supper hearing about the fearsome papists. For Annette's sake he said now, "You listen to the sisters—they're often right. When my wife died—" but he could not stoke up his grief a single time more. Benjy was digging holes with his tennis shoes and scuffing the dust high. "That'll stick to my wet clothes. What do you do in this school?"

"I built a volcano on a piece of plywood." He supplied eruptions, noises. "Have you seen a snake yet? I know somebody keeps a snake in a coffee can."

"Sit down and we'll make something." Things continued in this way a long time, the judge being almost finished with his second peeled slingshot before Nancy and J. Waldo Foster were heard calling. Benjy's answering scream lifted Clancy's front hooves off the ground.

Nancy came first into the glade saying softly to Judge Jolley, "You were exactly right about there being no hurry. Let's stay one more night in Bandelier with the Fosters. Tomorrow morning we'll see the rangers together." For answer the judge began silently to untie his horse. "Even Dwight will always know we gave him plenty of time." The two withdrew uptrail, Benjy calling, "Can I ride *now*? Why not?" He broke the slingshot and threw the pieces after them.

Nancy released the judge's arm. "You go ahead if you feel so strongly. I'll join you tomorrow and confirm everything."

"And then?" he asked—meaning the rest of their western trip together.

"Then they'll believe you and catch Dwight and it'll be all over."

"It *is* all over," he said, mounting. "I may not tell anybody a damned thing."

Her surprise changed to relief. "Whatever you think best," she said with what he recognized now as a calculated dropped gaze. "It would give me some leeway."

Most of the skin was off his left thigh. "But eventually you'll go home to tend your family again."

"Have I a better choice?"

"Not now." He looked down at Nancy's dark hair. Freshly combed. In spite of all he meant to say, what came out was "That child is spoiled!" At his slap of the rein Clancy almost bolted toward the mesa. The judge tried not to bounce but to look as if the gallop were both intentional and graceful. Once Nancy vanished out of sight it seemed too much trouble to slow the horse. If he could not shorten the next hard ten miles he might as well speed the time. Of course he would tell the rangers everything. Or, if he didn't, what difference would it make?

Soon he was sitting on one hip awhile, then the other; he would distribute his weight on the coccyx while counting one hundred, then shift forward. He had crossed Alamo Canyon and passed Tuonyi when he ran out of all possible rotations. Before the wooden bridge over the Rito de los Frijoles, the judge remembered Nancy was having her Time of the Month. He thought it a good joke on Foster.

Walking Clancy to park headquarters the judge lost count of how many of his parts were broken. In the paddock he remained hunched in the saddle until the boy reached to help. "Both hands, please," he said, and came heavily down as if the boy were a mattress. His knees folded.

"You all right?" The boy held on to the bridle. "Where's the woman?"

"Tomorrow," he said. The snack bar was at least fifty steps closer than the ranger's office. He turned slowly toward it.

"You want anything, sir?"

He shook his head.

"Are you just going to stand there, sir?"

"For a little while, yes." He was able at last to *see* his legs move more than to feel them. He worked his way between supports to the snack bar door. He stood at the counter to order iced tea.

"You're the one with the red suitcase?" Before he brought back the frosty glass the counterman called into the patio, "Your friend's back!"

The judge did not even have to wait for the screen door to open. "Hello, Dwight," he said through it, lifting his tea. He thought: Serves Nancy right.

10

As the judge rattled off on horseback like a small Quixote, much of Nancy's enthusiasm also went flapping over the hill. The last link broke between her and anyone she knew. Thoughtful, she walked toward Capulin Creek, where Foster was lifting his son astride the dappled horse. J. Waldo—a name suited to a disposable man. He'd said he was a successful pediatrician; his divorced wife ran a Mexican gift shop, also successful. Their only son, Benjy, might be emotionally affected by their divorce right now but he had from babyhood been hyperactive and was kept on a steady dosage of Ritalin.

Ahead she saw Benjy thumping atop the saddle as if it had bed-springs.

"Mr. Jolley left?" J. Waldo's teeth flashed white as plastic in his beard.

Benjy pumped the horse's ear. "I'm going to ride in front."

"Not doing that—you'll get hurt." Nancy uncurled his fingers. Though Benjy grabbed the reins, his father said he'd lead. "Hold on here," said Nancy, tapping the saddle horn.

"I don't want to hold there."

J. Waldo frowned. "Then do you want down? Benjy, it hurts the horse when you kick hard."

"Nobody holds the saddle horn."

"I could lead by the bridle, I suppose, if you give slack. Nancy goes first."

Benjy snickered. "So she won't step in manure shit." They started slowly up the trail the judge had taken.

"I can't tell you what a pleasure—doesn't this horse ever keep his head still?"

"Not when anybody's pulling both ears," said Nancy.

"Benjy, would you like your ears pulled like that? No, you would-n't." (She wondered if the boy had missed his morning medicine.) "Son, you want to let go now? At least let one go. Did you hear me?" Turning to wink, Dr. Foster repeated Nancy's "ears" with no "r." "Keep talking, ma'am, your southern accent is a treat for the ee-ah." (Nancy decided to tone it down.) "What's Greenway near—Char-lotte?"

"Maybe seventy miles west." She began improving her biography. "After my parents died I grew up on my grandfather's horse farm, all thoroughbreds." She thought of the judge's solemn list of facts. "That's how, Benjy," she said louder, "I know about ears; let go now."

"And after college, what? Where did you say you went to college?"

She chose and said Hollins. "I inherited the farm and manage it now." The inheritance part was true—her grandfather's one hundred red clay acres were growing a crop of broom sedge, sorrel, and dock, with pine and hardwoods around each field. When she could borrow Faye's car she would drive there to walk its tangled woods and weedy pastures, check the stages by which the old house was falling down. She could not afford to repair and rent the one place she had been happy.

Dr. Foster repeated, smiling, "Ah manidge tha fahm. Do you show your horses?"

"Of course," she said. "That is, the trainer shows them."

"Daddy's got a sauna bath and we go in it naked."

"You come to Sacramento, Nancy Finch, and I'll show you that sauna bath." Another wink. "Can you loosen the reins, son?" She had already seen J. Waldo behave as if all flirtation passed entirely over the boy's head; on the other hand he involved Benjy like a peer in serious, democratic discussions of the boy's behavior. "The sauna is very stimulating. Now let's not hurt the horse."

"My ass hurts," Benjy said. "This saddle doesn't fit." He poked his father for attention.

After resettling him J. Waldo caught up with her. "He's very intelligent."

Or just noisy, she thought. She stole a glance upward. Not since the coach left town had she made love to such a big man. His size and transience might be Foster's only appeal, not that she planned anything tonight, though she knew from a book called *She* that sex during menstruation was considered savagely good by some.

"How long have you been a widow, Nancy?"

She hid her smile. In Greenway everyone's well-known history prevented substantive lies. "He was killed in Vietnam."

"A waste of so many American resources," he began.

"I never thought of Randolph as a resource."

"No, no, I only meant that the insane commitment of that war made every loss—"

"He believed in the war," she said shortly. The dead Randolph Macon Finch was taking shape in her mind—six feet four, another big man like the coach, like her grandfather; the kind of man who, slow to fight, would beat the living bejesus out of anyone once he started. She led them into Alamo Canyon, perfecting Randolph in her mind. For one thing, he had never talked in bed. Patrick might think clever patter was fashionable but she and Randy had always found it distracting. Also he read no fiction except by Russians. He had promised always to look after Beckham. Travel—he liked travel. He thought all women should have freedom so of course she had needed less than anticipated. Aloud Nancy said, "I do miss him."

At the creek Benjy called, "Giddup!" and kicked the horse. The boy snatched at his father's imitation bush hat, catching the thong behind the beard. "It's hot up here."

"Wait, wait!" J. Waldo worked the chin strap loose so Benjy could drop it onto his smaller head like a mottled pot. "At least trade me yours." The tight baseball cap made him look overweight. In fact, the coach had run to fat but never Randolph. Nancy remembered the long streak of dark hair running down Randy's flat belly. Jesus! she thought suddenly. That was Dwight's belly!

They filled their tin cups upstream and drank slowly, J. Waldo stroking her back. "Want to rest while we've got a little shade?" He told Benjy there were probably arrowheads to be found in the canyon. The thought of tufa arrowheads shattering against buffalo made Nancy smile. Randolph had always paid closer attention to his surroundings. They tied the horse and Benjy followed them up a broad pink slab in which visitors had signed their names with pocketknives. Nancy sat on several crooked signatures and took off both shoes. Randolph seldom wrote his name on anything, had disliked monograms, i.d. bracelets, and belt buckles shaped into letters.

"Roger. Jim Thurlow," Benjy read loudly off the stone. "Sheila Fox. Fuck you. What with?"

His father laughed into Nancy's eyes. "Go play in the water, son," he said, still watching her. She thought Randolph might have favored spankings, at least on occasion. "With your dark hair, a tan makes you look very earthy."

He had grown the beard, she decided, to conceal his meaty mouth. She lay back on the warm rock, closed her eyes, and tried to collect his odor through this dry air.

"Trade hats again?" She heard J. Waldo talking to Benjy, scuffling, then a splash. "Don't go far!" She sensed the man was stretching himself beside her in the sun. Very long; she knew where his body would extend beyond hers if she should ever lie under it. William, the coach, had been concerned about his smothering weight and had usually flipped her on top, from which angle she knew her chin looked slack and old. Randolph was an experimenter—upright and sideways, reversed, catty-cornered, bondage-and-games. *The Joy of Sex,* Alex Comfort. Another book she'd had to find outside the library. She caught Foster's smell at last: mouthwash.

"You're a very attractive woman," he was saying near Nancy's ear.

None of them had ever spoken the right seductive words; she would never hear the talk that so smoothly filled the lines of books. For Joel she had once, half-teasing, composed in a long afternoon at the library a set of 3-by-5 cards with fine musical compliments inscribed, and threatened to hand him one at crucial moments. With a laugh he had snatched the stack and shuffled her preset deck. Even Randolph, she saw now, had no skill at seduction by words; out of bed, too, he was taciturn. The Russian writers were poor at love talk.

"Sleepy?" Nancy said no. Her knee was struck. "Throw them the other way!" called J. Waldo, sitting up, his body shading her face. More stones rained down and stopped. His shadow descended. "I'm often glad his attention span is short. I see you don't wear your wedding ring."

"There's not much point."

"Were you married long?"

"A year. We were separated a lot." Randolph wrote wonderful letters, though. Everything he couldn't say out loud he could put onto paper. Not like Oliver Newton!

He seemed to be fingering her ear, the hairline behind it. "Since Randolph, has there been anybody?"

What subliterate writes his cards? She knew how to match them. "Not really. Tell me about yourself."

As soon as he said there wasn't much to tell and launched forth, a yawn rose in Nancy's throat. She always hoped to hear some profound analysis of the malaise of the twentieth century, *within* which, from time to time, the chosen man would add murmurs about her beauty and desirability. The latter: almost Elizabethan. Thomas Mann, beset periodically by high grace notes of passion. Solzhenitsyn touched with the erotic. Not Nelson Algren, Jack Kerouac—the best she usually got.

She tuned in to J. Waldo's long paragraph. ". . . Hawaii was different then. My father worked for American Factors. Sugar? Have you ever been to Hawaii?"

Why not? Perhaps she had visited Randolph's grave in a field of graves above Waikiki? She decided to say no.

"It was so beautiful then that I took Adrienne back for our honeymoon. Now you can ride a tour boat into Pearl Harbor where the flag of the *Arizona* sticks out of the water. Worse than walking on a grave. Over a thousand men are under there."

She did not trust the catch in his throat to be sincere nor had she read all those *National Geographics* for nothing. "I didn't think it just stuck out of the water. Isn't there a monument?"

"On the ship's bridge, yes. The flag still flies at full mast since as long as a full crew is aboard any vessel, the Navy considers it still in commission."

"How old were you at Pearl Harbor?"

"Just a boy," he said evasively. "I thought it was an earthquake." His words sounded well rehearsed or plagiarized. "I remember blackouts and that every family was given gas masks. That spring we came home to San Francisco and stayed." He moved his fingers off her ear and began stroking above the elbow. "Is Mr. Jolley your uncle or Randolph's?"

"Mine. It's Judge Jolley." She decided the least she could do was say, "He decided some big civil rights cases in the sixties."

"He didn't want you to stay."

"Since Aunt Clara died he's been very protective. She had epilepsy. You get in the habit of being protective, I guess."

J. Waldo removed his fingers to call Benjy. A strange woman answered, "He's over here helping us take pictures."

I'll bet he is, thought Nancy.

In a louder voice the unknown woman said, "Your daddy wants you now."

Benjy yelled, "I'm getting my picture taken!"

Nancy turned her face from the sun to look sidelong into J. Waldo's, close and huge, a collection of pores and occasional shallow sweat droplets. He was still wearing Benjy's baseball cap. He gave her such a patent salesman's smile that she almost felt sorry for the hard work that still goes on between men and women. "Aren't you going to see about Benjy?"

"He'll be all right. Benjy makes friends everywhere."

Makes them what? "On vacation, some people prefer privacy."

"He'd know that—he's very sensitive. When we got the divorce, Benjy was quite grown-up, not a bit surprised. We talked everything over as a threesome. Children are exposed so much to adults now, at home as well as on television. They become sophisticated at a young age, especially in California."

With emphasis Nancy said, "When I saw adults they were *working*. They'd take me along to plant a field or to walk through the factory and speak to friends. That's different from dinner parties by the pool."

"I didn't mean just dinner parties." He called, "Benjy?" Nancy sat up. "Ready to go, Benjy?"

Downstream Nancy could see two elderly women in flowered dresses, both backed against separate trees. Benjy was probably playing Joans of Arc.

"Benjy?" One of the women at the stake pointed vaguely toward J. Waldo.

Behind them the boy screamed. They scrambled up the gritty rock and leaped off during his second scream to find him behind the next boulder, posed wide-armed as if crucified and staring between his tennis shoes. The crooked black stick arranged there did not resemble a snake at all.

J. Waldo patted one of the boy's spread arms. "You were feeling neglected, is that right, son? It's all right now."

Benjy whispered, "It's a rattler. I saw it move."

His father squatted and began snapping the brittle stick in two parts, then four, and so on. Slowly, almost fluttering, Benjy brought down his stiff fingers. "I fooled you," he said with nasal scorn, and vaulted past Nancy across the carved array of names. He ran into Alamo Creek with his shoes on. "Are we going or not?"

"If you'll lead." As he rose J. Waldo scattered the bits of wood. "O.k. if Daddy rides the horse now?"

"I guess so." Benjy splashed to the far side. "Not long. Come on, there's nothing to do here." His father's too-large hat fell into the water and J. Waldo had to chase it down the current. Nancy followed, remembering times she had been sent to the front shrubbery to choose her own switch and had thus learned that forsythia had hollow stems.

After J. Waldo beat water out of his hat and set it on his head, he mounted and clucked Mike into a walk beside her. She asked carefully, "What exactly does Ritalin do?" wondering if perhaps he should ask for his money back.

"It's methylphenidate, actually, and though in large quantities for an adult it would be a stimulant, for the hyperactive child it has a calming effect. His problem is a chemical difference in the brain, to oversimplify."

She knew schizophrenia was now thought to be the same. Perhaps the properties of honesty and sweet temper could also be identified by laboratory analysis and a prescription written for each.

"This is one of Benjy's medication-free periods," J. Waldo added, walking the horse by her. "We try it on summer vacations to see if perhaps he's outgrown the problem. By puberty most children do. He's must better than he used to be and, of course, being out of school is a big help. He finds school routine very difficult."

"How can you tell it's an illness? I mean, fifty years ago a teacher would have called it bad behavior."

"The difference is in degree more than anything else and too many teachers still call it bad behavior. There may be five million—Benjy?" The boy had gone out of sight offtrail among the scattered pinyons. From his seat high on the horse J. Waldo called, "I can still see you, son!"

"Now you can't!" Scuffling noises.

"Behind the rock!" They continued to shout back and forth, J. Waldo's voice falsely hearty, Benjy's growing steadily more cross as he failed to hide.

Between yells Nancy asked, "Are you born with hyperactivity?"

"Yes, although at first it's hard to diagnose since many babies have feeding problems, sleeping problems, colic. *There you are, on hands and knees!*" In a normal voice he added, "Most parents know something is wrong when the child is a toddler. They feel as if he has broken the bars of his crib and come forth to tear up the house. Something's always being broken, or you pick up the telephone and the child is running into the street." He called, *"Up in front on the trail! Now around the curve!"*

She could hear pounding noises ahead. "What's Benjy doing now?"

"Kicking a rock; that's fairly typical, to react against the world when it won't do his will."

"And if he keeps on kicking rocks, can you tell when it's still chemistry and when he's simply formed the habit?"

J. Waldo, perhaps not hearing, called, "I'm coming to get you now!" and toed Mike into a lope along the trail. Benjy's shrieks angled off cross-country while Nancy waited for dust to drift away. Grit had settled on her sunglasses until the crack across one lens became a row of magnified stones, like the edge of a parapet over which she was about to peer.

Well, Joel, she thought as she scrubbed the tinted glass with her shirttail, if I'm not competing with a wife I take on a Chemical Difference. She moved down the trail almost muttering aloud. I only want to be happy, Randolph. What's wrong with that? People promised me that. Everybody. I'm going to write that in *my* declaration of independence, not the pursuit but the capture of happiness. Heading west to Nancy's Manifest Destiny.

Ahead J. Waldo, holding Benjy in the saddle with him, rode parallel to the trail and waved. She lifted a hand as they tested Mike in short trots and gallops across the brushy mesa.

Instead of me having a baby, Randolph, let's you have a vasectomy.

From the highest point above Frijoles Canyon she looked down at the river twisting in and out of cottonwoods. The even stone ring of Tuonyi Ruins seemed so small and lost in the sweep of land it was as though a stale doughnut had melted there. Beyond, Nancy could barely see a beetle-sized dot inching up the river trail from park headquarters, perhaps someone's black hat, now gone under a bulge of greenery.

The trotting horse drew nearer, carrying an argument. Benjy was tired of riding double and wanted to ride alone with nobody leading him like a baby, like a baby on a merry-go-round. "Only if you stay on

the trail and ride slow," said J. Waldo, dismounting somewhere behind her.

In an instant the horse almost ran Nancy down as it pounded past
with Benjy beating on the neck.

"The reins! Pull hard on the reins!" Benjy reacted to his father's
shout by making the horse rear. Two girl hikers rounded a turn just in
time to leap away as the horse came down, was kicked, and raced
headlong down the trail. The one who twisted her ankle yelled about
a shit-ass kid. She limped to where Nancy sat cross-legged by the trail
waiting out this latest game. "Your little boy's going to hurt himself
or somebody else," she said, furious. Nancy nodded. The second girl
sucked a nettle from her wrist and spat it behind the Fosters.

"Maybe at least he'll run down the creep," she said. With Nancy
they watched dust and thrashing bushes mark Benjy's path, with J.
Waldo's bright orange backpack bobbing behind. "There's this creep
back there," she said to Nancy.

The red-haired one said he had asked them to go to Florida. Both
were in their late teens, lean, long-muscled, hair aglow, white teeth
straightened and filed to shape in their pink gums, with bodies so
healthy that if they should be squeezed even the sweat wrung out
would be potent with multivitamins. "He's just roaming around hoping to find some woman in a sleeping bag—"

"With a drop seat," said her friend, pointing to where the dust trail
had just stopped. "Your friend caught the horse."

Nancy asked if they had passed another horse, chestnut, with an
older man riding.

"Talking to himself?" At Nancy's nod, the girl said he had crossed
the main bridge while they were filling canteens. "I thought he was
asleep up there and talking the way old men will."

To them the judge *was* old. The girls, walking on, stopped while J.
Waldo led the horse into view with one hand and Benjy with the
other. His red face looked slick, the cup at his belt clanged against his
backpack with every stride. Until he came close, the girls straightened
themselves and smoothed denim, but when he walked into full view
and beyond their generation they slumped as much as solid protein
would permit. J. Waldo, muttering orders, pressed a hand on his son's

head and bore down, repeating, "Sit here, sit here," until Benjy sagged halfway, then deliberately hung there in a rubbery crouch.

The red-haired girl limped noticeably under Benjy's drooping face. "Fall off?" He barely swayed, aloof as a lily. "Break anything?"

J. Waldo dropped alongside Nancy, dragging the horse's head so low that he collected warm saliva down his collar. "Sit right there, Benjy," he puffed. He took Nancy's canteen and poured water inside his shirt front. "It's in my pack, Benjy; oh yes, you've made your choice, we both know it." He drank deeply. "You've violated our agreement." Unzipping a pocket he said, "You can have water in a minute but not by itself, Benjy; are you listening to me?"

The girls stared at the boy's hanging head, which had begun to mottle with congested blood. the blotched jaw slackened and fell; the tip of a tongue, excused by gravity, stuck into view. Nancy thought that for a boy with a short span of concentration, he was doing all right.

"Stand up now," said one of the girls uneasily.

From the pocket J. Waldo pulled an amber bottle and rattled its pills. "One now and another at"—glancing at his watch—"at four o'-clock; now you come here. Benjy? Do you hear me, Benjy?"

The red-haired girl could not stand it; turning back in the trail she called, "Of course he *hears* you—that's not the problem!" The other girl told her to come on and mind her business.

When they had gone J. Waldo swallowed another long, noisy drink from the canteen. "How cool! How sweet and cool!" His meaty mouth caressed the words; he dipped his head to show Benjy droplets clinging to lips and chin. "Tastes wonderful! You have some now, Nancy."

Though she shook her head, Benjy held still except that his darkening knuckles brushed the sand. His face, quite red now, was purpling around the nostrils. She had a horror of seeing pooled blood drip through his pores. J. Waldo sloshed water into his palms and laved both cheeks, murmuring, "Marvelous!" Benjy sagged even lower, poised, and crumpled so easily to the ground that each joint seemed to fold in sequence. He lay curled like a paper accordion, his face turned from them.

"Oh hell," said J. Waldo. "Nancy, hold this damned horse."

She led Mike down the slope toward Frijoles Canyon while he sat near Benjy's head talking in a sugary whisper, agitating the medicine bottle like a shaman's rattle. When she looked back Benjy had up-ended the canteen. Down the valley Nancy could spot the tiny creep with the black head, resting now that the two girls had escaped him.

Soon the Fosters caught up. Now medicated, Benjy seemed less calm than deliberate. Between softer arguments they nibbled gorp for lunch and did not stop walking until coolness floated to them from the shaded main canyon; then they turned offtrail to make camp before the tall clouds with thunderheads dropped their rain.

Nancy's shinbones hurt. Lactic acid in the muscles, hormone ooze from the uterine wall, a Chemical Difference staining a boy's cerebrum—all this diminished and depressed her. She felt no different than the Pueblo tribesmen, who, in this same countryside, had felt themselves at the mercy of sky/earth spirits with more musical names.

Though it was still afternoon, she unstrapped the tent and began driving stakes. J. Waldo, also depressed, helped stretch the fabric taut. "I had to do it," he said softly.

She glanced at Benjy lying flat on his back. "Is he better now?"

"Better?" He gave one stake a vicious blow. "The new studies seem to show a relationship with food dyes and flavors; did you know that? Grape soda, orange Popsicles? Something in the luxuries we made, the treats especially for children—" His voice waned as he squatted to zip the tent flap. "He'll go to sleep early; that's something. We'll have some private time together." She felt his warm look, made it ricochet. "I want to get to know you better. If you do decide to stay out west, come to Sacramento."

Maybe this climate would dry arthritic joints; maybe this sun would burn flat any peaks on her own encephalogram. "Do you need an office receptionist?"

"If she's receptive." At his father's chuckle, Benjy edged up and trickled sand inside the heel of J. Waldo's boot. "Very funny." J. Waldo sat down to empty it, stripping off both sweaty socks, one of which Benjy filled with dirt and began beating into his palm like a blackjack. To these thuds the two, finished setting the tent, now looked at each other helplessly. Ahead of them the evening sagged heavy with effort and politeness.

"I'm wearing that tomorrow," J. Waldo finally said. Benjy dropped the sock among thistles and shot Nancy a look she had seen in her mirror at home—bored, fretful, petulant.

J. Waldo was suggesting they take a swim; Benjy said no, he was tired. "We'll go by ourselves, then," said J. Waldo, leading her across the hot sand.

Just then, downhill beside the noisy water, somebody's black hat came into view and ducked behind leaves again. The Fosters saw nothing, but instantly Nancy knew Dwight was the creep the girls had met, that he was watching them from the brush of Frijoles Canyon, that for some reason he had come back for her. She snapped a look at the red tent, which must be functioning for Dwight like a bull's-eye in a large target.

"I'm tired, too," she gasped, pulling back, though she was uncertain whether the Fosters were safer with or without her or whether she was safe at all. Benjy ran ahead. J. Waldo insisted the cool water would soothe her sunburn. She wondered how her sunburn would feel with a bullet hole in it. Carefully she marked where the hat had disappeared as she followed them. Could Dwight tell she was staring through half a mile of greenery into his face? He hid like this at Linville, she thought, watching Eddie eat ham.

"Let's move upstream, son!" called J. Waldo. From the brushy noises she realized he was beating Benjy, like game, downwind toward the hunter. She screamed, "Downstream! Downstream!" She imagined Dwight enjoying her backward stumble; maybe he barked his humorless laugh and rattled his blue jacket. She ran after the Fosters and fell into step between them. "Let's hurry!"

On all sides downdrafts from the coming storm blew every leaf at once. J. Waldo settled his thick arm around her waist. Are you watching, Dwight Anderson? Benjy walked hard on Nancy's foot but she didn't mind; and quickly she wound her arm around the boy before he could pull loose. Benjy finally broke free and ran to the river's edge and jumped flatfooted among rocks in the shallow water. That splatting noise, thought Nancy, would carry a long way.

As if to play a scale, J. Waldo had spread his hand on her diaphragm—yes, C was in the cleft between her breasts and lower C under his little finger at her navel. Big men, like yardsticks, measured women. In Nancy's experience it was not true that big noses and big feet kept their promises elsewhere. A big man with a small penis, however, always proved a wonderful lover; he began seduction already abashed and tentative. He took his time.

She followed them into the fast, cold water. Ankle-deep, looking upriver, she was dizzied by the small cataracts rushing toward her. Nothing else moved except stray branches leaping out from the wind, sighing back.

"Nancy? Hand me that rock."

Until now, Benjy had not spoken her name. Hefting the stone, staggering forward, she rolled it into place atop the dam he had begun, found another, closed off a small torrent. With one scooped hand Benjy sent a sheet of flying water over her sunburned legs. Since he was smiling she flung back a smaller splash.

Uncertainly, then, Nancy began telling him about the last dam she remembered building across a smaller, North Carolina branch, under a footlog she had finally learned to cross alone. Into the pool she had transported frogs and crayfish to better quarters where they could be fed and offered an ideal life. "But they migrated through the rock wall and the toads drowned—I didn't know the difference from frogs, then, so I'd hold them under to give them time to feel at home." She left out the part about her grandfather chiding, "Quit trying to change it all, Nancy; roll with the world as it is." Well, I'm rolling now.

J. Waldo nodded, whistling. He was on the downstream side plugging leaks. Benjy said, "I saw this flash flood once and a dead cat in it."

Nancy hung on to a low limb, remembering. "I was afraid to play in the branch because it ran through the cow pasture. I thought all three cows would stampede or mistake me for a bullfighter. My grandfather knew I was scared; I'd say, I *hate* those cows, and he'd say, Tell them so. I'd walk along the feeding trough and whisper to every cow how much I hated it and later he'd ask me what the cows said back. Of course they paid no attention, but he'd shake his head and advise me to keep notifying them and to tell him when they finally understood it." Upstream she could still see nobody lurking in the leaves. "Most of one summer I told them before I got his point that the cows didn't care and couldn't change. If anything was going to change, I had to be the one."

"Pretty dumb," said Benjy.

"A little slow, yes." She jerked once. "What was that?"

"I thought you raised thoroughbreds. What?" J. Waldo looked at the underbrush where she was pointing. "I don't see anything."

"Somebody hunting deer out of season shot one of those cows and I found it in the branch. There's not a man in that thicket?"

"It's your ghost cow." Benjy's grin persuaded her they could be friends, especially when he said, "Moo"; but then he lowered his head and butted her painfully in the ribs, hard enough to send her floundering onto boulders as she sat down heavily in the icy current.

J. Waldo said in a mild voice, "You don't want to play too rough, Benjy."

Wet and angry, Nancy struggled upright in the river and rubbed her hip. She said under her breath, "Little bastard."

J. Waldo asked, "You're not hurt?"

"Yes, I am, and if you'd turn your head I'd box his ears."

He grinned. "Ee-ahs. I just love to hear you talk."

"You don't know the first thing about loving anything!" She watched Benjy hoist new stones for his dam. "The medicine he needs most is a dose of peach tree tea."

"Come on, Nancy. He's just a child. Show a little maturity."

Mature rage was what she wanted to show. "You teach him all about excuses but nothing about consequences!" Benjy made a nasty face. In the foamy water J. Waldo turned his whole body slightly away.

"Adults teach self-control by setting a good example," he said rather primly.

"Good yes, false no."

"You're mean, when I was just playing—you're not fair!" Benjy then shoved all the rocks they had assembled until the Rito de los Frijoles broke through the dam and tumbled downhill as fast as ever. He slung smaller stones in all directions. It was like standing too close to a Gatling gun.

"We know you were playing, son; be careful now."

Nancy sloshed to the bank, where she wrung out the sodden hems of her clothes. On all sides pebbles were flying out, pelting leaves, plopping into the stream.

"He *said* he was just playing." With a relieved smile, J. Waldo joined in throwing stones downstream while dodging others and glancing at his waterproof watch to verify how far away from the next pill Benjy was. "Find some flat wood, Benjy, and I'll make us some sailboats."

"He can lash sparrows on board and set them afire!" Nancy headed for the tent. Whether Dwight was coming through the pinyons hardly mattered; let him come. Inside, she lay on her back waiting to see which man would unzip the doorway first, the criminal or the doctor; as with most choices offered in her life, she wanted neither. Stone County's tenth-rate Hunger Artist. She did not even turn when metal buzzed down the fabric but waited until J. Waldo's voice chided, "Obviously, you have never reared a child."

"Obviously."

"I've explained to Benjy that you've had no experience playing with boys."

"I'll let that pass," she said.

"I also told him your husband died before you could have a little boy of your own."

Oh, this was not going to be worth it. "I was never married, J. Waldo. I only said so because I get tired of being asked why not."

He crawled nearer. "I can understand the general astonishment," he whispered, bending to kiss her.

Nothing. Bells or falling stars Nancy no longer expected, but how welcome would have been the simple physical reflex which wrung their mouths together. She rolled her cool neutral lips loose from his. He said, "What's wrong?"

That she was choosy? The calendar? Everything. "Nothing," she answered as women always have.

"Why did you come, then?"

I'm an idiot. Aloud she said, "To get away, to keep from going home."

"No, you wanted to be with *me*. Trust that impulse."

Again she turned her mouth into range but the second kiss had no better effect. As it so frequently does, failure made him moral. "Why did you lie about being a widow?" he said severely. "What need does lying fulfill for you?"

"It seemed harmless, that's all, a lot more fun than being a librarian on leave."

"No, the lie protected you. But how?" His face alight, he said intensely, "Having a dead husband disguised the real truth, that you've had no man at all! A virgin! In this day and time! Naturally in this age and at your age—the thirties?—it's embarrassing."

"Late twenties." If evolution had worked right, Nancy decided, the hymen would be a nictitating membrane by now. "I am neither virginal nor embarrassed," she began, but his third kiss stirred her slightly and she saw that the fantasy *he* had set in motion had begun its work, that if she could recapture untouched innocence with no experience to test against, even J. Waldo might look good. With fervor she kissed him hard but it felt like setting her mouth by will against a newel post. She drew back and stared at the tent's ceiling, thinking of Oliver Newton's rather thin mouth. She had always imagined his kisses as thin, too, but lasting—like unleavened bread.

He said again, "What's wrong?"

Patiently Nancy began to explain that they couldn't have made love anyway, wrong time, wrong week, closed-to-the-public and all that, moon and mense; but the more she talked the less convincing she sounded and the more his beard closed over his lips, until his entire mouth had disappeared.

"I see." See what a liar you are. In a sarcastic voice he asked if she'd join him in a little Scotch for her cramps? She shook her head. "I'll ease mine, then." Outside he rummaged in his pack and came back into the tent with a pint.

While he was drinking she said, "Maybe you shouldn't leave Benjy alone."

"He's playing World War Three."

"Now don't pout, J. Waldo. You didn't ask for a certificate of accessibility. It was my pleasant company you invited along, remember?"

"I can't believe," he said, "the lengths some women will go to, hoarding their maiden's treasure."

Good grief. J. Waldo drank again while watching her face, her ungrateful mouth. "Women like you should come into California and the twentieth century. I can help you."

"But not this week."

"I'll awaken you."

"You bloody well won't," she said—her joke wasted.

"Don't you realize that nowadays women can do what they please with their own bodies?"

"Except withhold them?" Nancy crawled out and called Benjy's name. "He doesn't answer."

"He's mad at you. I can hear him splashing. Benjy likes war better than anything." He had crawled behind her and now slipped one hand inside her thigh; yes, and she liked it there so long as it seemed detached from the rest of him.

"I hear the splashing. What if he's struggling with a kidnapper?" J. Waldo pressed close enough for her to discern that he had no erection despite all that panting against her neck. "Benjy?" she called. No answer. He leaned over her shoulder and bellowed the name and waited for the returned call, "Not now, I'm busy." "Satisfied?" He breathed into her ear. "Trust me and you can be."

Why should she be so fastidious? After all it was his—she started to giggle—it was his little red wagon. At her laughter he let go and headed for his pack. "It's time for Benjy's medicine anyway."

The rainstorm had moved until only distant lightning could be seen. They found Benjy sitting in the water, unwilling to take his pill. Midstream his father administered it by force, holding shut his mouth until the boy swallowed and tore away. Then J. Waldo waded onshore to sit by Nancy and whisper, "We have to wait so he won't puke it up." At first she was sorry the taste made him nauseated. It was explained that Benjy on purpose would put his finger down his throat.

While they waited and Benjy sat in the current, back turned, Nancy began to speak seriously and to enunciate like a Yankee. "It seems time to tell you that Harvey Jolley is really not my uncle"—J. Waldo said he wasn't a bit surprised—"and this isn't a vacation trip. It's imperative that you understand because you and Benjy may, even now, be in danger. What happened—"

"Jolley's a little old, but it fits. That's who you run with—queers and old men, right? We'll change that."

"Just *listen!* Last Sunday I was kidnapped back in North Carolina—"

"While riding your thoroughbreds to hounds, I know. You and Grandpop and your old roommate from Hollins, big girl with bobbed hair—honey, is *that* it? We're all bisexual, take it from the doctor. Benjy? Stop putting your head underwater. I've seen that trick before and I'll just give you another one. Was the kidnapper named Randolph?"

Stiffly she said she had been in Linville Gorge with her sister and her husband ("Three's a crowd, right?") when this man with a gun . . . She summarized the week's events: Isoline, the judge, the kidnapper's double names, their route west. At mention of Dwight's probably murdered brother, J. Waldo gave a fake yawn.

"That manicure has never groomed a horse."

"I told you, I work in a library; now listen—the man has followed me here. I saw his hat, Dwight—"

"His hat? Black, I suppose."

"Red," she decided to say. "He's carrying a gun. Didn't you hear the girl hikers?"

No, he had not. He smiled, shook his head in a kindly way. "Vicarious experience, it figures. What else to invent but a man outside the law who's good at heart? You virgins!"

"At heart he is terrible." Leaning against a cottonwood, Nancy pressed her teeth together. For years she had dreamed of a different life, *any* life; this substitute now sounded so implausible no one would rescue her from this one, either.

J. Waldo soothed her hand between his. "The truth is, Nancy, everybody gets bored and feels he could invent an existence better than the one he leads. I do myself. I'd have made one hell of an F.B.I. agent."

"I doubt it." She tried again. "He tied up my relatives. He steals cars. He has held a gun on the judge."

"I could tell the judge was terrified! Come on, Nancy. There's nothing wrong with being a librarian and unmarried. What you need to do is move your fantasies into reality." He slid his hand onto the small of her back.

"One fantasy will be walking into camp any minute." She scanned the countryside, wondering if J. Waldo might be correct in reverse; perhaps she was imagining Dwight *now*, had read him into a black-hatted *local* pervert.

"Repeat after me: Fantasies are normal."

She did, twice, while checking hills and trees. He said, "They become abnormal only when you lose the line between fantasy and real events. Many women dream of rape, of intercourse with dogs, all kinds of things. You've read Erica Jong? I knew you had. In California, we're much more open about such things."

An imagined orgy of women and Chihuahuas had made Nancy's mouth twitch and he nodded. "Smile, yes, because shame ended with Queen Victoria. When you're in Sacramento, I'll show my collection of sixteen-millimeter films—they helped Adrienne overcome her inhibitions. Even Benjy has seen the milder, heterosexual ones. Go ahead, smile. It'll cure your period."

Her smile was threatening to laugh. She said, "If you're right, Dwight must be a figment of my imagination." This was her best fantasy in a long time. "Mr. Jolley and I and a busload of other Sunday schoolteachers have come west together." His arm gave an involuntary jerk. "We've seen Oral Roberts University and we'll hear the Mormon choir and hold a sunrise service at Grand Canyon. Dwight Anderson must represent—"

"Satan! Who represents all you've repressed! My God, no wonder!" When he embraced her Benjy threw a few rocks to remind them he was there.

"My dark, irrational, selfish side, that's it!"

"*Now* you feel better." Nancy allowed herself the full laugh. "Never be ashamed of thoughts or dreams." He mumbled about bodies, temples of the Lord, while his fingers crawled downward. "In your imagination does this Dwight ever touch you? Do you perform with him the acts you've only read about?" Perhaps now he was getting an erection. "You've read the *Story of O?* And Frank Harris? I knew it. The fear, the theme of kidnapping only add to the thrill, isn't that so?"

From the river Benjy yelled, "When do we eat?"

The roving hand leaped away. "In a minute, son! Some women, Nancy, mark or mutilate their fantasy men. I need not analyze a wooden leg, for example. But a scar?"

"Or a broken tooth? A tattoo?"

"And the murdered brother? Maybe you've felt some sibling rivalry? Envied a real sister or brother of your own? Wait. That's who was with you at the so-called kidnapping. Your *sister.* Your sister's *husband!*"

"Amazing."

He nodded. "So true of us all. What was your father like?"

She said he was dead.

"I knew that; he *had* to be dead, but how long ago? What happened?"

"He worked for the railroad. I was nine when he had his heart attack."

"Just before puberty, yes, and *heart.* Poor Nancy."

She had never known Leon Finch half so well as her grandfather nor missed him one tenth as much, but J. Waldo's voice made her feel bereft.

He said, "It wasn't a good marriage."

"My parents'? Average. I don't think I ever thought much about it."

"We never *think* we think about it. Only complete candor can prevent a trauma. Benjy here"—he smiled at the boy coming to them from the water—"Benjy knows Mama had a lover; he's accepted that fact as well as I have. Benjy has shared our lives fully, haven't you, son?" The boy seemed to look at Nancy with hatred. J. Waldo threaded her ringless fingers into his. "Tonight," he whispered as he drew her to her feet, "I'm going to be your Dwight Anderson, but I'll be good to you."

Nancy wondered if a quick Enovid tablet would stop her period. While J. Waldo was milking more human kindness from their twined hands, she took a last look at all the green hiding places. There was no black hat in view.

She let J. Waldo lead her up the path she could climb perfectly well by herself. In a minute I'll simper from autonomic femaleness, she thought, while her drawl thickened like molasses pooled low in her throat.

The freeze-dried porkchops tasted like pulpwood. After supper they sat around the tent smoking, waiting for twilight to end. Benjy had found a traveling ant column in which he was mashing every other one. The returning storm blew an occasional spread of chill bumps under Nancy's sunburn while nearby J. Waldo watched her with the smile of a therapist.

At last she politely excused herself for a trip into shadowed underbrush. She flourished the blue box where a smiling J. Waldo could see and identify, wanting to tell him no tampons would absorb periodic mild neurosis. Though he acknowledged the swoops of her package, his nod was patient, understanding. "Soon you won't need these psychological crutches," he said.

Coming back, Nancy was not really surprised to see two men by a half-struck tent. "Perfectly, I understand perfectly," J. Waldo was saying earnestly to the man in the low black hat. "Here she is now! Ruby Kaye?"

"What's that?" She stared into Dwight's flat, expressionless face. "What is he calling me?"

"Your brother's come," said J. Waldo in a strained tenor. "Took him a while to find us."

"My brother. Well, well. Is that *your* fantasy, Dwight?" Half-frightened, half-resigned, she stood between the men. When J. Waldo continued to gaze at his cowboy boots and Dwight only curled his lip past the gap in his teeth, devilment overcame her. "Benjy Foster?" She did not turn to the seated boy. "I'd like to introduce my dear brother. Benjy Foster, meet Melrose Lee Shelton."

The broken tooth went out of sight; Dwight's chin jerked as if hit.

Very slowly she said, "From Virginia. Roanoke."

"I don't care," said Benjy. "Can we keep the horse?"

"If I was you," Dwight said, "I'd save these people trouble by coming on and keeping quiet."

Though he was half a foot taller than Dwight, J. Waldo had no intention of arguing. She said, "I've got another brother who looks just like Melrose here. Just exactly."

"Mister, uh, well?" J. Waldo coughed. "I wouldn't want you to get the wrong impression here."

"He doesn't care what you want. Would one of you roll the tent, please?" Nancy began gathering her things and zipping compartments in her pack. "Think about what I've said," she told J. Waldo with emphasis, adding, "We owe an extra day on the horse."

Dwight did not move to do anything and J. Waldo started dismantling the tent without thinking at all. Like a bumblebee he hummed a nervous one-note as he lowered and folded. Several times he repeated that it didn't matter about the horse, glad to take care of it, glad to. In his haste the nylon tube turned out unbalanced and lumpy and he laid it across Nancy's arms as if getting rid of an illegitimate child. She had difficulty strapping its odd shape on her backpack. "Are you going to carry this?"

"Didn't plan to, no," said Dwight. Benjy said he would ride that horse all day by himself tomorrow.

"So it's only fair that I pay." J. Waldo laughed heartily. To Dwight he said, "He's my *son,* so his presence should make perfectly clear the innocence of everything." He caught sight of Dwight's tattoo and forgot to close his mouth.

Nancy hefted the unframed pack onto her shoulders and reset the straps and waist belt. "Is the judge all right?"

"Was when I left."

"He won't wait for you like a package. I know where he's gone."

"Not if he plans on ever seeing you again, he didn't."

J. Waldo had not been listening and his words spoken to himself grew more audible. "Suppression deeper than . . . hint of incest so shocking, well . . ." He came over to shake Nancy's hand and to gaze wisely into her face. "Remember, Ruby Kaye. Face up to your thoughts. You are no longer a child." Trying to decide whether to offer the hand to Dwight, he hung his fingers in midair near his belt buckle. "Nice to have met you, Ruby Kaye. You're a real lady. Yes *sir.*" He sent the emphasis toward Dwight.

"Keep healing the sick," answered Nancy over one shoulder as she led the way to the trail. Were it not for the rhythmic sounds of walking, she would never have known Dwight followed. He did not speak and she would not. In the pale early evening they marched silently alongside the flickering river. A long turn sometimes brought his shadow sliding along the ground toward hers; once she smelled his burning cigarette; when the light rain began she heard him swear. She could not guess what time it was. They were still walking through the cool rain when the gray colors turned black around them.

Her shoulders felt raw long before the far lights of the lodge came in view. Only then did Dwight ask her back, "Who was that man?"

"What man?" Nancy slid her thumbs under each strap to cushion the load. "There was nobody. I made him up."

Again rain made the only sound. When they finally crossed the bridge she stopped to rest the pack briefly on its wooden rail and tried to see Dwight's face through the rain. "Where in the world did you get a hillbilly name like Ruby Kaye?"

"Come on." He pushed her ahead of him under the tall black pines. His car was waiting down the empty street; with relief, she could pick out Judge Jolley's profile through the back window.

Behind her Dwight said, "You don't ask me anything about names and I won't ask you." If the backpack had weighed less, Nancy would have shrugged.

11

After flinging objects into the trunk, both Nancy and Dwight had slung their bodies inside the car as if discarding themselves on the seat and now sat rigid and silent while the speedometer passed seventy-five. Had anyone spoken in the speeding car, a rush of air would have whistled the words away. From behind, the judge squinted through his wildly blowing hair at Dwight's hat, Nancy's upturned and imperial profile.

Had Dwight brought her out of Bandelier at gunpoint? Were they being pursued? Though the judge doubted J. Waldo Foster could send the police down the right highway after the right car, Dwight's reckless driving should soon bring sirens.

"Dwight?" He leaned forward. "Uh, Dwight?" Surely a frightened parent in some car they flew past would report this dark car rocking from side to side in the rain almost grazing their doors. The judge's uplifted hair whipped forward to blind him. In the middle of another roaring downhill loop he slid spread fingers under his flying hair and lunged against Dwight's back with one elbow. "For God's sake, Dwight!"

Nancy heard him but her locked mouth was dry, the passing whiz of pocked cliffs with blurred amoebae of vegetation both fearful and exciting. She supposed Dwight raced downhill to punish her, to prove his control.

She was wrong. Motives lay beyond Dwight's analysis. For years he had faced a sequence of serious expressions laid over minds unlike his own, and for years professional strangers had been asking him, "Why?" He decided young that this searching for cause was done only by people at desks who earned salaries for it. "Why?" Always their questions were patient; always they wrote down the answers he gave whether these were right or wrong. Any answer seemed not only acceptable but dignified by their solemn interest. Any boy "rehabilitated," Dwight quickly understood, would be turned into a stranger like those behind the desks who could then draw weekly wages asking "Why?" of other boys.

"Why not?" became Dwight's favorite answer to their patient question, got written down, and caused them to ask next, "Why do you say that?" At first he had been making a serious inquiry because he could not understand their question; a search for meaning had never occurred to him spontaneously. Before fourteen he understood that the clash lay simply between what Dwight wanted and what deskmen wanted him not to want, their side no different from his except for words, words, and words, spoken and written down. None of his actions escaped the cosmetic improvement of their words. If he beat the piss out of another boy it turned into "hostility." You could make a tune out of a word like that. "Genevieve." "Hostility, hostility, the years may come, etc." For a while he enjoyed seeing them bring up new musical words and write them after his name like a string of shining fish.

Then he worked at deliberate confusion, petting the same dog he later hanged, inventing contradictory dreams, reading the prism's colors in reverse, only to watch some solemn "why" written down in polysyllables to account even for that. Though one stranger tried to explain Dwight's negativistic pattern, it was too much trouble to keep that one out of phase, since breaking an order involved first Dwight's effort of learning to think in it. He returned to his original intent to do what he wanted when he wanted. Period. Why not? Behind their word fog, officials must do the same, he decided.

Let him drive fast. I won't submit to being punished by this man, Nancy was thinking.

And Dwight drove fast out of Bandelier only to feel the damp wind in his face. Why not?

Nancy thought: But I've proved I can control him and use him. And I'll run now first chance I get. The judge will have to look after himself, like Mama now, like Beckham.

"Nancy, tell him to slow down!" the judge was yelling.

No fear, she thought. She said nothing. Through Santa Fe in early dusk and out of the rain down to Albuquerque without a policeman glancing twice at their car, they drove onto I-40 west again toward Arizona. When their speed dropped the relieved judge began looking at places on the map where they could eat. They were reduced to the basic rhythms of food, sleep, westward movement, having no stake in this landscape, no house, no work, no faces to recognize. The judge thought they were as loose from their surroundings as a meteor flying across these reservations of the Laguna and Acoma Indians, and this made them like Dwight—an accident choosing its location.

"If you've quit trying to make this thing pull up its landing gear, I'll drive," he offered, but Dwight said Nancy was next.

To the judge's shock she said with malice, "Clara was killed but you lived through it. There must be ways to wreck a car so only half gets sideswiped. When I'm driving, Judge, don't sit on Dwight's side." Dwight called her a whore, putting an end to further conversation. Nobody was talking when they ate beef barbecue in—a joke?— Thoreau, New Mexico, and watched the evening turn darker blue.

The judge felt static was crossing their silence. "We're almost at the Continental Divide," he said nervously. The others chewed; the air crackled. "It runs with the Zuni Mountains here." He had gotten a grim picture in his mind of Dwight stopping the car on some dark road, gunning him down, saying to Nancy over the dead Harvey Jolley, "Now will you act right?"

Staring at the phone booth Nancy said, "I'm going to call somebody."

"You're not." Dwight smelled of a Los Alamos barbershop; his hair looked clean.

"Beyond it the streams flow the other way." The judge spread his travel guide on the plastic counter and slid it toward first one, then the other.

After arranging her coleslaw flat in the dish Nancy said, "You could listen in, I don't care. It's to Detroit."

"I don't care if it's to Jesus."

"Why," she said sharply, "do you drag in Jesus all the time?" Dwight said he never did that. She dropped a pat of butter on the judge's map, complaining, "He opens his mouth and Jesus falls out every time, have you ever heard of anything so ironic? Pass me a muffin. Just like Hazel Motes." She went on talking with corn bread in her mouth. "They're the worst kind, those people with a ghost for a god, a rumor. And you? You change the subject. That's all you can think to do. That's all you've been doing while you were in orbit around Somerville, and him!" She snapped a nasty look toward an invisible image on the windowpane. "J. Waldo Foster," she said slowly to herself.

"That's it, Somerville. I can always find Somerville," said Dwight.

The judge said angrily, "And hers is Greenway, don't forget that." Now electricity flew everywhere.

"It's just a vacation call to an old friend," she said to Dwight. "Having wonderful time; wish you were here."

"We don't wish he was here."

She held out her palm. "Lend me change for the telephone, Judge. Surely those satisfied defendants gave you plenty."

"You couldn't hold a candle to Clara Elaine Jolley!" cried the judge.

Nancy began pawing through her pocketbook until with one hand

Dwight swooped it from her and hung both handles on the foot he had crossed to one side. "Now let's *eat!*"

Too angry to eat much, Nancy eventually said, "You should have called police from park headquarters and you know why you didn't? Jealous. You were jealous as hell." The judge said *to Dwight* in a prissy voice he hardly recognized that he had never known Clara to use an unladylike word.

When they paid, the purse was swinging from Dwight's hand; something in his face kept the cashier from laughing. This time Nancy took the driver's seat while Dwight sat beside, zipping and un-zipping her purse and watching her angry face. Once more their speed through the darkening craggy countryside so worried the judge that he concentrated on how the vibrations sought out the tenderest muscles in his body, for he was afraid to sleep and trust Nancy to manage an expert sideswipe that would leave him unhurt. In time fatigue snatched him into short sleeps. Gallup was a set of intermittent flashes. It was black dark when he heard Dwight say from a great distance, "Now you're in Arizona, Nancy Finch." The continent, he remembered drowsily, had divided someplace behind them.

Waking still later he found the car parked on ground that slanted backward, saw Nancy drooped asleep in the front seat, Dwight smoking. In his next dream, Gulliver-sized, Harvey Jolley lay strapped to a huge rolling platform and small creatures, not Lilliputians but Houyhnhnms, were tapping him everywhere with miniature farrier's hammers. They had dragged off his massive clothes and where he could see his skin it had crazed like porcelain from all their tiny blows.

Next morning his body felt beaten. Some fault in the morning light seemed to mute the gold and magenta terraces of the Painted Desert. Beyond, in a Holbrook restaurant, he barely reached the men's room in time to vomit his first cup of coffee.

"Are you all right?" Nancy was knocking on its door. "Judge Jolley?"

He let her worry, retching up pale stomach juices next, then white globs and foam.

"I can come right in there if you need help." He could not answer this time, heaving dry. "You know Dwight wouldn't; he's ordered seconds."

"Send the first policeman you see." He flushed the commode and rested his forehead on the cool translucent window. Window? It was sealed shut for air-conditioning with paint clogging the lock. After much strain he could turn that latch and began working up the sash. Below the window was a dumpster full of kitchen garbage whose stench wrung his stomach again. Beyond? It would be a long exposed run to the first house. He unfastened the screen.

"I got worried that—Judge?" Nancy froze in the men's room doorway.

"Close it for God's sake. Will it lock?"

"No." Quickly she joined him to look down upon heaped lettuce leaves and rotting meat. "You'd fall in."

"I can walk on the rim by leaning into the wall, at least I hope so." He gagged in spite of himself.

"Let me." Nancy stepped first on the toilet tank, then felt outside with one shoe for the edge of the garbage bin. "I don't know. Give me a hand now."

When Dwight came in Nancy was half out the small window with the pale judge trying to support her while she strove for balance. She squealed. At sight of the level gun the judge let go her leg and retched.

"Get back in here."

She sat straddling the sill. "You won't shoot in a public place. You'd never make it to the door."

"I always make it to the door." He was smiling. "Who's going to get up from breakfast to risk his life for you?"

"Some may."

The judge said, gasping, "You know they won't."

"Would you?"

At Dwight's question she slowly drew in her leg and sat dangling them both by the commode, saying to the judge, "I hate what he's done to me, to my values, to everything." Jolley, spitting up clear fluid, could barely nod. "Can't you see the judge is sick?"

"It's probably his heart. He might have a growth on it," Dwight said. "Let's go sit down now."

The judge tottered into the restaurant, Nancy following with her eyes alert for the one who might have come to her defense. The nominees seemed unlikely.

"I'm too sick to smell this food. It must have been the barbecue."

"Don't smell, then, but sit down. It's Nancy I want to talk to."

She arranged herself very formally in the booth, sipped tepid coffee, and got ready to contend. Where were you going? Anywhere. What is it you really want? To be happy, she would say, then embroider. He'd ask how she knew about Melrose. Perhaps as one of God's running jokes he would say, Will you marry me? Over my dead body; no, scratch that. When hell freezes over. She waited.

Instead he asked, "Who's in Detroit?" Her cup stopped at chin level. "A man," he decided. "What's he doing there?"

"I don't know; we're out of touch."

"You want him?"

Joel? Now? She discovered that she did not. "This isn't what we need to discuss. We need to talk about separating now that we've come to Arizona. You could leave the judge and me right here, for instance, and just drive on."

"I'd have to steal a different car and change clothes and give up my new hat. Arizona's a big state."

"You said *to* Arizona; you never said *through* Arizona."

"You never said you'd be going out toilet windows."

She flung up a hand. "Why—do you even know why you are doing this?"

"Why are you letting me?"

Nancy recoiled, mistaking this for a serious, even a probing, question, not guessing how often it had deflected guilty counselors and moved them by its deep implications (actually, their inferences) of a textbook cry for help.

"Don't answer him; don't pay him the compliment," muttered the judge.

But she, who was uncertain why she had not by now escaped this dangerous man, mumbled, "What difference does it make?"

Since the answer might have been one of his own, Dwight was pleased and said for reward, "O.k., you can call Detroit." He almost pushed her to the nearby phone booth.

She no longer wanted to telephone Joel, whose face she had suddenly forgotten. Dwight insisted, thrusting the directory into her hands. Not wanting him to overhear anybody else's name and address, Nancy found the number in her address book, a number obtained from an operator two years before but never dialed. Dialing it now she suddenly thought of the time difference. "They're asleep!" she cried, appalled by the thought of Joel in bed by his wife when the telephone rang.

"Wrong. They're eating lunch." Dwight blocked the booth door. "You chickened out on calling police, admit it."

"No, look." With one finger she covered the name but showed the digits she had dialed. "I don't carry around the number for Interpol."

"You could be calling the F.B.I."

"Or Jesus, I know, but it's neither one."

"Let's see the name, then." He jerked her book, read quickly a number aloud, and reached past to dial it himself. Nancy thought he had chosen the wrong number but the book had dropped and she did not recognize it. "I'll need change."

She said, "Use your own change, smart-ass." Dwight listened, deposited quarters. "We'll see; you wait, we'll see." His broken tooth flashed, then disappeared as his face altered. "What? Wait just a minute." He held the receiver away as if to cool or quiet it, then shoved it into her face.

Nancy juggled against one ear. "Second Presbyterian Church," a man's voice was saying. "Hello?"

She breathed, "Oh God."

There was a chuckle. "Not quite but we have connections. This is the minister, Mr. Newton. Can I help you in some way?"

"No," she said. "Maybe. I'm calling you by mistake. He did it."

After a wait he said, "Nancy? Are you here? In town?"

With a glance at Dwight she said, "Out west."

"Your voice sounds strange. What's wrong?"

If Dwight had been a star Sunday school student she was in trouble. "Like Jesus, I've gone to the wilderness. With the same party."

"What? Look, is anybody there at home with you? Let me speak to Mrs. Finch."

"*After* this call," Nancy said. "You got that?"

"You're in some kind of trouble. Tell me what it is." Nobody said anything. He added, "I can do that much, at least."

"Listen, you mean? Is that all?" Dwight was fingering her shoulder as if searching for tender wounds. She said wildly, "The denizen from Gehenna instructs against details!" Dwight's eyes enlarged.

"This isn't like you," Oliver said. "I don't understand what you need, how to help. Calm down a minute, dear, we'll talk of other things awhile. How's Beckham? Are you still working at the library? Did they buy a new steeple?" Dumbly she stared through glass at Judge Jolley. "I read the Iris Murdoch. What about William Golding?"

Dwight, who had touched his face to hers in order to eavesdrop, looked bored. He took the phone from her hand, blew into the mouthpiece, and handed it back. She could feel his gun pressing her hip. Oliver Newton was saying, "Trouble on the line? I couldn't understand that last."

"Help me," she said. Dwight pulled the phone. "Help me, police—" It was slammed into place. Nancy clamped her teeth and bore down against any likelihood of crying. "That was cruel," she said. "You don't know how cruel that was."

"Who was he?"

She shook her head. "I won't tell you anybody else's names. I'm sorry I ever told you Faye and Eddie."

Softly he said, "I never told you mine," but his push toward the door was hard. He said, "If that old man pukes in the car, he goes out." Once at the wheel Dwight repeated this condition to the judge, who denied his stomach had anything left to lose.

Alone in the back, stuffing the address book into her purse, Nancy felt the compact of Enovid and paused to tap out days. "Is it Sunday?" she asked aloud. "Is that all?" No wonder Oliver was in the church office, reviewing his sermon, posting the hymnal numbers. Perhaps after the benediction he would call Greenway and ask for her, perhaps only remember her welfare in a silent prayer. "Only Sunday," she said again, only a week away from Linville Gorge, which meant she had bought the pills in Texarkana—Wednesday? Five days or seven? Five seemed more than sufficient.

While Dwight drove out of Holbrook she worked the first orange pill through its slot, lazed it around in one cupped palm, finally swallowed it dry. Though she had half hoped to feel internal fallout of radiant hormones, another promised event fizzled without igniting. This whole week of her kidnapping—or her freedom, depending on your point of view—had been the same.

But either the pill or Oliver's resonant voice sparked her wish to shampoo her hair, to change these rumpled clothes. In her pocket mirror she found extra freckles in the new tan. Through that image she could visualize Oliver in the pulpit: tall, lean, a little swaybacked, looking down on his single-breasted wife in the front row. At lunch he would describe Nancy's strange call; the wife would urge him to do nothing so that Nancy would seek counsel from her own pastor as she ought. They would be eating something cool and congealed, the wife having learned to cook by exchange of recipes at Bible Circle meetings. Sylvia still wore a high permanent wave that leaped off her forehead and circled her head with brown cylinders of hair. Under the curls her head was full of Bible quizzes, for which she was famous at Presby Youth. Oliver might say, "I'll just call Mrs. Finch, that's all." And Sylvia, serving chicken salad in a patty shell, would sweetly ask their two sons, "Which character said, 'Whither thou goest, I will go'?" Oliver would get the point.

Immense and monotonous, the stony landscape passed under Nancy's dark stare all the way to Flagstaff, where the mountains had come into the city and thrust themselves between gas stations and stereo shops. Maybe she would live out her life in a city jostled by Nature, her eye always being carried past roofs to rocks, then beyond to the San Francisco Peaks. Whither I go, no man knoweth.

Then it was her turn to drive through the city alongside the bleached sour-smelling judge, who finally said, "You called home?"

"Wrong number. Judge Jolley—if you'd gotten out that window by yourself would you have sent back help for me?" He said of course. "I wonder," she said.

"He has made you paranoid," he said with several injured breaths. He felt able to drive near Williams but before they had traveled far north Dwight stopped them at a commercial campground. He planned to reach the Grand Canyon early Monday morning.

"I thought you never planned," she said.

"I'm doing this for you and it's the last thing. Who was that preacher?"

"He was assigned to my region for instant sacrament and dial-a-prayer." She was afraid Dwight believed her.

At the campground, portable comforts were for rent separately. The judge, still sick, paid for an aluminum lounge that he carried into the air-conditioned laundromat. Nancy rented a ratty black bathing suit and bought a swim in a crowded pool tasting of chlorine with a soupçon of urine. Through the chain link fence Dwight watched her so intently that she stayed submerged until her eyes were burning. He had rented a transistor radio to play unknown tunes through his earplug. That's the last they see of *that* one, Nancy thought. She stayed in the water until he wandered off.

While waiting for a shower, she listened to a woman crooning inside the stall, "Stop that. Now sit." She expected a mother and child to emerge, not the tiny gray-haired woman in a duplicate black suit leading a wet brown dog. "Oh my!" she said at the sight of Nancy seated so near; the large dog, on cue, shook himself of flying water, which fell with a hair or two into Nancy's open mouth.

"I'm sorry." The woman tossed a clean towel off the rack and hooked the leash to a low pipe. "At least he's clean."

Nancy scrubbed her tongue and patted drops off her face. "It's all right. What kind of a beautiful dog is that?"

"Chesapeake Bay retriever." With another towel the woman began drying the wavy fur on the dog's shoulders. "He's on the way to an assignation; two, in fact." Squatting, her hip bones sharp as a child's, she could hardly have outweighed her pet by much. Her short hair was set in the same tough wave, her skin sunburned nearly the same rosy brown. Unmoving, the dog watched Nancy with eyes as yellow as Dwight's.

"Is he friendly?"

"Yes, but not demonstrative. I breed them." She guided Nancy's cautious hand onto the wooly back, which felt barely damp. "They're duck dogs with a coat that's almost waterproof." As Nancy stroked, the dog rolled back its lifted upper lip into a wrinkled sneer. "See? He smiles. This is Tanner, top stud and CDX." At Nancy's blank look she added, "Companion Dog Excellent, never mind. He'll look wonderful to two bitches up at Valle."

Nancy turned from the high window where she had gone to look for Dwight. "Where's Valle?"

"North," said the woman. "Thirty miles. You'll pass it going to the canyon. Or are you coming back?"

"Going. It's my first visit."

"Then don't listen to a word people tell you in advance. Don't read books or look at pictures. Just go. And don't go all the way to the bottom right away; save something for your second visit." She held out a damp hand. "I'm Chan Thatcher."

They exchanged other facts—that Chan was widowed with a middle-aged son, Nancy unmarried; that the dog was named for a river rapid in the Colorado and came from a kennel the Thatcher family had operated for twenty years, the late Mr. Thatcher having been a judge of sporting breeds; that Chan's friend had a litter of pups in Valle.

"I'd like to buy a dog like that," Nancy lied.

"Maybe you ought to stop in Valle and look at Lewis' pups." Chan said that her friend Lewis—"boyfriend, really, but in your sixties?"—used to fly for Bonanza airlines but now sold canyon rides in his own light lanes. "Not just for tourists, either, but local people. You can look maybe ten miles and see all the way across the canyon but there's only one bridge and it takes two hundred miles of driving to cross. He raises dogs on the side." She bent out of sight, rinsing shampoo from her thick hair. "When I'm in Valle I make a few flights with him just to see the canyon change into a postcard and then into a contour map. If it doesn't change into something artificial like that, the imagination can't stand it. Mine can't."

"Lewis who? Maybe I'll call him." Nancy had already learned that Chan was driving an Airstream trailer perfect for her getaway.

Chan wrapped the towel around her hair instead of her slim body, which was smoother and more youthful than her face, padded to her bag hung on a nail, found a business card, and scribbled on the back.

"I know Lewis' dogs as well as my own if you want to stop by unit twenty-one this afternoon. These are Tanner's pups. I've got a photograph of the bitch and her pedigree."

Nancy took the card with its dog-head silhouette and AKC emblem and dropped it into her purse. With a growl the dog suddenly leaped toward one wall.

"Some sickie," said Chan, flicking her towel toward a shadow outside the window. Tanner rose barking on his hind legs and propped himself on the damp bricks. She stepped into jeans and improvised a terry-cloth halter before reaching to slap the high window screen. "I'll sic the dog on you!" she yelled outside. Nancy closed her eyes. "Pitiful," said Chan.

"You're parked where?"

"Three spaces down. He's gone, I guess. Do come by." The woman left with a brisk wave, Tanner heeling close and carrying a wet rolled towel in his mouth. Nancy dragged over a bench and climbed to the window but she could not see Dwight; still, instead of showering she decided to use a washcloth in one of the toilet stalls. It did not seem possible to clean herself in that small space, in that smell, between walls on which outsized cocks and Jesus crosses had been drawn and interlaced. Even when her skin was washed, the lining in her throat felt darker; flecks of excrement seemed to obstruct her lungs.

She came into the campground coughing. No sign of Dwight. She hunched herself small as a child in the first telephone booth, reaching overhead to dial Joel—no answer—and Stone County Library, which of course was closed on Sundays. Rejected money rained onto one shoulder. Evaline was probably out at the Katsewa River Power Plant drawing generators. Since she was still holding exactly the price of a call to Greenway, she dialed home.

Beckham answered. She went into harder consonants an octave down. "Mrs. Finch, please."

Through the background music for "Lamp Unto My Feet" Beckham said his mother was at church. He seemed preoccupied from the effort of trying to follow the Savior's will by audio alone.

Rarely were Mama's knees pliable enough for all those Presbyterian stairs. Now she is kneeling, for me, thought Nancy with reflexive guilt.

Homesick not for that house but for more innocent parts of herself she said, "I'll speak to Nancy, then."

"Who?" Suddenly items rustled near the phone. "Who is this?" asked Beckham, louder. "Who's calling? What do you want?"

His usually serene—vacant?—face would now be twitching and frowning as by muscular effort it tried to pull forward his thoughts. She could hear him mumbling about wires, switches. Something clicked softly, then she heard an even hiss. He had turned on a tape recorder! Silence. On his end Beckham could think of nothing to store on its whirring spool.

She said helpfully, "This is an old friend of Nancy's. In the west."

He whispered, "Is she there? Is she all right?"

The booth was cramped, hot. Nancy slid quarters off her stack while she said in a Pharisee's voice, "Be thankful she has not been harmed in any way." Perhaps when they played back this tape later they would recognize her tone and accent, though it was probable Beckham had switched the machine to "play" and not "record." "Soon Nancy will be released in the western states," she said sonorously.

In a nervous rush he asked, "Where do you want the money sent?"

She bumped her head from surprise. All he knew about kidnapping, she realized, he had learned from television.

"And we won't tell a soul," he said since she had missed her line, "not about the money, not even about this call."

She snapped, "Beckham, you know you don't have any money, or Mama either!"

His tape filled itself with background television dialogue—an evangelist, from the melodious ring. "Nancy?" he finally said.

"I'm all right, Beckham, that's the truth, don't worry now." The telephone operator intervened and clanking quarters hid part of Beckham's answer.

". . . kill him if he hurts you," he finished. Her peaceable brother.

"We are not the kind of family that does that," she said in her mother's way. Her mother had drummed home this message over and over because of her secret fear. *Someday I'll die, Nancy, and he's a man. What if he, after all? Maybe little girls? I dream of this.* The Finches did not discuss rape, much less do it.

By habit Nancy fell into the old speech. "Remember we are civilized people. And where in the world did you plan to get ransom money?"

"From the life insurance, Mama said."

"Daddy's? You know that's been gone for years. It is gone, isn't it?" She closed her eyes wondering if she had come home from college for nothing. "Has Mama had a secret bank account all this time?" Her throat was choking itself. "Beckham? Answer me!"

"How did you get away?"

"Did Mama tell you she still had money?"

"You were smart to escape."

"I was dumb not to do it sooner," she said, and hung up. She thought Beckham would not remember to trace the call but would, in a while, unplug the tape machine before the television alcoholic had quite come to his John 3:16 senses. At a station break Beckham might even think of telephoning Faye. They would play back and analyze her conversation on that tape recorder bought from a nest egg that had never hatched once when Nancy needed anything.

Angry, she raked coins into her purse and looked again at Chan Thatcher's business card.

In the laundromat she found the judge dozing, his face covered by newspaper. An honest stranger had piled their dry laundry on a table. Nancy folded and stacked clothes into a paper sack before waking him. Through newsprint he mumbled about flu and botulism.

She began, "I've met a woman here who might help," but the judge said even penicillin wouldn't help.

When Nancy lifted the newspaper he squeezed his eyes tighter saying, "Where's Dwight?"

He looked old. "I don't really think he'll hurt you," she said softly.

On a sour breath: "What a comfort."

Her forefinger could not flatten the crease in his brow so she pressed her hand flat to cover his wrinkles. For a minute his face had looked like Mama's. "Are your maps in the car?" He nodded. "I'm borrowing them, o.k.?" She set the bag of laundry between his shoes and stood indecisively in the doorway watching him sleep. "Dwight didn't hurt Eddie, he wasn't even interested in Eddie." A snore. She turned into the afternoon sun and sprinted toward their campsite. At a jog she finally half fell inside the black car and panted there. Wherever Dwight was, they were in Arizona and Nancy had kept her word. He might be deliberately tempting her to escape. She felt like a mouse when the cat once more withdraws its paw.

She had barely time to refold the judge's map around Montezuma Castle and the Paria Plateau, with Highway 180 running above Williams almost straight to the Grand Canyon's South Rim. She crumpled it into her pocketbook and counted money—not enough. There was nothing inside the glove compartment except the rented transistor radio wrapped in a shirt off some camper's clothesline. Nancy swept one hand under the front seat for the cache the judge had described and grabbed from a paper bag a handful of green-backs. Below were wallets, watches, a row of rings aligned on a tube of rolled paper. She was staring at these when the loud talk of passing campers made her hands shake. Trembling, she sorted out higher bills into her full pocketbook and kicked the bag under the seat again. She sat nodding jerkily to people who passed the car, her heart in panic, her legs drawn up to spring and run.

Though she knew her last act was foolish she yanked loose Dwight's boxing gloves from the mirror's stalk. The string snapped, dropping one mitt to the floor. She kicked it underneath with the money, slammed the car door even if Dwight should hear, and took off running past people who were sitting on overturned boxes drinking beer, girls applying Band-Aids, women hanging wet lingerie across twigs. Nancy plowed through these temporary backyards with a wave, knowing she would be well remembered. A poodle chased her. She slid on garbage. Beside a tent two children listlessly twanging a shuttlecock back and forth watched her pass under its flight. Beyond the shower house she found space twenty-one, but the rounded silver trailer had no car attached. Nancy thought: Of course. She's driven on to Valle and left the trailer here. Half-crying, she slapped the aluminum wall and shook the locked side door.

Then she stumbled helplessly to the rear of Chan Thatcher's space and dropped to the ground, her shoulders against the trailer's convex metal skin. She was still holding Dwight's boxing glove and now flung it as if it were hot. The sight of a lone man walking toward her down the asphalt drove her lower until she rolled underneath the trailer and flattened herself in the sand. There were only two wheels. She pillowed her head on Dwight's stolen money and watched the man come closer, every step slow, lingering, sometimes pivoting so he could look to this side and that. Her flesh crawled. He would take vengeance on the judge for sure. The man wandered by and grew gradually small down the road. Soon he was the height of a cricket; her thoughts turned to the judge's unwarranted cowardice. She lit a cigarette.

Later, when tires rolled into the space and stopped, she waited past the sight of narrow ankles until a dog bounded from the car. Before she could call, Tanner, at full speed and bark, circled the trailer and stuck his snarl close to her face. "Chan! Chan Thatcher!"

"Ho, Tanner, easy." The woman's voice was mild though one of her hands came into view picking up a stone. "Who's there?"

"Nancy! We met in the shower! the one who wants a puppy?"

The woman squatted. "What *are* you doing?" She yanked the dog's collar and made him sit.

Nancy rolled past his bristled back and sat at a distance brushing off sand and barbs. "Can we talk inside? Please? It's very important."

"You're some dog lover," said Chan Thatcher, not moving.

"Please help me."

Frowning, Chan unlocked the door and sent the dog inside. "If you weren't hiding from me, then who?"

"Please." Nancy hurried them both indoors between couches. The rounded metal skin of the trailer curved free of corners. With Tanner watching, Nancy flattened her back against the closed door. "You've got to give me a ride to Valle."

"The hell I have." Chan rinsed and dried her hands on a paper towel. "Until today you'd never heard of Valle. What's going on?"

"Any place will do. I have to get away from here without anybody knowing—it's very urgent."

"Why?" said the woman with a frown.

Nancy could not help looking past the curtains but the man no bigger than an insect was out of sight by now. "I'm with a criminal," she said.

"You've committed a crime? Forget it."

Nancy shook her head, since the theft of stolen money didn't count.

"Who is the criminal? What crime?"

She thought about J. Waldo Foster and which was worse—to tell a lie or too much truth. "Please, I'm not even sure about all that. I just know he'll come after me and I need to get away."

"I'll drive you to the camp office and they'll call the police."

"Not yet." She thought of St. Augustine—"Lord, save me! But not yet!"—and quit thinking of him. "There's somebody else he can hurt. I need more time."

"Are you married to him? In his family? Then what?"

Nancy felt angry and impatient. "None of that matters; I need to go and I'm trying not to involve you too much. Please help me do that much."

"Sit down." Nancy dropped by Tanner on the couch, stiffening when he lifted his head and then eased it onto her leg. Chan said, "If you think I consider a dog a good judge of character, you're wrong. I can get in trouble, then, by getting involved?"

"Not if we hurry. He doesn't know about you."

"At least you don't overpower me with reassurance. What else should I know? You didn't answer me about the police."

Nancy only stared. By now she was convinced the sight of policemen would guarantee Dwight's turning on the judge, while her disappearance would only send him after her.

"And what will you do in Valle?"

She could send back help, then, once she had time to explain Dwight to officers, to warn them, to give advice. "Please."

The woman stepped out of both shoes and moved into the rounded toilet cell at the far end. "I'll think it over," she said before closing its thin door. The dog relaxed and allowed his head to slide away.

Nancy called, "I'll be glad to pay."

"You can pay a taxi," came the answer when the door reopened. "He's a lover then. No?"

"Just an enemy," Nancy whispered.

Chan came rapidly down the trailer and sat on the opposite couch.

"Look up at me. You're not drunk. You're not high on some chemical?" Uneasily she examined her foot soles for splinters. "How long have these people been after you, dear? What is it they say to you?"

"I'm not crazy," said Nancy.

Chan gave her another long and serious look. "One of us must be. You're saying it isn't the law pursuing you? Then I don't understand. I'm so old-fashioned. I understand husbands and lovers but . . look, I'm so old-fashioned I even obey bad laws until we can get them changed, as a kind of moral taxation. Most civil disobedience seems to me a lack of fiber." Nancy tried looking fibrous, reliable. "So I won't even be sympathetic if you've been damaging nuclear plants in the name of ecology, is that clear?" She blew a short, irritable breath. "All right, but I've got terms. You don't want Valle as such but to leave here, is that so? And I can choose to take you on but Lewis can't. He thinks intuition is a high-class word for guesswork. Look at me, Nancy. I've got to trust something and it might as well be your eyes." Nancy gazed. "So I'll take you all the way to the canyon or its airport or a bus line there, even to the mules at trailhead for all I care, but I won't let you out in Valle, where everybody counts heads, not when you won't say exactly what's coming behind you. I owe that much to Lewis."

"Thank you."

"You're not welcome, not one damn bit." She rose and looked out the window. "Is he fat?" Nancy said no. "If he finds you here, what will he do?"

"I don't know. I'll pay all expenses, more, whatever."

"I know you will, every drop of gas, and I don't want to drive till it's cool. After dark. Are you going back for clothes, anything?"

"Nothing. The sooner we go the better. I don't want to go outside."

"You mean to ride back here? In Arizona it's legal but I've never even allowed the dogs—is it necessary?" When Nancy nodded she said, "You stay here and let me walk to the office and call the police."

"Please, I know him and you don't." But she didn't know Dwight, nor what he used to be; she only believed he would abandon the judge in Williams and come after her alone.

"You're not going to cry, are you?" Chan asked.

"I hope not."

Chan walked around barefoot. "There's no air-conditioning back here and if we have a wreck I never saw you before and that's what I'll say to my insurance man and that's what I'll swear in court."

"Fair enough."

"You want a handkerchief?"

"No," said Nancy after one thorough snuffle.

"One thing more—if any policeman asks about you, during or afterward, I tell him everything. You still want to go? From this moment on, anything you tell me is saved up against the time somebody official may ask me about it."

"Entirely understandable."

"And I call you Nancy—?"

She took a deep breath. "My real name is Ruby Kaye Foster."

"Is that so?" After a moment Chan Thatcher's mouth turned up. "There's not a stray dog between Flagstaff and the Mexican border that doesn't know what a sucker I am."

12

Chan, whose family had valued ancestors and surnames especially if they preserved a history of livelihood, had been named Mary Susan Chandler Webb. Like Thomas Carlyle, her forebears believed self-identity was found only by finding whatever work one did well; they favored action as the route to essence and names that recorded the acts.

The Chandlers had once made candles. As a hobby the aunts still poured wax into elaborate molds in honor of the dead who had bequeathed every cell of their bodies. On the paternal Webb side, old English weavers had turned wool into cloth. Even now when Chan did needlepoint it felt memorial.

Chan's earliest male callers were subjected to immediate genealogical research, for no young man who took lightly the genes and name he had received in trust could be allowed to procreate with the Webbs and Chandlers. They did not admire names that gave addresses rather than professions—Milford, who dwelt by one; a Norwood who was known for nothing more than living in the northern forest. They disliked the excesses of foreign names: the French penchant for description or the arrogant Hebrew habit of hinting God's presence in the least newborn child.

But Richard Thatcher, a mining engineer who had found his work young, met their criteria. His name recorded what skilled grandsires had done with their own hands, laying yelms of straw from right to left on Devon roofs. To the Webbs and Chandlers he spoke respectfully of the heritage of honest work, could even describe the hazel pegs his ancestors had bent into place and the ornamental patterns of runners and spars set above eaves. He knew such facts because Chan, seventeen, who liked his looks, had warned him to read up on thatching. They were married at her home in northern Michigan.

There and in central Canada Dick Thatcher worked at prospecting and ore analysis during Chan's first snowbound pregnancy. She named the baby Alisande, from *Connecticut Yankee,* hoping her daughter would always be in love with pragmatic ingenuity, not knowing the girl would always be called Alice and would fall in love with no one. The next baby, stillborn, left Chan weak and depressed.

The Thatchers moved to old Apache country in Arizona partly because Dick hoped the climate would improve Chan's health. Here she was sure the sun that reached everywhere would finish drying up her unreliable womb. The excess of light and air made her porous, insubstantial. The second child surprised them both, seeming fragile as an object baked for years in a latticed oven. Chan feared her delight in this late son would ruin or smother him, especially now that Alice, six, was fiercely independent and already rode her pinto alone far beyond the black and yellow artificial hills the copper smelters had thrown up. They named him Hunter.

"Don't let me spoil him," Chan would beg her husband as she sat rocking the baby in her arms. "I'm Mother *Goose* this time, it's terrible."

"I'll see that you spoil me instead."

But she turned her face away to keep him from seeing how much greater was her passion for the son than for the father. From the first Hunt proved too good-natured, with eyes more black than they ought to have been, a smile too wide. She imagined her love binding him to her forever, perhaps turning him into a chaste homosexual with courteous habits. Her husband, who understood in his practical way, bought her three dogs at once, English setter pups, with needs that diluted Chan's avid attention to the boy. Sometimes she called them to his crib and crooned to them as if they were intermediaries. She also disciplined herself to give extra devotion to Alice, whose cold jealous eyes were not deceived.

Like many women before her Chan threw herself next into projects, tasks, crafts, and chores. By making her days too busy she further diluted the intensity secretly concentrated on her son.

"You worried about spoiling him for no reason," Dick Thatcher said one night as they passed Hunt's open door toward their bedroom.

"You're right. I think we should get more dogs, honey," said Chan, straightening the rug they crossed, "and I could learn bookkeeping if you want out of the mine and into your own business." In bed she made love to him. He slept immediately but her voice kept calling him back. "Let's build on another room for the children." He was afraid she meant right *then,* that the hammer and nails were under her pillow.

When they did add to the house, Chan helped with the manual labor. Cash was short. Just before Hunt's birth, when old equipment, low-grade ore, and national depression all worsened together, the old Dominion Copper Mine had been closed. Its pumps were stopped; water rose in the pits and tunnels. Thereafter Richard Thatcher, with most other men in Gila County, worked for the W.P.A. if he worked at all.

On idle days Dick and Chan would sometimes walk the winding road through Pinal Creek Gulch past slag dumps and tailings. Sight of the almost inactive town of Globe reinforced worries Dick kept to himself. Chan would pace ahead in the hot sun trying to visualize the girl somewhere predestined to marry her son, trying to imagine a crowd of grandchildren on whom she might safely release her full matriarchal force at last.

So she barely heard Dick's increasing talk of dogs, of heredity, of how their species rhythm, naturally faster than his, went visibly forward. In the thirties, men seemed at a standstill, poor as ever, stingy as ever, greedy as before.

"That's true," said Chan, knowing her own grandchildren would be different.

Dick Thatcher could see the characteristics of one dog breeding true for succeeding generations no matter who reared the pups, could watch one trait override another, see the pale coloring swept away by dark; until he felt like writing overdue letters to surviving Webbs and Chandlers to notify them that he understood at last.

"You do think the cook will hear Hunt if he cries, don't you?" said Chan.

"Of course," said Richard, for genetics had given him the sense that his children and their lives were fated.

Evenings he sat studying canine eugenics. Chan did crewel embroidery and pretended not to care that Hunt's homework was difficult, his cold worse, his silence a sign of bad behavior. From an amateur biologist, Richard became a fanatic who could read Mendel into the human world as others could perpetually trace the presence of Freud, or Marx, or Jesus, *absconditus*. Eventually even old friends who liked to drink with him would empty their glasses as soon as a chromosome was mentioned.

When at last the Miami mines provided work again, he raised Welsh corgis, then pointers, became active in the American Kennel Club as a show and field trial judge. Laughing, Chan would accuse him of using an ordinary social introduction as an excuse to touch human strangers and read their conformation against some breed standard for *Homo sapiens* he had charted in his mind. With the Italian criminologist Lombroso he agreed that most criminals were of a distinct anthropological type whose physical and mental flaws could be measured. By forty he had become a philosophical determinist, a political conservative, and a strict but loving father.

He was also a loving husband. The marriage was happy. They balanced each other's extremes: Chan, who could read courage and honor into the reflexes of every dog; against Richard, who saw beyond every human action the power of surviving instincts and animal hungers. Without her he would have grown cold and melancholy; she, in another setting, might have been all gush and babytalk. Between them some vaporous Golden Mean shimmered in the domestic air.

But their children illustrated their differences. Alice, taking her father's view, believed environment merely expressed or made difficult one's natural inclinations. By her teens she had concluded she loved horses by natural temperament, decided to become a veterinarian, and did. Since this was as natural as weaving cloth, laying roofs, or melting tallow, she never understood why journalists later interviewed her as a representative feminist pioneer in a male profession. "People do what they want to," she would say impatiently in interviews that bored everyone. "Men beat horses because they are cruel." And so on.

Some people, however right, dismay you, Chan often thought—never having expected to give birth to one.

Their son, Hunt, had a harder time in the world but not because his mother loved him intemperately. That love like a fire in a stove had become safely encased to warm but not burn. All mothers loved, he thought, for he had a Victorian's sentimental awe of mothers that prevented his knowing Chan at all.

Something also prevented his learning other lessons. In college he was attracted to psychology but repelled by behaviorism. He wrote home that Pavlov had obviously never owned a dog. Next term he switched to anthropology but disputed the collapse of kingdoms over a few failed corn crops. To be called simplistic insulted his teachers. For two months he kept a murky diary about a dog-faced boy in the circus exhibited to crowds who paid admission in books and articles. He lasted half a semester majoring in social science before he began to smother in a tight box known as the Middle Class. What he wanted from college was a single comprehensive vision of life; what he got were assorted specialties.

In his junior year, feeling like a blue marlin waking up in the Mohave Desert, Hunt Thatcher left school with no degree. He apprenticed himself to a Globe old-timer and learned how to shoe horses, finish wagon wheels, and fashion wrought-iron gates for suburban driveways. He hung a sign with flowing scrollwork, *Hunt Thatcher,*

Farrier and Smith, between Globe and the San Carlos reservation and opened for business.

Both Chan and Richard tried to talk with him about his depression, but since he considered his case unique he could not credit their comments.

In a year he married a girl who had without marriage already brought grief to a dozen local men and still had plenty left over for Hunt. They were quickly divorced.

"Are you ready to grow up now?" Chan spoke in this stereotyped way because it was the only phrasing Hunt could hear. As he did not want a mother who read Kierkegaard, she cooperated with cliché. "And clean up this place!" she snapped. "Get a haircut!"

His despair began to respond to treatment by homily. By then Richard Thatcher was raising Chesapeakes, a solely American breed small enough to focus his genetic interests. He enjoyed setting these ice-water duck-retrieving specialists on the high dry sands of Arizona without detriment.

"Thank you both for sticking by me," Hunt said one night as they were touring the new kennels.

I can schedule my menopause now, Chan thought. She allowed herself a pat on her son's shoulder. Immediately her husband caught her hand in midair, returned it to Hunt's back and held it firmly in place while they kept walking between fences. She was always to remember that generous and understanding moment and the heat which her palm drew outward through Hunt's shirt to meet their joined pulses.

Richard Thatcher died in late May 1960, heading home from a Chesapeake specialty trial in Reno, Nevada, where champions Nelgaard's Baron and Atom Bob had starred. At night where a steel bridge crossed a dry wash he lost control of the car and drove it through the rails. A policeman had to shoot the dog on guard inside the dangling car before they could cut his body out with acetylene torches.

They had been married thirty-five years. Chan thought then only a third or a fourth of her own life survived the loss of his, and that part was blotched by her guilt for the favoritism shown the son. Yet she had healed in a year merely by keeping busy after the habit of Webbs and Chandlers. Life, going on, erased life with inexorable disregard, she found, and her house, the neighborhood, the ongoing generations of dogs, and even—at last—another man rolled easily forward to fill the space her husband had occupied. Nature has no sentimentality, Dick Thatcher had often bragged; no, nor any sentiment, either. As she had been happy for most of her married life she was, in a while, on the average, happy again.

Whether a conjunction of genes preset her so, or her past history had trained the skill, the timeless ordinary motions grinding on had all the mystery for Chan that they had held for Helen, forgetting Menelaus on a larger scale. Penelope's behavior, she was certain, had been invented by a male author with greater optimistic ego than powers of observation.

Something about this young fugitive woman, this Nancy Bird or whatever her name was, reminded Chan of Hunt's long numb recovery from the University of Arizona. She watched Nancy while she swept maybe a teaspoon's worth of shed dog fluff out the trailer door, saying, "Once when my son was as jumpy as you look, I called up my daughter—she's a vet—just because I needed somebody to talk to and Alice said—she would!—She said, 'What do you want me to do, worm him?'"

Nancy smiled politely. "Our delay makes me tense. I'm afraid you'll change your mind."

"Even if I did I'd keep my word." Nancy paced twice the trailer's bounds and paused before a set of photographs. "My children at different ages. They look like their father." On its own Chan's eye automatically measured Nancy's height, as many women prospects had proved to be taller than Hunt.

But Nancy's look had burned through Hunt's picture and on through the trailer wall. "If we wait until dark he might come knocking on the door, at least I hope he'll knock."

"You trying to scare me?"

"I know him but you don't. Yes."

Chan decided at least she could get ready for departure. "Tanner, stay!" she ordered when the dog's ears sprang forward as she walked carefully to the door. She had broken both major bones in one leg some years ago and usually allowed herself to limp late in the day if she were alone. Not until she was outside did Chan now permit the slight dip that, though it did not relieve the ache, acknowledged its return. She bobbed toward the trailer hitch, tested it and the brake lights, disconnected the hookup lines with surreptitious haste. The sight of a gray-haired man carrying a folded chair made her leap behind the trailer.

When she went inside Nancy was crouched at one window. Chan said, "Don't tell me that old man was him!" Nancy shook her head. "Then before we leave you'd better describe the man I'm not looking for."

"Black cowboy hat. Broken front tooth," said Nancy crisply. "Brown hair, eyes like Tanner's. There's a tattoo on one arm."

"Cute boy, I can tell." While Chan moved through the trailer settling drawers back on runners and storing those objects which might fall, she debated taking her .32 automatic out of the bread box and then driving straight to Valle after all, to Lewis. He would ask pointed questions of this frightened young woman and, if her answers were right, could even fly her across the canyon and leave her troubles marooned on its south side.

She sat by Nancy and straightened her sore knee with care. "Look, I don't know what your friends are like but let me tell you about Lewis. This is a man who's done everything, from working in a mine to looking for gold himself. He used to be a calf roper, the real kind, though he tried rodeo awhile, too, and he was a volunteer in World War Two." She could have mentioned medals but, since Lewis never did, omitted them. "He learned to fly there and he's a fine pilot, not as reckless as he used to be. But even what looked reckless to others just felt relaxed to him, although I'm just as glad I never flew with him under river bridges." Were these the right details to give? "After the war he made money down in Mexico but nobody ever asks him how. I'm sure it wasn't dope; guns maybe. Nobody even knew he had money until the Internal Revenue Service filed a claim for unpaid taxes. A big claim, very big, I guess. Lewis said he'd lost everything gambling in Las Vegas except for his charter planes, and that whole argument has been banging around in the courts for several years." She reached beyond Nancy to stroke Tanner's ears. She must now convey how long she had known him, though she need not describe how well.

"My husband brought Lewis home from a fishing trip in the White Mountains; that's how we met, years ago. If you have any need for a friend, he's a good one to borrow."

For a few minutes she quite forgot Nancy, carried back to the sight of two dirty, bristly men coming into her kitchen; Richard Thatcher, who was tall, and behind him someone even taller who was bumping the light fixture. Richard had bent as always to kiss her cheekbone. The stranger's smile almost folded out of sight. Though he turned out to be Chan's age he looked older, with a creased face of tanned skin unevenly quilted over the bones and a deep squint formed by long days working in the sun. His torso looked off-balance above the waist, his shoulders curving forward too much. The hair, a reddish stubble with some gray, seemed to have been yanked straight up and chopped off short. Its uplift made his green eyes, going brown on the iris edge, flare through the facial lines as if they were more surprised than the squint could quite reveal. Looking past Richard, Chan felt she had just startled the man in some way, or the world steadily had, and he had withdrawn farther below the surface of that sunburned face than most men need to. She had smiled and reached a handshake toward Richard's new friend. Her longtime friend, too, as it turned out. Years later, when she woke the first morning in Lewis' bed and felt too much at home to care that her hair looked like a bird's nest, she had watched him sleep with his upper lip whuffling. She shook him awake to announce that they two had ripened to this harvest, somehow, without ever passing through a stage of bloom. "I don't even remember finding you attractive, back then." Lewis knew when that blossom was, he said. "It only takes one to know."

At first he wouldn't say when. Then he reminded her of that flicker of possibility quickly extinguished out of loyalty, or maybe duty, or maybe just a dread of complications, one year, two years, beyond that fishing trip. In Arizona, La Reina de la Noche blooms like that, only at night and only once a year. Between times doubtless its roots forget why they are there.

Into her silence Nancy said wistfully, "You've been lucky, haven't you?"

Chan nodded at the memories blurring past. "I'm only trying to say that he's competent and loyal, that he doesn't sermonize and he won't blame you for any fix you're in—that is, unless you *are* the fix."

"In a way I always have been," Nancy said.

"He owns a plane that would get you away faster than I can and he has some money plus a lot of friends in different places who owe him favors. If we asked Lewis to help, he'd probably try."

"Why? He doesn't know me."

"He'll help if I ask him."

"You *have* been lucky! But you were right the first time about not involving him. Other people"—she began wondering aloud—"they complicate everything, but if you can cut loose from even the last one you can start over. One part dies and the larger part comes to life. You know?" She saw Chan's disapproving stare. "In a few weeks I'll find a job; I'll send money home."

"Where is home?" Nancy did not answer. "Send who money?"

"My mother."

Nobody hated to pry more than Chan Thatcher, who thought everyone blabbed too much in public nowadays. "I'm going to tell Lewis all about you anyway," she warned. "You've got my address and his if you need them." She started to the door but turned back to the kitchenette. "I just hope I'm not making a mistake and you're not just out of the loony bin."

"What's that for?" asked Nancy as Chan started out the door.

"I always keep this bread box with me, that's all." She was limping badly now and as usual Tanner made his quick adjustment and heeled closer to cushion any fall. They settled into the front seat, Chan opening the bread box on the floor so the gun handle stuck up between wheat and white loaves. Slowly she drove the narrow asphalt drives, gazing under every dark Stetson and guessing about the owner's dental work.

Then they were crossing the plateau beyond Red Lake, lumpy with lava flows. Chan knew this road well, knew how the land rolled so that no wide view northward was possible, as if the earth had deliberately arranged itself to let the great precipice and its silent deeps burst on the eye without warning. Now there were scraggly residential developments on this once-barren southern approach. Chan wondered how anyone could bear to live so near a gorge of that magnitude, or mothers endure an awareness of its open mouth in the edges of their imaginations.

The Grand Canyon, in fact, had driven Chan back into the Methodist church though she had never admitted that aloud. "I'm getting old," she had said to Lewis and Hunt when they asked, "and I want death to be one more experience to live through." They understood this reason with a certain affectionate contempt.

But actually her reconversion had more to do with the unseen chasm ahead that already brooded indistinctly in her thoughts. Any deist could look down on that gulf crammed with tumbled mountains and the Colorado River far below like a dirty string—but not and go on thinking God or Nature *reasonable*.

No, she had run straight from those depths to a human story she understood: Mother and Baby, carpenters, fishermen, and tax collectors.

In the rearview mirror Chan checked the car behind. She should have asked Nancy to describe what this Enemy was driving. Nervously she patted the dog and murmured. "She's some kind of crazy woman, Tanner; they let them out of the hospitals now with pills they forget to take. And the man with a black hat is right out of a Hollywood western; why didn't you bark at her more? Why didn't you bite her once so I'd have known to call Lewis?"

The dog dozed under her hand and voice as they passed the familiar road to Valle without turning and entered the evergreens and aspens of Kaibab Forest. "On the other hand, if she's not crazy she might be resourceful. Why can't Hunt find a resourceful woman, Tanner? Hmmn? God, your breath smells awful."

They had been driving less than an hour when Red Butte rose nine hundred feet on her right. Now she could turn toward Grand Canyon Airport or Moqui Camp, she thought, braking, hesitating. "She may be all right, Tanner, and me the crazy one—this is the craziest thing

I've done since the horse ride that broke my leg, and Lewis warned me that time! How did I want to look to him—Mother Courage? Much did he care. Let's take her to the canyon and see what the sight of it does to her. Cutting people loose, she said; did you hear her, Tanner? Maybe she's sane but stupid?"

The dog slept on and in late afternoon Chan joined the line of cars and paid the entry fee at the Visitor Checking Center, promising to leave before dark. Under the ponderosas, pine needles on every road softened the sound of their wheels past the train station, the busy headquarters crowded with tourists, the paved circle at Yavapai Museum. The trailer felt heavy from the burden of this girl for whom some enemy was searching, perhaps in these very crowds.

Not permitting herself to look toward the misty nothing that she knew broke open just beyond the road, Chan drove nervously along East Rim Drive. She was beginning to feel desperate to park, to empty herself of obligation. In part she wanted to see the sweep of the Grand Canyon again, but also to turn from that to the sight of Nancy's face when it first lay vulnerable to all that rocky emptiness. This is what you've escaped to, Chan would think but not say.

At Mather Point a long bus was spilling dozens of Japanese tourists with cameras hung from their necks. Tanner woke and stretched when they parked. There was little to be seen yet, a distant level of irregular rock mountains on the other side notched somewhat above this one into a ragged cliff, and a vague apprehension of swimming air between two vast edges.

Chan limped to the trailer door and rapped three times. When it gave way in a thin dark line she said, "Come on out now. I can't stand the suspense, I want you to see it."

Gingerly the young woman stepped down while staring everywhere at once. "Are we there?" she asked, and then, "Where?"

"A mile from park headquarters. This way." Though Chan had advised Nancy to listen to no one in advance she babbled, "There's a handrail; this is Mather Point and they've cut all the trees back here." At nearly a run she pulled Nancy through the Japanese to the low parapet and the edge.

Where creation came to an end. Chan only looked from the corner of one eye into that luminous abyss. She had never—close up—seen anyone view the great chasm for the first time and she wanted to watch all innocence drain from such a face.

Nancy jerked backward once as earth opened the size of her eye, her mind, and exploded beyond; then she bent to hold the rail and sway across it as if she might wing out on that silent air. She opened her mouth but no words were in it. In stages going downward for a mile the sunlight gilded and bleached and reddened and finally failed among the rocky cliffs and walls. She stretched half her body above the top slopes that could still be recognized as earth, with pebbles and clinging plants, and watched them give way to distance fit only to dream about. And wide as forever, from her right hand and equally far to the left, the stone wilderness rolled endlessly in streaked slopes and terraces and bright towers until mountains turned blue without ceasing and drifted out of her sight.

At first as stunned as she, the tourists broke into new chatter. Like click beetles the men darted here, now there, snapping photographs they could bear to contemplate in a safer place. Each time their tenor words subsided, that thickened, tangible stillness swelled up almost visibly from the unseen bottom of the gorge. On the rim a bird occasionally whistled but from the deeps down there not one single sound came floating up.

Now Chan's eyes left Nancy, survived their first giddiness, and followed the red miles of chasm into haze. She had been right in sensing that Nancy would not spoil what was vast by conversation, however unbearable and barbarous she might find this indifferent beauty.

No, not even beauty. Better or worse than that.

The other visitors had turned quickly from the precipice, shivering, recoil still showing on their faces, and backed to a spot where translators with folders were repeating Carl Sandburg's first description of the Grand Canyon. "There goes," said the guide, "God with"—intoning slowly—"an army of banners." He nodded and rendered the line into vibrating Japanese.

"Oh hush," Nancy breathed. But the crowd was repeating the line while some posed on the rim at an angle where the falling away of two hundred miles of sheer gold cliffs and red formations could be suggested flat on film. One twosome set up a humorous pose in which a companion seemed held above space in his friend's spread hand.

Chan, not minding much, sat on a boulder and watched. Nature did not even ignore tourists, she thought, but was simply present in a way no mortal had ever been. While Nancy paced the jagged edge Chan looked east, but the rim-to-river trail, the side canyon, and the rapid which all bore the Tanner name could not be seen. Hunt had hiked those switchbacks to the river once and explored mine shafts between Tanner Trail and the alkaline blue Little Colorado, down the same steep land she had surmised while looking upward from a raft on the river. Yet when they compared the same terrain from different angles, mother and son seemed to speak of different planets. She knew the bedrock shore terraces with dark talus trickling down to the cold water; Hunt had only one lukewarm canteen left at the halfway Redwall point, and had to decide whether to cache it there for the climb out and search for a seep or plan to drink heavily at the river in the bottom of the gorge. Chan was rowed past three faults in the igneous rocks downstream. On foot Hunt passed the Tapeats sandstone, found no way through the lower basalt, and clambered aside across red shale. By the time boatmen rowed her into Tanner Rapids, Chan had floated seventy miles down the deepening canyon and gradually adjusted to its rising walls and the worsening white water in the river's plunge. In an instant she was flung past Tanner Canyon and soaked by flying waves as she bounced across its frothy scoured-out fan of scattered boulders; but Hunt had come twelve hot rugged miles and picked his way down the dry stream bed of that same Tanner Wash to sit by the same rapid for an hour, resting, while it foamed before him like a sculpture. While she was poured past the spot in seconds and soon swept ahead into coarse debris at Unkar Creek, he rested and planned the hours twice over he would need to climb Tanner Trail to the rim again. "Twelve going down, but twenty-four back," as experienced hikers said.

Chan saw they had passed each other on land and water like a pair of spirits—and in their lives as well.

Tanner gave a slow bow and wagged his tail as Nancy bent to whisper, "Thank you, Chan." She nodded. In a last moment of fellowship they looked together at the North Rim's horizon where it crumbled, broke, threw up a brilliant blocky cliff, dropped off sheer, and at last rolled in a series of blunted cones shadowing far away. Then Nancy opened her pocketbook in which bills were tumbled. "How much for the gas?"

Chan gasped. "Well, of course I can't leave you *here!*"

"It's the best place."

"In the village, where there are hotels," Chan brushed off her jeans as she stood. "Everything's there; the schedule of the mule trains if you want to go down, everything." She wanted to grab Nancy's arm and shake loose the canyon's spell. "You'll need to buy some things if you do, a shirt with long sleeves and a hat, and your sunglasses are broken." Nancy shook her head. Louder Chan said, "Absolutely you cannot just stay *here*. In the village a big store sells everything. Suntan lotion, don't forget to take that; it's a hundred and twenty down there in daytime. If you think he's coming after you, you don't want to be standing at Mather Point after dark."

At last Nancy agreed and joined her in the car, Tanner wavering on all fours in the back seat. "You can get folders at headquarters to help you find your way around. Can you afford a hotel?" Nancy rode silently beside her. I knew I should have called Lewis. "In the morning you can see some of the early boats that went down the river and also in the museum—the geology?" Nancy heard nothing. She waited quietly while Chan hurried into the visitor center before it closed and scooped up a set of all printed material marked FREE. Dropping the folders into Nancy's lap she said, "You seem to have plenty of money."

Nancy laughed almost bitterly. "And I don't even have to be sensible about it. I've been sensible all my life! Every dress I own is in a color that won't show dirt!"

They agreed she would get out at the supermarket and walk from there to El Tovar Hotel or Bright Angel Lodge. "See?" Chan said uneasily when they were parked at the store. "The whole village is mapped out here." She pushed back Nancy's handful of bills. "Oh keep it; maybe I've done you no favor. Now remember the park rangers have police powers here. You'll be all right? Maybe I shouldn't leave you." Nancy insisted. "My home telephone number and Lewis' are on the card. Promise you'll call if you need anything."

Nancy took the map and climbed from the car. "You've been very good. Can't I pay you?"

"When you looked at the canyon the first time—that paid me." To Chan, the face of this grown woman looked suddenly like a lost child's. She lifted herself awkwardly into the car window and muttered, "Well, hug my neck," and then pulled back like a turtle. "Be careful, good luck," she said. "I hope you find . . ." She pulled quickly away, already worrying. At the corner she waited until the young woman had safely entered the brightly lit store. She knew nothing else to do.

All the way to Valle she talked it over with Tanner and was almost talk out by the time she was mixing drinks for Lewis and herself in his living room.

"I slowed down for every car looking for him, Lewis. Of course, he'd likely leave off his hat inside a car, what do you think? I sometimes keep mine on." She set their glasses on the low table. "I'm not used to finding every face sinister; it's depressing. I know you'll say I shouldn't have gotten involved."

"How could you help it?"

"She's a runaway wife, probably, and he beats her. But what if she really is mentally ill? If anybody wanted to jump off the edge of the world and kill herself, there's not a better place." Chan slumped on the sofa and let his hand settle on her far shoulder. "She acts younger than she is. I've always thought that when the Prince kissed Sleeping Beauty she probably said, 'Move out of my way,' and took off. Nancy looked like that."

Lewis called this feminist revision. "But you must have thought she was abnormal or else you'd have left her on Hunt's doorstep, just in case."

"If her body turns up in the rocks in a day or two, I'll never forgive myself." She settled her neck against his arm, knowing the worst was that she would forgive herself. That was the second cause of her Methodism: the abyss at the center of herself.

Lewis squeezed. "A suicide who wants to be stopped gives a clue but nobody can stop a suicide who's serious."

I'll forgive myself starting from there. "If she should call us, can't we help her?"

"I could take her to Mexico. I'm glad you've come."

"Actually she might suit Hunt exactly. He thought he was rescuing that other one, you recall, that hussy, that tramp."

"Because with the best of intentions you've kept him from understanding women."

"As you do?" Sometimes this archness in her voice, left over from youth yet never quite outdated, embarrassed her own ear. "I'm glad I've come, too." His body was stretched warm beside hers in a length she knew and often needed, the voice warm, too, and his good opinion of her loose in the air like radiant heat. In a few more minutes her thoughts disengaged from Nancy and returned Chan to her own life, which resumed its steady movement.

"I don't believe she's married or ever was," Chan murmured once, but that was the last connection before she brought the small eroded curves of their faces side by side and closed her eyes. Comforted, that's the word. And comforted late in your life—best of all, Chan thought.

13

You have to check in with the rangers before you hike down. They told Nancy that in the noisy store and told her what time Monday morning the office would open. You have to fill out a form about equipment and state when you'll return—just in case you don't, and somebody needs to come down after you.

She ate in the store's snack bar, afterward chose purchases, and paid with Dwight's crumpled bills. Then she walked out with the new pack on her shoulders, the new hard boots laced stiff on both feet, two plastic bottles already full of water strapped to the belt of her new denim shorts. In her backpack hung twenty-five pounds of freeze-dried food, small camp stove, nested pots, hard chocolate, tissue pack, tooth-brush, matches, utensils, raisins, trowel, a candle, teabags, sugar cubes, a packet of salt, skin lotion, and a tiny first-aid and snakebite kit. She was carrying extra socks, moleskins, Kool-Aid, flashlight, new sunglasses, and one change of clothes. It was barely dusk.

You may not be able to camp overnight in the canyon; they keep count of how many hike down from either rim, the clerks had said. People make reservations now.

They told her these things while they rang up her long tape at the cash register. If you get hurt or sick, they'll carry you out by mule or chopper. Cash in advance.

Regarding the other hikers clomping about the store in similar boots, Nancy tried to guess who had just come out or was going down. She decided none of them had been into the canyon yet from the lack of something that should have showed, but did not, in their faces.

The Kaibab Trail is harder and drier, not as long but very steep, said the clerk, and touched on Nancy's pink leaflet its starting place at Yaki Point. The rangers will have more detailed maps tomorrow. But the clerk recommended Bright Angel Trail instead, closer by, which merged with it down by the river. The rangers will give you that map, too, when you sign their roster. Bright Angel Trail will be better unless you're in top physical shape, the man said, running a critical eye over her body. Indian Gardens comes only four or five miles down, and the mule trains water there; also, there are two drinking fountains between the rim and that oasis. He did not tell her that new boots would blister her feet.

"It's almost eight miles to the river and nearly three more to Phantom Ranch," added the girl wrapping Nancy's old clothes in paper parcels. She herself had never been down.

"Neither have I," said Nancy, "but I've read everything Colin Fletcher ever wrote."

She discarded the clothes she had worn—they were Faye's—in the first litter can she saw, keeping only her pocketbook with cash. She shouldered the backpack and walked the paved rock path between the last cabin doors and the edge of the chasm, slopes of it speckled and purple now, one curving cliff lit up and brilliant from a late stray slant of sun. She passed the roof of Kolb Studio tucked into the curving rim. Mules browsed nearby in their small corral.

The unobtrusive point where Bright Angel Trail started down looked like only a short path that probably ran to a lower ledge. People were sitting all around, drinking beer; one guitar player thought it appropriate to lead his friends in singing (badly) "You Gotta Walk That Lonesome Valley." Frowning, Nancy threaded between feet as if along a theater row and took that easy path slanting gently down. Though soon the singers fell upward out of sight beyond stone, the harmonizing still sounded close by. " . . . your trust in the Holy Bible/And you'll NEV/-ver go astray/Oh, you gotta walk/ . . ."

She might have been in a city park. On the trail, too, talkative crowds were passing in both directions, mostly in city clothes, just taking a mild stroll barely underneath the edge. "Valley valley valley/you gotta go/ . . ." She passed photographers trying to preserve in color the way every rocky cliff had changed since afternoon, gone red and lavender with bright horizontal streaks that appeared molten. Edging behind one man with tripod and light meter, Nancy stepped into a small unexpected tunnel, trailed her hand along the knobby wall, came out again. Overhead the thinner voices sounded less human; soon only the tune came down and then not even that. It was that stillness, felt first as an almost physical pressure at Mather Point, that Nancy wanted to enter. She took her time descending the incline, which bent back and forth along the plane where Bright Angel Fault had separated and offset the strata of the cliff. Plodding the zigzag trail pocked with hoofprints and littered with stones, she could already feel her toes jamming steadily forward into the hard curve of the new boots. She had to invent a stiff Frankenstein lurch to get them lifted and set down. The soles felt like roof shingles.

Such sensations came early in her descent. As she thumped lower down, passing not only through rock layers that recorded past eons like high-water marks but also leaving daylight behind and walking deeper toward the dark, Nancy felt herself shrink and grow denser. The great rock face beside the trail and the great rock abyss below seemed to alternate endlessly from right to left.

No one can marvel for very long. Too many shifting lights and rich movable colors, vistas too large and hills too massive all overloaded her senses until they went as numb as her feet had felt when she last remembered them. Slogging on, she also passed the last upward hikers. Even in dimming light the muscles were ridged in their hard necks and red faces; their weariness did not seem far from terror as they saved breath by only nodding as they gasped by in the thin high twilight air. Beyond them and farther down in more shadows she began to feel, despite her rhythmic motion, almost inanimate—a small rolling rock among the rocks. Rocks, rocks. Valley, valley. Go there. By yourself.

The switchbacks of Bright Angel Trail were a prehistoric Indian route, improved by prospectors, later maintained by the county and now by the park. It and the Kaibab Trails wind down from the South Rim, join and cross the Colorado on a footbridge near a sparkling creek a mile deep in the earth, then the North Kaibab runs up again and ends on the farther rim. No other direct foot trail goes all the way across. Nowhere else but in the Grand Canyon can a man in two days—though trained long-distance runners have trotted the whole 20.6 miles in less than four hours—walk steadily down through the record of earth's biography and then climb slowly through it into his own century again. He starts where marine shells and sponges remain in the limestone, passes the Permian dune sands still marked with reptile tracks, sees where the red and gray floodplains settled, then under the Redwall descends into time back through the quartzite, the sandstone, and lower shale. In the Bass limestone he descends among pre-Cambrian stones where the first traces of plant life have been found. If he could walk to the deepest inner gorge downriver (and its walls are so steep that only boats penetrate there) he could also go down below granite, at last could lean out from his raft to place one hand flat on the lowest stage of Brahma and Vishnu schist, azoic, laid down before any life on earth is thought to have existed. Minus-One from the first page of Genesis. Cold.

Not many go through these eras and strata with all their nonconformities and geologic faults the full way to the spot where perhaps the world's first virus had not yet twitched. But even a visitor following Chan Thatcher's advice, one who does not read too many conclusions in advance, who has not seen charts where the ages are traced out and labeled in layers of stone, becomes oppressed by a sense of his double passage. "Old" and "deep" fade in his mind into "ancient" and "endless."

Somewhere during the long descent he can feel himself forced to let go the whole notion of man; then the apes and chimpanzees are wrenched away and the fishes dry up and the path is still dropping. At last his heart sinks from guessing that here is the slime, hardened now underfoot.

Or it lifts. People vary. Some of them sing David's Psalms. Sandburg saw God strutting by. The Havasupai look toward pillars that seem to look back at them down on their green valley floor. They ask stones to grant them good harvest.

John Wesley Powell first ran the river and first saw the canyon from inside-up. When his boats had been rowed past old lava wastes he wrote in his journal, "What a conflict of water and fire there must have been here! Just imagine a river of molten rock running down into a river of melted snow. What a seething and boiling of the waters; what clouds of steam rolled into the heavens!"

Powell, who had read *Paradise Lost,* named the canyon and trail down which Nancy Finch was walking, also the creek far ahead of her. Rowing through water too muddy to drink he had called an earlier side stream Dirty Devil, and angrily named its three tributaries Starvation, Muddy, and Stinking. This stream ran clear with its waters ashine on the stones; Powell, for balance, called it the Bright Angel Creek.

That was in 1869, a yesterday hardly worth noting on the scale of the canyon into which those fresh unchanging waters still poured.

Though the night seemed constantly pooling ahead of her, each time Nancy walked into the dark it receded lower. She had pulled out her flashlight because of the black depth off the trail's edge, yet she kept walking without turning it on, the sides of the chasm making a steady moon reflection before her feet. She could even see and avoid the mule dung. The rustling, she hoped, came from large lizards with red speckles on their backs. At one of the fountain shelters where she had drunk, such a lizard had scurried away with a similar noise.

Ahead in the evening rose the surprise of tall cottonwoods. Their size on the easy plateau where she found herself meant she had come down over four miles to Indian Gardens, where she would sleep, hiking on tomorrow morning while it was still cool. Lumpy sleeping bags lay here and there under the trees, where moonlight could barely reach. Nancy followed the sound of running water and at its edge wearily unlaced both boots. Her foot soles were covered with unbroken blisters in odd locations. She left the light off, too tired to examine the damage in detail, and stuck both feet into the cold water. Everywhere rose the odor of manure; perhaps she was sitting in it; no doubt it seeped juice to the stream and would give her tetanus. She was too tired to care.

Nor did she care if a flash flood roared tonight down this same stream bed. With feet still in the water, throbbing, she flung off her pack and unrolled the sleeping bag behind her like a snake dropping its skin, then pillowed her head on its down while her blisters soaked.

The sky seemed gray through the small interlaced leaves. Many stars. This oasis could be anywhere. Nothing in view suggested a vast canyon dropping away on all sides.

Nancy crawled inside the bag with her feet still wet. They beat below her ankles like two turgid hearts. She could not sleep.

With the stone towers and great stained amphitheaters out of sight, the thought of Dwight Anderson recurred. He would look for her, yes, and this time she had robbed him. But since she had signed no list of hikers' names at the top of the canyon, how could he guess she had taken this trail to its bottom?

Nancy dreaded to sleep for fear he would break and enter her dreams, but he was absent from the strange land where a dark people were naming her queen and draping her in a robe of many colors. In the dream she freed by royal edict the miners' canaries that burst forth singing from underground.

Nancy slept late. A cool morning rose out of the dry canyon and escaped above her; the hot sun beat down and still she slept. Campers awoke and repacked and set out. She heard no talk or movements. Only the sound of the day's first mule train thudding to water and the loud complaints of riders groaning their way off the saddles woke her. She felt groggy, one eyelash crusted. In daylight she could see that the bare earth was deeply trodden near the few small buildings and a long table on which bag lunches were now being spread. She looked for her watch before remembering Dwight had taken it back.

At first she could barely stand. When she did several blisters broke and oozed flat. Both feet looked swollen, the inside of one arch felt raw. Blisters in all sizes had sprung up under and between toes, on a heel; the ball of one foot had a single taut blister all the way across. She sat there with the worse foot in her hands and called, "What time is it?"

"Noon," said a man leading mules into a pen to be fed.

Nancy counted people and mules; they matched exactly except for one pack animal. "How about taking another rider down?"

"Can't do it."

She began to medicate her painful feet. It took a long time to sterilize with a match the tip of her pocketknife, break each blister, and press moleskin flat after the antiseptic had dried. There was not enough to retread both feet. With two pairs of socks she could barely work the boots on.

Nancy rolled her bag while eating raisins by the handful. The trail riders had fried chicken. Some waved their napkins as into the hottest part of the cloudless day Nancy set out, stiff legged on feet that felt like blocks of cement, alone, crossing the easy plateau at first, then starting downhill again. When she broke out of the first shade and winced she had to take off the sunglasses to make certain they were still the old ones, still cracked, still bisecting the world for her.

She gasped the first time her foot soles slid forward in the shoes. The trail forked, one branch to Plateau Point, Nancy's winding below Tapeats sandstone on switchbacks that inched slowly down a narrow gorge. She could hear Garden Creek nearby until she passed the brown Cambrian rock marking the edge of the canyon's inner gorge, the rim below which all stone had first been melted liquid, which finally boiled into these high shapes.

Her hat was too loosely woven to hold back the midday sun. Nancy rolled down both sleeves. Already she felt very thirsty. She thought of turning back to spend the afternoon awash in Garden Creek, especially the way her feet burned with pain; but she was already halfway to the Colorado with a string of tourists soon to be riding behind. Should she drop with heatstroke, one of them would fold her across a mule for that second half. She moved slowly and picked her path toward the hope of more cottonwoods ahead. The trail, five feet wide, blazing with sun, seemed smaller and rougher in daylight than the night before. She had a tendency to lean away from its edge.

Like the judge from Clara's death, she thought. If he got to the car before Dwight he's hitchhiked away by now, riding anywhere in other people's cars and in that way raising the likelihood of dying in a wreck of his own. Or maybe the higher statistical risk is a cure, the same used by Graham Greene when he played Russian roulette over and over until at last he no longer needed to.

Nancy stopped midtrail, surprised. Last evening she had been so numbed by the sight of the canyon that she had entered it like a somnambulist. She was awake now, to people and that terrible substitute for them—the books! the books! the books!

Her descent became more rapid. Sometimes she skidded downhill on pebbles. Any mental coolness she had maintained while water bubbled nearby burned off when the creek at last fell away into a steep chute. Turning sharply east, the trail meandered as if to carry her miles to the canyon's eastern end before doubling downhill again.

Nancy was curled to rest in a block of hot shade when the mule train caught up. She was thinking that nobody in North Carolina would believe in "hot" shade, like furnace air in light and dark colors, as she limped from the wall displaying pain. She opened a face of utter exhaustion to the man in the lead, but he passed with a nod while the line of tourists smiled, waved, and called, "Isn't it beautiful?" as they bounced by. In a few minutes the whole smelly crowd of Levites would be gone! Nancy broke in between mules and chose the third man from the end, who looked like a lifelong outdoorsman. She blocked his path. His mule veered toward trail's edge and the yawning gorge. "Father in Heaven!" the man breathed, shuddering, as he dragged on both reins, "Whoa, whoa, you son of a bitch!" From perversity the mule hung his head over the precipice, gazing down. The man cried to Nancy, "Get away!" His tan was from sunlamps; the shoulders he had acquired in gymnasiums.

"I need a ride!" she said. The mule jerked away from her outstretched hand. "Give me a ride!" she begged the last two riders. They pushed by, saying she could pay for a ride herself.

The last man in line turned to say kindly, "No need to panic, ma'am." He pointed to the plastic bottles at her belt. "You've got water and Pipe Creek is ahead, you'll be fine."

"I won't!" she screamed. "My feet!"

He rode on. She was shaking; the very word "panic" had created itself. She hurried after but the row of mules like a linked chain wound east and then lower west and lower east, lower west still, as the trail notched down. She rested while from far below two riders pointed back to show how impossibly small she'd already become. The rock wall threatened to burn through her shirt. Nancy drank water and trudged on.

By now she had come down into Archean rocks—dark, metamorphosed, flowing, old. Their tall surfaces, struck by sun, like a reflector oven magnified the heat. Chan's warning of 120 degrees came true. On sore feet and through a stench of fresh manure Nancy avoided the heated walls and moved rapidly for a while, hoping to keep in sight the last mule.

No other hikers were on the trail. Had better sense in this heat this time of day, she supposed. More water. Its taste did not cool.

Stopping to rest again on a boulder that felt like a red-hot stove, Nancy breathed too deep of the mule droppings and gagged. She swallowed the reflex hard but too late. Chewed raisins and fluid rose pungent in her throat. She could not hold back vomiting, though it would dehydrate her. Should she drink water immediately? She would lose it again. Well, she could sit while her whole body baked drier in this sun or could mutilate her feet even more on the way to Pipe Creek. She spat, wiped her tongue on a sleeve, and got up.

Below, the mule train vanished around curves, reappeared tiny at greater depth, and at last was gone behind a new mountain and never seen again. She walked slowly under more than heat and light—a growing overhead weight of both. Grimly she began to count steps the way as a child she had counted ceiling tiles while the doctor stitched up her foot. Marching she called back other stoic survivals: the time she got stuck in a culvert, her long run for help when Grandfather dropped onto a barbwire fence from stroke. Once a strange man had appeared in the library, unzipped his trousers, and laid out his penis on the edge of her desk—only to bolt when she made a move to staple it there.

Still her nausea grew. She began to wonder if Pipe Creek had been an invention, a placebo against terror, for no shade could be seen ahead. When she turned to see if any shade behind was worth returning to, the first hiker of the afternoon showed very far uphill, the size of a thumbtack on the trail's winding ribbon. A dark thumbtack. *Black?*

Nancy ducked trembling into a crevice and closed her eyes. Not possible! Her heart would not go back to normal, even after she had patted moisture on her face and wasted a handful of water underneath the hat. She decided to call out, "Hello! Hello!" but she waited a long time in silence afterward. When she stepped out, rocks hid the other one. "Hello, up there!" she called. The long echoes of her unanswered voice were frightening. She moved quickly downhill on her painful feet, snatching up one of a billion pebbles to suck for the sake of moisture in the mouth. Hot as a coal.

When she was farther down, looking back, Nancy could see the hiker again, no nearer, and although it couldn't possibly be Dwight she decided not to call out again but to hurry on. The water she drank seemed to rush through and steam off her skin. The dry air kept her skin dry, the feel as foreign as parchment. For a few yards she trotted until her nausea increased.

Suddenly she came on a narrow with the path winding between walls of rock into a blessed gloom. She could literally touch a long block of cool air ahead! One hand plunged in to the wrist before she stepped through its curtain into shade, real shade, and cool. She dropped flat on her stomach against that cooler ground. Was that the sound of water? Not much, but the trickle that must be Pipe Creek flowed past in a wide sandy bed. Nancy rolled gratefully atop it and luxuriated in the slow wet path it took through hair, shirt, down her back, along one leg. I am going to stay here till the food runs out. Nothing will drive me into that furnace again!

Ugh. She could smell that the mules had also rested here. Nancy rolled to wet her other side and then out again with a little scream. Tiny white worms were whipping everywhere in the shallow water.

She shuddered at even the possibility that they had crawled through her clothes, that they were under her waistband and into her flesh. Nancy tested her hair, under the shirt, the crotch. She itched everywhere.

But she had finished her bottled water and this supply would not be drinkable. Even if she boiled it, the worms would cook, would disintegrate, would become a white mush—her thoughts were too vivid. Nancy bent and vomited most of the water she had drunk.

Panting, she sank onto the shaded sand. Pick out the worms first, dummy, and then boil. You can do what you need to do, is that clear? And be ready to hike on by sundown.

After she felt solid again, Nancy was able to sweep a hand through the water without looking at the movement in it and wash her red skin everywhere. She kept her gaze averted. Death. To her the worms said Death.

Cooler then, she moved to check damage. Both thighs were specked with white blisters. In a self-fueling aura her burned skin kept radiating heat like a stovepipe. She used the lotion from her pack, took off her old cracked sunglasses, and buried them in the sand. The new ones were a relief but they admitted too much light.

She felt strong enough to step out to look up along the great cliffs and towers but the following hiker was gone, perhaps only nicked by imagination into the stone through the break in her glasses. To reassure herself she called again; this time the silence was a relief.

"I'm free," she said aloud several times as she reentered the shade. Bushes and grasses grew among gravel. Since she had been accustoming herself to barren rock, it amazed her that seeds had lodged here, found life, turned green. And now that her strength was coming back and she was alert again, she spotted the small log shelter that the park service had built on a ledge in this small oasis. In case of rain? It could rain into this caldron?

She lit the camp stove to boil water and strained it through the tail of her shirt. Whatever disease I catch they can probably cure, she thought, setting a full pot in place. The air felt so good that she left off the shirt, even dropped her bra into the stream to store up coolness. A bare-breasted Indian, she hobbled up the creek bed but the route was too steep. It must flow into the Colorado. Downstream, the bed looked equally wild and strewn with boulders.

She found inside the shelter a paper sack of trash. Since like Crusoe she could use anything, Nancy sorted food wrappers down to a torn sheet describing Bright Angel Trail. Squatting, she stretched the map between boot soles. Pipe Creek, and below it a section of River Trail—blasted from solid rock in the wall of the gorge, it said. On to the footbridge. Then across the Colorado and 2.5 more miles to Phantom Ranch. When climbing Bright Angel, said the paper, allow five to eight hours since the rise to the South Rim is steep and the elevation high. There was no advice for hikers going down except to travel in cool weather with companions. Nancy was sorry the other hiker had not been real. She would have had someone to go with her to the very bottom.

From above came a sudden noise. She sat down hard while the paper sprang to wrinkles on the sand. The noise rumbled but could not be thunder. It rose and fell but could not be voice. I would not recognize an avalanche if it *did* give warning.

She rose and stepped past her pack, listening. The small stove roared; the water bubbled in its pot; nothing more.

There! A wailing animal, surely, or some kind of horn. Again!

Because the sheer walls must be distorting the sound, Nancy limped along the trail and back out of the narrow canyon into the vast one. Sun struck in a solid sheet. Blinking, she waited in the hot glare. The sound—a voice, she decided—was just dying away. Someone in trouble? They don't know how bad off they are if I'm all that's here to answer. Though she strained, the echoes had died away without making sense. The sound came again, and twice. Again.

Now she heard it. Her own broken, echoed, bounced twist of a name. "NAN-cy" came over the heated air. "Nan-CEE?" Slowly it looped and fell down the rocks to her. "Nay-un-see?" Then long and wheedling in slow, mocking decline: "Naaan-ceeee."

She slapped her arms across both exposed breasts, though she could not see him yet; the word had fallen to her from far away. She ducked out of sight, threw on the shirt, again went to that cool curtain of shade and looked through it into the stony wilderness. Someone was moving on the high trail above.

Though her mouth was filling with screams of rage and fear, Nancy set her teeth, ran her eye along the switchbacks to estimate the distance Dwight had, the time she had. Never must she answer back; otherwise he could not be entirely certain she was below, hearing him.

She picked up a rock, but there was no good place for ambush. In Pipe Canyon she could not go far upstream or down; even if she were able to walk the creek bed to the river, where would she be then? And he would be looking down from a vantage spot on all parts of the trail she had already covered, not that she remembered any cutoffs.

If she was tired, he must be tireder; must have come straight through Indian Gardens with a short rest stop. Suddenly Nancy ran to turn off the stove's loud roar. Two miles to the river, to tourists, park rangers. Travel light, leave the pack but hide it—mustn't confirm his guess that I'm down here. He ought to give up and decide I'm in Reno by now, but he won't turn back. Climbing out must be worse.

Nancy stumbled upstream through pools in which strings of moss were drifting and slung the pack overhead into a notch in the wall. New injuries were stabbing her feet. She tied on the straw hat, poured some of the hot water into the plastic bottle, which softened in her hands. The stove and pot she rolled under the shelter.

In high lingering tones he called her again. "Oh hell," she whispered at sight of her wet bra in plain view, and she snatched it for quick burial under stones. Though she knew she should run ahead, something called her back for one last look at the figure moving so inexorably down toward her. Its growing clarity, the hat, the lean shape and jerky movement, drove all sense from her and by reflex she whipped up the nearest stone and slung it overhead toward him.

As soon as it left Nancy's hand she pulled back, dismayed, for of course the stone fell far, far short. So harmlessly did it rise and decline, so quickly go, that she hoped Dwight might take it for some kind of bird but rock struck rock somewhere, echoing. She crouched lower. At once behind her something smashed into the doorway to Pipe Canyon, landed with a dusty *thunk* on the trail nearby; something else flew overhead and on into the abyss. He had located her! One rock, striking uphill, showered her with dust and pebbles. Another took a wild bounce and then hit hard above her eyebrows with a thud.

She rolled herself into the canyon shade, was immediately up and running for its other end. Her hand came away red from where the rock had struck, though her head felt numb. Into the blazing light she ran, at first believing he was pummeling her back with many small stones, then remembering the pocketbook tied to her belt and bumping wildly behind. Hardly had she run a hundred yards in the searing sun when a wave of sickness slowed her, and she was retching. Now that the upper wall slanted outward she could not see him or the higher trail. She moved as fast as she could. Sometimes she stopped to heave dry but she tried to keep trotting toward where the trail turned out of sight and along a ledge explosives had blown in the dark curving walls. These would hide, maybe shade her. Around the first turn she found no shade, but more in-and-out coiling of the trail along solid black rock hotter than ever before. She pushed off from the hot walls as she ran on, panting.

Two miles would take forty minutes on level ground? How long in this heat? And sick? Where were all the hikers supposedly crowding the park these days? She walked down a long interim stretch of bright sand, staring overhead, before passing between more walls of schist.

The trail seemed to wind through the black stone endlessly. Though the rock felt too hot to touch, her fear that nausea would make her dizzy enough to topple over the edge made her lurch against it. No river wound below that edge, just further shelves, other cliffs. Where Dwight's rock had struck her, the forehead bulged out and overhung one eye. Out of rhythm it throbbed; her feet throbbed; her breath roared in her ears.

Each time she rounded a curve to face more monotony, more serpentine bends in the massive black stone, she would pause to listen for sounds of Dwight coming behind her on the trail but she only heard her own breath, a vague sea roar. She needed water but could not yet bear drinking from the warm bottle bouncing from her belt. Several times she lifted and shook it before her face; the water seemed full of small dartings and twitchings.

Maybe five hundred feet below she saw at last the brown river, slow and sluggish. No one could climb down solid cliff to its edge. She stopped to look out into space, toward a beach with rounded stones on its far side, before that bank also went sheer and vast with still no sight of the bridge. Through the shimmer she imagined herself jumping, floating down like a thistle, her descent borne up by angels lest she dash her foot against a stone. Both feet are dashed already? Until now she had not once thought of praying for help but—finding that her only petition would be to kill the son of a bitch—she gave a kind of inarticulate moan toward Heaven and turned back from the edge to walk on.

With each turn in the face of the mountain she expected to see the bridge, but the trail only swooped in and back to another blind curve, and in and out to a wider one still. Maybe she could pray about moving mountains? She was in danger of hysterics and began counting the false promises that each new turn made her. Was she staggering? Five. Seven. It seemed to her she could hear Dwight now, a faint distant scuffle back trail, a dislodged stone. Nine. Ten. Her whole stomach tried suddenly to get out. The spasm bent her over against heated rock, dry, painful, deep as bone. Closing her eyes she rinsed her mouth with warm water and spat quickly before anything could swim across her tongue. She stumbled on. Thirteen. Sixteen. To a fingertip her lips felt paper-dry, puckered. Seventeen. The feet—better not think about the feet. The air she gasped was too hot to give help to her lungs. Eighteen and a fall. She rested on one knee.

I'll make it to twenty, she decided seriously, and then I'll just die. Better move the bridge there, Father.

It was hard to stand. Perhaps in a flood of grace He would skip one turn and move it even closer. Nineteen. No bridge. She took a deep breath and pressed toward the last outcurve of the trail and its turn. Twenty. Nothing. She got to twenty-and-a-half and sat down with her back to hot stone. Enough. Let it come.

Huddled there, she watched the last jagged curve she had passed, had been looking back at it a long time when the heated air swam once and Dwight came through it. He looked awful. She must look worse. At sight of her he stopped and leaned into the wall to rest, lifting one hand to point to her. He moved it as if accusing. She did nothing.

Under the hat brim his long face flamed so red its lines seemed about to burst open, the way overripe tomatoes will crack their length. The dry bottom lip was pale and had split in the middle. He still wore a sport shirt and regular shoes; through their thin soles the bottoms of his feet must be on fire. He did have two almost-full water bottles lashed to the top of Eddie's pack. His hand continued to blame her. For an instant she felt pity for them both.

When his breath returned he said hoarsely, "Lying cunt." Nancy waited. The hand wavered as he moved slowly toward her hunched against the black wall. "Why?" he said. "Oh, you dumb bitch. Listen to me."

Both her hands were moving but on this part of the trail there were few loose stones. Originally these walls had been fused into single sheer towers or solid cliff faces; whatever debris had been made by the dynamiting had been blasted over the edge and lost in the river. "Stay back," she warned. She found a chunk of hard coal too large to hold in one hand. She dragged it over the trail toward her. Dwight stopped to watch and made a noise that might have been a laugh if his throat had not been so dry.

"You never will," he said.

Into her lap with both hands she heaved it and waited. At that action Dwight stood with his feet wide, shaking his head, ten yards away where the trail swooped wide above the river. She waited in the pocket where it turned in again.

"I will," she said.

He moved closer. "You can't."

She managed to lift and threaten with it. He sat down. Neither said anything else until she was able to croak, "Give me some of your water."

"Come take it."

"I won't," she said.

After a long time, it seemed, he moved his split lip enough to show where the tooth was broken, the pair of injuries making a sardonic grin, and slowly untied one of his water bottles. He took a long drink, poured some down his shirt, even poured a dark stain into the trail between them. He capped the bottle, watching her. Nancy shook her head. With a shrug he rolled the bottle along the trail. It stopped halfway between them. Nancy hunkered forward and carried it back, the heavy rock in her lap making scratches as she went. Though she could not get enough, the tepid water did not slake her thirst and her stomach groaned and cramped as she swallowed. The sunlight felt thick as brimstone.

It had occurred to her that she might go on living. "Thank you," she said in a whisper.

Dwight took off his hat, jerked his head and then a thumb upward. Come with him? Come *back*? Back up those eight burning miles? "You're crazy," she said, and drank a little more.

Then they slipped into some kind of dream, for she could not believe he was tugging from his pants pocket the same gun she had seen before. Nancy giggled although she could not explain why. It was an incongruous object in this place.

Dwight did something with the gun, probably loaded it.

The ease with which he could handle the gun without taking his stare away made her ask, "Judge Jolley?"

"Dead."

Oh surely not! No! but if so, she had abandoned him to die! "Lie," she said. "Lie?" He waved the pistol while she hefted her stone. Everything shimmered. The pantomime seemed to last a long time, its movements very slow and spangled.

"What do you want with me?" Her voice broke during the question. "Why are you doing all this?"

"Why not?"

In their silence the river could be heard far below but Nancy could not see it. He put back on and settled his hat and once more thumbed up toward earth's surface.

She started to say, "Go to hell," but the notion tickled her—since he had. If ever she started laughing she would not be able to stop.

"Either come," said Dwight with a dry cough, "or go." He laid calmly that free arm on his flexed knee as a brace and over it he leveled the gun straight at her, much as he had aimed it at the windshield a week ago.

Didn't he see that Nancy couldn't care less? She was too sick? With her rock she made new languid pantomime of threat. Besides, there welled in her a sudden irrational confidence that she would get over dying, would recover from it. That somebody good would wake her up afterward.

Nancy turned placidly aside to offer him a clear shot to the head. He seemed to tense for it. Everywhere, she felt too painful and nauseated and burning and giddy to move any farther, even to stand for her own execution.

A giggle escaped her. Dwight had come all this way for nothing and could now complete his sunstroke climbing out alone. Baffled by her laugh, he got to his feet with the gun held stiffly in front, and moved a few steps. His face looked dim to her except for the clenched teeth that shone in the sun.

"Stop it," he said.

But no other threats were now large enough to reinforce his order. Nancy could not keep from laughing, her lungs so dry she was afraid of sounding like a mockery of him: *huh-huh! huh-huh!* She, who should be saying the Twenty-third Psalm, was in a reactive fit as persistent as hiccups. *Huh-huh!* (This is awful! she thought.) And a *huh!*

"You hear me?" Dwight had walked closer, now made thin long shade fall across her.

She tried but a new wry joke had hit her, that she had come all this way for nothing, too! *Huh-huh!* she barked, though some degree of anguish had set in. *Huh!*

Looking furious, Dwight drew back the gun hard, not to shoot anymore but to strike her on some tender sunburned place, to club the wound he had already made on her head; and Nancy changed in an instant. He came into very sharp focus. To die was one thing, but to be hurt any more? No, enough of that, no. Did she growl in her throat? Long before Nancy had decided what to do about that slowly falling gun butt, her body had lunged upward; she felt the stone pushed out stiff-armed from the level of her chest. It flew away black in the air.

He was not hit. But he jerked aside, too much of his weight already displaced to one side with the uplifted gun. He stumbled. Maybe inside that dusty shoe his foot was entirely raw and undependable. That ankle turned. The next step he made to catch balance was right at the edge of the cliff.

There Dwight hung, almost was standing in air, something ludicrous in his air of expectation as he posed slightly swayed out with gaze fixed on the opposite cliff beyond the river. Maybe one degree past the balance he leaned, and on the brink he shouted once, "No!" He lifted his back foot then and stepped, lightly *stepped*, into the space he had been seeking and went home to his brother.

14

People are always crossing the Kaibab suspension bridge over the Colorado with a tired wild look on their faces. Nobody notices this normal response to too much space, light, rock, heat, insignificance, and thirst.

Four trail loops before the bridge, a husband and wife passed Nancy on the hewn rock ledge. They answered her tense questions about how much farther she had to walk. "Did you fall? Is your head all right?" She nodded. She looked hot and sunburned, naturally enough. Her lips were peeling and she admitted to nausea, but she was carrying two water bottles and a large black rock. "Souvenir?" the husband said. She heaved it over the edge.

Five ecology majors stopped in a row on the footbridge to let Nancy work her way by. Knowing that older Americans were flabby and mentally slower than college men, they asked after her welfare politely. The way she breathed, she must smoke cigarettes? Too bad! She nodded, clutching the rail. Below them drifted black rubber rafts in which boatmen planned ahead for Horn Creek Rapids three miles downstream. Passengers waved hats overhead at the bridge. Nancy stumbled over that river procession like a sleepwalker, but nobody noticed. It's hot in the canyon.

Even if all seven of those hikers had later happened to look off River Trail at the very spot where Dwight Anderson had fallen, his body lay far below, almost invisible. No one could reach him down that long sheer drop. Talus had rolled to the cliff's foot where his body struck, and had mounded dark atop him on the sharp shelf before the slope to the river's edge. Only from the river could any unusual shape be traced in the rubble. The canyon is full of unusual shapes and the boatmen were busy.

Someday a passenger who was not teetering in the raft snapping pictures nor trying to read from his river guide what a number ten rapid was—someday such an unusual passenger would notice a shoe below the pile, or maybe a white bone in it. Or maybe a jaded boatman who had rowed many times through the canyon would be loafing on his oars below Bright Angel Creek and spot something new among gravel along the south bank of the upper inner gorge. Nobody saw it yet.

Beyond the college students, Nancy hung on to the bridge railing with both hands all the way across the muddy river. Most people do. Once in the late 1950s a priest on the Tanner Trail became irrational from thirst, threw his shoes over an eighty-foot cliff, tried to climb down its face, and was killed. If any hiker fears that after walking eight miles beside hundreds of beckoning suicide leaps he might now, on mad impulse, succumb and for nothing leap straight into the Colorado—this is an ordinary concern. Though Nancy held tight to the rail even for an instant after she had stepped onto land, nobody on the north side of the river thought a thing about it.

Nor did she think. She could not. She was still in the dream.

Downstream from the bridge, Bright Angel Creek poured clear and sparkling across its large fan of debris and bubbled into the larger river. Beside it, the sandy path on which Nancy walked skirted empty buildings.

Families passed her with friendly remarks. At first she said,

"There's a man . . ." but they smiled past before she could finish. Not that she wanted to finish or to remember.

She came to a spigot dripping a slow waste of water, sat by it, turned its tap wide open and held her head under the gush of cold water. She forgot to remove her straw hat but people do that; the cool crown and brim keep soothing heads for a long time afterward. She drank, spat it out, drank again. Couples in love went by. She became part of the sweetness they saw everywhere, temporarily. Numbly she watched them float past.

Next came a neat ranger's house with a brilliant green lawn one would almost be tempted to graze. On it a stationary sprinkler opened out a great bloom of silver water. For a few minutes she stood putting her hand through its petal and out, then walked on with that wet palm pressed to her cracked lips.

She fell automatically into step behind others headed upriver to the campground. She was walking more stiffly than they, as if upon stubs. One girl called over her Coca-Cola, "You must've had a hard trip!" as she crossed the musical creek. The water was flashing the way it always does in dreams.

Under a cool limestone overhang Nancy followed the path to a flat shaded creek bank with its long row of cottonwoods. Here the banks of the stream had been paved with round river stones held in place under woven wire. There were many shelter sheds with people underneath, eating, talking. Dreams omit detail and favor background people with no faces. Had she approached one of these picnics, Nancy was certain everything would have dropped away like a tapestry and left her staring off that cliff where pebbles still trickled down. With care she dreamed every thread of the picnickers safely into place, though for a minute there burst through the fabric Dwight's "No!" and its spinning echoes: No!—No—no—o—oh.

She seemed to be swimming now through the thickest air of the dream until far down the campground she came to a tree with nobody else under it and dropped by its trunk. After ten minutes or so she managed, slowly, to ease off both boots. The socks would come only partway. Fluids dried in the cloth had stuck fast. Nancy lay flat, shuddering, and threw one sunburned arm hot over her eyes.

Other campers walking to Phantom Ranch or back simply stepped over or past her. It's natural to sleep soundly by the song of that clear rushing water. Probably John Wesley Powell's face looked wild and tired just before he slept here on another August night under, as he wrote, "a great overspreading tree with willow shaped leaves."

After a while Nancy dreamed she was asleep.

Dawn? Dusk? Summertime, she knew that much.

Even raising her head made her sick. Nancy woke disoriented in a twilight she could not recognize, hungry for some rare food her stomach could retain, perhaps communion wafers. She took a swallow of lukewarm water and decided she was safe at Indian Gardens after a nightmare involving fire and snakes.

Something bulky—pocketbook—poked into her back. Head down, fighting cramps, she worked it under her neck for a pillow. In the nightmare a king had thrown her into the fiery furnace. Parts of the crucible had survived in flashlights, flickers. Distant people were talking in voices softer than the river noise, voices lost in it until the river itself said something long and foreign.

She felt hot and clammy at once. Her grandfather bent through this steamy mixture her skin was exuding. "She isn't dry enough behind the ears yet," he said over his shoulder to Daniel and the Lions. Probably they raised the thermostat.

Though she lay still with eyes closed her mind kept running headlong through a petrified orchard with some blackbird that flew along behind her crying *know-know-know!* An enlarging pillar of fire caught up and burned past; a voice out of it said her grandfather was dead but the red shoes wouldn't let her stop. Things were the wrong size; you'd have to eat figs with a shovel here, and they would be stone. She went through the mirror to Oliver. He was the height of a pill bottle and burned a hole in her pocket and rolled down the steps. As she ran after, the stairs opened farther and he tumbled ahead like a scorched gingerbread man.

Than it was night, the tree trunk cold to her inflamed arm. The figs had fallen off the tree as rocks and pebbles. When she opened her eyes the dark and the stars made her dizzy. She carefully stood, holding the tree while her stomach convulsed. Slowly she picked her way down the stony bank, the wire mesh cutting her feet with the socks attached and dragging, toward the sound of water. Trembling she lowered her body among rocks in the shallow moonlit splash of the creek. Hydrotherapy. She slid deeper. There were things she must not think about. Wash me whiter than snow. No, she refused. HYDROTHERAPY.

"Attagirl!" said J. Waldo as he sailed by on a large bobbing slice of bread. It was buttered on his side.

She slept awhile in the water, never did remember crawling back to the tree. The locusts and other plagues sang to her. In daylight she found herself on land, clothes still damp. the eye below her injury was swollen shut. Out of the other she watched silent people packing camp gear in the early dawn. The odor of their coffee was poisonous and made her stomach heave. Hikers began moving out of camp.

Nancy thought she must be invisible, perhaps dead. She propped on her new sunglasses though they hung crooked; anyone could see that a ghost would not wear sunglasses. Feeling in a wider circle she found her pocketbook with sand now mixed with the money. She declined to think about whose money it was. Though the movements had made her nauseated and faint, only sour spittle came up. She called out to one of the hikers but her voice was so dry and sore that he took it for greeting, and waved. She was not certain where she was except that she had fallen from a height and hurt her head.

Later the morning sunlight stretched under her tree and drove her back to rocks and their paler shade. By midday she had chills. Shaking behind her screen of boulders she did not see the ranger walk along the creek until he was well past; then she shrank away as if guilty, as if he might punish her for something.

By afternoon she had remembered the hike down and the necessity of telling someone there was a man broken on the rocks beside the river. She stumbled onto the path and looked vaguely around.

A boy came up wearing a big pack. "Are you sick? Do you need anything?" She said yes. He led her back to the tree, filled her canteen with tepid sweet tea and made her drink.

"It was a fall, just a fall," she began when her throat was wet.

"I can see that," said the boy as he fingered the lump and her swollen eye. "It looks worse than it is, though. You could use a stitch."

"Not me, not me!" she said, but he was promising to send back the ranger when he passed the station. "Eat these, too." He poured out salted peanuts. "What are you doing down here by yourself?"

She spoke at some length.

"You're feverish, too. Well, if I see your friend on the trail I'll tell him you got a little too much sun. Is he carrying your pack and supplies? You should have stopped when he did and not pushed yourself so hard!" the boy said sharply.

His misunderstanding of her frantic talk made Nancy gape. Even as she stared she pictured the edges of her life seamed together more neatly than any wound; she saw a way to pluck Dwight Anderson out of her life as if she were cleaning dirt from an injury.

"Now who is it uptrail that I look for?"

She drank tea and took a long breath. "My sister and her husband. The Rayburns."

He said if she didn't feel better by nightfall she should consider a chopper lift-out or at least wait several days and recuperate. He squirted burn lotion onto her hands. "If I don't see the ranger, I'll leave him a note. He'll check by in the morning at any rate."

At long intervals Nancy ate peanuts one at a time while watching him disappear down the path. Slowly her throat stopped trying to erupt. She sipped the sugared tea. At dusk the ranger had not come and she lay again in the creek's tumbling current. Even by the stream the air was not cool; the canyon was an inferno; only water was cool. Waist-deep in its flow she let herself urinate through cloth—anything to avoid the long walk to the camp toilets. It was Tuesday; how long since she had urinated last? She was asleep on the bank before dark.

Wednesday morning, though weak, she stood and made herself walk. The cut soles of her feet drained through her wet socks. After finishing the peanuts and tea, she combed her dry hair and ran lipstick over the peeling rim around her mouth. Apart from sunburn and the gouge Dwight's rock had cut in one eyebrow, which was going to scar, the mirror showed some new expression in her face she could not name. She saw the ranger coming under the limestone overhang. No, she thought; no, it's over; no! and she snatched her pocketbook

and limped in the opposite direction, tugging the hat low. By following the others she could find Phantom Ranch, not far, over a route as
smooth as if laid through a city park, with patches of shade here and
there. Much sun and heat still made her gag, though, and she was
grateful to approach the grove on the canyon floor with buildings,
penned mules, a dry swimming pool, and three tame deer grazing.
I'm not dreaming now, she told herself. She walked slowly toward the
nearest deer but it did not believe in her innocence and twanged away
gracefully.

At the small store she bought ginger ale and soda crackers with . . .
with *her* money. She sat apart from other canyon travelers, eavesdropping on who had found a scorpion in her shoe, who had nearly
stepped on a pink rattlesnake in Nautiloid Canyon.

Nancy seemed to be painfully relearning the English language from
what they had to say. One party group of paying tourists from a mo-
torized raft chattered about their steaks, kept cold on dry ice, and
about the electric toilet that consumed their luxurious excrement. She
moved farther away, feeling deranged, and tried to remember the
world a mile above them all. Through the trees, she could see a telephone wire which came down that full mile.

The longer she sat, the more the tourists talked to one another, and
the longer she looked at the high spot where the wire grew transparent between the farthest posts, the clearer it became to Nancy that no
one except Chan Thatcher knew she was here and that even Chan had
not seen her go down. If on the rim she had not signed her name,
Dwight had certainly never signed his. If one more hour, one more
mile had separated the two of them, he would never have caught up
with her on the trail, never been sure she was there, nor would Nancy
have known he was following. Speed up one clock, or slow Dwight's
stolen watch, and she could produce a dimension in which she never
did see him, a space through which if he had called out, the sound
would not have been heard. Although some stranger lagging far behind her might well have fallen to his death, she—who was crossing
the bridge by then—could not have seen him go over the edge.

Normalcy was all overhead where she had left it: the books, the library, Beckham, those tiresome dates with Patrick, the hall clock that

was always gaining or losing time when there was no advantage either way. Her eyes smarted; Nancy would have cried if her whole system had not been so dry.

A hiker had joined the float passengers. He had just come down the North Kaibab Trail, steeper than Bright Angel—he was telling them—but easy to follow, with a creek nearby. Nancy looked past him and upward where the trail and the telephone wires disappeared. This time she did not have to get heatstroke since she could step aside at will and lie down in that creek.

And what if she took that trail, climbed out the other side of Grand Canyon as one more in a line of hikers no one had time to check? She could still decide, on the North Rim, to tell the rangers she was the weary and frightened woman who had fled from her kidnapper at Williams! that was as much as she had to tell anybody.

She filled her canteens, *her* canteens, at the tap. She bought more ginger ale, bread, two tins of potted meat in case she should ever be able to eat meat again. She did not have to decide yet what she would tell or to whom she would tell it. She circled the small building and sat with her back to its wall, alone, listening to the wires singing in the hot wind and wondering whether there was anyone overhead she really wanted to telephone.

On Monday morning, Judge Jolley had turned from the man in park headquarters and said to Dwight, "Nobody named Finch. He went through the whole roster."

"She's down there," Dwight said. "Wanted to see the bottom. Well, she's going to see it." He was breathing rapidly; sometimes he slapped his left chest with the flat of one hand as if to awaken his heart.

"She's gone," said the judge firmly. "Let me go, too."

"I'll show her some bottom," Dwight muttered.

He had been mumbling like this ever since he practically assaulted the judge, tearing the chaise from his grip with a heave and then throwing him into the car with its engine running. They had roared out of the campground to this mumbling: Nancy was gone, nowhere in camp; she had robbed him. A thief! She had robbed him and run!

While they sped toward the Grand Canyon Dwight said under his

breath several times, "My mama, she looked at the bottom." The
rearview mirror he had broken with one swipe of the gun barrel as
they drove. "Took them to the bottom with her!" he said wildly. The
judge was afraid to do or say anything.

They arrived after dark Sunday to find the entrance gate to the
Grand Canyon closed. Dwight half stepped out of the car onto one
leg and propped himself to stare at the road barrier.

The judge thought it safe to say, "Uh, if you drive through it that's
sure to bring somebody."

"If I was you, I'd hope so," he said, rubbing his chest. Then he
pulled the car off the road among trees, but neither of them could
sleep. Most of the night Dwight chain-smoked while the judge gazed
at stars until they all ran together. Monday morning they were first in
line when cars were checked through.

The judge thought Nancy was halfway to Sacramento and Dr. Foster by now, leaving him as the hostage on whom this psychopath
would wreak revenge. Even if her name had appeared on the hiker's
roster, he had not decided whether telling Dwight would do good or
harm.

"That's so? She's not there?" Dwight asked behind him now. The
ranger shook his head. Dwight pulled the judge into the parking lot.
"She thought if she went down there I'd let her go."

"You don't look well," the judge decided to say. "It's this altitude. Is
it bothering your heart?"

"No," said Dwight nervously. "What makes you ask that?" He
shoved his hand into a pocket. "There's nothing wrong with me."

"You look white," the judge lied, "as if your blood doesn't reach
everywhere."

Dwight poked him toward the car. "It's been fine all week," he said,
"while she was here. You shut up."

"You go right on after her if that's what you want," said the judge
with a placating spread of the hand, "and just hand me my suitcase.
I'll take a bus home, straight home, I promise you. That's the only
place I want to go."

"You'll go to hell if I say so." He waited till the judge slid under the
wheel.

Around them people climbed in and out of cars and talked about the broken dinghies and rock specimens displayed in the museum. Never again would the judge believe such people even noticed their temporary neighbor, much less loved him as themselves.

"Well, turn it on!" Dwight growled. "Find a hotel." As they drove he said, "Let's say you did go to police and let's say they arrested me. Even from jail I can send somebody to see you, remember?"

Jolley's persistent fear was that every man he had ever sentenced had subsequently purchased the death of the judge from every free-lance murderer in prison. Once near Somerville, in fact, a bullet had struck the rear window of his car; the sheriff said it was a rifle bullet from great distance, only a hunting accident, but the judge knew better. Often he had heard hit men thrashing around and whispering in his shrubbery.

They checked into the El Tovar Hotel. "Ask him," said Dwight.

"Do you have a Nancy Finch registered?" They did not.

Upstairs he made the judge dial every other hotel, but she had not checked into any. Then he stood too close to the judge, listening, while Nancy was paged in the small terminal that served the train and tour buses. His breath was hot, its smell bitter. Nobody could find her. The judge moved the phone away from Dwight's odor, watching him knock one fist against his ribs. "I don't want to go down in that ugly place," Dwight said, rapping himself. "Look up the airplanes."

Obediently the judge had carried the phone book to the bright window to find the listing when he saw into the canyon for the first time. For the hour they had been on the rim he had been sensing its depths but not at this size nor in these brilliant colors. For an instant he thought it might suck him through the glass. She's down there; he's right! he thought instantly, backing off. And it's all the fault of that fool woman and her color slides back in Tennessee. "Why can't you do some of this telephoning?" he complained.

Dwight said, "Because I've got the gun and you ain't."

He learned that the airport restricted itself to sightseeing routes or rescue trips for the Park Service; it referred him to a telephone number in a nearby town.

A man answered. "Lewis McKinney, help you?"

Eyeing Dwight, the judge invented a family emergency, a deathbed situation. Was it possible to take a helicopter down both canyon trails and drop low enough to pick out the face he was looking for? Dwight whispered to him. And how much would it cost? Where would one land to intercept?

The man said no way. "You hover there very long and a hot wind will slam you into rocks. Now I can take you all the way to the bottom and land in a field near Bright Angel Creek or I can take you all the way over to North Rim if your party's hiking out there. But, mister, you'd do just as well to telephone the rangers and send one down to the footbridge. Everybody's got to cross that same bridge."

"Thank you." He relayed the information.

In his ear the man added, "I don't mind making the hundred bucks, but if it's a real emergency the rangers can do the job better."

Again he spoke to Dwight, who said, *"She's* got my hundred."

The judge started to hang up when the man said, "If they find your party? Remember I can always pick up down canyon or cross, and my night listing for Valle is in the book."

Dwight snatched the phone. "Did you fly a woman anywhere last night or today? By herself? O.k." He hung up and walked to the window. "Ugly place. Did you ask about people that signed for both trails?"

"Yes, and the ones for Hermit's Rest and Clear Creek besides."

Staring out, Dwight slapped himself again. "It's getting worse," he said. Onto the dresser he emptied his pockets, counting bills as he made a roll. The judge could not estimate the cash after Nancy had— Dwight claimed—cleaned him nearly out; but his gaze was distracted by the handful of packaged condoms that Dwight had dropped carelessly under the lamp and that in the end he scooped up and returned to his pocket. He saw the judge watching and showed the broken tooth in a grin. "Yeah, and she likes it," he said.

The judge rushed into the toilet, slammed and latched the door. Through it Dwight said, "Time we went down there."

"I'll never make it even on a mule." Seated on the tub's edge, the judge watched the doorknob first twist one way, then the other. The door rattled. "I'll just slow you down."

"Come on out."

His courage mounted now that he could only hear but not see

Dwight. "Or what, you'll shoot through the door?" Just in case, the judge got into the tub and lay down.

"I'm not going all the way down there to hurt her and make trouble for myself." Coughing. "Come on, now. I don't want to hang around all day."

"Can't you get it through your head that she's in Las Vegas by now? Go away. I'm not coming a step farther."

There were more movements and metallic noises beyond the door. Was he unscrewing the hinges? The judge looked wildly at his arsenal: towels; plastic toothbrush glass; Kleenex holder.

With a creak Dwight sat down and leaned against the other side of the door saying in a conversational tone, "How I feel about killing is this—I try the easiest stuff first, see, because killing is going to make me trouble." Despite his soft voice he seemed restless. There were noises of movement and once a coin dropped and rolled. His breath sounded rough and uneven. "But I'll be glad to kill you if that's what you want, if that's what you make me do."

Then there was silence. He heard Dwight walking through the room, to the window. Drawers opened and closed, then the room door opened and he imagined Dwight standing there till his heartbeat felt normal. "If you make me do that," Dwight said, "I'll hurt you a long time first." The door closed.

After a few minutes Judge Jolley sat up in the tub, certain that Dwight had slammed the door as a trap and even now was listening and waiting. With care he unlaced and slipped off his shoes. Still no sound from the bedroom. He stepped onto the cool tile and took a quick hop to the door. His ear against wood, he strained to hear whatever noises Dwight might make with his own ear pressed to the other side. Both men probably stopped breathing so each could better hear the other. For a long time he tried to outwait Dwight before easing out the lock button. He decided to snatch open the door all at once and stood back for the gesture. With a quick turn and jerk he brought away, astonished, the entire knob in his hand! Dwight had somehow unfastened it from the other side, and the door—he tried—but now it would not open.

After a shocked moment the judge called out, then banged sharply. He knew immediately why Dwight had been opening drawers; he had hung outside the sign asking that the occupant not be disturbed even by the maid. He banged and called, then walked around all the walls beating steadily with one shoe, but no one heard; the other guests were out of their rooms walking along the precipice. He clanged his shoe heel against the water pipes in S.O.S. code. He flushed the toilet twenty times in succession, pause, and twenty more, but the noise kept him from hearing the faintest footsteps in the hall. He wondered how long Dwight had stood out there double-checking how well or poorly the judge's noises carried through the thick walls. They must carry poorly, he thought, or else Dwight would not have gone on downstairs and followed Nancy into the canyon.

Nobody helped him. From the adjoining room Judge Jolley in late afternoon identified the noise of many children. When these siblings were not shouting or fighting or playing the television set as loud as it would go, they did hear his knocking and knocked vigorously back. They set up a knocking contest among themselves. Then they checked out with their parents and forgot him.

Later, between spells of calling for help, the judge took several baths. In the close, steamy room he studied his vulnerable body with its extra ridge at the waist, every blood vein in jeopardy under the thin white skin. His penis seemed smaller than in his youth, smaller even than the night Clara had not cared to touch it. His body hair was more sparse. As he lay naked in the tub he thought about the police, about testifying at Dwight's trial, being pitied for his wife's death but judged for his neurotic reaction to it, being tried himself for those unimportant cases he had handled independently. Yes, and handled well! Touching himself, he remembered Dwight's condoms. Nancy had left him here to be killed; Dwight was still willing to kill him; both of them, strangers to him. In this small cubicle devoted entirely to the care of the body, Judge Jolley could see for himself how fragile this body had already become.

Even on our honeymoon, Clara would never bathe in the same tub with me!

He thrashed in the water at the pity of it all, the pity of the things he had never done and now would never do.

There was no conscious decision. By the time he was out of the tub and dry the last time it had become clear to the judge that Nancy had chosen to please herself and Dwight himself, that life was short and terminal, that an accidental encounter need not determine its course.

Besides, when the maid finally heard the judge call, when the hotel repairman had come and conversed through the door as he worked, when the manager and other guests had joined the waiting crowd, when at last the toilet door was opened and he stood there—a very clean anticlimax—his emotions had dwindled to those that suit trivial embarrassment. Because of them he blustered about hardware and lawsuits. Asked about the man at the desk with him, the judge called him a mere acquaintance, someone met on the bus, a tourist.

Under the circumstances, the manager said, one day's lodging would be free.

"I won't even need that much. Excuse me, but I've another bus to catch."

Not until sunset could he board the next eastbound bus. His wait in the bus station clarified how many travelers departed every day for every place. The milling crowds convinced him Nancy had never come to the Grand Canyon at all but like these other hurrying people had gone sensibly on with her life as he intended to go on with his.

As the bus rolled past Dwight's parked car near the museum, the judge saw that its broken windshield appeared the result of a flung pebble. At Yavapai the bus stopped for one last look into space and the judge stood among companionable travelers close to his own age while they made final snapshots. At this hour the canyon was turning a misty purple. For the first time he saw the Grand Canyon as it was meant to be seen, with its great depths and heights turning beautiful and serene as they grew steadily less distinct. He thought of Psalm 121. He thought of the shadow of a mighty rock within a weary land.

Riding away through scrubbier unchallenging country, the judge fell into such a deep dreamless sleep that his seatmate had to shake him awake in Flagstaff. Sometime on Tuesday his uncertainties began and, by Wednesday, when he was riding a different bus much farther east, he feared that he had abandoned Nancy in the chasm after all.

He might then have turned back, or at least at a rest stop telephone the police with a late report; but since it had now become clear that for two days his conscience had really been sending him home to Somerville for confession, trial, possible disbarment, or worse, the judge, brave at last, allowed himself to hurry toward that shame and restitution. He thought of them both as the banquet being spread for him at the end of a long journey.

Nancy meant to start hiking out of the canyon by dark, but by then she had vomited the ginger ale and dropped into a dizzy sleep. When she had strength enough to go, it was close to dawn on Wednesday, and though she found the North Kaibab Trail amply watered, with campsites nearby, nothing compensated for the rising temperature and her growing weakness. Because other hikers spoke pleasantly she concluded she must look as normal as they, and she summoned a smile for each one.

An hour north of the ranch, in a narrow corridor through granite, her thin scabs wore through and her feet began bleeding in her shoes. Clothes and all, she lay in the creek until giddiness passed. Her head ached. She floated out her hair in a corona like Ophelia's but the ache was too deep to cool.

Maybe it's now, she thought, that the lesion in my own brain is tearing loose and will give me a seizure many times worse than Beckham's.

But she was able to start dizzily uphill again. The wavering vision recalled her frequent faints as a girl, pre-menarche. Injury, sudden pain, seeing a blood sample drain from her arm, taking in a dentist's chair the full crash of a strong dose of novocaine—such physical shocks had always caused the young Nancy to faint. Probably fear played a part. In every case she would feel prickly, then cool; then she passed into pleasant dreams among enormous but uncertain vistas where great music reverberated and cosmic events occurred that she never could recall.

In time, she connected these faints with Beckham's epilepsy, saw them as its milder reflection; and although she did not faint after puberty the similarity frightened her. The "falling sickness" had many gradations. Perhaps her grand mal had only been delayed. In the library she read Alvarez's strong case for epilepsy by inheritance. Still, she grew older than Beck at the onset of true convulsions and even her faints did not recur. In fact, sometimes she missed them. She had read that patients pulled back by doctors from the brink of death sometimes recounted bright visions, sweet voices, a floating along a tunnel toward light and space. What Lazarus withheld, they now gave interviews about. Their loved ones met them, they said, but embodied in light. Nancy would have passed God Almighty at a dead run to see her grandfather again.

Whether somatic or not, entry into that great and ethereal world made fainting a secret pleasure. She thought of that other world as being always parallel to this one, with a doorway which traveled with her body, standing by. Each time, a foreknowledge cooling her skin would warn Nancy that doorway was swinging open, and she would have time to announce to the dentist in a calm voice, "I'm going out." Out of it. Outside me. Over there.

Even though reason told her those caverns and panoramas must be caused by physiology, a condition from which aromatic ammonia could always summon her back and resign her to wherever she might wake, Nancy could still recall each last dim reluctance before she let go that radiant void to return, as if she agreed to go back to earth, but of necessity. Vaguely she trusted the door to wait for her till the next time.

Something resembling that cool threat of faint rippled repeatedly over her skin now as she hiked uphill. At each warning she stumbled aside to lie flat in the creek until this world again settled round and solid and stony on all sides. Otherwise she might walk off a cliff into Dwight's secret world and not hers.

Dwight? Who? Not yet, not yet.

The sun rose higher and probed more hotly everywhere. She was panting, though the chill still tickled her flesh like a summons. Nancy forgot how many times she had washed herself during the climb. With a whisper the fine hairs of her body rotated in each pore; she shook with a brief but hard chill. Next she was touching the great Paleozoic Redwall, which meant she had climbed halfway to the surface. Though Nancy had meant to eat at this midway point, she knew she would vomit.

She walked on in the heat, trying to control the persistent sense of falling. She would analyze and thus control this longing to faint—she decided. If her blood pressure fell, surely that caused the sensation that all her cells drooped toward earth. Then the vessels would go lax in the brain so it could process fewer sense impressions from the outside world. Its thought activity closed up on itself. The depths she had visited in her faints might be the size of her skull, though when she had first stood with Chan looking off Mather Point, Nancy had almost recognized the place, felt she had been a speck in it before.

With surprise Nancy found herself seated against a shale wall in the blazing sun. Time has passed, she thought, and I have been in far palaces. The remembered clamminess tickled her arms. She was, yes, very sick, homesick and sick, but she had to hurry somewhere in order to stop a man from falling. To help herself struggle to her feet Nancy set the bag of food aside, then forgot it, walked a few yards up a steep incline, and sat down again.

She drank from her warm canteen. Water surged back up her throat, thick with white sodden fragments. She could not remember eating anything. No doubt she had swallowed the secret papers. She was glad to see their fragments, partly digested, unreadable. Forcing herself upright she held to the gritty wall and worked her way farther uphill.

While walking—when was this? Days later? While walking, she finally remembered the other papers inside her pocketbook that could be used to send her back there forever. She began shredding all she could find—cards and sales tickets and loose checks—letting the bits drift off the trail on the hot air above the gorge. It was correct that the light should be so brilliant in this dream place, she decided. To receive that full light she took off the sunglasses to remove the air's last green dilution, threw them down a cliff and stumbled on, much slower. Inside the pocketbook she felt for and pulled out wadded bills the same green color. As she moved she tore all these into pieces and scattered them over the side. Around the next switchback the wallet flew out almost by itself and fell among gravel below. Everything she found she slung off the trail as she hobbled on, and she would have reached a last small card in the zipper pocket, too, if her dizziness had not grown too thick.

To the high wall of limestone behind her, Nancy said with a pat, "I'm going out now."

The wall seemed to soften as she slid down its surface. As usual the door was there. She was sitting on pebbles with her back pressed to its heat. Then through stone she sailed off like a dust mote into endless space.

As soon as Nancy had flown out of it, her body toppled aside and fell sprawled across her footprints on the sandy trail.

In the Oklahoma City bus station, unable to read, the judge finally threw Marcus Aurelius into a waste can and persuaded a stranger to place a phone call for him. "It'll be the easiest five dollars you ever made."

The man seemed slightly drunk. "Fits so easy," he answered, and then thrust himself taller. "If it's so easy, why ain't you calling free?"

"As I said, it's a police matter. Now I've already gotten Mrs. Finch's number from the operator—right here, see?—and all you do is ask one question no matter who answers. The question is: Have you talked with Nancy since Sunday? The part about Sunday is very important; it's crucial. Have they talked with her *since Sunday?*"

"She get converted?"

"Just ask the question, nod or shake your head to me, and then hang up."

The two men crowded into the booth. Halfway through dialing, the wino asked to be paid in advance. Judge Jolley gave him two dollar bills and two quarters and an angry headshake. He lined up the receiver between their ears.

"Hello?"

"Have you talked?" began the wino obediently but Judge Jolley clapped one hand over his mouth because—my God!—it sounded on the other end like Nancy herself!

He whispered, "Ask who it is," and replaced his ear to eavesdrop.

"It'll cost you more money," said the drunk loudly.

On the other end Faye with wild flappings of one arm silently summoned the family into the hall while she tried to make out an exchange of whispering.

The wino recited, "Who is this that talked with Nancy, Sunday?" though the judge was gesturing *no-no-no!*

But Faye answered breathlessly, "I know who this is! I well remember you, and we've been expecting you to call us." The judge only heard the last part as Faye withdrew to shove Beckham aside so Eddie could work the tape recorder this time and not erase half the conversation.

The judge tried to claim the telephone to find out what message Nancy had left for him.

"Not yet!" barked his assistant, waving it overhead while Faye's voice floated down: ". . . all right when she talked to Beckham but now . . ."

Even that fragment was enough to make the judge slump from gratitude. So Nancy *had* called home; she was not in the canyon!

The wino got between him and the mouthpiece, announcing that he wouldn't turn over anything until he got his two-fifty.

"What? How much? What did you say?" In Greenway Faye dropped the telephone to the hall floor, crying weakly to Eddie that the kidnapper wanted a ransom of a quarter of a million dollars!

Eddie Rayburn scrambled for the dropped telephone while only the turning tape heard the judge's angry, "Here then! And shut up!" Faye had entangled herself with Beckham and her mother, still crying.

"Be quiet, Faye, or I won't be able to hear him! Hello? Hello?"

The judge did not know whose the new voice was, much less what it meant. Nancy had made the Finches sound somewhat peculiar. That, plus the recent strain? "Get out of my way!" he snapped as he flattened himself to the telephone so the drunk could leave the booth with his five dollars.

". . . speak to her," said Eddie's voice.

"I'm glad you have," said the judge politely. "Just what did she tell Beckham?"

But by then Mrs. Finch had snatched the phone from Eddie and she, too, almost wept at this callous question, since the kidnapper had evidently not realized Nancy had made a call until now. They had betrayed her to his vengeance! "No detail," she began to babble, "but she spoke very well of you under the circumstances; you mustn't be angry." ("You're wasting time," Eddie said. "Give it back and let me find out when and where he wants the money.") "Surprisingly well of you, I thought," she whimpered before she surrendered the phone.

The man's voice was hard, tense. "As Beckham told her, we've said nothing. We were just glad to know she was alive. You understand, Beckham thought she was alone, that she wasn't with you anymore, so . . ."

"That's true," said the judge happily. He was confused to find Nancy was keeping him out of it, perhaps because he had hinted to her his own legal difficulties? "But there's no need for secrecy anymore now that I'm prepared to deal fully with all the consequences." Midway in this sentence he saw it was time for his bus to leave.

"What?" Eddie barked. "Listen, we'll get it somehow!"

The drunk was pushing in the booth door. "Quit that! Get back! Right now I've got to go—"

Eddie shouted, "Don't hang up!" Eddie could hear scuffling just as the judge could hear women somewhere crying with near-hysterical relief. But there wasn't time to explain; Nancy could do the explaining. So he hung up hurriedly and pushed by the man who was now offering to call the President for him at a reduced price.

He had to run to make his bus and sank into the seat and spread a handkerchief across his face. Nancy was free! She had called Beckham. She blamed him for nothing.

Back in Greenway, the Finches and Rayburns huddled around the recorder, rewound and then played back the tape. "That's him, even trying to change his voice at the first!" Eddie Rayburn vowed. "That's the man in Linville Gorge! I'd know his voice anywhere. And listen."

"Shut up!" the voice said to someone invisible. "Quit that! Get back!"

"He's still got her," Eddie said. The women cried.

Beckham kept asking of everybody, "But I thought she escaped. Didn't she get away?" He caught hold of Eddie's arm. "When is she going to get loose?"

"You've started to hop to the bathroom at night. I woke up and thought some burglar on a pogo stick was in the hall. Last summer I could still hear *two* feet touch the floor."

"Naturally I'm a little stiff when I first get up." She reached her fork to sample his enchiladas: poor.

"I thought Hunt was coming up this summer for another hike into the canyon."

"Probably he thinks the canyon will come to him. He worries me, Lewis; it's as if he's a settled old man with lowered expectations."

"You don't think he wants his wife back, do you? I had her tracked down."

"You didn't! By now nothing should surprise me, but where did you find her? Don't ever tell Hunt—he'll think I asked you to."

"The way you kept worrying without a word and with your teeth gritted—in a way you did ask me. She's in Denver working the switchboard for a big bank." When Chan said she doubted Ilene was smart enough to remember five digits, he said, "The way she's built, they've put her in the lobby as an art object."

"Hunt was too old to have made that particular mistake." For no reason the runaway Nancy appeared in her mind; Chan wondered if her pursuer were handsome and stupid.

"Some dog breeder you are," said Lewis, laughing. "You know how little sex has to do with judgment. To *marry* Ilene was the mistake." He touched her ear as if its shape were rare. "Since you think he used his mother as a model, it insulted you that he chose Ilene, didn't it?"

"Puzzled," Chan corrected.

After dinner they drove to his house, with its high round beams and heavy Spanish furniture. She admitted his rooms were larger and cooler than hers. "I'll come someday. Since Ilene left, Hunt has seemed so withdrawn I just couldn't leave. It's as if he's given up on humans. I'm one of the last two-legged creatures he even notices."

"You exaggerate. Hunt Thatcher sees customers all day long."

"Horse owners. He walks past every one to get to the horse. And the attention he pays those wolves is creepy, Lewis. Both my children have chosen to have animals instead of babies and I don't understand it."

"Don't approve, you mean." Automatically they had moved to the door and out back to check the kennels. "They both grew up in a family that loved animals."

"In addition to people, not instead of," she said as they walked along the runs speaking softly as each dog came to the fence. Chan knelt where Tanner whimpered to be let out.

Lewis laughed. "At home that dog sleeps on the foot of your bed. I call that instead of." He added that he had some sympathy for Hunt and his animals. "In Jefferson's time America was run by men who were still in touch with animal husbandry. They saw the strong and weak strains, the different dispositions, the work of instinct and heredity, so naturally they didn't have so many airy-fairy ideas about equality. That's why Jefferson said the pursuit, the *pursuit* of happiness, no more than that."

"It's just that they meant equal before God." Chan faced him through the mesh. The big difference between them was Lewis' fascination with human history versus her conviction that all events if rightly understood were theophanies.

And maybe that's why I don't move to Valle, she thought with a pang. when she rose from the squat her hip joint had frozen.

"Careful," he said quickly. "Take my hand. Does it hurt?" She shook her head. Inside the house the telephone rang. Lewis grunted. "It's that man with the deathbed; I've been half-expecting him. Now that it's dark he wants to go down in the canyon in a hurry."

"You wouldn't take a chopper in there at night?"

"The wind currents would probably be better. Don't look like that, Chan. Of course I'm not going. I'll get it—you take your time, go slow."

She stopped to refill a water bowl and had turned to follow when he called from the patio, "Chan? It's for you."

Right away she was certain a horse had fractured Hunt's skull; no, his pet wolf was loose and the ranchers had formed a posse—he was doing some brave, outdated thing as a consequence. Despite the hip she began running. "Who? Did they say?" Lewis held back the door. She hurried across his Navajo rugs remembering the night she had stood half-asleep at the telephone trying to figure out who else was dead besides two dogs. "Hello? Yes, this is Chan Thatcher. Ranger who? I don't believe I—where?" She had to orient her thoughts with a plunge and a high swoop again to realize she was speaking to a ranger on the North Rim, not South, and that he was asking something long and complicated.

". . . maybe in the late twenties and dark haired"—(but Alice was blonde!)—"wearing blue denim shorts and a blue shirt, and apart from one business card with your name and this telephone number, nothing to help us identify—"

"Yes," Chan broke in, "I know her. Was she murdered?"

"Ma'am?" Chan changed it to "hurt." A group of three hikers, the ranger said, had found the young woman unconscious maybe one third down the North Kaibab Trail; whether she was coming up or going down nobody knew yet. A very bad case of heat prostration, maybe heatstroke; it was uncertain how long she had been lying in the sun when found. She was feverish and delirious, under medical care now, of course, and they couldn't even get a name from her yet. Just this one business card in an otherwise empty pocketbook. The number in Globe had reached a—just a minute—a Hunt Thatcher? He didn't know her. Who was she? Who should be notified?

"I said I know her—listen, she's not hurt except for the exposure? Will she be all right?" Lewis' eyebrows were jumping but Chan only wobbled one elbow in his direction.

"There's one deep cut on the forehead which may have been re-opened when she collapsed. What is her name, please?"

She whispered to Lewis, "He clubbed her!"

The ranger was adding that the boys were experienced hikers who bathed her as well as they could, then rigged two poles in a sleeping bag and packed her uptrail while the third ran ahead for help. "Who is she?"

From surprise Chan could not remember the name. "She's my cousin. Has she told you what happened?"

"Nothing coherent." Her temperature was still almost 105 degrees, though the pulse rate was slower. Doctors thought she'd been drinking liquids but not eating for several days. In the clinic the usual treatments had been applied—a cold enema, ice packs; probably she'd had glucose intravenously by now. "If I could have her full name?"

Chan was trying to recall their talk in the shower room, Green, or was that her hometown, Green something? "It's Nancy," she said to prod her own memory. "She's from North Carolina. I can come over there tomorrow." Lewis was putting a pencil and paper by the telephone.

"Nancy who?"

"Thatcher, of course!" she said impatiently. "I'll get a private flight, helicopter, something." Lewis nodded. "Where did they take her?"

"Would it be better, then, if you called her closest relatives rather than we?" Very cautiously Chan agreed that this would probably be better, though she did not actually promise she would call.

Once you've seen Miss Thatcher—it is Miss?—you'll give us full information for the report?" Yes. Chan slapped the air for Lewis' attention; he could fly her? She copied the ranger's instructions on the pad. "And you're sure nobody was with her?"

The ranger's voice grew sharper. "Was anyone supposed to be?"

"No, no. It's just that I told her to find a companion before she started down Bright Angel in this heat."   .

He sounded angry. "You should have told her a good deal more than that. She didn't have the equipment for a backyard sunbath much less a cross-canyon hike." She heard him telling someone else that evidently the poor woman had hiked down as well as up!

"She was buying equipment."

"If she did it's back on the trail somewhere and nobody has turned in anything. I tell you she had one empty pocketbook when the boys found her."

"That's not my fault," said Chan tartly. "I'll be there early tomorrow morning." Lewis was nodding again. "Listen, if a man wants to see her, don't you let him. Wait till I get there."

"What's that? You'll have to be more specific, Mrs. Thatcher. Your cousin did not check in at south headquarters—I've already inquired—so I hope you'll explain to her family that the Park Service cannot be held responsible for bad judgment in this matter. Now, who do you think may be looking for her?"

"Newsman, I said newsman. Her family would want no publicity. Will she be able to travel?"

"Not for forty-eight hours at the earliest," he said. "Much depends on how she feels tomorrow. She's very sick, dehydrated, very badly burned. You should tell her family that."

"I'm sorry it happened. Thank you for being so kind," she said meekly.

As she hung up Lewis said, "You're in the thick of something, if that's the girl you sneaked out of Williams. Why didn't you just tell him that?"

"I would have, Lewis, but at first it was such a surprise and then he kept talking so—he seemed to blame me for letting her do such a dumb thing. You know I'm no good when people fuss. I even forgot her name. Even if I'd remembered, she went to a lot of trouble not to be recognized, even emptied out her pocketbook."

"All the more reason not to adopt her. Maybe she's the kidnapper—did you ever think of that? Maybe she left a victim in a burning car someplace! Maybe the F.B.I. is looking for her."

Chan dropped among sofa cushions saying she needed a drink. She listened to his noises at the bar while staring into the huge black fireplace. "Lewis, her pocketbook was so full of something that the zipper was bent out, and I left her at that big store that sells everything. Why would she go down with no more than that unless she was running?"

"She could be, for instance, a mental case who took you in with that story—not that it was much of a story."

"Greenway, that's it. Where's your atlas?" She took the wet glass but didn't drink. "It's some kind of bird—her last name. I was going to remember it by remembering she had flown out of her gilded cage."

They looked up North Carolina, where the town was listed, population 4200, but too small to appear on the state map. "If she hadn't said details like her hometown, I'd think amnesia. Nancy Jay. Crowe. Nancy Martin? That man was so irritated! I never expected a call like that."

Lewis sat with his own drink on the couch. "I don't even believe amnesia exists. I don't think people back in history ever got it before the suggestion was made." He thumped the atlas. "She could be from five hundred other towns. Nancy Swift? Parrot? I've got it. Nancy Robbins!"

"You're right; if I'd told him the truth, they could have handled the whole thing." She shook her head. "I've blanked out on the name."

"Right. Nancy Crain? Would you rather drive over or fly?"

"Fly. Thank you, Lewis."

"Nancy Oriole," he tried. And once in the night he woke her with a shake and said, "What about Nancy Plover?"

That was about two a.m. At three she woke him. "I've decided we'd better drive and take the trailer. We can bring her back in bed if that's necessary."

He flapped and blurbled until his mind was working. "Why would we bring her back?"

"Because there's nobody else, of course; she's a stranger here."

"When you take a bird out of the bush into your hand . . ." he said, pleased to be so clever when half asleep. "What about Lark? Dove? If you'll think a minute you'll know you can't put a woman with heat-stroke into a trailer that isn't even air-conditioned and drag her through more high temperatures for hours on end. Besides, I thought they said forty-eight hours at the earliest."

"With you driving," she wheedled, "I can ride in the back and keep sponging her off. If I'd brought her to you in the first place, this wouldn't have happened."

"That's true." He grunted. But he added that if he met this bird woman it would be strictly to save Chan from herself; he hoped she understood that. "She won't take me in with some cock-and-bull story. Cock? Hen? Nancy Gosling?"

"A smaller bird," she said. As a result they were both lying awake visualizing kinglets and chickadees when the telephone rang at three-thirty. "Oh Father, what if she's died?" Chan groaned as she stumbled toward it. "Hello?" She spread herself, appalled, against the wall when the telephone said in her ear, "Mother? Is that you? What are you doing there?"

"Certainly a surprise," she breathed.

"I was calling Lewis because I had a funny telephone call early this evening and I couldn't sleep—Mother?"

"Just a cough, Hunt," she said, making his name very loud. Lewis sat up in bed and decided to join her. "We were out so late I just decided—" Well, this was ridiculous. She said in a furious voice, "Do you want to speak to Lewis or not?"

"I guess so."

She banged the telephone into Lewis' chest. "Tell him whatever you please," she whispered. What Lewis told him was that a night this hot was far too hot to sleep; it was a shame Hunt could not be in Valle with him and Chan for the bacon and eggs she was fixing. They'd been up late with a sick dog, he said.

"I thought it might be a sick woman after I got this call from the North Rim—somebody found half-dead with Mother's name in her pocket?"

"You know how your mother is always taking in orphans."

"I'd come by to feed her dogs and water her plants when they called—she's not going over there, is she, Lewis? You wouldn't let her get too involved?"

"That's why I'm going along."

"You remember that guitar player she bailed out of jail? The motorcycle freaks who camped out back for a week? Remember the Mexican with the allergies?"

"I said I would see to it, Hunt." In a few minutes Lewis summarized everything they knew about the woman who was so sick across the canyon, Nancy Dove or Shearer or something. "Yes, Hunt. I promise I will. Your mother wants to speak to you again."

Chan stood like a soldier and made her announcement. "Hunt Thatcher, Lewis and I are . . . we are . . . we are not platonic."

To her surprise he laughed. "I wondered how long before you told me. My felicitations."

"You're not upset?"

"No, ma'am." The politeness seemed contradictory.

"Why aren't you surprised at least?"

"Because you've always had a secret life. This is just one more part of it."

"So you didn't know."

There was a silence. "Now that I think about it, I did know. Will you stop worrying? I don't feel shocked and I don't feel critical. Maybe a little . . ."

Surprised, she thought. Amused? "You thought I was too old and too good?"

He waited before saying, "You won't force me to fight with you. I like Lewis, Mother, and I love you."

"I love you, Hunt." She was pressing the heel of one hand against her forehead, wondering what the mother he loved was like, whether the son she loved bore much resemblance to the way he saw himself. "I love you more than you know."

"Good night then, Mother. Listen to Lewis, now, and don't mortgage the house or anything."

In bed she would touch no more of Lewis than his hands, but lay on the edge of the mattress staring down, down, down at the black floor and trying to decide whether to cry or not.

When Chan woke at six, Lewis was already up, dressed, and busy. Crisply he explained that at the field they were padding the narrow foot space in the back of a helicopter, not much of a bed, but any woman whose knees would still bend could lie down there for a short trip. A friend would bring a car when they touched down above Kaibab Lodge, where they were to eat breakfast. The dogs had been fed.

"This is all strictly to reassure you," he finished, "and not because I really intend to bring her back here. Did you get any sleep?"

"I think so." Without even coffee Chan put on the only dress she had brought to Valle and finished closing its buttons in his station wagon. "Do you still want to make an honest woman out of me?"

"You're too damn honest already."

"There's no need to drive so fast. It's just like you to complain and complain and fight the whole thing and then take over and run it."

"She's still not coherent," he said, driving. "I talked to her doctor."

"At six a.m.?"

"Five. She was definitely hiking up to the North Rim. They've found food downtrail where she left it." He eyed Chan. "What they found closest to where she passed out was lipstick and birth control pills. The trash detail picked them up close together along with two dollar bills in the brush. They *said* only two."

"She had more money than that, but it's a big place." It began to seem to her like a mundane love affair, almost as mundane as she and Lewis must seem to her son. "Did they do a rabbit test?"

"I'm sure they never thought of it. Let me tell you one thing—if you marry me, it's to be because of you and because of me. Not Hunt. Clear?"

"Clear." But now she felt rebuked by both men, as if she could not win for losing. She stared straight ahead and fixed her mind on the canyon to come. She could visualize it (1) in the bottom or (2) off the rim or (3) far below an airplane window—what she had never been able to do was fuse those vantages, keep all three functioning at once, and see it steadily and whole. When she almost glimpsed that entity with its great levels joined, something in her mind would rebel and cast the vision out; she thought the human imagination, like the optic nerve, could not sustain such a view.

"Now when we get there," said Lewis as they parked, "let me talk to her. I'll soon have the truth out of her."

"You think I should call Hunt before we take off?"

"No. Do you?" He watched her. "And say what?" They crossed the landing field. "Maybe I ought to try talking to him."

"And *you* say what?"

After Lewis had lifted off the helicopter smoothly Chan watched their dust cloud spread and settle. This first noisy rise always seemed jerky, as if the machine yanked itself up overhand on an invisible ladder; then he leveled off north above uneven land that gave way to dark and chunky treetops. To the far east broke the great ragged gash through its bas-relief map, looking gray in the morning light. From this height the canyon's mountains were aligned as almost identical receding pyramids, each the same rose gray, with the toy river blue from this distance. Any sweeping view would shrink the canyon safely down to a small ingenious labyrinth that some trickster by reflection had falsely doubled in size. Though Chan tried, she could not call to mind the shocking abyss off Mather Point, nor the look of the land upward from Tanner Rapids.

Lewis shouted as the village roofs appeared underneath, the high chimneys of the oldest hotels. Then they flew over the rim. As usual, her stomach dropped into it.

To please her, Lewis always lowered them inside its walls. For all of a minute everything was lovely—these first stone turrets, a yellow cliff backed by a red with a brown one behind; but almost instantly the hot air bounced their craft so hard that any one of a thousand projections might shear off their rotor blade or shatter the helicopter's tail. Cliffs loomed and seemed to rush toward the windshield. She thought of Nancy on foot in this arid and dangerous beauty—and Hunt, of course.

When Chan signaled thumbs-up Lewis took them higher so slowly and in such lazy swirls and spirals that the whole canyon spun. Now they flew straight ahead and seemed likely to smash into the North Rim under its edge. At the last minute as if on a lucky breeze they hopped up to miss it and climbed into morning sun.

The North was higher, cooler, greener with forest than the South rim. Two cars waited where Lewis set down. He helped Chan through clouds of stinging sand to shake hands with two men who quickly left in the second car. Lewis said they were old friends. Often he gave the impression of being a former gunfighter, a retired Mafia man. "I've got some other friends asking around in North Carolina about this con woman."

Knowing what he wanted to hear, she said, "You're still pretty good handling that chopper," as Lewis pulled onto the road toward House Rock.

"I'm the best," he said, "for a while yet. You look just as scared as the first time I took you over."

"There's always a scream in my throat, but it isn't fear."

He said, "Sometimes I take a Cessna down where the river is wide enough to buzz the riverboats. . . . It's a fool thing to do," he added with satisfaction. At breakfast when she grew preoccupied, he took her hand to say, "Look, I'll move down to Globe if that's the only way."

It wasn't, of course. "I'm acting like a schoolgirl who got caught."

After breakfast they found the small clinic, basically a first-aid and emergency station with one private room and a hallway of cots. Nancy was in the private room with the door closed. Doctors said she still talked deliriously of falling and death.

In the hall Lewis told Chan again to let him do all the talking. "But if she contradicts anything she's already said, you let me know. Touch your hair or something."

"This is silly, this spy stuff, and she's out of her head anyway."

"It's a good time to get the truth. If I seem to browbeat her, you hear me out," Lewis warned. He stepped ahead of Chan and opened the door.

Poor Lewis.

He could not know that when Nancy Finch was eleven her grandfather—a very tall man—had been much his same age and size, had also been burned to brick color though by a southern sun, was seamed down both cheeks in much the same way, and had then only a little more gray in his hair. He had died in that year. To Nancy he would always look exactly thus—neither older nor younger, no more and no less accurate a rendering than anyone else's last-known photograph.

Now the sickroom door opened on someone the grandfather's shape, height, age, coloring. Her fever was high. Both inflamed eyes stung when tears made the man even more indistinct. Nancy smiled. She whispered, "I thought you were gone." She opened her arms.

PART
3

15

In 1876, after almost 5000 unwilling Apaches had been forced into the worthless San Carlos country, where a ring of harsh mountains could form their natural prison, a silver strike was made on their reservation. Just inside its western boundary white men found a boulder of almost pure silver, shaped like a globe, its surface scarred with a resemblance of the outlines of all earth's continents. This may be legend; the replica did not survive the smelter.

The silver boom brought Globe, Arizona, into tent-and-shack existence along Pinal Creek in violation of treaty and at the Indians' expense. Rich copper deposits later turned it into a western boom town. Besh-ba-Gowah—the metal village—was the name Apaches gave the stolen land with its growing businesses and hills of waste. By the turn of the century most American copper coins were minted from bullion produced in Globe by Old Dominion Copper Mine, one of the largest in the world.

When Richard and Chan Thatcher moved to Globe those diggings ran deep into lower-grade ore and below twenty-seven levels the water kept seeping in. New mines competed just seven miles away in Miami. By then the town had survived a bitter union strike and two years of army occupation under martial law. At last Old Dominion, closed by the depression and never again to be a great producer, sucked the last water from Pinal Creek into its wandering shafts and ended as Globe's fortuitous municipal reservoir. Thereafter Richard commuted the seven miles to Miami. And the nearby Apaches, once the west's most warlike tribe, who had long since buried Cochise and Geronimo, saw their descendants become cattlemen and truck gardeners.

"Globe?" Lewis complained when they had lifted off the North Rim with their patient mumbling in the back. "Even your trailer's up here. I don't see why we have to take her all the way to Globe!"

"Because I've got everything there the doctors advised for looking after a sick woman." Chan's guest bedroom had been home to Richard's mother the last five years she was home to a burgeoning cancer. "I've even kept Mother Thatcher's bedpans and her old wheelchair."

"I'm glad you got some benefit after nearly killing yourself serving that ill-tempered old woman."

"She tried my soul."

"She tried souls in a radius of fifty miles."

"I meant that for one of the benefits, Lewis, and you know it."

They continued to argue at the airfield in Valle. Soon Lewis went to the telephone and canceled a profitable charter so he could commandeer one of the planes. He stood to one side watching his men shift a delirious Nancy out of the helicopter and onto the new mattress, thinking glumly that now Hunt would have two reasons to blame him.

"Rocks," Nancy murmured as the stretcher was carried by. "All those rocks! But he didn't miss." She raised her head to look back at Lewis while they maneuvered the stretcher onto the wing. "I wish you'd been there!" she called.

He went forward to help them fold down the seat and ease her onto the braced mattress in the back, returned to Chan shaking his head. "I don't know. It's me she notices—not you. She seems to know me."

"Otherwise the doctor would never have taken us for family," said Chan drily. "But that's all the more reason you'll stay in Globe a few days, won't you? She trusts you and she's forgotten me."

"What about Hunt?"

"One thing at a time," Chan said.

"And here's one of the things we're going to settle at *this* time—that I'm not going to pretend to stay at a motel anymore and you're not going to pretend that in Valle you sleep in your damned trailer."

"Clear," she said, trying not to think of fellow Methodists as he helped her into the plane.

Much as Lewis loved flying, it scared him to have Chan for a passenger, to brace her small elbow and support the weight of a mouse and settle it into the front seat. He fussed with her seat belt. He slammed the door, opened it, slammed it again. He made her test the lock. He had never meant to stake so much affection on anything so mortal and frail at an age when every day could be his final bonus.

They talked little on the flight, his concentration fiercely determined to get her safely to ground. The van marked HUNT THATCHER, FARRIER was parked at the landing field outside Globe. As he came in low Chan shouted above the engines, "I thought you were renting one!"

Lewis did not answer until after he had landed the plane without bruising her and had taxied closer to the man who waited, shading his eyes. "He isn't your husband."

In the back Nancy said to no one, "Did I fall? Was it my turn to fall?" She paid no attention to Chan's murmurings, but when Lewis reached back to touch one shoulder she seemed to fall asleep.

Hunt came forward to open his mother's door. The two stared, as if much looking would wear the other's face to transparency. Hunt called past her, "Good flight?" Lewis said it was bumpy. "And this is the victim?" His voice took a drop. "You sure she should be out of the hospital?" Even after helping Chan out, he balanced on the step to look again at the woman with the head bandage. "She's unconscious. You still don't know her name?"

"In the hospital records she's Nancy Thatcher," Lewis said drily.

"I see you kept Mother from getting involved."

Lewis could not decide whether or not the words were double-edged.

Hunt backed the van close and the two men slid the stretcher onto padding spread in the van. "Every bit of friction must cost her some skin," Hunt said as he looked through the open doors at Nancy's bruised and peeling face. "I expected her to be awake and stronger. What if she rolls?"

Chan said she'd ride in the back but Lewis with a glare said, no, she would naturally ride up front with her *son* and he would stay with Miss Starling. He took his seat on a toolbox listening to Chan explain about bird names while Hunt drove them slowly toward town. "It's some small bird."

"Peewee," Hunt suggested.

Lewis thought they both sounded stiff and polite exchanging news about the dogs, a letter from Alice, what drought had done to Chan's late tomato plants.

"So I had to have Tanner shipped overland; there wasn't room," she was saying. "Did your new mare come?"

"And she's no more in foal than I am." They drove along Ice House Canyon Road to the Thatcher home, where, at Chan's suggestion, he backed across some of those tomato plants to a patio entrance. "The sheets looked clean enough to me," Hunt said, fishing out keys he had kept for her. He caught her hand. "You should have left all this to the Park Service, of course."

She let her hand rest limp while she said firmly, "What's done is done." They looked alike, Lewis thought, in the tense moment neither moved in the front seat.

Then Hunt said, "By the way, you've never looked better. Maybe you've changed your hair?" Their hands were still locked on the key case when he leaned forward awkwardly and gave her a hug. "I'm glad to see you."

"I'm gladder," said Chan with her eyes closed. She hurried off to check the bedsheets herself while the men carried Nancy into the house, down the hall and through the long living room with its belligerent elk's head, and into the room Mother Thatcher had used—in Lewis' opinion—as a spider uses the center of her web.

The feverish woman moaned when they slipped her onto the bed and said it was falling, Beck was falling, London Bridge was falling down. "Go on out, I want to get her into a different gown," Chan said. "You're in my house, Nancy. House. In a house."

And the House of Usher was falling down, Nancy said back.

• • •

Lewis followed Hunt into the long low living room full of book-shelves, photographs, dog show trophies. Over the stone fireplace hung a stuffed elk's head whose golden and vengeful stare still resented death. This part of the sprawling adobe and timber house was all stone with a long stone and cushioned bench built the full length of its back wall.

Hunt dropped onto that bench and looked out the long window. "Mother's limping."

"This time of day she always does." Lewis was thinking that years ago he had come through this room, through a hall and then a dining room, not knowing that ahead in the kitchen his Fate was stirring soup. The elk had been alive then.

There were no paintings in this room nor anywhere in the house. Richard had disliked their extravagance, whether they distorted or abandoned Nature. No phonograph—Chan said music clogged up her mind with sound until thought became impossible. The elongated window that ran just above the stone bench showed another paved patio along the edge of a rocky gulch. Beyond rose the mountains, "the only mural anybody needs to look at."

"Are you sure that woman's really unconscious? She's found the softest touch in the west so she could be faking it."

"I read her chart, Hunt. The fever's high enough to justify delirium." He was thinking that it should be obvious to Chan why he could not move to Globe and into his friend Dick Thatcher's house, that for him it would be genuinely haunted. He walked nervously under the elk's head to get away from its yellow stare.

Noticing, Hunt said, "That's right. You shot it, didn't you?"

"No. Your father shot it." He and Dick had stalked the cold Hualpai mountainsides in the only way that works, deer-fashion—a few steps forward, a long patient survey of winter terrain, another slow cadence of steps and another expectant sweep which would spot any flip of a tail, that twitching V inside a restless ear, even the smallest white spot which might move against that white field.

"I was in college then."

"No, just out. Your father said he couldn't persuade you to come."

Only old friends know how to move evenly as partners, only one friend was left to remember the small elk herd from which this five-point bull had slowly raised this great head and looked steadily back at them, not with the present manufactured glare but a gaze calm enough to measure just how much danger was standing there in the snow. The elk weighed over six hundred pounds yet every movement including its last plunge uphill seemed delicate.

"He always said it was your elk."

"He brought him down. I think I fired the killing shot." The nearby gun rack probably still held the very .300 Savage Dick Thatcher had fired. Afterward they had not shot into the brown explosion of the other fleeing elk nor, at first, even walked to where this one fell. The kinship of death, the hazard of who did the killing or dying at any particular moment, suspended them both. Then Dick yelled in celebration and both men ran forward and knelt where the snow was turning red. The elk thrashed and Dick told him to finish it.

Though under the elk's head hazard overhung him again, Lewis thought even the taxidermist's glass eye might be easier to face than the examination Hunt now gave him—his face only briefly, then long speculations down the limbs and trunk. Hunt's black eyes were flat as an Indian's.

"When are you leaving?"

"I'll stay on a few days." With the elk's rubbery nostrils behind one shoulder Lewis made his face innocent, harmless, but he could not quite meet the black eyes before him. Instead he looked at the roof of the Busy House downhill, so named because when Hunt and Alice were small and their mother could not be found, someone would mutter, "Busy," and point toward that tile roof. Once a bunkhouse, it was full of the leftovers from years of Chan's enthusiasms—a weaving frame, pottery wheel, stacked animal cages against the door to a dusty darkroom, machinery to cut and polish gemstones, clay pots of calcified house plants, a leaning metal detector whose corroded batteries had stopped oozing, woodworking tools, electric kiln, miner's gold pans.

"If she's not faking, that woman will be here a week or more."

"And I'll stay as long as Chan wants me to." He was remembering how one winter a red-tailed hawk had knit his wing bones in the Busy House while shitting all over Chan's wire dress form and clawing the heavy wardrobe she had been planning to refinish since 1951. Here, too, she had kept for some months a Mexican with food allergies who had to live off soybean milk substitute. She had found him in the bus station. Like the motorcyclists and the teenage kleptomaniac, he had been a project undertaken after Chan's float trip down the Colorado.

Hunt, too, gave the roof of the Busy House an accusing stare and said, "Mother's got another one."

Lewis nodded while his heart (or maybe a touch of indigestion) tweaked his chest once. He was always on guard lest Chan's good works be too contagious. Sometimes after one of her visits he would rush out to the Red Cross and donate blood—if you weren't careful, where might such generosity lead? So he said in a hurry, "Last time I was in Denver I saw Ilene."

"At the V.D. clinic?"

"Now see here, it's time you got over that woman," Lewis said. "Don't interrupt—I know you're not living a monk's life out there no matter what Chan believes, and now you know she's no nun, but you might as well sleep in the city dump from what I hear about your taste." His superior taste, said the silence, was for Hunt's mother. He said defensively, "I've been asking Chan to marry me for three years."

"Oh, Lewis, I know you and I've realized that. Underneath I've realized everything, but you don't pay good attention to other people when you're feeling sorry for yourself."

The moment seemed so fragile that Lewis went straight to the window himself so they could look at something together with reduced embarrassment.

"Ilene's all right?"

"She never will be. You know that." Lewis looked beyond the Busy House to the Pinal Mountains. "I didn't know you were sending her money—the judge didn't award her a dime and she's got a good job." Hunt said nothing. "And I apologize for that crack about the city dump. You've been dating a schoolteacher from Peridot, I'm told."

"You get told a lot."

"She's Apache?"

"Mostly Apache. I met her shoeing horses on the reservation."

Lewis was trying to figure out how to suggest he marry the girl so Chan would marry *him* when Chan carried in a basin and sponge and set them on a hassock. "Nancy's asleep and still talking to people nobody else can see. Sometimes she calls out that she had to, she couldn't help it."

"What's under the bandage?" asked Hunt.

"Five stitches, right through the eyebrow. That's not too bad—you can fill it in with eyebrow pencil, but you can't paint in an eye." She lifted her head like a dog catching a sudden scent. "What's going on in here with you two?"

"Nothing," said Lewis and, simultaneously, "Good conversation," from Hunt. "I was telling Lewis it's good he can stay a few days or else I would have moved in myself to protect you."

"Oh," said Chan, smiling. "Stay for dinner." Lewis watched her face bloom into that smile, thinking that if there was anything to Freud, sister Alice should by now have an envious ruin for a psyche.

While Chan went to the kitchen, he and Hunt paused to look into the guest room at Nancy's bruised and burned face on the white pillow. In a clear childish voice she was giving a recitation to the walls though her eyes were closed. Lewis caught it on the second repetition. "From morn to noon he fell, from noon to dewy eve." She said it over and over in treble singsong. The words sounded familiar.

"Is that Mother Goose?" he asked.

"No." Hunt stood in the doorway, frowning, until Lewis called him to have a Scotch.

The delirium of heatstroke is one long hot current of dreaming on which (1) memories, (2) fantasies, and (3) real events float dreaming by. It washed up a feverish Nancy onto the high bed where Chan's mother-in-law had died. Sometimes its ornate headboard leaned into her sight, an impending avalanche of dark pineapples, so she went to the tropics where Oliver was running around in a loincloth. Often when Chan heard her speaking to phantoms, Nancy behind closed eyes was trying to separate the real Oliver (3) from the man climbing the coconut palm (2). And some of her dreams contained so little verifiable fact that she felt like Samuel, who rose from his dreams and responded to Eli, who had not called.

Eighth grade science. Miss Hendrix asked for a creative paper, giving these examples: "Is being in a cocoon like live burial?" "One day in the life of a mole or wildebeest."
Near-plagiarisms of Peter Rabbit were the typical result.
Nancy, who already had a premonition that without much luck or much effort she would end up ordinary, labored on hers for weeks. She chipped her way out of eggshells. She became Popocatepetl and rose smoldering through a farmer's field. She personified a thinking reed from the Nutcracker Suite *who, in the final surprise paragraph, metamorphosed into papyrus.*
Then at great speed, dazzled by the sudden blaze of Ultimate System seen as panorama, she started on her real paper. Perhaps she was a prodigy! All birds are fragments of Bird, she scribbled rapidly; only one Giant Bird is alive in the world on any given day. The same held true for Dog, Monkey, Man—each individual was a cell in a single planetary organism.
She chewed her pencil eraser. Therefore, Noah naturally needed only one male and one female of each to restart zoology after the flood! She worked on details and with pride presented the finished essay to the ghost of her grandfather, intending that he should react in the style of Pierre Curie. "That's awful," he said in the old way.
"And why stop there?" He insisted on spitting his unforgettable tobacco juice. He went on to ask why not have only one creature in the world altogether? With bugs for the worldwide feet and so on until men constituted parts of the worldwide brain, seeing as men were the best candidates available. "And he's God? Slow-witted, maybe, but God?"
"That's awful," said Nancy.
"If you're going to improve on your common sense," he said, "you might as well go whole hog." Mostly real (3). Her grade on the volcano paper was B.

• • •

She had stowed away on the Ipswich before it sailed past Lady Liberty. The captain, who had climbed Fujiyama and the Matterhorn, swum the Hellespont, and hunted Bengal tigers, had secretly admitted that Nancy was his illegitimate child; but he could only, at sunset, throw tinned sardines to her under the lifeboat cover, as he must not endanger her mother's reputation. She was discovered; the captain pretended ignorance and ordered her thrown in the brig. Animals caught on his travels were penned in the same quarters, hard to identify in the dark but large. Many had tunneled to other parts of the ship and fed there in secret. They could be at home anywhere. Some, she knew, entered the ocean at night and returned to the ship at dawn, full and satisfied.

Invented (2). Though the captain, except for his paunch, was a ringer for Richard Halliburton.

Age nine. Her father's coffin was in the front parlor.
Mother: "He never gave me a minute's trouble."
(1).
She would not let the memory progress to the moment of standing on the box with Beckham for she did not want to fall; she did not like to think of falling; she hated the sound of the word.

A small gray-haired woman fed Nancy salted soups. She bit the thermometer; mercury ran down her throat burning. She melted the snowfield they rolled her across. Her grandfather, or maybe his emissary, stood by the bed. Her age was uncertain and changeable. She managed to say, "You're not from Heaven, are you?"
For her sake he hated to answer. "No," he said, "I am not."
Did this happen by her sickbed or not?

She was a Blackfoot woman by the Teton River, walking by that very water where Old Man rested from so much work of creation. And she said to him, "Will we always live here, with no end to it?" Old Man had never thought of this; he offered her a bargain. He would throw into the water a buffalo chip and, if it floated, the dead would always arise after four days' sleep; but if it sank their deaths *would last forever. Then Nancy turned from him and chose instead a stone to throw, saying in Blackfoot language that if the stone floated all would live forever; if it sank in the river, people must die and— knowing that—be always sorry for one another. And threw the stone.*

When after that one she lay half-awake, Nancy knew she had read the story somewhere in Stone County Library, knew it was true. Was able to remember the Navajo story as well, in which she had climbed with the others through that hole in Earth's center behind Begochiddy, remembered how she had blinked to find everything in place but immobile. On all sides the Earth, Sky, Sun, and Moon stood still; Coyote said they were waiting for someone to die. Then the first man died and the Earth, Sky, Sun, and Moon moved out along their appointed paths. The Sun said he was always glad when death came, because death was what kept him moving; and he slid behind the people and shortened their shadows on the hot sand.

Yes, they were real, both those dreams. Real.

The truth was, her grandfather had always thought Leon Finch a weakling. It was a family story that once when he came in from treating Buck's sores in the barn and found Leon out on the porch courting his daughter he said to Grandmother in a very loud voice, "That mule is sicker than I thought. They've sent for the next of kin." Memory (1). True.

Church. Age ten. If Nancy knew, error-free, the most memory work, they would give her a week of more memory work at camp in the mountains. She was ready, could breathe out the Psalms in her sleep. Twenty-three. One hundred. Rivers of Babylon. Corinthians 13. Luke 2. Isaiah 53. Exodus 20. Given a key phrase she recited the full verse and reference. Before the congregation she listed the books of both Testaments, the Tribes, the Major and Minor Prophets, the Kings, the Apostles. She traced the lineage of Jesus, with variants. Only three girls had missed nothing when both catechisms were brought out, only two when they opened the harder one.

Waiting her turn for the next question, Nancy saw a strange and in-

tense expression spreading across faces in the congregation. It multi-plied there while she kept rattling answers easily forth. Their faces changed as if the audience was affected by meanings she did not know she had spoken. These rolling sentences in her mouth were, said their faces, as much truth as Nancy was old enough yet to bear. Adam and Eve and the Fall—she did not like that word—and her ready-made sinfulness: what could be worse than these? Something was.

She omitted a word and Sue Witherspoon won the prize. Nancy got another Bible.

This one was true up to the part where Nancy and Alice went down the rabbithole to find the omitted word.

Seventeen. The car's back seat was much too short for comfort. No good at all. If babies come out crying it's because their memory goes all the way back to this. The threat of disease showed itself in a hickey on Alfred's chin.

(1).

Not the last one, Thank God!

She was back in front of the church assembly again and it was time to admit that David had hit him with a black rock in his sling, but she felt too sick to answer the question.

?

Eleven. The big year. Beckham was slow in school. Nancy had even heard one teacher say, "If you let Beck Finch go out for recess he'll have to start the whole grade over." The teacher visited Nancy's mother and discussed Beckham's slowness with greater tact. Mrs. Finch cried. She began a campaign to prevent the girls' showing off at their brother's expense. Nancy ran off on a Greyhound bus the full six miles to the farm, and over the footlog where she could be herself. Grandfather drove her back. "You just do. Stop asking me why."

Yet, maybe for Beckham's sake, maybe because a widow's pension was small, her mother sent her again to the farm when school was out and she stayed until January. He lived alone; Nancy did not remember her grandmother. He allowed her to drink coffee. He only cooked one dish per meal but they had to eat it all. He complained that Nancy was so skinny she would have to run around in a rainstorm to get wet.

Eleven. The last year of his life. Surely he had taught her important lessons that year; certainly. Hundreds. Happiness made her mind a sieve. She could recall not one serious talk, only the regular days and their steady routines and chores through which she trotted beside him, radiant without cause.

At twelve she stormed at his ghost for never once saying he loved her or making her say it too. He kept taking off Nestor's robe. "No, and I'll not tell you now. Baby talk."

A man with a mustache and black eyes stood over her with his arms folded. "You have taken in my mother," he said, "and she has taken in Lewis, but I'm telling you three days is your limit here."

She might be inside the whale?

"I've hiked in that canyon," he said, "and the trip is not that bad, especially on that trail—unless you're stupid."

She did not want to think about canyons, where even the shadow of death was hot. Moby Dick was cool and white.

"Personally I think you're a clever actress. Go ahead, change my mind like the others', say something soft and sweet."

"Marshmallow?"

What category was this?

Eleven. She was with him when he died. Had gone into Greenway to spend Christmas holidays, which lasted too long, and was glad to be back on the farm and riding that orange bus to the rural school where she could outread everybody.

They had gone to the stable at night in case Chinchy's calf had come. Maybe by morning. The calf might be small like its mother, who had been no bigger than a chinch bug herself.

On the edge of the feedlot her grandfather fell without warning across the top strand of barbwire. He was big. Nancy could not unfold him though he was still alive, merely hung in abnormal sleep. If she did not run for help he would die; if she left he would die all alone. Finally she ran to escape from the hopeless effort of trying and trying to drag him off the fence, ran through the dark pasture, over the footlog and fence and highway and beat on the door of the nearest house.

Flake Woodward and two boys came in a car. He had not died yet but as soon as they got him inside the hospital he did, and left her in the hall. A stroke. What struck him?

Her mother, the aunts, the crying and questions. She knew he was scratched on the outside of his heart from all the times she had tried to pull him off the wire barbs. (Like who? Who? Nobody living, she thought.)

Faye and Beckham had each brought a toy to the hospital.

In the waiting room she tried very hard to faint but could not. Her grandfather hated to see Nancy faint. The one time she had hoed her own foot and almost did he had shaken her out of it until the lighted space in which she was almost loose turned solid, and rattled on all sides and fell out in the corn rows as fieldstones and clods lying right by her open eyes.

When he was doubled over the fence Nancy kept shaking him, too, but he did not come back.

This dream was surely invented.

Nancy called for the man resting in Abraham's bosom to come down and lay a drop of water on her burning tongue, but because Lazarus was keeping his ear cocked in case he should be called forth from the dead, he could not hear her voice.

Then she called Abraham himself but he was busy trying to make Lazarus hold still and be quiet in case angels were at his door unaware.

She opened her mouth; yes, she had a tongue of fire when it wasn't even Pentecost. She stuck it out at them both like a torch.

"Give her some crushed ice," said Grandfather Abraham, and they relented in Purgatory and fed her pleasure in a teaspoon.

Chinchy's calf was two days old before anybody knew about it.

Since now she was thirty-four and knew it, this dream had to be a (1), yet nothing seemed real. Beside the still waters but hot as the streets of Gomorrah. Adam was pushed.

I do not like this dream and will leave it down there.

The only garment of Chan's that Nancy could wear was a green silk caftan which ended halfway down her shins.

Hunt had given it to her for Christmas. Chan said with false enthusiasm, "It looks fine!"

It would look better over her head. "Even if I can stay vertical that long, who wants to see this face at dinner?" Gingerly Nancy touched both red puffy cheeks, which were peeling. From forehead to nose, where she had landed on stones, her face was swollen in yellow and blue, her left eye sealed shut under color behind the bandage. She lurched away from the mirror. "No, I'm too dizzy to be out of bed."

"The doctor said bed itself is weakening. And we're civilized people who can avert our eyes." Chan pointed with the hairbrush.

"Let's try the left side one more time."

"My scalp will slough off."

"What we can't fix we'll cover up." Chan wound a green scarf over the dark hair and made Nancy face the mirror again.

She looked like a scarred radish. "Besides, I'm not hungry."

"At breakfast and lunch you were, come on. I want you to meet Hunt."

"If he's the one with the mustache we've already had one very confusing talk. Later I realized he meant feigning when I meant fainting."

"That's all right—Hunt's never been drawn to women with large vocabularies. But he's handsome, isn't he? Just down this hallway, now."

"He's not drawn to me at all," said Nancy. "He wants me to leave."

"That's because Hunt thinks I'm fragile and he thinks I'm a dupe. See there? Dupe—another word Ilene never heard of. We couldn't discuss anything but cosmetics." Chan held back the door before hiding her limp as she led the way into the long living room. Behind her Nancy limped unevenly on both sides. Two men turned to them from the long window with its view of darkening mountains. The older one—who seemed a longtime friend—stepped forward with a smile, but with his black eyes the younger one measured her injuries rather than regretted them. He had both a mustache and a pipe—one affectation too many, Nancy thought.

"I've told you all about Lewis McKinney, whose plane brought you from Valle." There were light scabs on the hand he shook so carefully. "And this is my son, Hunt."

Lewis was saying cheerfully that she certainly did look terrible. With a nod the younger one relit his aromatic pipe.

"We've met," he said with some sarcasm. "I'm the one you talked to about Humpty-Dumpty's great fall. And pride's, too, as I remember." She turned away quickly to stop herself from thinking of his words. "I know you, don't I?"

"Just from the plane ride," Lewis said.

She remembered no plane ride.

"I believe you said something, too, about the apple not falling far from the tree and that led you to the tree in Genesis."

"Hunt, that's enough. None of us wants to know what we said in delirium. Nancy is still weak so I've promised she can listen and not have to talk," Chan said. "She doesn't need a drink strong enough to dehydrate her, either, and I know how Lewis fixes them, so would you pour her a small sherry? It's awful to talk in third person as if you're deaf, Nancy; I'll get over that in a minute."

"I want to thank all three of you—you didn't even know me—"

"From Adam," Hunt finished as he opened a carved cabinet.

"From Eve," Nancy said with more chill than intended. Though Hunt was taller than his mother he was barely Nancy's height, with very black hair that peaked at the center line, the edges sweeping upward on each side. Bald before fifty, she thought, and why so sarcastic? The ends of his brown mustache were trimmed against any tendency to curl. He handed her the wine with a look that totaled her pounds and freckles.

"What happened down there?"

"Give her time, give her time." Lewis led her to the window. "You look south here to the Pinal Mountains, the tall one is Signal Peak."

"I don't remember everything that happened," said Nancy. As she tasted her sherry she thought that even her fingerprints were scaling off.

Chan said, "I'm gradually bringing her up to date. Maybe you'd better sit, Nancy, and put your feet up."

"Has Nancy been bringing you up to date as well?"

Though Chan's touch seemed only to move Hunt aside so she could slide an ottoman nearer, actually she pinched his arm hard. "She's barely out of bed. Stop pestering her and come help me a minute."

She yanked his sleeve. In the hall she said softly, "What's wrong with you, Hunt? And what good were your own problems if they didn't make you any kinder to other people?"

"Time somebody forced her to open up."

"Of all people you should know better than to force. Remember she doesn't know you from Adam, either."

"But she recognized Lady Bountiful on the spot, didn't she?"

"You were taught better manners—call on them now."

When he reentered the living room, Lewis was explaining that the woven frieze on the hassock was of three Yei figures standing in four longer stalks of corn. Nancy propped her bandaged feet there looking around at the elk, the crowded bookshelves, the trophy boards. Hunt asked about the sherry.

"It's wonderful. I saw your picture in Chan's trailer, didn't I?"

"Alice, too. Here they are." Lewis passed her a photograph of the two, younger, posing with a basketful of puppies. "These aren't ordinary retrievers, though, but Hunt's wolf pups."

"You raise wolves?"

"If I bore you," said Hunt, puffing on his pipe, "blame Mother. Alice treats many pet dogs, many of whom by breeding or contagion from their owners, or both, develop neurotic symptoms. It seemed obvious that if we could learn about humans from watching chimps, we could find the sources of canine behavior in the wolf. He's the closest ancestor, not the jackal, as Lorenz first said. So several years ago I got a young male wolf but because—because other things took too much time, I quit any real study. Now I own a female and serious scientific studies have already been published. I've come to like wolves, that's all."

"He listens to records of wolf pack howls."

"So they're tame?"

"With me, not strangers."

The better to eat you with, my dear. Lewis said to her, "Last time his bitch was in season Chan kept her here and from frustration *her* dogs got neurotic."

"She-wolf," Hunt corrected. "You don't call her a bitch."

Chan came back from the kitchen to ask for a drink to carry with her. "You spend too much time with those wolves and too little with people."

"They are so placid and self-contained," Nancy recited.

"Whitman?" Hunt frowned. "Isn't that Whitman?" Regretfully, she said it was. Chan had begun giggling at the bar. She was still giggling when Hunt followed her to the door and hissed, "Just what's so funny?"

"You! You're not sure," she whispered and wheezed, "that she could be a villainess and still read Whitman! Oh Hunt, Hunt! And you think I'm gullible!"

"You'll make her think we're laughing at her."

"At least you've got your manners back, you snob." She carried her Scotch down the hall, shaking her head.

But Hunt, thinking to use books to win Nancy's confidence, sat carefully by her bandaged feet on the hassock and gave her an encouraging smile. "I believe you were also quoting Milton during the fever."

She seemed to withdraw. "Was I?"

"I don't read much except history myself, especially Toynbee," Lewis put in. "Barbara Tuchman and Howard Mumford Jones, people like that." The silence grew uncomfortable. He added, to help, "Milton who?"

"Perhaps you teach literature," Hunt offered.

Nancy said no, pointing out that even a blacksmith was allowed to know Whitman and Milton. He got up and went onto the patio. She told Lewis, "He's easily offended."

"Pay no attention; he's mostly cleaning his pipe," Lewis said. "Hunt has always been devoted to Chan and at the moment he probably thinks we're both taking advantage of her." Through the glass they watched Hunt balance on one leg like a crane and knock out the pipe against his lifted shoe.

"I'm a librarian," she murmured, still watching Hunt pace outside.

"A librarian! Interesting work—did Chan say Greensboro? Oh. Greenway. All this time I've been concentrating on Greensboro thinking she got it wrong." Lewis kept nodding. "There's probably someone in Greenway we should notify."

"I'll call in the morning. Chan says he married a trashy woman."

"Hunt? Ilene thought she'd get some of his money and I guess she has. I don't know what he expected to get that she didn't already give away."

"Probably he wanted to be happy."

"But we all want to be happy."

"Oh no," said Nancy. "Some want to be successful or rich or wise or famous. Any one of those would be better."

"Better than what?" asked Chan as she joined them and set her tinkling glass on the long windowsill.

"The pursuit of happiness?" Lewis gave an uncertain shrug but she did not hear, having stepped out the doorway and closer to Hunt.

"More sherry, Nancy?" Mother and son came in together. From the bar Lewis announced, "She's a librarian, so you were close, Hunt."

"Too much time with books, too little with people," Nancy admitted.

Hunt said he'd take his wolves over books any day because "Nature triumphs over all abstractions."

"How can you say that in Arizona and mean it? And be so smug? That's not all your landscape triumphs over—why Grand Canyon alone!" She waved a peeling hand. "Grand Canyon alone is enough to—"

"Scare the pants off anybody," said Lewis with a nod while Chan was saying, "Humble you."

"In time this landscape would show you that it's beautiful," Hunt said.

"Magnificent maybe. Not beautiful." Nancy frowned at him over the sherry.

Chan began pointing out the parallel between parts of this landscape and the wilderness around Sinai and how both would have a similar effect on anyone living near those rocks, near all that desert. But the disagreement seemed to lie between Nancy and Hunt.

"Evidently," he said, "you read down the shelf to Whitman but not farther along to Wordsworth."

I'm beginning to fear he really is a snob, said Chan to herself.

"There was more excuse for Wordsworth," Nancy argued. "He saw the Lake Country and Tintern Abbey and pleasant places like that."

"He saw the Alps," said Hunt.

Well, well, she thought, come into the spider's parlor and bring your wolf along! Like a prissy librarian she said, "In *both* texts of the *Prelude* he looked at Mont Blanc as if into the open book of Nature. At first he read tenderness, but forty years later, when he was doing a version with the aid of all that recollected tranquility, he was even able to read in brotherhood. Wordsworth saw something, all right, but it wasn't the Alps." They eyed each other like wrestlers a referee has just separated.

"But you've seen the real Grand Canyon without reading into it?"

"Yes."

For no reason the other two could specify, they began smiling at each other, though the movement hurt Nancy's mouth. His smile widened and held, then he said through it, "And anybody who remembers both versions of the *Prelude* remembers everything that happened in the Grand Canyon and remembers why she was running away from Williams in the first place. Doesn't she?"

She nodded and turned away that part of her shredded face which was most discolored.

"Let's start with your name."

"But I told Chan my name! It's Finch, Nancy Finch." She eyed Hunt, wanting him to think well of her, wanting the truth postponed—no, be honest!—wanting it expunged. Chan was nodding.

"Now tell us about the gilded cage."

"What?"

"We can get the details over dinner," said Chan, rising. "If you'll help Nancy, Lewis?"

"No, Hunt is right." Nancy had not spoken his name before; she liked it. They waited. "Where to begin is the problem," said Nancy, secretly wondering where she could stop. "What day is this?"

"Sunday."

"Two weeks?" She repeated it to herself. "Two weeks. It seems as if I've been outside time." Where Dwight is, she thought. She set her wineglass on the windowsill, where it blotted out one of the foothills, then said flatly to Lewis McKinney, "If you will call your local police, please—this is Valle? Globe. Ask them to check with North Carolina.

You can report that Nancy Marie Finch, who was abducted at Wiseman's View two weeks ago today, is safe now in Arizona and able to answer their questions." With another long breath she shot a look at Hunt. "After that I had better talk directly with Mrs. Leon Finch or Mrs. Eddie Rayburn, either one, in Greenway." There. That wasn't so hard, was it? Yes. It was. Now she would go home and home would be the same while she could never be the same again.

"Right now?" asked Lewis. He got slowly to his feet when she nodded.

"Why didn't you say so in the first place?" Chan wailed. "They could have caught him by now."

"They won't catch him," Nancy said. Hunt reached past for her glass with a broad flat hand that must be calloused. "I want to get this part over with."

"Scotch or blended whiskey?" She chose Scotch.

"Make it light, as weak as Nancy is." Chan followed Lewis to the hall telephone.

"So you've had more than one terrible experience. Nancy Marie." Hunt poured and stirred her drink. "What happened to the kidnapper, Nancy Marie? Does anybody call you Nan?" She said not yet. He put the cold glass into her hand. "What happened to him, Nan?"

Her grip was weak; she went weak everywhere and had to adjust the glass to several small injuries. He had been at the campground, she said, when at last she saw a chance to steal money from him and escape. "Later I thought I saw him in the crowd at Grand Canyon and it scared me, but maybe I imagined it. I went down that trail fast, though." She drank deeply. "Was it you talking to me about Bright Angel Trail? You were right. It's stupid to panic."

He said drily. "And maybe a little out of character."

From the hall Lewis called to ask if Raleigh was her state capital. Instead of telephoning the Globe police or the Gila County sheriff, he had decided to go straight to the Arizona highway patrol.

"Did he hurt you?" Hunt reached up as if to chin himself on the elk's head antlers. She said yes, Raleigh; and no, he didn't. "Then his motive was ransom? Or he needed a hostage?"

Nancy shook her head. "He had no motives I ever understood."

"You seem very resourceful. I'm surprised you didn't hurt him."

"I wanted to." His sharp gaze was making her feel more tired by the minute. "I wish you wouldn't keep waiting like that. You can hear the whole story when the patrolman comes."

"Was he crazy?"

"I haven't been able to decide if he was sick or just evil."

"Don't let Mother hear you say *just* evil. But you never saw him again after you went down into the canyon."

Nancy took a deep draught of the Scotch and let him accept her silence as agreement. If she told everything she might have to face again not only the fact that Dwight was dead, but the barbaric pleasure with which she had watched him fall. "I wish you wouldn't stare. I can't even focus very well out of one eye."

"Do I make you nervous?" Hunt gave the elk a pat before sitting across from her.

"I'm sorry you think I've misused your mother's kindness."

"It's just that I'm allergic to the nervous martyr. I've known very well one woman whose nervous headaches occurred every night, but they could come on in daytime, too, if there was any chance of her hairstyle being disturbed or her makeup smeared." He looked as if all womankind had some disagreeable share in his memory.

Chan came in frowning. "He's having some trouble getting through and you're starting to fade, Nancy. Not feeling dizzy, are you?"

"It's just a normal helpless attack of southern womanhood before western hospitality," she said irritably.

"See?" said Hunt. "I believe that kidnapper may have been glad to see her go." As Lewis' voice rose in the hall they listened to his attempt to speak being passed from one distant desk to another, forcing new starts and repetitions. He called to Nancy, "Where's Wiseman's View? Whose jurisdiction?"

"Tell them in Linville Gorge." More softly she added that you could drop the whole Linville Wilderness off Mather Point and never hear it hit bottom.

"Fine," Lewis was saying. "Fine. Yes, that's the address." He came to the door to say that an officer would be out in half an hour. "You already look tired. Shall I go ahead with the other call?" Nancy nodded.

"She has reserves of strength," Hunt said.

"We should have fed you first," Chan said vaguely. "And you'll want to talk in private."

Now Lewis' voice came to them almost shouting. "No! No, ma'am, that's not—Nancy? Can you come here? Just a minute, I'm getting her now. No I am not!" Again he appeared in the doorway thrashing both halves of the telephone above his head. "Mrs. Rayburn thinks I'm the kidnapper himself!"

Forgetting her sore feet Nancy leaped forward and had to catch Hunt's quick outstretched arm. She refused to lean for more than an instant, bracing against the door frame to untangle the wires. "It's Nancy, yes, really. Yes, it's Nancy. Faye? Be quite a minute, Faye. No, Lewis is just a friend who had nothing—Faye? Will you listen? All right, get Eddie then. No, I won't hang up. I promise."

As hysteria faded from her right ear, Eddie's brusque voice blew in. "I knew he'd call back and he'll keep you from saying much but, my God, Nancy, give us a clue to where you are!"

Call back? "I don't understand. I'm in Globe, Arizona," she got out before he interrupted in a low, tense tone.

"I know you can only say what he's ordered but, listen, you can ask me about people by name, see? And the first letters of each name will spell the place where you are. I've been thinking about this system and it'll work."

She said patiently. "Globe. Arizona. And I'm free and police have been called. And I'm all right, Eddie; everything's fine now. Can you explain to Faye and the others?"

Aside he said, "Nancy says she's loose," and into the phone, "Arizona? The *state* of Arizona?"

"It's a long story and a long trip but I'm all right. No, not hurt at all. Let me speak to Mama."

After a long pause he whispered that if Nancy was really free, why didn't she even know whose house she had dialed? It took more time to soothe his new suspicions. Then she was telling him, "No, nobody knows for sure where the kidnapper is now. I've been through Grand Canyon, Eddie." She did not look at Hunt, who was leaning against the wall beside her.

Noise blew into her ear. "Oh, we know where he is!"

"On foot—I walked through it." She bumped her own chin with the telephone. "How can you know where he is?"

"Oklahoma City!" cried Eddie. "He called from there." Nancy's mind reeled as she visualized Dwight rising from the rocks and floating across two states. "Our police know that. Say, he took you over state lines—it's a federal crime, did you know that?" He broke off to pant, then asked with control, "Did he hurt you? Did he, uh, anything?" Nancy said he didn't. "That's good; your mother has thought the worst. What? Faye wants to know when you'll be coming home. She's been staying over there nights."

"When the police are done with me. Unless they find him right away"—she looked at Hunt—"it won't take long."

But Lewis shook his head and took the phone from her hand. "Mr. Rayburn? Lewis McKinney again. Write down this number." He read it off the plastic label. "That's the home of Mrs. Richard Thatcher. Nancy will be safe here until she feels well enough to travel, maybe another week. You can reach her—what?" Very gently he tapped the paneling with a restrained fist. "Just a little heatstroke. I said *heatstroke*. Yes, as Nancy said, a long story. I don't know that; no, sir. Now let me give you our local state police number; you might feel better if you could independently confirm that I am who I say—yes. Of course. Quite right. Nothing a little rest won't cure. I don't mind a bit; you do that." he raised his eyebrows, but Nancy shook her head that she was finished so he banged down the receiver, plainly offended. "Mr. Rayburn doesn't trust any number I might supply, says he'll have the operator place the call direct to our patrol office. I do believe he thinks I've had you staked out on the desert."

"Is that your husband?" Hunt asked. Nancy said she wasn't married.

"He wanted me to be aware," Lewis complained to Chan, "that every word I spoke had been recorded on tape for the F.B.I."

"The whole family sees too much television." Was she getting hiccups? "Where the plots always fit together." With no warning Nancy's giggle turned into crying. "I hate television," she groaned, trying to swallow. Lewis wrapped an arm around her shoulder and across raw skin. She could not stop crying. "It's so damn boring." She turned furiously to Hunt and said—perhaps she was a little drunk— "And I'll never *get* married! Not now!"

"Come on . . . shh . . . sit down." Lewis and Chan got her back to a leather chair, Chan saying, "You cry like that and your whole face is going to feel like it's on fire."

Even Hunt looked dismayed but that did not stop her from saying to him angrily, "They're real tears, not glycerin!" She snatched his proffered handkerchief and managed to gasp in a voice part wail and part squeak, "There's nothing to cry over *now!*"

"Things catch up." Having made her sit down Chan slid the ottoman under her feet. One had begun to bleed. "I keep forgetting that when they took off those moleskins half your feet came with them. I promise I won't let them question you long."

While she sniffled they stood over her, worrying, but Hunt left the room and came back carrying a plate. He was eating a steak sandwich and had brought one for Nancy. "Medium-rare, do you good." He set it into her lap. "Very few people can chew and cry at the same time." She moved it aside onto a table but again he put it on her knees saying, "Besides, I expected a librarian to have mostly those thoughts that do often lie too deep for tears."

In spite of herself a giggle got into her snuffling. She tasted the sandwich. After a first bite the size of the lump in her throat she had custody of her voice again and thanked him. "And, Chan, I'm afraid Mama will call next. I'm sorry to put you through all this."

"All what? I'll tell her the facts so you need only say a few words, enough to let her hear your voice. I understand exactly how I'd feel if Hunt had been missing. Or Alice. You don't want to be crying, though, and scare her. Now here," Chan said. "I've put in more Scotch."

It tasted good with the steak. Sniffling once, Nancy said, "Eddie's such a fool."

Lewis agreed. "And if you're crying he'll ask for Lewis McKinney dead or alive." He dropped in more ice cubes. "Nancy doesn't want to drink too much of that Scotch too fast with the police coming."

"That's why she's having a sandwich, dear. Now." Finding no further action to take, Chan perched on the sofa arm. Hunt stood at the darker window, eating.

"Please, Chan. Have your own dinner."

"In a minute." One of those silent spaces occurred, Chan on the sofa, Lewis pacing, Hunt over his half-eaten sandwich. Nancy looked at his back remembering that Joel had actually been a bit skinny. Outside a dog was barking. With great deliberation Nancy chewed. The long glass panes, which at first seemed to have turned black, slowly let show a few bulky mountains and high stars. With her good eye fixed on spaces between those stars she began mentally to go over the sequence of events since Linville Gorge. What about Judge Jolley? If he was alive, he must know that Dwight had come after her to the canyon. Dwight said he was dead. You couldn't believe Dwight.

"All right, but I'm too excited to eat anything," she heard Chan say. Nancy hardly noticed her and Lewis leave the room. The Scotch was refreshing. She felt stronger. Was Dwight's car somewhere on the South Rim? Maybe the judge had escaped, or been murdered, in Williams. Nancy put down her sandwich to count days and cities on her fingers.

Low laughter made her look away from the night sky. "It's clear why the south lost," Hunt Thatcher was saying as if to himself, though he looked at her while his mustache curled up. "All those women they left behind—so delicate, so much like Aunt Pitty Pat. Must have been demoralizing."

She started to counter with something smart-aleck about how the wild west was tamed, but what was the point? In a few more days she'd be in Greenway and all their preliminary sparring would come to neither enmity nor intimacy. She rose, finding herself more weary than expected. "I believe I'll get another sandwich."

"Might keep your strength up."

Until she was out of Hunt's sight she would not wince or lean on the furniture.

In the dining room Chan was exclaiming, "How do you manage to find out so much? And just what does this little Apache teach?"

"Art. Primary grades," said Lewis.

"Well, I'm not choosy, not anymore—just so he's satisfied. Lewis, do you think he's really satisfied?"

"Not yet. Ah, here's Nancy; let me pull out a chair." With special gallantry he seated her and passed the meat platter. "Now when your mother calls, allow for a week or two rest at least. After all," he said, smiling, "we *all* want to get to know you better, Nancy. We want to see how you look when you're well and the bandage is off, don't we? Chan?"

"Oh my!" she said, beaming. "Oh my, yes!"

Before the officers arrived Chan had the idea to fetch from the Busy House a wheelchair once used by the elder Mrs. Thatcher, "Just to reinforce how far Nancy still is from recovery."

"By all means," Hunt said mockingly. "Let me get it at once." On the patio they swiped cobwebs from the spokes and hastily scrubbed the seat. It still felt damp through Nancy's borrowed robe, which, Hunt suggested, might better have been white. An uncomfortable hour went by before Sergeant Art Hollis and Patrolman Cleo Lillagore arrived. They had been on the wire the whole time since Mr. McKinney's call, they said, hats in hand, darting quick glances at the invalid until Hunt rolled her fully into their sight and into their murmurs that she had been through so much already; yes, a pity, these circumstances; try not to tire her too much.

Everyone found chairs and Hollis sat formally on the couch and opened his notebook. "You might like to know that quite a manhunt, ah womanhunt, has been under way in your home state," he began. "After the man was so violent with the Rayburns a great deal of the Smoky Mountains Park was searched for your body. I understand that he both struck and shot at Mr. Rayburn."

Though it could make little difference Nancy said, "No. He did not."

"That so?" He made a mark. "Now the latest report indicates the kidnapper has left Arizona and made contact from Oklahoma seeking ransom money from your family."

"That doesn't sound like him at all!" said Nancy. "No. It's not possible."

"Here it is—he called them Wednesday. You had already escaped by then."

Again she counted on her fingers. Not possible. "I escaped Sunday from a campground near Williams." He wrote down place, time, their hour of departure in Mrs. Thatcher's trailer, when she had left Nancy at the supermarket at the Grand Canyon. "I must go back and tell you"—Nancy hesitated—"about Harvey Jolley, a hitchhiker he picked up in Tennessee. He was at the campground, too." More questions, her description of the judge, his Somerville origins, mild surprise at the reasons for his hitchhiking. Patrolman Lillagore asked Lewis if he could use the telephone, calling him Mr. Thatcher by mistake. Immediately Hunt led him out.

"So there's a second missing person. The kidnapper was still armed? Why didn't Mr. Jolley escape with you?"

"He was sick. We weren't able to plan anything, not being left alone together much. We tried once before, from a restaurant." He wrote those details in his book, then frowned as he balanced his hat over one knee. "I should have gone straight to the police but I didn't want to endanger Mrs. Thatcher, and afterward?" Hunt was standing in the doorway watching her. "Afterward I kept seeing him in the crowds at Grand Canyon and I panicked. At least I thought it was him." Hollis asked if she had no concern for the second kidnap victim. "I thought he'd come straight after me and then Mr. Jolley would call police. By the way, nobody's heard from the judge?" Tears washed her eyes suddenly. Perhaps two men were dead because of her. She shivered.

"You felt the kidnapper preferred . . . uh . . . did he assault you?" Hollis looked at the ceiling, adding, "In any way? Then why would he come straight after you?"

"It had to do with women in general, not just me. I can't explain him to you."

Politely the sergeant said abnormal behavior was hard for anyone to explain. "So you ran down into the canyon."

"Besides," she said, breaking sequence again, "I had stolen his money." She mentioned Dwight's sprees in Los Alamos and Texarkana, the judge a forced accomplice.

"Judge?"

"He said so—retired." She decided to leave out Bandelier and Dr. Foster. Into her preoccupied silence Lewis said anyone could see Miss Finch was still under strain.

Nancy looked brave. "I'm sorry things sound disjointed, but that store was crowded and everybody looked like him. Everything I bought is down in the canyon."

Returning from the telephone Lillagore shook his head once and sat down.

Nancy said thoughtfully, "Why did I even go down that trail at all?"

"I had given you those tourist folders," Chan prompted.

"And it wasn't dark yet. The way people were still on the path it looked like an easy place just to step out of sight and hide. I was going to hide in the tunnel."

"I've been down there; she's right," Lillagore said.

She gave him a grateful smile causing Hunt to roll his eyes. Without intent, her words were growing slower, blunter, more southern. "I only stole Eddie's money back but I knew he'd be furious to find me gone and money, too, and he could shoot from a distance so I went into the tunnel." She touched the rubber wheels of her chair and turned herself slightly to look full at Hunt. "And I had just seen the canyon for the first time. It was like wanting to touch the Ark of the Covenant."

"That part I understand," he said.

But the lawmen raised their eyebrows at each other; seeing their faces, she went back to facts. "Some boys started singing on the rim and that collected a crowd with flashlights. If he was waiting there, I couldn't come back up without being seen. So I went on down."

"You didn't ask any of these hikers for help?"

"Would you have tried explaining all this to anybody who had just climbed a mile?"

"In altitude," Lillagore said helpfully. "The trail is really longer and the top part very steep."

This time the smile she sent was caught by Hunt and deformed in midair. She moved the chair again, saying earnestly to Lillagore, "Even if one had listened, they were all too tired to help much if he was really waiting there. I was too frightened to think clearly." She ignored Hunt's coughing spell. Lewis interrupted to say there was a call for Patrolman Lillagore.

"So you went down where?"

"Well, not knowing the landmarks . . . I rested at two water fountains and the trail cleared out. There was supposed to be an oasis."

"Indian Gardens," said Chan. "You must have missed it!"

"And if you took a wrong turn there it carried you to Plateau Point and just quit at the edge, didn't it!" said Lillagore sympathetically as he returned to his chair. "Art, they did find a car in the lot, registered to a Dwight Anderson, Fullerton, Maryland, being checked now. There's no money under the seat but the watches are and a stack of credit cards from nine different states. They've sealed it for prints. And Miss Finch's medical report is in from the North Rim." He said kindly to Nancy, "Tore your feet up, didn't you?" She nodded and touched her forehead lightly.

"If she went down to Plateau Point she wandered all night without any sleep, it looks like," said the sergeant to the others. He had stopped writing in his notebook. "No wonder your mind played tricks, all you had been through. When you finally got back to the trail it was one hell of a hot day."

"I rested at a creek but I was vomiting." Ahead, in her mind, ran the River Trail between Pipe Canyon and the bridge; she swept her mental eye along it once and then decided, no, she would leave Dwight out of this part altogether. He was dead; it made no difference. He would disappear from her life as abruptly as he had entered, like a pattern of wallpaper, and only she would know where the design stopped. All this she thought in an instant, remembered that some unknown hiker might have heard voices call, and added, "I seemed to keep hearing him call my name and I screamed some—it must sound crazy, but it's so quiet in the canyon that everything echoes and I was sick."

"Terrible," the sergeant said in a soothing tone. "Our heat is hard to get used to even if you're in top condition. Nobody strolls into the Grand Canyon. You've been lucky, Miss Finch." He clicked his ballpoint pen again. "I'll need his full description."

But the impetus to finish her story was irresistible and the black River Trail opened in Nancy's mind without end. "It was very hot and I was trying to run. The water in that creek has worms in it—does the Park Service know about those worms?"

Hollis patted her fist where it had hardened on the arm of the wheelchair. "We know you've been through a physical ordeal. Though it won't comfort you now, going into the canyon probably *did* hide you. That's where the kidnapper abandoned his car and gave up. Our job is to find him before he does something worse to somebody else. What name did he use?"

Hunt said, "Maybe he's in the canyon, too. Maybe he's down there still."

She said quickly, "The name on the car, Dwight Anderson." Patrolman Lillagore said he doubted the man would go *down,* lacking any certainty that Miss Finch had done so. "And she never signed. It would be too easy for Anderson to be his real name but we can always hope."

"Here's Edward Rayburn's description, if you'll correct or add to it." Reading slowly, Sergeant Hollis looked up after each phrase. "About thirty-five. Black hair, dark eyes. Approximately two hundred and ten pounds. Six feet one or two inches—"

"Smaller," said Nancy wearily. "Younger. Not black, not even dark brown. Besides, he had on a cap back in Linville."

He made notes and before she could correct eye color read on. "No scars or marks. Very deep voice." Was it deep? He spoke so little. "Sharp featured. Cleft chin. Carrying a thirty-eight?"

Nancy didn't know the caliber and she doubted Eddie knew, either. She mentioned the tattoo and the broken tooth. She told him about Dwight shooting out the windshield in case a bullet hole size revealed anything. Lillagore said any man that had shot at him once he would run from himself! His clothing in Williams? Short-sleeve shirt and a black cowboy hat. She added, "One of his driver's licenses was for Shelton, Melrose Lee Shelton, and the picture looked like him." Looks?

Again the telephone rang; this time it took so long for the patrolman to come back that Hollis stopped questioning her and stared toward the hall, waiting. Chan took the occasion to whisper to Nancy, "What you said about the Ark of the Covenant—are you Jewish?"

"If anything, Presbyterian."

"Now isn't that nice! She's Presbyterian!" said Chan to Lewis.

"Naturally," said Hunt.

Lillagore came back saying a Harvey Jolley had been registered at one of the South Rim hotels, had gotten himself locked into a bathroom, in fact; but since then seemed to have, ah, seemed to have—

"Dropped off the face of the earth," said Sergeant Hollis grimly.

But Nancy, after making Lillagore give days and times precisely, knew that the judge had to be alive, and she slumped in the wheelchair and closed her eyes in relief.

"Worn out, poor woman." The sergeant stood, folded his notebook, and tapped it against one palm. "We'll find them both. Miss Finch, I hope you'll soon feel better. Sorry you had to come to Arizona in such an unpleasant way." Walking with Lewis and Chan to the hall he promised to keep in close touch.

In a weak voice Nancy called—determined to sponge off her conscience at least—"Maybe he fell."

"Falling's too good for him," Lillagore said, following.

Hunt waited nearby. "Headache? Could you use another drink?"

"Could but better not." Though both eyes were shut she could tell when he came nearer.

"I go down into the Grand Canyon," he said softly, "to relearn what the scale of measure really is."

"It'll do that, all right, and drive your own life off the bottom, smallest end."

"In one way." The telephone was ringing. "In another way you realize you'd kill to get a drink of water and save that puny life of yours." Hunt answered the phone since the others had walked out to the patrol car. "This time it's your mother." He rolled Nancy into the hall by a table. Mama was already speaking as Nancy lifted the phone toward her ear.

"Nancy? You there? Is it really you this time? Nancy?"

"I'm fine now, Mother. I know you've been worried—"

"Worried! They wanted to put me in the hospital. I just hope they hang that man two or three times for what he's done to all of us. Eddie talked with the police out there and they say the people you're staying with are all right; that's a blessing. They must have money to be able just to take in anybody."

"About average, I guess. I never did find out when Eddie got the ropes loose."

"You ask Mrs. Thatcher if the desert is good for arthritis; you never know. They were there all all night and Faye swears a bear came and looked in the car—you know how her nerves are. This thing has been hard on her, Nancy. She's not as strong as you are."

"So you keep saying, Mama. Is Beck all right?"

"Now Nancy, this is your mother, now. Did that man do anything?"

"Not the way you mean." Her gaze flew down the hall and after Hunt, who was in the dining room pretending not to listen.

"He put his hands all over Faye, she says. Don't you be brave if he did, Nancy, because doctors can do things nowadays."

"He didn't. In a few days I'll be starting home."

"You want Eddie to come out there?"

God forbid. "I'll call if I need him, Mama."

"Beckham is fine but he grieved for you so. You know how he depends on you and when I'm not well . . . he's wanting to talk to you in a minute. Now I just thank the good Lord and so should you."

"I will, Mama." The truth was, she had not yet thought of it.

"Well, I hope so because you've drifted away from the church since Reverend Newton left. Here. Speak to your brother."

"Beckham?"

Nobody answered at first. Heavy papers slapped. Mama said at a distance that he'd better put that book on the table before he dropped it.

"I did just what you told me to," his voice at last. "Now you'll be coming home." He sounded sweet as a choirboy but she was through crying.

"Very soon. Is everybody all right there?"

"We are now. I've got the atlas right here. It's wider than my hands to where you are." He was moving—she knew too well—the lamp with the slag glass shade and its crochet scarf. "I thought it would have the time zones."

"At the top of the map, Beck. Where the longitude is." In the dining room door with another sandwich Hunt was looking quizzical.

"The print's too little. What time is it there? It's two-thirty in the morning here and the late late show is still on!"

"I didn't realize." She covered the phone with her hand and asked Hunt the time, then said to Beckham, "We're in different days but it's late here, too. Get some sleep." He asked her which day he was in. "Tomorrow," she said.

16

Four states became involved in the search for Dwight Anderson: Arizona, Maryland, Oklahoma, and North Carolina. Each asked Nancy to hold herself available for hearings that would indict him for theft, auto theft, kidnapping, whatever; but the Arizona authorities were the most concerned, believing him still in their state, like an imported pest that had slipped by their border inspectors. Arizona coordinated the interstate reports and the search for the missing Harvey Trace Jolley.

Maryland reported the black car stolen in Fullerton from the son of Dwight Anderson, Sr., almost a year before. The son—age twenty, blond—was stationed in Bremerton, Washington, but known to be at sea. Unsolved robbery cases in nearby Lutherville and Bagley had been reopened.

Oklahoma policemen carried the fugitive's description, since he had reportedly telephoned from that state. "No," said Nancy when asked by the sergeant," I can't believe that; it's someone else." Hunt asked later why she was so certain. "He wouldn't warn or make a bargain—there's not a promise of any kind in him," she said, forgetting what the two of them had pledged about Arizona.

Two national park services had to be consulted, also their county law officers, also the F.B.I. Conflicting reports were filed. Dwight had been seen at Yosemite exposing himself to a troop of Girl Scouts. A lunatic wearing a dark Stetson had pulled a handgun in a Dallas shopping center, shot up a candy machine, and escaped.

"Also the wrong man?" Hunt asked. She said probably.

A fingerprint check now awoke the state of Virginia, where Melrose Lee Shelton had a long police record, mostly armed robbery, twice with assault. Both assaults were in gay bars in Norfolk. He had served several jail sentences without incident. One psychiatric observation: able to stand trial. One arrest but no conviction in West Virginia. His criminal record ran back to age twenty-three and then stopped. It developed that although a Shelton birth certificate was on file in Roanoke, so was the record of the real Melrose's death at sixteen from multiple sclerosis. The astonished Shelton survivors wanted to sue someone for malign use of his name. Their lawyer stood by and awaited emerging defendants.

Meantime, Dwight was arrested by a zealous policeman in Greenway, North Carolina, for suspicious behavior on Crosby Avenue, but turned out to be an advance-need salesman for cemetery lots who had fallen asleep in his car between calls. Beckham had notified the police and then gone out bravely himself with a broom handle to wait in the nearby spirea.

Besides, Dwight had already been picked up in Tucson in a vice raid and admitted all, including rape of the kidnap victim. I know that isn't him," Nancy said, "because he didn't."

"That proves he was crazy doesn't it, Hunt?" said Chan with a shy giggle. He stared at her, blinked twice, and then turned to examine Nancy with even more measurement than usual. He folded his arms next and stared his mother down.

The confessed rapist turned out to be a fifty-eight-year-old doctor, under great mental strain while defending a malpractice charge involving the death of a primipara. Soon after, another Dwight in another stolen car, black hat and all, was stopped near Tulsa for speeding. His laconic manner, height, spare credit cards—these matched; only fingerprints proved him a different thief. Unfortunately for him, this man received a mild concussion during arrest and in a prison clinic passed into his bedpan fourteen condoms full of heroin tied shut with dental floss.

The day Nancy's wheelchair picture had briefly appeared on television news. J. Waldo Foster wired her a potted geranium with his professional signature attached and Benjy's name below. Nancy supposed he now had quite a vacation anecdote for mothers at well-baby checkups, though he evidently made no official report.

"I see you've got flowers from your boyfriend," said Hunt with a meaningful look at his mother.

"Didn't you say he was your retired family doctor?" Nancy said yes.

Nothing came from Joel, of course, nor William. Patrick's telegram was so flirtatious that she left it lying around on various surfaces without its being read by either of the courteous Thatchers.

Of course Oliver Newton wrote to her special delivery—her telephone call clarified now and a burden on his conscience. He discussed at length (Nancy skimmed several paragraphs) the nature of conscience as Luther saw it, the doctrine of synderesis, the view of Heidegger; he referred her to Psalm 137 and the Babylonian Captivity—she sped through the words to the end of a letter that had so much to do with others and so little to do with him or with her.

That day Chan found her in the long living room, depressed, with her gaze fixed on the elk's belligerence.

"Something wrong? Not in your pastor's letter, I hope." She looked guilty. "I didn't mean to meddle but I noticed the church address."

"It would be ironic if he was right all along about what I was in love with." Nancy glanced aside to the window and the rugged mountains beyond, almost with a shudder.

"In love?" asked Chan uneasily.

"Just a figure of speech. And he's not *my* pastor anymore."

"If you feel up to it, Hunt's coming to show you the sights this afternoon."

"It's so hot out there."

"Nancy, you can't live in air-conditioning forever. And Lewis has run the last reporter off."

"But regular clothes scratch. Admit it—Hunt's doing this only because you asked him." Nancy shook out the loose caftan. "I can't wear this."

"Why not? There's nothing wrong with asking. From what you say of your life at home you should have done more asking yourself."

"I still look awful to be out in public."

"Horses and wolves won't notice."

"Oh, all right." She felt irritable, dissatisfied with something she could not name, and she tore up Patrick's letter and Oliver's both.

Her sunburn could endure only a loose polyester dress with soft seams and her feet were still scabby and sore. She combed hair over as much of her face as possible and would have worn Chan's largest sunglasses but they kept sliding down her blistered nose.

When Chan had left for her church meeting, Nancy arranged herself in a large chair with a book open in her lap, since books seemed to serve symbolically for Hunt. She had chosen Bandelier's novel about prehistoric Pueblo Indians, *The Delight Makers*, and got interested in spite of herself. The Koshare clan was required to fast and pray for harvest but primarily to make the rest of the Queres people happy by dancing and merriment.

She had looked up again at those ragged rocky mountain peaks when Hunt's voice asked what was making her so pensive.

"Thoughts of happiness." She put the book aside. "You don't have to show me the sights unless you really want to."

"Mother thinks you'd better get away from these crank calls."

"Some people honestly wanted to help. They thought they'd seen him." One man, though, had whispered that he was coming to get her again and had breathed hard and ticked his loud watch in Nancy's ear.

"Mother said you'd be glad to associate with something as civilized as a wolf after some of those calls. I've parked close so you needn't walk far on those feet."

The outside world felt like a conical oven. "You couldn't pay me to live in Arizona unless I was a rock."

"No library can be paying you very much to live in North Carolina. You'll like this country when you get the mildew out of your lungs. How far can you see from your house—a block? Through trees? It's miles to those mountains and they top out at eight thousand feet," Hunt said. In his car, Nancy found herself leaning against the passenger door. The last time she was in a car . . ." Here the land is stripped of everything superfluous."

"I don't consider trees superfluous."

"On the way, since you've been reading about them, I'll show you

the ruins of a real pueblo village, Besh-ba-Gowah, the same name Indians give the town. I don't know how much delight they made here."
Hunt wore a wide-brimmed woven hat; she did not like the shadow it
cast. "I hope you're not bothered by Mother's obvious matchmaking."

"Not if you aren't."

"It's natural of her to think Fate, or maybe her own telepathic
powers."

"You could do worse."

"Probably have. Nobody seems able to find your kidnapper. Do
you think he followed you down into the canyon?" When Nancy said
yes he kept his eye on the road, asking in a casual tone, "What would
you have done if he had caught you on that trail?"

"If there had been no other escape, I would have tried to kill him."

"Yes. I expect so." Across a flat stretch of cat's-claw and cactus
Hunt drove to where rubble walls broke the pale mesa into even but
unroofed squares. "We won't get out because this surface would hurt
your feet. There were two hundred rooms here once. What's wrong?"

"The light. My eyes seem hypersensitive these days." He adjusted
the visor, pointing to the creek whose stream bed had supplied the
building blocks, using his pipestem to indicate fire pits and open
courts. "The Indians buried their dead under the floors of the patio,
some of the graves breaching others. New graves had priority, it
seems. If they came across pieces of older bone they used them for fill
dirt."

Nancy didn't see why they had needed a special clan to pursue happiness; they were already calloused against loss.

"We'll move on before you overheat." When he had backed into the
road and turned he said, "I'm told I owe you an apology."

"Something else your mother has said?"

"This time it's Lewis. All his reports came in from Greenway."
Nancy asked what reports. "I thought you knew he'd sent detectives
from Charlotte to check you out."

"Check *me* out!"

"For Mother's protection. Now calm down, Nancy. You'd understand if you knew more of the history Lewis knows. Somebody even
left a baby on her doorstep last spring, taking for granted that was the

choice place to abandon babies. And of course it was. Anyway, the detectives say you're exactly what you claim to be. You're all over the Stone County newspaper this week—did you know that?"

"I trusted Lewis McKinney on sight." Hunt said she had good instincts. "But now I feel hurt."

"Don't let it hurt that he puts her first—so he should. Now the other thing Lewis wants me to talk to you about is his intention to fly you home when the doctor and police say you can go. You've sent for traveling money but he does regret mistrusting you and snooping in your past and, besides, he loves to fly."

"How much snooping did he do?"

"He didn't say. I didn't ask." They were crossing Globe's residential outskirts under trees made greener by their rarity.

"Flying. That's so fast. I had hoped for more gradual transition."

"Once he flew Ilene to Texas because late one night she remarked she'd like to Christmas shop at Neiman Marcus. Ilene? My former wife." Nancy already knew about her from Chan. "Probably she made a pass at Lewis in midair," Hunt added. "She liked to be pursued but she hated to be caught."

"Since you're so clever and can see straight through any designing female, I'm surprised you married one like Ilene."

After a silence Hunt said, "Was that nice?"

"Have you been?"

"Granted. But at the moment I'm trying."

Then she would hold up her end of a truce, Nancy said. Their car was climbing gradually north toward what Hunt identified as the Globe Hills and the farther Apache range. After a while he said, "I married her because it was time for me to get married. It was late."

"I'm years beyond late and though I've made mistakes about men I still haven't legalized any."

"Were you invited to?"

"What the hell kind of truce is this?"

But when Hunt began to laugh she couldn't help it herself. "Not lately," she admitted.

"I'm laughing at myself, Nancy. I'm the fool who did the inviting, bought the ring, and so on. There were reasons but none good enough. I got lonesome. Ilene was pretty. She seemed to be a tramp only by default—in fact she said so—and I was convinced that devotion and emotional security were all she really needed to change her."

"You weren't old enough to be out after dark much less to get married."

"I'm Methuselah now by contrast. But you're not married because of good taste and good sense—is that it?"

His question set images clicking in her mind—alternating pictures of William, who'd done karate workouts Monday nights and made love to Nancy on Fridays, and of Patrick, who was probably winked at by cohorts in Kiwanis. Joel going home to his wife and probably scheduling sex by odds and evens. Oliver having his cake and *not* eating it, too—the acme for a Calvinist, she thought.

To distract herself she pointed through the windshield to a strip of sand white as talcum. "Is that Old Dominion mine?"

"Tailings with no ore left," he said, "and that black cliff is slag. My father used to walk me around the mine and tell me about the big fire in Interloper and the man who climbed all the way up the ventilating shaft to where rescuers could just touch his hands and then fell and screamed all the way down. For years I dreamed about it."

Nancy did not want to think about falling.

He saw her squinting and adjusted the visor. "Did the doctor check your eyes for damage?"

"He said there was no physical problem. He offered me tranquilizers but I said no. Are we going to the mine?"

Hunt shook his head. "Just out to my place. But see that notch way back there on the ridge? That's where they took out the first silver. The only way into this valley then was from the east and through the Apaches. Are you still having those dreams?"

"A few." Once the floor of Mother Thatcher's bedroom had rolled back so a very bloody Dwight could beckon her down his deep black stairs. Once she was trapped atop a burning building and forced to jump.

"You don't think those pills would help?"

"Not as much as living through it," Nancy said—a Calvinist herself.

The distant mine was sliding beyond their side windows when

Hunt said, "One of Old Dominion's early owners, as you must have guessed, came from Virginia, so it's possible for southerners to adjust to this western landscape."

"Oh, I could adjust!" said Nancy. "It might send me to a nunnery, for instance! New York City would never do that."

"Mother would say it could send you to Globe Methodist Church just as well."

She asked, "Did your father's stories about fire and cave-ins keep you out of the mines?"

"Not just that. I'd seen his hard years starting over with a new company and never assigned any work of first importance there because methods had changed but he wouldn't. Here we are." After turning off the highway he parked underneath his wrought-iron name. "The Thatchers aren't flexible and they cling to old ways and natural rhythms. Alice hates to spay female dogs. She says stable horses chew wood from boredom and the Tennessee Walker has been forced into a gait no horse ever ran in nature. And I'm the village smithy after all the chestnut trees have died." He opened the car door and took her right elbow. "Get out; come in."

"On the other side, please, that foot is the worst." She was surprised by Hunt's strength, but under the smithy shed among long bars of iron and scrap sheeting, great callipers, rusted wheels, andirons, tongs, fencing, old saw blades, boilers, and shafts, she understood the weight that had hardened his arms and shoulders. He checked the brick hearth and did something with shovel and bellows to make the fire glow. Heat passed burning over her skin.

"Now we go through this shop—arc welding," he said with a wave toward dark equipment. From its back door a path led to his small house. Hunt guided her straight down a dogtrot hall outdoors again to a chain link fence. From one shaded corner an animal rose—very long, gray with darker torso, its tail somewhat tucked, sharp ears erect. Hunt unlocked the gate. Silently the wolf sprang.

Nancy had time only to use the gate as a shield. In three high bounds the wolf reached Hunt, dropped, rolled near a shoe and sent a strong yellow spurt of urine onto his pants. When the fountain stopped, Hunt squatted to rub with both hands the gray head and long muzzle. He laughed seeing Nancy flattened between layers of wire mesh. "I wish I had a camera. This is a wolf's greatest compliment, no matter what they think at the dry cleaner's. Akela submits his will to mine; this is his deferential version of tipping a hat in respect. Come on in; I'm watching him."

Nancy's first movement made the wolf crouch almost flat and snarl.

"Akela!" Subtly the haunches relaxed till the wolf seemed to lie at ease in the sand but both forepaws were still taut, the hair in a streak of arousal along his backbone. Nancy looked uneasily along the fence.

"Where's the female?"

"Down in her den. I dug them a slanting shaft and put in a big terra-cotta pipe. She keeps cool under the roots of that cottonwood."

"I thought dens were for foxes. Thank you, but I'll wait outside the fence." Though the wolf remained still under Hunt's spread hand Nancy saw Akela's hind legs flex for any attack she might force him to make. She latched the gate while Hunt walked to a grass mound near the tree, knelt, and thrust one arm below ground.

He called, "Ruth's shy with strangers." The male wolf remained stiff, legs spread, tail flat out, watching her with narrow golden eyes that seemed slightly misfocused. She had seen such eyes before and they bothered her now.

Hunt brought Akela water and watched the wolf trouble its surface with one paw before drinking, "so it will seem like running water," he explained. Then he patted the lean back before joining her outside the fence. "Most people fear wolves but I didn't think you would, even on his territory."

"Akela didn't know me from lunch. Besides I'm not as brave as I once was—or as good, either." They started up the path. "Where'd you get him?"

"He's an Alaska gray wolf I bought as a cub and so tame that if I was alone he'd be going inside the house now to his chair. Don't you think he's handsome?"

"No," she said. "He looks"—what was the word?—"remorseless. All animals are, I know that, but I don't often have to know it in such close quarters."

"That's why raising wolves will reconcile you to your own species. You can't take much of this sun yet, can you?" He led Nancy into an undramatic living room—cheap furniture, desk, brown curtains, nondescript floor lamps. Dark triangles of dust in the room's corners. Books. She thought: Ilene didn't live here long or stay here much.

Hunt said his bar was the kitchen. He selected gin from a row of food packages and canned goods along a counter that always— Nancy saw—got wiped but not washed, just as the floor tile got swept but not mopped and never since installation waxed. Around every cabinet knob were whorls of gray fingerprints. A kitchen so empty of female attention made Nancy almost comprehend the territorial sensations of the wolf, not that she cared for housework except under conditions so bad any improvement would be vivid, the way a lightly stroked sponge on this greasy wall, for instance, would leave a streak white as new paint. He said, "What are you thinking?"

She forgot to lie. "That Ilene couldn't cook."

"Not much. But we lived in Phoenix, not here. I had to hire people to run this shop while I tried to learn to sell advertising. I never learned. Crackers?" He rattled a box from the counter collection. "Must be all crumbs." He slid the box back into place, perhaps because the garbage pail was full. It had been full yesterday. "I'll bring drinks into the living room. Take off those boots and cool your feet. I'm told your blisters came out by the roots."

She still had to wear the fateful boots because Chan's shoes were so small, though under bandages her foot soles looked like overripe melon someone had been sampling with a tablespoon. "How long," said Nancy as she stepped over a broom propped in the doorway, "did you live in Phoenix?"

"Even the first day was too long." He moved one shoulder impatiently. "In spite of Mother's matchmaking I don't mind living alone and as you can see, I manage a house very well."

The poor man meant it. "May I use your bathroom?" He sent Nancy into disorder even worse, though some visiting woman had left a jar of caked bath salts. A large grasshopper was spending a hungry afternoon in the dingy tub.

Carrying her boots back to the living room, Nancy sat by him on the brown sofa, and since Hunt was already resting his feet on the glass tabletop, she put hers alongside.

"The only reason I've talked so much about myself is that I don't feel right carrying around this knowledge in my pocket," he said, and unfolded some papers in his lap. It was the Charlotte detectives' confidential report. She snatched and began reading nothing but dreary facts about Nancy Finch, more residue than she had expected to leave behind even at death; and in a few minutes she had flung the sheets onto his table. The facts were both true and irrelevant. She was indeed an old-maid librarian, respectable, a good credit risk, an alto, the support of her family. She owned life and health insurance but no car. Her largest outstanding account was with Sears Roebuck. She played bridge at three women's clubs and won. She was 5 feet 7 and 34, weighed 128 pounds, had headed the Greenway Community Chest one year and the Girl Scout Council for four, and also she had associated with the specific male friends duly listed in sequence. And wouldn't Joel hate it to know that all his care and secrecy had gone for nothing! In fact, Nancy hated it, too.

Hunt said quickly, "I have no questions."

"But I want to explain some of this."

"No," he said. "Drink up. If I ever do have questions I'll ask them. I was getting ready to tell you more about Akela and Ruth."

"You weren't," she said.

"I am now. One reason for Ruth's shyness is that she's been badly treated. She's a darker timber wolf from Canada caught in a trap up there, still has a damaged hind leg. At first she didn't like Akela, either. They're monogamous, you know, and will mate for life like geese. He wasn't her chosen mate. When I put her in the lot they fought so much I doubted the fence would hold them."

There was a silence while Nancy tried to decide how much she was reading into his words. She chose to mention only the scattered hairs and parallel slits in the green chair. Hunt said yes; at night he read and Akela guarded in his chair.

"Do you ever think of setting them free?"

"Sure I do, high in the mountains in good weather on a dark night with their bellies full—sure I do. Once instinct took over they could live off the javalinas. If Ruth has cubs and they organize into a real pack with Akela at its head instead of me as a substitute, I'd want to turn them all loose." He frowned. "Some mechanized sportsman would probably shoot them in a week. Anything you tame will own you. I don't even take vacations anymore."

"I thought Chan would look after them."

"She'll come to sling meat over the fence but after all she's a dog breeder—to her, wolves seem like the Jukes and the Kallikaks." Now that Hunt had made her smile, he said, "Promise you won't blame Lewis for asking questions or for showing me what he found out."

"I don't understand why he showed you."

"Oh, I do." Hunt smiled as if at a secret. "It's because they both like you."

Puzzled, she said, "Funny way to show it. And Chan likes everybody."

"You're not taking the matchmaking seriously enough. Besides, Mother would argue and say she *values* everybody, that there's a difference. That way she can pretend to herself she isn't sentimental."

"But it's outrageous that Lewis decided you were entitled to know in advance everything that I—that's outrageous! And unfair! Nobody's told me everything about you!"

"Come now. Think back."

"No, my information has been much sketchier. I just think Lewis was trying to scare you off."

Hunt thumped the papers farther away, saying, "He knew this wouldn't scare me off," and he looked at her so long the nape of her neck prickled.

Nancy took an interest in her drink. "You say you have no questions but you and Lewis stare at me so, as if you've read the report and I don't fit it."

Hunt nodded. "Although you were kidnapped and under threat for days, carried across the country, all that, much of the time you seem like a woman who stepped out for a loaf of bread and just made a wrong turn. Too calm, or maybe numb. Yet at other times you'll pull back and your eyes look at something none of us can see."

At the suggestion, part of her pulled back, threw the rock, and rejoiced when Dwight went over the edge.

"Like that, but more so," Hunt said pleasantly. "Mother tells

Lewis it happens because you don't have things sorted out yet, and that no experience solidifies until a person has decided what it taught her; but you know Mother. She thinks everybody's real name is John Bunyan."

"I learned I'm not frail."

"I told Lewis that we just didn't know everything yet and that maybe you didn't either. So he gave me the detectives' report."

"It's not that I'm numb or still in shock."

He prompted her. "But what?"

"But I'm not as surprised as I expected to be."

"About kidnappings?"

Maybe Chan was right and her explanations were still incomplete. "Remember the night the patrolmen came? And you said that somebody lost in the canyon would kill to get a drink of water?"

He started to answer but car noise drew him to the window where he pulled back a drapery, cobweb and all. "I've got to shoe this horse that's just over laminitis but I want to talk more about this. Bring your drink."

Following him to the shop Nancy could hear the wolf rumble behind her; I have spoor, she thought; it seemed ominous. Hunt, in the smithy shed, shook hands with a man called Chunk and the two men backed a pinto from a trailer. First running one hand down the foreleg Hunt lifted and straddled the foot, brushing off dirt with one hand. Chunk said the vet had finished treatment, trimmed the hoof and cut back the frog. "He says to lighten the shoe."

"What was he carrying before, eleven, twelve ounces? He's skittish but let's try first without a twitch." Nancy sat on a keg. After he checked the ready-made shoes hung from nails on rafters he muttered, "Go to a nine," and took down four horseshoes. He tied the horse near her and put on a black apron. Chunk came forward, too, trying not to stare at Nancy as he was briefly introduced. With a grin he said he sure hoped the other woman looked worse.

"All right, hold him now." Hunt finished rasping and picking clean the hoof, saying, "Won't be fit to carry anything but old ladies for a long time." When he black-heated one shoe and seated it to the front hoof, sudden clouds of smoke made Nancy recoil; her movement alarmed the horse. "Be still, Nancy; it doesn't hurt him."

Chunk bore down on the horse's head and calmed him with whispers but his face turned apologetic. "I just realized you're the Nancy Finch in the newspapers. I'm sorry. I hope they catch him."

"I don't much care," she said. "It's all over now."

"Well, you may *say* that but you wouldn't want him to keep carrying off innocent people. Maybe kill one." He watched Hunt work on the other front hoof. "I heard they found the old judge."

"What? Found him where? Is he all right?"

"It was on the car radio that he's been visiting some orphanage all this time."

"Oh, I hope so. Hunt, is there a radio in the house?" He told her where. She hurried away, half-hearing Chunk answering another question. "No, I think he really is old—he was retired, they said. He took bribes."

Nancy found the radio on Hunt's dresser in his bedroom, a box of corroded batteries. She dropped onto his unmade bed with its yellowish sheets, disappointed, then slowly lowered her face into the hollowed pillow to test his smell. She was lying there in a vague melancholy when through the nearest window she saw that, near the fence, the wolf with fangs in view was watching all she did. She leaped up as if surprised in something shameful and hurried out back. Now she trusted the metal mesh enough to sit close while every inch of Akela's gray body sent out warning. Before, the animal had seemed walleyed, his look piercing air beside her face; in Hunt's absence the gaze became direct, fixed.

Yet Hunt had said wolves only needed a clear-cut understanding of who in a pack was dominant over whom else. A wolf, Hunt had insisted, almost never killed another wolf. In a fight the loser would drop flat and bare his throat as Akela today had bared his own; such surrender would be honored by the victor. Nor were there any recorded unprovoked attacks by the wild wolf, alone or in packs, upon a human being. So rare were renegade wolves that these passed into folklore by name—the white Custer wolf, for instance; and even he had never ravaged humans or his own kind but had become a mutilator and wasteful killer of livestock. A psychotic wolf, Hunt said.

Akela continued to gaze and to drink Nancy's scent. Never had Dwight's yellow eyes burned with such energy. Never could? Never will. Almost mesmerized, Nancy waited by the fence until Hunt's customer had gone.

On the way home they stopped at the patrol office in Claypool. Sergeant Hollis said he'd just notified Mrs. Thatcher that Judge Jolley had turned up safe in an orphanage in Ruston, Louisiana. Seems he'd grown up there and on Friday appeared at the director's door in an agitated state and asked to be taken in, promising to work as a janitor and watchman. No other details. "Miss Finch, you look better every day," said Hollis gallantly. He reminded her that Zane Grey had recovered his health in this climate.

Afterward in the car Nancy said, "So the judge did go off and leave me without knowing whether I was safe or not!"

"Didn't you do the same?"

Yes, but that felt different, Nancy grumbled.

At Chan's, Nancy—made hopeful by the sergeant's compliment—hurried to the nearest mirror but found her face still shocking, the lavender bruises touched up with added gilt. Full or profile, it barely resembled her old face. She held the bruised cheeks in both hands. A tourist legend which nobody believes says that a cowpoke (or heiress, or schoolteacher, etc.) on seeing the Grand Canyon for the first time exclaimed, "Something happened here!" With those words in mind Nancy stroked the healing face that was molting into what?

In the new face her eyes looked darker, more enlarged, yet more secretive. Perhaps Dwight had avoided mirrors because his dead brother waited there. Sometimes now the raw head of Dwight himself waited for Nancy in the looking glass.

She took off the bandage and reduced the new one to a patch that would hide her puckered stitches. She could have told Hunt how she had crawled to the high edge of River Trail and looked down the cliff, had found far below a new rubble pile still raising dust in its track with something protruding that was not stone. And how she had struggled shakily upright, drawn back one boot and by reflex kicked Dwight's pistol high into space after him before stumbling on toward the bridge alone. Except it was not by reflex. Celebration?

After Nancy had changed into the green robe she tried coating her gaudy eye with makeup, but the effect was bizarre. Her scrubbed face tingled when she joined Lewis and Chan for dinner.

"We're so glad you got out of the house!"

Lewis agreed because "it'll make it easier for you to see today's paper." Six reporters had pushed into the hall the day before, forcing Chan to sic Tanner on the group. "Look at it." Lewis handed her the newspaper.

Even while tumbling ahead of Tanner's teeth in a flurry, they had been popping flashbulbs to get this awful picture of Nancy from an angle which made the blotches on her face resemble a wandering birthmark. Underneath, the headline said KIDNAP VICTIM WON'T SET FOOT OUTDOORS.

"I know where I'd like to set a foot," Lewis muttered.

"It doesn't matter," Nancy said, though she had never looked uglier in her life. "I want to read about the judge." She flattened her thumb over the wild contorted face ascribed to her, but Sergeant Hollis had already told her more than was reported here. She had trouble keeping her attention on the copy because of wondering whether or not Hunt subscribed to this particular paper. Too bad no one had used the one good, even flattering, snapshot she owned of herself, but it was in her wallet and her wallet was somewhere in the Grand Canyon.

After dinner Nancy called the orphanage in Ruston and asked for Judge Jolley. The man spoke to someone, exclaimed, "Still!" and then said Jolley was still in the chapel. Meditating. He had been there a lot since arrival.

"We really have no facilities," the official said to her, "to keep him on the premises. He offers services, of course, but he's untrained in work with children and they find him a bit, well, emotional? If you could encourage him to go home now, and to make his contributions right there in Somerville, I'm sure that would be for the best, Miss Finch."

She said she would try and left her number for the judge to call, but he did not.

• • •

Hunt, carrying the Globe paper open to Nancy's pop-eyed photograph, called down the hall next morning, "Just leave your foot in a drawer and come on. Unless you'd like to put it in your mouth? Worse?" In midstride he snatched the hall telephone on first ring. "No. No, she's not. Who is this? You go to hell."

"It wasn't Judge Jolley?"

"It was a nut," he said, slamming down the receiver. Chan came out to kiss the edge of his mustache. Nancy could guess that Chan had summoned him. Now that Eddie had transferred her funds, the two women had gone out early to buy Nancy clothes. Bank tellers had stared, salesclerks whispered; and since the newspaper photo appeared the telephone calls had begun again—some urging a trust in Jesus, some conveying sympathy or recommending sodomy. Those voices seemed to heat up the folds of her ear.

She grabbed her new western hat with its wide brim, pale tan, not at all like Dwight's; and pivoted. All Hunt said was, "Pants, good—I was going to suggest them."

"Have all those cars gone?" asked Chan. "Especially that boy wanting an autograph!"

"If his is the van with stars and moons painted on the side, it just pulled off. A lot of pedestrians, though, are watching the 'spacious Thatcher home.'" Hunt frowned again at the article before dropping the newspaper into a waste can. "And how are you this morning, 'well-known local dog fancier'? How's your 'longtime family friend and companion' Lewis?" He adjusted Nancy's hat brim forward on her brow and nodded. "You're looking better, 'hysterical victim.'"

"Lewis flew back to Valle this morning," said Chan, "before he hurt somebody. Can you believe famous people live this way all the time? I'm so glad you came, Hunt; I was going to ask you."

So! He had come without prompting!

"It's good to see you smile. I hope that means you feel well enough to ride a horse. Turn around. We'll make a westerner of you yet."

"I haven't worn jeans in years and a bandanna shirt—never. Just look at these boots! I could kick through steel." Nancy stuck out a pointed leather toe with fancy stitching. Her cramped feet were already hurting.

"You do ride?" He was opening the front door for her.

"Pretty well."

Hunt shook his head. "You must have had very little practice lying. Ilene was an expert."

"Some tell lies, some live them." She stopped in disgust. "All these people! What do they expect to see!"

With arms folded, Hunt waited until passersby moved on. "Good liars volunteer details and know exactly when to stop," he said as the watchers dispersed. "Inept liars—they just fall silent. They lie by not finishing sentences. They only hope to avoid any direct question because one of those will fold them up every time." He smiled at her silence, adding as they drove away, "Perhaps inept liars have scruples. They may think avoiding truth is better than violating it."

"Not unless they missed instruction in omission and commission. O.k., so I've been on a horse maybe four times in my life."

"Four."

"Well, twice. A westerner wouldn't count two times on my grandfather's mule." While Hunt was laughing she wondered in which direction she would fold if asked: Do you know what happened to Dwight Anderson?

Without talking they drove south through the forested Pinal Mountains and down curving unpaved roads. The dry air smelled resinous. Hunt parked before a washed adobe stable with sliding double doors.

"Speaking of deception by silence," Nancy said, "until I read the newspaper I'd never have guessed you were an 'independent businessman and breeder of fine western horses.' Chan says you own fifty registered quarterhorses and hire other farriers now and hardly ever shoe a horse yourself except to impress visitors.

"You weren't much impressed. I'm just half owner." Hunt led her into the barn. "If you knew how much money a man can lose raising horses you'd show more sympathy." From the wide center aisle between stalls Nancy could count feed and tack room and twelve stalls on each side. Grinning, he said, "Mother left out those details in case money might attract you—she's a bad liar herself." Overhead skylights dropped blocks of sunlight on the wood shavings. Hunt hauled out two western saddles while horses, nickering, stuck their heads over the half doors.

"I don't count fifty."

"Maybe she's right and you're a gold digger. Most are on pasture. Two have been brought in and groomed for us." He haltered and led out an Appaloosa mare. After brushing the saddle area, he smoothed with a palm the mare's back from mane to the spotted blanket pattern on the rump. "Come meet Tattooed Lady."

Born to boogie. Nancy was acquiring a positive distaste for coincidence. She clumsily patted the sparse mane while Hunt settled pad and saddle into place. He absently moved her hand onto the mare's neck and shoulder and changed its movement into a long, slow stroke, murmuring to the mare as he tightened the front cinch, then came around Nancy to replace the rope halter with a bridle. Before sliding the bit into the horse's mouth he said, "I'm just giving you a snaffle, not a curb, until we see what kind of hands you have. Lady's very sensitive."

Nancy picked up the bridle he had set aside for himself. "If this is a curb bit, that's what I used at Bandelier."

"When did you ride at Bandelier?"

Sure enough, the direct question hit low in the stomach and threatened to fold her in half. "He made us stop there; I told you."

"No," said Hunt. "You didn't." He walked Lady in a small circle, then readjusted the girth. "You can mount now."

Nancy could not lift herself aboard and Hunt, who continued to examine her face, wouldn't make a move to help. Like a pogo stick her right leg bounced stiffly until at last she was able to spring off it high enough to reach the saddle and sit. "Big horse," she mumbled, evening the reins. She could feel blood seeping into her new boot. "If we waited in Bandelier for twenty-four hours without calling police, he said he'd let us go. So we went horseback riding."

"That was cool of you. Walk her up and down and get the feel while I saddle mine."

Nancy reined the mare toward sunlight at the end of the corridor. At the exit she halted Lady and looked across paddocks to fenced pastures with perimeters of pines, but she could not pose there in silence forever. When she rode back indoors, Hunt was brushing a sorrel gelding larger than Lady and watching her across the withers. "I told you when the time came for questions, I'd ask. It won't be long."

"Naturally you'd start with the very hardest, like why I didn't run like hell in Bandelier."

"Why didn't you run like hell?"

"All that time I *was* running, but running away from home." She'd had overnight to think about what she wanted to say, something about becoming like Akela and acting instantaneously on one's best interests. "People are wrong," she began earnestly, "if they think women want to be raped—they don't—but the very thought of it, the thought of just having matters taken out of your own hands releases all kinds of feelings." ("I'll remember that," he interrupted.) "No, no, I'm not even talking about sex, Hunt, I'm talking about being free of all choices, about taking a vacation from conscience."

"To where? Childhood?"

She said intensely, "There was a big flash flood out here a couple years ago in a canyon, and maybe fifty or more missing afterward, remember? I think it was Big Thompson Canyon."

"I remember. Colorado."

"You know some of those missing people lived through that flood. They just walked away. They just broke off one life and walked away into a new one. If you were leading a certain kind of life when the opportunity came to disappear, you'd disappear."

"Or if you were a certain kind of person."

She did not mean to jerk so hard on the reins. Lady leaped, causing the second horse to shy aside into Hunt as they galloped by. So sudden was the headlong bolt that Nancy was riding out of the stable before she knew it on too loose a rein; she felt herself tip forward awkwardly. Screaming "Whoa!" she pulled back hard on both reins. Lady reared, came down with a heavy thump and stood there, snorting, while Nancy hung on to her neck with both arms. Hunt ran up to grab the bridle then and—without checking Nancy's condition at all—he began instead to calm the mare and loosen the bit at her mouth corners. "Easy now, damn it, I told you she was sensitive, easy girl, all right, ho now," he murmured, leaving Nancy to disentangle her own embrace, spit out mane, and balance herself in saddle and stirrups again.

"What is the matter with this horse!"

"You." He untwisted both reins. "Lady did exactly what you told her." He caught Nancy's fist, unwrapped the fingers, and positioned leather in her left hand. "This will be a riding lesson. Heels down. Just sit still and do nothing while I get a saddle on mine. No." He pushed her hands forward over the withers. "If you jerk the reins she can only do two things—back up or rear up. Got that?" Nancy nodded. "Romal," he said as he slapped the tapered rawhide into her left hand, which he had snatched off the saddle horn. "If you've ever ridden anything more spirited than a Confederate monument, it'll surprise me."

Shaken, angry, she stared at Lady's ears until Hunt had ridden up beside her. "Feel better?" She remained motionless, a granite Roberta E. Lee. "Sorry I lost my temper. My fault for not treating you more like an amateur." Nancy gave a stiff nod. For a few minutes he talked generally about gaits, how to get the horse in and out of each without being a mere passenger, and about neck-reining, adding they would mostly walk the horses along smooth trails. "Now relax your waist so it will go with the movements of the horse." His hands were suddenly flattened just above her belt, one front, one back, to emphasize rhythmic flexibility when the saddle began shifting beneath her, and they were as quickly gone. He rode ahead to hold back a gate. By then Nancy had meant to apologize for clumsy handling of his horse but as she drew near Hunt said, "If you hadn't surprised me with Bandelier I'd have paid closer attention."

Silently Nancy passed through the corral gate with her waist flexing like a snake.

Their hoofbeats brought other horses out of ponderosa shade to form a small herd that grazed while watching them cross the broad plain. The sun was dazzling, even through the new glasses. Nancy held the mare in a jog, thudding high in the saddle, to follow Hunt out of sunlight along a forest trail. Easily he trotted ahead without bouncing. As she gradually relaxed she more nearly fit the shape of horse and saddletree and, for the first time since the canyon, thought her body was returning to her, sore but responsive, healed.

As if he understood a happier rhythm in Lady's hoofbeats, Hunt looked back. She thought he was going to smile or praise her but he said, "What did this kidnapper look like?"

"You heard my description!" Then she cleared her throat. "He was ugly. No. Nothing like that. Nothing I wanted."

"Nothing? Sure?"

"Except that he had no conscience and I did envy that. Yes, I did, I do—and so do you if you tell the truth."

"What do you know about my conscience?"

"I know you're Chan's son." Nancy removed an imaginary thistle from Lady's poll. For a long time neither spoke.

Both horses picked their way among stones on a trail that ran by a small creek. At a spot where a fallen pine had dammed up a pool, with bright strands of water trailing down the slimy trunk, Hunt swung down, watered his horse, and dropped the split reins in a patch of grass before reaching to help Nancy. At first she caught his hand but he would only steady her arm while she dismounted in the regular way to his advice and corrections. She had to swing up and down several times before her posture and ease satisfied him. Finally Nancy pulled away and bent to drink a handful of water. Her altered face vibrated on the flowing stream. She thrust her fingers through it and watched them waver there, insubstantial.

Behind her Hunt said, "He's down there, isn't he?"

"What?"

"He's still down in the canyon."

Nothing changed except her rate of breath. "Yes."

"He's dead." Nancy nodded. On the stream's surface just above her own broken reflection, his even less definite face appeared. "Was he dead when you left him?"

"I never wanted *that* much vacation from conscience. Yes. He fell." Her reaction started; the hand underwater turned icy. She felt detached as she shook droplets off and at last pushed that cold hand, like a dead trout, into the opposite armpit.

"Did you push him?"

Nancy teetered in her awkward off-balance squat. "He pointed the gun. I threw a rock. He fell." She sank onto damp sand, adding, "It didn't hit and I didn't push him but I wanted to. I would have."

"Then in God's name!" Hunt dropped to the ground beside her. "Why didn't you say so right away?"

"I don't know." Her system felt badly organized, some of her nodding, some shrugging, some running her heart to uneven rhythms. She felt shame and relief. "The moment passed," she blurted to his disbelieving face. "They keep passing. There comes a time when you could easily leave home but let three such times go by and they don't come anymore, or you don't recognize them, or you do but can't act on them. I didn't tell at Phantom Ranch and the moment went by." Her voice sounded whining, she thought. The way Mama whines. "I didn't escape from home and I didn't escape from him and after a while I just didn't tell, either. It's easier just to keep on and follow any action to its natural conclusion, you know; it's not premeditation and planning, just that some endings are innate, the blossom in the bud and all." She groaned. "I'm babbling."

"You certainly are," Hunt said.

By watching the water run she calmed herself. He asked, "Were you never going home?" She made uncertain gestures with both cold hands. "If rape is inevitable, relax and enjoy it?"

She began arranging pebbles in a line. "When Dwight got caught I'd have to go home. Or go free."

"I don't know what anyone over sixteen means by free."

"Now I don't either, but nothing much had ever happened to me before." She pushed away his hand and stood up. "I don't even believe my own explanations, now that I might be inventing them after the fact."

"Most of us do. You might as well practice on me because you'll have to tell the police eventually." Nancy said oh no, she could not. "Or someone will find him."

"I'll face that when I have to."

"That's been your usual method, hasn't it?"

She said rather irritably, "Nobody at home thinks I'm indecisive or weak—at home I'm the strongest. Faye's always telling me, 'I could never live at home like you do, Nancy, but then you're so strong!'" The falsetto sounded worse than Faye's. "The weak view strength as

an unfair advantage you've taken and ought to pay for. There's a grad-
uated income tax on strength, justified at home by scripture. To
whom much is given, much shall be required? I didn't think I had
much given and I got tired of having so much required. If you knew
my family, Hunt Thatcher!"

"I've read the report. I can figure out the rest."

"What they thought was strong and good was just silent and angry
all the time."

"Maybe. It's fashionable to believe only your worst feelings are the
real ones."

"It's been fashionable since Calvin. Maybe it's even true." If so, she
was furious.

"Faye's the sister who was with you. I wonder why the kidnapper
took you instead of Faye."

She had never wondered, though Faye was pretty. Faye wore a 36 C
brassiere.

"Just lucky, I guess." She was thinking that if Faye ever risked her
figure enough to have her two carefully spaced bottle-fed babies,
they'd be sent to Aunt Nancy's regularly. "One reason they sent me to
stay with Grandfather was to save enough so Faye could have dancing
lessons. I'm drifting a long way from Dwight Anderson."

"Take your time. I guess it all goes together."

But less and less did the pieces seem to fit. "Even the report you
read—when it's true, it's misleading. I know my brother, Beck,
sounds like a burden, but he, but he's the only . . . you know what I
probably thought? I probably thought I'd run loose awhile and I'd call
home from time to time and the first day that Beck didn't answer I'd
know Faye had put him into some kind of institution and I could still
rush home and get him out." She scattered her row of stones. "I'm
not saying what I mean at all."

"Want to ride awhile?"

"Yes, oh yes." She rushed to swing onto Lady's back and lead the
way down the trail. Behind, not hurrying, Hunt steadily followed.
She wanted to tell the whole truth to Hunt Thatcher, was afraid to do
so, and wondered immediately what anyone over sixteen meant by
"the whole truth."

When the trail widened and the pines thinned out among boulders they rode side by side. Though Hunt asked nothing, she said, "Dwight did exactly what he wanted and if he was never satisfied, he was never guilty, either. It was fascinating. What makes some people turn out that way and some others become such nasty martyrs?"

"You're not a nasty martyr."

Remembering Persephone, Nancy understood her sampling the pomegranate. "I'm like him," she said shivering. "Part of me is like him."

"Who isn't?"

"The degree," said Nancy, "was news."

For perhaps ten minutes riding alongside, Hunt talked to her in the soothing tone he used with horses. Softly she answered his steady, gentle questions. By stages he began to admit that as Nancy's silence had gone so far, perhaps it was best maintained. Like a prosecutor, Hunt probed. Where exactly did Dwight's body lie? Where was the gun? Who saw her when? Had anyone seen them in the canyon together?

What she felt, responding, was the sheer physical relief of confessional—the twitch when unknown muscles relax, the emptying out of the weight upon the chest and its pressure on the windpipe. In time she only half listened, answering automatically. The excuses he made for her she arranged as a bouquet.

And it stopped being necessary to say that in the moment Dwight Anderson teetered aside and walked forth on the heated air she had sprung forward hoping to see him strike stone and break, intending to guarantee that he did. Nothing but luck sent him over the edge in advance of her pushing hand. When he fell, there had rushed forth from Nancy's throat a noise in which—to this day—she could not separate laughter from roaring, as if the cries of lion and hyena had been electronically mixed and repeated and played on her vocal cords loud enough to start the rock avalanche under which he eventually lay.

She could not bring herself to tell even Hunt about that roar, although once or twice she touched her savage throat while he, riding beside, kept speaking in so rational a manner. The roar was stored deep in her throat. She imagined it was tangible, red and black, folded somehow into a pharyngeal pouch like a vermiform appendix.

"You must quit assigning moral blame to your natural instinct to survive," Hunt was saying.

Above a rocky canyon they dismounted and led the horses down-trail, then rested under trees that had broad leaves like the purple quince. The confessional—though incomplete—had left them intimate, a new softness in both voices. Each was more willing to look directly into the other's face. All the clues, she thought, that Chan and Lewis wished for—but the real cause is our hope that now there's nothing worse to learn.

"Let's spread this blanket. You talked to Beckham Sunday night so it's safe to stay on in Globe awhile."

"I can't keep imposing on Chan."

"We'll send her to Valle, where I've only recently realized she belongs. And I'm entitled to see the final face you're peeling down to every day."

They sat in the shade, Nancy working off the tight boots. "If only Judge Jolley would call. He's going to tell police Dwight went down that trail—I just know it."

Hunt passed his canteen; she was delighted to find it full of gin and tonic.

"All you have to say is that he never caught up. I don't mind a limited amount of loving you for yourself alone, but I'm still curious about how you look without bruises."

"If Dwight's ever found, they'll probably bring me back for the inquest. What did you say?"

"If you ever want me to, I can hike down and find him myself. By accident, of course."

"Did you say loving me?"

"It's possible. Don't you feel it's possible?"

But she was imagining him rappelling down the cliff to kick aside stones and find first an arm dried to leather and an etched leather rose. She saw, suddenly, the magnitude of shared secrets. "I'd be embarrassed even to think about loving anybody my mother threw at me."

"Your mother may have worse taste than mine. Come on, Nancy. Laugh. The joke might be on her and Lewis after all."

"I'm nobody's joke; pass that canteen." She drank deeply and slid to the edge of the blanket. "One reason I wouldn't let Lewis fly me home is that I want to rent a car and drive, and by starting soon I can stop in Isoline. I want to ask about twin brothers."

"Ask who?" His face was lazy, almost drowsy.

She didn't know who. Perhaps the housewife in one of those tract houses, the one whose pastel sheets had been blowing on the line.

"Even if you find he left a dead twin somewhere, since they're both gone now, what's to be gained? Oh!" He looked past her as if at an insight he had seen sculptured in the sandstone wall. "Oh, I get it. If Dwight was a definite murderer, you'd feel justified about everything, including the silence."

"I want to know who he was."

"Why? He didn't care who *you* were. Trying to understand him or what made him is just trying to pump up regrets or good reasons— that's indulgent; it's sentimental." He touched her arm, the one that had heaved the rock. She did not move away but said as she pushed off the second boot, "I hate leaving things in a state of senselessness."

"Even if that's the most accurate state? Would you rather read in a pattern?"

"Probably. That's how I am." She watched his fingers sliding up and down her arm.

"Stay here awhile, Nancy."

"When somebody dies, you ought to know his name."

His hands went where they had pressed her waist when he was telling her how to move with the horse. "I don't want to hurt you," he said. "You'll have to tell me."

"I doubt you can," she said as his hands began moving.

"It doesn't matter who Dwight really was. Who we are—maybe that's going to matter." He kissed her then as she had long ago intended that he should.

Both her eyes stabbed once and then reabsorbed tears she refused to shed on behalf of this kiss, this ultimate male argument, this final reel of the story; and long fibers tightened in her throat where the roar was nested. So much concealment, she thought, slipping her arms around him. Nothing quite as it should be.

But pretty good, she decided, as the kiss went on. All these compromises, sometimes compensations. She would, yes she would, lie now with this man in the sun in this small wild canyon and claim her compensations.

This was the last intention clear to Nancy's will, which was already blurring into sound and touch. He was almost too slow and too deliberate for her—she saw right away that Hunt knew sex was a power and that he wanted her given over to it, lost to it, made helpless by it. Maybe with Ilene he had been the lost one.

She wanted to touch him, too. But her body forgot and moved only for itself as he touched and teased her. She had to close her eyes on the bright outdoors as his sweet delays controlled her until she was spread open and starved. She looked at him fiercely when her climax was becoming real, perhaps premature, and found Hunt staring directly into her face, which no doubt had altered even more than before. That she should be panting while he watched so coolly, perhaps for ascending symptoms, almost threw Nancy out of phase but as he entered her she lowered her lids again and took her full twisting inner wrenches of pleasure in the dark.

17

Five days later Nancy parked her rented car outside the science museum in Los Alamos to stare at Ping-Pong balls glued into a nuclear chain reaction. Leaving Globe she had planned to retrace Dwight's route west and thus erase in reverse the effects of the trip, but halfway to Phoenix she had swerved onto the first route east. She did not want to look off Mather Point again and know some of that silence rose up from him. From now on she did not want to see even a photograph of the Grand Canyon.

Outside Albuquerque she realized that only events she had not witnessed retained any mystery for her, but she had come to Los Alamos without conjuring up Dwight's thefts secondhand or imagining his activities. Actually, as she looked at this toy representation of destruction, her mind was on Hunt Thatcher.

In her motel room she reread his farewell letter:

Dear Nancy,

If I had come to the house Mother was willing to collude by going out for two hours of fresh air and she was disappointed to be handed this letter instead. Probably you also expected me to come and try once more to persuade you to stay. You have not explained yet how briefly we've known each other and may have worked up that one to try. Instead of to me, practice saying no to Faye and Eddie, who sound like a pair of leeches. I'm still waiting for a yes.

It may have been too soon to speak of marriage without adding that I have mixed feelings, too. If I'm not your ideal, you are a long way from being mine—and I've already made one mistake. Besides being smaller and gentler, my ideal was also the kind of horsewoman who could ride a stallion using sewing thread for reins. She had less brains than Nancy Finch but more animation. Afternoons she would have met me at the door, and so forth. I've already missed her once, and it confirmed the criteria and how they would have brought out the man I was always meant to be.

But I'm not that man and I don't expect to become the one your own best self has been waiting for, either. If you're still waiting, don't answer this letter. I'm too old to enjoy unattainable romances by mail. Or by telephone, for that matter. We're both lonely—a waste. Maybe one more year and we'll harden into the people we already are. Together we'd have to change and grow. I'll ask you again to marry me so don't write back unless you know that and the door is open.

No, these letters won't tell the "whole truth" as you advocated last night before even you laughed. (You're more humorless than my ideal, too. You substitute sarcasm.) Keep Oliver Newton to yourself—we're too old for confessions as well. You said you weren't an Augean stable that had to be emptied, not now, and that's good because I have no place to store all that. I've decided that living with a librarian's allusions could be almost as good as living with wit. I'm almost as good as something you had your heart set on, Nancy, and I'll make you happy. Promise.

But your nasty analysis of our motives, which has you forced into my arms because I know where the body is buried—phooey. Horse-shit! I dread the prospect of living with a woman who will be pick-ing her scabs forever. Martyrdom with a rearview mirror. There's truth in pessimism but no one can bear very much of it. Mrs. Thomas Hobbes has my sympathy. I have gloomy tendencies enough but I trust Mother to patch her Wesley on top of your Calvin toward the kind of earned optimism which already knows the worst and hasn't quit.

One important thing you never asked, so I'll answer it anyway. We could always build a house large enough for Beckham.

Travel carefully, Nancy, and think about this last week. You were happy. I couldn't be wrong about that. Our matchmakers were right when they decided I'd learned at last how to love somebody and they saw you as a good candidate. We all tried to hurry you into making a big change in your life when you hadn't digested the oth-ers yet. But when you do, if you decide you also know how and that I'm a good candidate, I'll come to Greenway and ask you again.

Love,
Hunt

P.S. I'll bet your ideal resembled Heathcliff. Sorry.

That night instead of love Nancy dreamed she was taking a long, slow, soundless fall off an airplane wing and inexorably toward the open mouth of a heated smokestack, but she was not much fright-ened. In the dream she thought she could pull a parachute when she chose or possibly fly. Good, she thought in the morning. My mind is cleaning itself.

When she called Ruston, Harvey Jolley had left for Tennessee. Now that he was ahead of her in Somerville and now that she saw that nothing would explain Dwight except perhaps facts about Dwight, she threw away her marked map and drove fast across the country-side toward whatever answers the judge might have. She tried to phone him but the number was unlisted.

When she came out of the booth into the busy drugstore, on im-pulse she walked to the counter and asked for a year's supply of Enovid. The dozen compacts were handed calmly to her across the counter with no mention of prescription. She felt foolish standing there with the wherewithal for twelve safe lunar cycles in her hand, no questions asked, and it made her wonder how many of her other long-term wishes might have been as easily granted if she had only requested them with firmness.

Down the long slope of Oklahoma on I-40 Nancy was approaching Weatherford when a rear tire went flat. She thumped off the highway, rolled out the spare, and posed helplessly by the open trunk with the jack sagging from both hands, though not as breezily as she might have before knowing that someone like Dwight might always be driving by.

The Indian who changed her tire was headed to Okeene, a town she might know because of its annual spring snake hunt, he said. Above his elbow were two scars he said a diamondback's fangs had dug last April. They looked like cigarette burns.

"We milk poison out and then kill them for meat and leather," he said, tightening the lugs. "The poison goes into medicine to treat snakebite." He used his biceps to vibrate the scar tissue for Nancy's benefit; she knew then that her bruises were no longer ugly.

In Oklahoma City, sleepless that night between sheets as unnaturally crisp as bond paper, she thought about Hunt, who would brood, who would hold things back, who was subject to melancholy. Under his busy fingers she had felt like a console being played—worse, she had understood Faye at the mercy of Eddie's hands.

Already she had complained, "Hunt, I'm never going to know you."

"You know me." She shook her head. "Women usually mean by that that the man is withholding his weaknesses, leaving her no weapons that can do him damage if she needs to."

"You're cynical."

"Yes," said Hunt. "I promise it's going to be a relief to you."

"But I told you about Dwight and you haven't trusted me with a damn thing."

"See?"

That's when Nancy brought up emotional blackmail and the bond of knowing the worst. "Let's take self-interest for granted," Hunt said. "If you plan to spend your days culling real reasons from good reasons—go right ahead. I'll settle for what people do and judge those acts." He knocked out his pipe in the car's ashtray and turned on her that languid look of sex. "We haven't harmed each other so far." Proving his point, he had slid one hand casually from her breast to pubis, though they were parked in downtown Globe at the time. Her thighs quivered. "No matter what your essence may be," he said in a soft, half-mocking voice, "I'm satisfied to deduce it from your body and behavior."

She felt belittled, her soul canceled. "That's not what I want!"

"No?" His hand was roving again.

"Not all I want," she amended.

The next day Nancy crossed Oklahoma and pushed on through Arkansas to Memphis late Friday night, and Saturday she arrived in the quiet county seat of Somerville, once the heart of Tennessee's western plantation country. She was directed to the judge's house near the Loosahatchie River by a mechanic who said, "Watch he don't shoot you now that he's a nervous wreck!"

After hardwood forests and long, orderly cornfields, Nancy took a curving drive through a pecan grove and into a semicircle before his large white house. High and low piazzas had become two floors of screened porches with green awnings and window fans filling the long side windows.

While Nancy parked, a young black man ran a lawn mower toward her and left its handle blocking her car door. "Give the judge your name, please, ma'am?"

"He's expecting me." The man waited. "Could you move this mower?" She finally shouted over its engine, "Nancy Finch!" While she stayed blocked in the car the man carried her name onto the dim lower porch and a shadow climbed more stairs into the house in relay until at last Judge Jolley, red-faced, came running out. On a chain around his neck hung a gold cross the right size for the Pope. As Nancy got out he touched the Band-Aid above her eye.

"I did that," he said mournfully, "as surely as if I'd struck you."

"Of course you didn't." She felt awkward with Dwight gone and gave him a light hug. "It happened in the canyon."

"But he might have caught up with you there for all I knew. What a coward I am! All the time you saw straight through me!" Before she could disagree he called as the mower roared by, "Thanks, Bruce! Fine boy. One hundred and ninety-five pounds, on the wrestling team, in case Dwight ever shows up here. I'm trying to get him to go to seminary. At night his brother comes. But you're traveling alone? He could be anywhere, Nancy. He could come to Somerville with a machine gun under one arm and ask where I lived and somebody would tell him the shortest road." He led her to the wide porch and a white wicker chair. The main doors and ground-floor windows, he told her, now had a burglar-alarm circuit. "You do the same when you get home. For years you won't hear a board squeak in your floor at night without wondering if he's standing on it. Have some of this iced tea. I've quit drinking."

"You're wrong," said Nancy as she took a glass. "I wish I could reassure you that Dwight is never going to bother you again."

"You can forgive me for deserting you that way?"

"I deserted you, too."

"It's in my blood, I think—my mother left me and my father left her and I keep leaving, too, but that's no excuse. I went back to Ruston in case she was alive somewhere and very old and needing something and I could break the pattern, but they never had any idea who my parents were. I talked to the children a lot about standing firm in adversity, at least I could do that."

"Why didn't you call me from the orphanage?"

"I was ashamed. So much is clear to me now, Nancy, that I don't even know where to start. For instance, when Dwight locked me up and I had plenty of time to think—that was the beginning. The place was just like a prison cell."

"Well," said Nancy. "Not exactly." The judge looked much older. "Do you think Dwight went into the canyon? Did you see him?"

"I didn't but I'm sure he went and I hope he stepped on a rattlesnake. Probably it would kill the rattlesnake."

"I'm headed to Isoline to learn more about him. Maybe you know someone there in the register of deeds office."

"I don't see why the police can't find him. He didn't just walk off into thin air." The judge wiped his forehead on a handkerchief. "Maybe he's hiding out in Isoline deciding whether to come west for me or east for you."

"We'll never see Dwight again, I'm sure of it."

Judge Jolley walked past a potted fern and stood watching Bruce mow grass. "People can change, even cowards," he said. "Simon Peter did." She agreed quickly. He said, "I'll be going to jail, Nancy. They're going to charge me with misuse of judicial office. I'm ready to go."

"I'm sorry. Are you guilty?"

"I'll be able to think in jail. Peter did. Peter had his name changed, too, did you know that?"

"So did Paul but I can't see what you mean. What about Isoline?"

"In Tennessee my name won't do you any good. Besides, it's Saturday. Everything's closed. You can stay here for the weekend." His mouth closed into a knot. "You'll be chaperoned. There's Bruce's brother and a live-in cook." Nancy said she didn't know. "I want you to hear this evangelist who's only in town this week."

"I doubt I can stay." The conversation seemed difficult. Away from Dwight they did not know each other very well.

"As soon as I got back I went to see the sheriff about Dwight and the foreman of the grand jury about the other case. I'll be glad to go to jail; I deserve it. What if you'd died down there?" But she didn't, said Nancy. "Clara did."

"I'm sure you'll only get a suspended sentence."

"Oh no! They wouldn't do that!" he said in dismay. He took a small notebook from his shirt pocket, extended it so she could see several columns of phrases and pick up: *Appian Way, Quo Vadis? Capernaum, Jerusalem,* before he took it back. "In prison I'll be able to do some writing."

"Can't you write here?" She swept a hand at the green peace and isolation on all sides, even Bruce's mower a soothing distant sound by now. He looked doubtful. "Right now I'm more interested in learning about Dwight Anderson than Simon Peter."

The judge said, "I plan to write my autobiography in prison. I see a pattern in Saint Peter, that's all. Maybe I was meant to be a Catholic anyway; my mother always thought so. I mean my mother Annette Jolley." He located the wicker chair in some definite spot on the porch floor, sat in it, and turned up his chin. "Haven't you always thought there was something unusual about my face?"

To say no seemed unkind. "In what way?"

"Look closely now. And remember my hair used to be much curlier than this." He set a forefinger to the tip of his nose and pushed in. "There. Now you see it."

"Where? What?"

"I might never have realized it but for going back to Louisiana and taking a good look around. I may be mulatto!"

"What?" She laughed and stopped laughing. "You're no such thing. You're a boring Anglo-Saxon like the rest of us."

"Until I got back in the really deep south I'd forgotten that nearly everybody there is black. The numbers alone, the statistics alone, would make it likely! And if I was a mixed baby why of course he would leave her and, naturally then, she'd leave the baby. She'd be bitter."

"Judge Jolley, your hair has been blond all your life and nobody's face could be more Caucasian. Take your finger off your nose."

"Dark blond. Once it was curly, very very curly." He looked cross. "When you get older you'll find a partial plate will make your own lips look thinner than they are now." He blew lightly to drive his mouth forward. "I don't see how you can fail to see it."

"Surely you're not going to make such a claim in your autobiography!"

"It'll sell the book if I've lived my life on the white side of the color line and sent white men to jail and married a white woman. I'd be," he said triumphantly, "the first colored judge in the state of Tennessee, no doubt, and you know how firsts and mosts sell books. *Then* we get to Saint Peter, you see. Repentance and turning. Have you tried the profile?" He showed it, Roman nose and all. Nancy shook her head, smiling. "I never felt really settled anywhere."

"You were an orphan and could remember it. Sometimes I've felt as if I belonged somewhere else, too, but I can trace my family straight to the Scottish Highlands."

He stood over her, cocking his head this way and that. Now she saw why he looked older—he had shaved off the blond mustache and uncovered lines by his mouth. "You'll be able to see it after a while," he promised, "once you start looking for it."

He looked zero percent Negro. "Are you telling people in Somerville?"

"I've told Bruce. He can't see it either."

When they went indoors for supper the judge showed her how to activate the electric alarm by flipping a simple light switch.

By the stairway, where you would pass them morning and evening, hung dozens of photographs of Jolley ancestors and kin, wearing every uniform and regalia. In the most recent row she found Harvey and Clara at their wedding altar, Clara with an elongated face and holding her mouth as if it enclosed buck teeth.

Though the table was too long, the chandelier too low, the room too overpowering, eating together made both more comfortable. "This feels like my home—the sideboard, the big mirror."

He passed the fried chicken. "And you're going back there, you who were more entitled to run away than I ever was."

"I'm going back different, though," she said, for she had been making plans. "First I'll rent an apartment and see how well Mama and Beck can really get along by themselves, or maybe I'll live on my grandfather's farm and look for a buyer. You see"—she waited until he had lifted his head—"you see, I met a man out west."

"Not that awful Doctor Foster!"

"No, someone in Arizona. Maybe someday I'll move where he is."

"Not that airplane pilot?"

"Lewis is old! No, Hunt Thatcher, the son of the woman I've been staying with. You've seen the papers? In Globe. Maybe he's forty, divorced. You'd like him."

The judge repeated, "Forty." Without warning he exposed rows of many teeth. "How's that for a natural minstrel grin?" Nancy said he looked like a crocodile.

"I know black is beautiful nowadays but there can't be many rewards in Tennessee for changing color."

He seemed to be losing heart, said to her he probably resembled "the man who burned down the temple of Diana in order to get into history. You know. What's-his-name."

That made her laugh. During a tour of the farm she agreed to stay overnight, drive east on Sunday and stay in Monterey, and take all of Monday to search the public files. "And you're chaperoned here," he repeated, "though I must be as old as that airplane pilot!"

Despite his enthusiasm, that evening she found the tent revival like a hundred others, the preacher intense in the usual ways, the band too brassy, the crowd too desperate, the quartet on "Heavenly Sunshine" sounding ironic to her now. The judge seemed deeply moved. Sometimes, touching her with his elbow, he would say "It's all right if you want to go forward," and fidget in his seat while the preacher called once more for converts.

The many songs of pilgrimage had some cumulative effect. "I Feel Like Traveling On," sang these farmers, who had rarely left the county. They were bound for Canaan; they were "going/to where the fountains are overflowing"; they were marching to Zion. Gospel ships and mountain railroads also carried them upward.

After the congregation had sung all the verses of "Oh, Why Not Tonight?" Nancy was not surprised to see that Judge Jolley had rushed down the aisle to the penitents' bench; her surprise came when an old woman down the row whispered to her husband, "That's the same one that got saved Monday night." The husband said, "The preacher needs him to prime the pump."

Afterward Nancy could not figure out what to say to the judge. He drove home in his usual tentative, anxious way, pulling onto the shoulder for passing cars, remarking uneasily at last, "I thought you might come forward with me, too, but you're not carrying my guilt."

"I have my guilts."

"You'd find it a wonderful experience to be changed by the Holy Spirit."

To her the judge didn't seem changed enough.

Nancy slept poorly in his house, not because of wood creaks or banging clocks but because the judge flew down the dark hall after every noise. One owl hoot—his flashlight beam swept by her window. If a shutter blew the bodyguard was called.

Though she said, yawning at breakfast, that if she ever did get married she'd invite him, she was thinking that she and Harvey Jolley would probably never see each other again, and not just because he had hidden himself in the Rock of Ages. Before noon they ran out of talk. He thought of showing her Clara's grave but someone had marked on her tombstone with Crayola crayon. He had been almost speechless from anger. Nancy decided to leave early.

Bruce was pruning all the lilacs below man-height as he watched them say goodbye. "You write me," said the judge. "Do me a favor now—take off that tape and let me see."

With resignation she peeled the bandage and put it in her purse to show him that the stitches were healed, the eyebrow growing hairs. "My fault!" he cried, and leaned forward to kiss it with a spiritual kiss she found distasteful. "I want you to have this." Though she made aimless protest movements he took off his cross pendant and hung the chain around her neck. The whole thing was so heavy she decided it was made of lead with a fake bronze patina. "I have others," he said. "No, I insist." She got into the car with the four points banging into her chest until she expected to end up as bruised as Dwight. "I envy the man in Arizona," he said as she started the car, and then called him Chase and not Hunt. She was glad to wave and go.

Monday morning, turning off the highway north to Isoline, Nancy was surprised by a vague fearfulness she had maybe caught from the judge. His picture of Dwight trying to decide between coming west or east to kill one of them made her imagine Dwight working out painfully from under his heap of stones, hailing with bloodied arm a rubber raft, wading into the Colorado River to be dragged aboard. Not possible.

Yet she was nervous and stared at everyone. After the cluster of stores she decided Dwight had turned off this road right, then left. Dusty fields, trumpet vines—here? She bounced on stones a long way before looping back to the same spot. The next turnoff crossed a creek and ended at a fill-dirt and gravel business.

Outside a grocery store she asked a man sitting on an overturned bucket if he could help her find the courthouse.

"Didn't know it was lost. Little joke? Lady, where you from? Does this place look like a county seat? The courthouse is in Cookeville where it's always been. You know where Cookeville is?"

An earlier exit off the interstate—damn. She drove back to Cookeville and the Putnam County Courthouse. She told the Registrar of Deeds the year she was interested in—assuming Dwight had told the truth about being twenty-nine. The clerk said she'd never heard of any county that kept separate records of twin births. "I'll have to check them all then." She was ushered into the vault.

"I never knew," said the clerk suspiciously, "you could trace a genealogy without knowing the surname."

"If the family stories are true, the twin boys were illegitimate." Nancy lied so smoothly she was sorry Hunt had missed it. "They're probably under the mother's surname but I don't know what that was."

"You plan to read through that whole year?" The ledger on its metal shelf was two inches thick. Nancy nodded and lugged it to a high table. Doggedly she began turning pages. After the F's and G's she dragged over a stool and smoked two cigarettes. For a long time after her dehydration in the canyon she had not smoked at all. The only twins she had found were stillborn girls. She stood up to stretch, beginning to think that Dwight and his brother had been born in Illinois, Kansas, Maine. From the doorway the clerk suggested she try the *Dispatch* office.

"I thought this would be easier than going through three hundred and sixty-five newspapers."

"The Putnam *Dispatch* is only twice a week if their files go that far back. They might have written up any twins." She looked thoughtful. "But I doubt they'd put in any illegitimate twins; this isn't New York City, you understand."

"Maybe the mother got married later." Nancy took a walk to the nearby newspaper office. In an alcove in the large newsroom a teenaged boy explained how the card file was cross-indexed to bound volumes of old *Dispatches*. Nancy drew out the T drawer and pulled a card, TWINS, with a long list of headlines, dates, and page numbers. The dates showed how many articles were linked to holidays. JEAN AND JOHN WEAR WHITE ROSES must be a sad Mother's Day feature.

Nancy made herself counter space among paste pots and rolled newspapers, looking for headlines with male names. GHOSTLY DOUBLETAKE *w/photo, Oct. 31)* was too recent.

The boy who was taking classifieds by phone said between calls, "We've got one set of triplets if you need them. One is deformed?" Nancy shook her head, reading, CHUCK AND CHICK CONFUSE SANTA— also too recent unless Dwight had kept his illusions to advanced age. At last the only unusual entry stopped her sliding finger: GRANDSON SOUGHT—not a word more, not even about twins. Ten years ago. She was afraid Chick or Chuck might have been lost overnight in the woods, yet everything else on the card could be instantly dismissed. The boy watching her asked, "Is this a heredity study? Are you from the university?"

"North Carolina. It looks like a dead end." But since the bound volume was near her chair, even stored crooked to catch her notice, she spread it and leafed toward September. GRANDSON SOUGHT. *Page 5. Col. 3.*

Beneath that headline the article proved to be a chatty county correspondent's newsletter, a collection of one-sentence paragraphs about who had visited whom, had surgery, or harvested vegetables with funny shapes. At last she found:

> Friends of Mrs. Willard Apple have been unable to assist her in locating her grandson Ervin Childers. His twin brother Edwin sent letters to newspapers in Chattanooga, Memphis, and other large American cities just after Mrs. Apple had her stroke without success. Since leaving home some years ago Mrs. Apple has not heard one word and his whereabouts are unknown. Mrs. Apple is reported to be sinking fast in spite of visits and cards.

That was all. In the next paragraph Lacy Whitfield was having his elbow cast removed. Nancy copied the paragraph and showed it to the boy, asking what area of Putnam County this correspondent covered.

"You're from the Charlotte *Observer!* The TV?"

When Nancy said it was just family research he became bored and

showed her the large county map on one wall and a road between Isoline and Monterey.

"May I use your telephone?"

"I take classifieds on it! Well, if it's short."

She called the Registrar of Deeds and asked to have her open ledger
checked. No Childers twins. Would she try a year on either side?
Nothing. Discouraged, Nancy walked through the humidity and ran
the car engine till she could feel the air-conditioning. No matter
where the Childers boys had been born, Dwight might have been a
Smith in a different state. The Isoline house could be one Dwight had
robbed, or a cell mate had robbed, or—

If I don't check, Nancy thought, I'll always wonder.

North of the interstate past dairy farms, across Obey Creek, and
under trees so tender a green she felt like airmailing leaves to Hunt,
she drove to the right county road. Something about the row of small,
nondescript houses alerted her. She stopped by the roadside, examined them, and again her nape tingled. What she half recognized were
not these flat front yards but their partly seen backyards; once she
had raised her eyes the meadow sloped uphill beyond just as she knew
it must toward somebody's abandoned homeplace turning gray in a
grove of oaks. With its dead chimney swifts inside. Nancy hurried to
knock on the nearest door.

The woman who answered did not look capable of choosing lavender sheets but this was the house. "I'm trying to locate a Mrs. Willard
Apple."

"She's dead. I don't miss her, no offense."

"I'm mostly looking for her grandsons."

"I don't keep track of the generations, especially hers." She was
closing the door but remembered. "Those twins? And one of them
never came to her funeral? Serves her right."

Nancy nodded rapidly. "Ervin Childers."

"Oh, *those* people. I don't have anything to do with people like
that." She stepped onto the cracked cement stoop. "The Apples
owned all this land." She waved a blotched arm. "What's left of them
lives at the end of these houses in the biggest one and I don't have a
thing to do with those people. Be a waste of your time, too." Nancy

stepped in line to see the far house with its extra wing. "I hope they got rich off of these houses we got poor off of," the woman grumbled.

"Who lives there? Edwin?"

"And friend," said the woman with a sneer as she closed the door.

The house was eight doors down at the end of a row of seven dry front yards. Bermuda grass was at work breaking apart the seven cracked driveways Nancy crossed. From the last mailbox she took the walk and climbed to a white front door with a peephole. As always, she rose on tiptoe and put her eye against that peephole, not because she could see in but because she liked to imagine some nervous resident recoiling when her giant iris swelled into view.

Then she rang the door chimes. A front drapery wavered. She waited, noting that this house had no more individuality than the rest. No ornament had been added. The same incompetent horticulturist had sold these five sick boxwoods and stuck them into hard clay. Her second ring brought a soft flap of bedroom slippers. Nancy shifted her purse to the left hand and got ready to smile.

Dwight Anderson opened the door.

18

A scream burst halfway up Nancy's throat before she realized the man in the satin bathrobe was Dwight's double and not Dwight. She could not muffle the cry that blew the stranger back against a foyer table. He staggered forward to slam the door.

"Wait!" She pushed the panel with both hands. "Edwin? Wait!"

Hanging on to the door's edge he looked unbelievably like Dwight—only, she thought, not Dwight, not even Melrose, but Ervin, *Ervin*. Like Ervin this man was lean, brown haired, sharp boned, plain, forgettable, an inch shorter. His front teeth were unbroken, the face blanched, his hazel eyes only yellow tinted. He pushed the door against her saying nervously, "Scream all you like, I won't buy any magazines!"

His eyes were both paler and smaller. "Edwin Childers?"

"Wrong house."

She said rapidly, "You're Edwin Childers and I've come across the country to find you. I'm Nancy Finch; please let me in." He kept the door under pressure. Inside the robe he wore cotton pajamas, perhaps recuperating from the bullet wound his brother had paid him for the car. "I know your brother Ervin."

At that he groaned and pushed the door harder, forcing Nancy to block with her shoulder. Their braced feet alternately lost and gained leverage as they threw their whole weight against both sides of the door.

"I hate Ervin," she wheezed during an equilibrium in which each leaned evenly. The man's jawline looked slightly blue from struggle. She gasped, "I thought you were dead."

The word jerked him off-balance. "I mustn't exert myself or I will be," he puffed. "Go away, let me alone." But Nancy's extra power now made his bedroom shoes slide.

"I hate Ervin," she said again.

"Go hate him someplace else."

"He kidnapped me."

He also responded with new strength until gradually the door began shutting again, Edwin's face bone-hard from strain. "That's not my fault."

Her cheek was against the door and she feared the healed stitches would split. As it slammed she shouted, "And you're alive while Ervin's the one dead."

Immediately the door swung back no wider than his face. He was clearly the second boy in the photograph, the weak facsimile. All along the fish had been Dwight's. "Dead?"

Since twins were alleged to have a sixth sense about each other, his surprise was disappointing. "You're deeply grieved; I can see that."

"If you knew him you know better. I doubt he was any different with women." As if from an air current the door drifted wider. "I'm not well. This excitement will set me back. What was your name— Byrd?"

"Finch." Nancy pushed harder than necessary to guarantee getting past him and the foyer table. He could only follow saying, "Surely I'll be notified officially? There's no need!" They half ran down the hall into a large early American den containing many dried flower arrangements. Every scrap of fabric in cushions, draperies, and up-holstery showed the same pattern: pine cones on tan. She dropped into a rocker.

By the cold hearth Edwin stood tying his sash while he reset his face into regret. "Dead. Ervin is dead." His voice and mouth turned up. "Are you certain he's dead?" Nancy said she was, though some weren't. "It's his turn." Under his thumb the fringe was trembling. "Tell me exactly how you know."

Nancy took from her pocketbook the first long clipping from the Globe newspaper and handed it to him. He read aloud in disbelief, "'Bizarre kidnapping ends in flight across canyon?'"

"Grand Canyon. Whenever it says Dwight Anderson read Ervin Childers."

He absorbed a paragraph before asking, "How do you know his real name if this newspaper didn't?"

"Until today I didn't know." She was staring past the pine cone draperies through the window and uphill to the oak grove. "He brought me to your Grandmother Apple's house. And he had a pho-tograph of twin boys who had caught a big fish. It's a long story but that's where it starts."

"Ervin kept that picture? I burned all mine and then Grandma died and left me a drawerful." Reading, Edwin said, "He never changed," and at the clipping's end, "Was he caught? Is that how he died?"

"He disappeared. I believe he went into that canyon and never came out."

"What do the police believe?"

"That they'll catch him. They still don't know who Dwight really was. Is. Was."

He laid the clipping down with a gesture she was later to mark as habit—releasing it, then looking with evident puzzlement into his own empty hand. "He's not dead."

"I'm sure of it."

He said bitterly, "Ervin has already climbed out of a wrecked car. He has already made it to shore when most of the other people in the water did not." She watched him pace before the brick fireplace, finally asking, "Must the police know his real name?" Surprised, Nancy began to stammer but he insisted, "Why? He's caused me enough trouble!"

"But to catch," Nancy faltered. "In case he survived? But just because; just for the sake of the facts. To have things right!"

"Right? It's not right that I have to live Ervin down again. I despise policemen." Across the table he pushed her clipping away, took back his hand, and studied the palm. "They spy on people's private lives."

Perhaps some righteous look on Nancy's face made him add angrily, "This wouldn't be the first secret you ever kept in your life. If the police track down his identity, that's one thing; but why must you volunteer?"

She admitted it would hardly be her first secret.

"He won't come back here. If he did, even I would notify the police. I'm afraid of him. So life will go on as it has gone the past few years, for I've had no way of knowing if Ervin was alive or dead."

"Let me think about it. Lying becomes so complicated."

Edwin, now standing by the window, said, "When he came to that house I was probably sitting right here in this room. Ervin would have known that and liked knowing it. He probably looked toward this house. No?" Quickly Nancy reconstructed the episode for him with the interruption of Judge Jolley, and though Edwin nodded periodically he seemed hardly to hear details. "He wanted to show you to me, I'm sure of that, but the old man prevented it."

"Why?" She thought suddenly of that scene in the bare kitchen, that she might have been brought downhill with her clothing in disarray, hurt and crying. She said angrily, "What if he had?" Edwin shrugged. "You wouldn't even have interfered, would you?"

Very lightly he touched himself on the left breast. "I'm getting over a serious operation. I went to Pennsylvania for open-heart surgery and came home with a pacemaker." Now Edwin almost limped to the cluttered chaise across from her and arranged himself under an afghan. "I can't seem to regain my strength with this electrical device, perhaps I mistrust its workmanship."

"Did your brother know all that?"

"He didn't believe it. Ervin always insisted that he was the one with heart disease. To know he was dead now would cut my blood pressure in half." Unclenching his hand, he glanced inside seeking a trace of pity. "Your secret could help the life of a sick man, Miss Finch." She said firmly, "Sick people have already claimed fifteen years of mine. Persuade me another way."

"You must have given Ervin a lot of trouble." He smiled, sinking into his nest among magazines, books, radio, food packages. "What persuades you?"

"Tell me everything about your brother. Tell me what caused him." His high giggle was nothing like Dwight's. Ervin's. "The same things that caused you and me—one sperm, one egg, and carelessness." He had begun to exhale behind every word, making his speech falsely strained and hyperbolic. "I'm only drawing you away from emotional interpretation to mere facts, to an observation of facts."

"Facts, all right; let's hear them."

"In a scientific sense, life arranged certain control factors. We're identical, not fraternal, twins. Concerning environment, our early experiences were the same except I was physically weaker. Oh my!" Again the giggle. "Perhaps it relieves you to find me sick?" It was a happy discovery. "Miss Finch, you were afraid of me!"

"Twins are usually alike."

"No, no!" He opened and upturned his right hand, shook it—nothing concealed, nothing up his sleeve. "No, Ervin and I were absolutely not alike from the very first, no similarities, none. He was a cruel boy who grew into a cruel man." From the afghan's folds he lifted *Time, Reader's Digest, The New Yorker.* "I've educated myself. And this house—can you imagine Ervin in this house?" His swinging arm rocked a vase of dried wheat and seed pods. Nancy decided to sit quietly and listen. "The only book Ervin ever read voluntarily was about those awful Siamese twins in the mountains, Chang and Eng something." Edwin drank in quick agitated swallows from his glass of ice water. "I wouldn't read it."

The silence went on too long. Part of Nancy wanted to hear good and happy memories but part did not. "When you were little boys," she prompted.

"I had rheumatic fever as a child, I had—in fact—every disease it was possible to have. If they find his body"—he giggled—"if they find his corpse it will weigh twice as much as mine because he has tonsils and I don't; he has an appendix; he has adenoids. He may have several adenoids!"

"He was tattooed."

"Not that I know of," said Edwin vaguely as he swept on. "If he got a swollen ear and was well overnight, I'd be in bed with mumps for three weeks. I was allergic. Only his nature was . . . was deformed."

"Even as a boy?"

"You want a trauma, don't you? Yes, there was a trauma but it didn't make me kidnap women! No, that's too easy. His parents died but they were my parents, too!" Nancy asked how. "In a boating accident. We were twelve and afterward they sent us to Grandma's. We were all in the water—I nearly got pneumonia." He shook his head at her next rush of questions. "It was near the Gulf but how our parents got down there and how they first met and got married and who *their* families were and which aberrations *they* had—well, those eggs and sperms and circumstances run back forever, Miss Finch. They tell you nothing, nothing."

Nancy said grimly, "I haven't come this far to settle for nothing."

"On a normal Sunday we were taking a family boat ride after church—"

"Catholic? Protestant?"

"I barely remember, something primitive, I've never even wondered." Without thinking he displayed *The New Yorker* again, saying, "Holiness? It's irrelevant. The boat on the lake turned over and Ervin"—he stroked his breastbone as if to soothe the pacemaker—"Ervin swam to shore. I made it partway before some man swam out to get me. Our mother couldn't swim. Father may have hit his head; I'll never know." He continued to caress himself without looking up. "That's them on the wall in the first and last car my father ever owned. I had the snapshot enlarged."

The young couple with grainy faces was posed between headlights. The man looked British and stringy in tweed clothes, the woman mousier, more like her sons, but too small and thin to support the large flowers in her print skirt. When Nancy stood closer both faces turned to blurred dots of all sizes. "Had you been born then?" They were almost two, he answered, and ten years later Ervin turned over the boat.

"So he made his own trauma and blamed himself."

"Made it on purpose. You can see how delicate my mother was. The ordeal of giving birth to two of us!"

"What do you mean, on purpose?"

"Ervin was rowing with my father since I was just over the measles. I was here, in the front, in the prow." Making his hand into a crescent, Edwin located himself tiny on the fingertips and floated himself slowly through the air. "My father had just used the word, prow, so I've always remembered. Ervin was tired of the attention I'd had at home while he went every day to school. They kept arguing behind me about school, some punishment he'd gotten there; I forget. Ervin always said later they had no argument but I heard them. I was looking for fish when"—he jerked his hand sharply in midair—"when the boat rocked and overturned so fast I was wet and then under the water before I understood anything and my mother—it must have been my mother—fell on top of me somehow. Screaming. I hit at her in a panic, you know, not understanding what was all over me. It couldn't have made any difference. Still."

"So Ervin swam for help."

"Ervin swam somewhere but he didn't send any help. See why I don't trust him to be down in that canyon? The man who hauled me in had seen the overturned boat. Everybody thought I was the only survivor. They found Ervin the next night miles away under a dance pavilion."

"Sick? Hurt? In shock?"

"Sound asleep. I've always thought—" Suddenly Edwin interrupted himself by snatching up the nearby telephone. He dialed and asked someone how soon he would be home, then listened. "A little nervous, yes—you'll see why." He turned his head away saying ominously, "Yes. A woman! All right. How soon? Good."

The call revived him. In a stronger voice he said to Nancy, "I believe Ervin hit Father with the oar but they were behind me; I didn't see it.

Later I did accuse him. He said I was delirious with pneumonia but I was not. I told the rescuers but of course not knowing Ervin they couldn't believe him capable. I told Grandmother Apple many many times, many times. All she would say was: God's will, God's instrument. Imagine my poor mother growing up in such an atmosphere if you think that will explain anything!"

"Did you accuse him many times?"

"He always denied it. When I kept on he would hit me. The principal would bring us home often in his car and I wouldn't even get to show my test paper because he had to talk over Ervin's fighting. They had to stitch up one boy. They had to stitch me." He showed Nancy a scar curving behind one ear into his hair. "Usually Ervin tried to hit somebody's head and to hit it *with* something so as not to bruise his hand. This was a croquet mallet. The boat had heavy oars." He found a medicine bottle and swallowed a capsule. "Even remembering him is a risk to me."

But Nancy said, "What if it was Ervin who fell on top of you in the water?"

"Ervin? Scream? Are you crazy?" With eyes closed, he waved toward the window. "So we grew up with Grandma Apple and for a widow in hard times she did her best. She was no thief, now; at worst she was a community pest. To her, everything she did was justified so don't you dare blame her for how Ervin turned out."

"He never mentioned her."

"No wonder, the way he worried her to death. My sweet neighbors have given you an earful, I'll bet. What time is it?" By reflex Nancy looked at the wrist where Dwight had put the watch. Edwin kept talking. "Grandma Apple just invented her own form of welfare payments and forced her type of tax on those sweet neighbors, every one of whom had plenty of money. For example, she had a schedule of people to visit and welcomes to overstay; she kept a list distributed on her Pinkham calendar. She would carry us boys to sit in different living rooms talking about nothing, smiling, I can see her yet—not many work any harder for their wages. She could keep talking and talking until it got to be eight o'clock and then eight-thirty and nine and at last people had to offer us supper or starve themselves. By that method we all got one free meal a day, usually supper." He stopped his short giggle. "Eventually nobody would answer the door when we knocked so she would walk right in and call. Finally those sweet neighbors locked their front doors against her. She had them spaced so they could have spread one little supper every two weeks—they all had plenty—but they locked their doors against us."

"I thought she owned a lot of land."

"You can't eat land or wear it in the rain and she wouldn't sell off an inch. She'd ask people outright for clothes or furniture but she had her code—you don't ask for money and you don't sell land." He peered long into his mysterious hand. "It's a marvel what I've come through."

"You and your brother must have felt embarrassed."

"It was clear that people hated to see us coming. The gall she had!" His imitation of a lady's soprano whine was almost too accurate. *"Now that you've added a pound or so, Mrs. Whench, if you decide to get rid of that little blue dress, I've always admired it!"* He had trouble lowering pitch for the next sentences. "And she could get up just as calmly and walk right into that woman's bedroom to show her which dress she meant, which hanger she kept it on. I've known her to carry a bicycle out of anybody's front yard if it was lying within twenty-five feet of the garbage can." Easily his voice rose again to treble, *"They've thrown that perfectly good bike away, Er-uh-vin!"* And he'd carry it home."

"You never carried things home."

"I wasn't well. It was better to leave me in bed and talk about being a poor widow woman with two orphaned boys to feed and one of them stricken."

"She made him a thief."

"I told you not to blame her. If things were missing around here, the first step was to send to Mrs. Apple's and ask if she happened to have seen it. Usually she said no, but sometimes I'd take it back later as a found-object because I looked sick, see, and they might give me some reward or at least a snack. She had a good business in missing dogs and cats when a reward would finally be advertised, but Ervin didn't get in trouble for that, for earning his meals—no, he got expelled for setting fire to the school. He set several fires before he started stealing, really stealing. Grandma Apple was shocked, let me tell you."

"He stole money?"

"We could have used money—no, he stole cars and took off in them. The sheriff got to know Ervin very well and by the time the third car disappeared he had the papers half filled out. When they chased him, he probably wrecked that car on purpose so the owner wouldn't get it back. So the state sent him off."

"She had to sign papers calling him incorrigible or something."

"You're hoping he felt rejected! He felt nothing—believe me. The way albinos get no color traits he got no real feelings. He forgot our dead mother in a week and when they sent him to juvenile detention he forgot us in less."

"No," said Nancy. "He didn't."

"All he got at that place was a first-class education in crime before he went over the fence. The second time he was gone two years. He would call us up using different names asking for money. He called himself Children, Childs, Irwin, Appleton. I don't believe his I.Q. added up to ninety. All he ever read was about those Siamese twins joined together on the side and how they could swim in perfect rhythm." The doorbell chimed. "There's Andy at last." Barefoot he started to the door, stopping to hand Nancy a covered basket from the coat closet. "Grandmother's pictures."

She had only lifted the lid when he brought in a younger man carrying a grocery bag. "Bedroom slippers," he was advising when he saw her. "So this is Ervin's girlfriend."

"Not at all," said Nancy. Edwin introduced "my roommate, Andy Wright," who was handsome though fattening from the armpits down in a way that made his head seem a small afterthought. He wore a white summer suit.

"I'm relieved," he said, extending a damp hand. "He'd require a Jezebel or a Borgia."

As they shook hands she asked if Andy were short for Andrew or Anderson.

"Anderson. I am going to mix some old-fashioneds before I even sit down."

"Good. Oh. Oh, I see what you mean," said Edwin slowly. "Anderson, Dwight Anderson! It could be that the similarity would have struck his fancy. Andy, just read through this clipping while you're making drinks and you'll be caught up. He's probably dead."

"That catches me up with all I care to know." Andy let the clipping dangle. "Edwin is making a terribly slow recovery from his operation. I'll bet you skipped your nap." Holding the news item to one side as if near his stronger eye he skimmed the main facts in silence.

"If Ervin's dead, I'm going to sleep like a baby tonight."

Andy's polite smile was shrinking. "There's nothing here about dead." Nancy explained again while he was helping Edwin back onto the chaise. All he said was, "If your brother died without making the F.B.I. most-wanted list he might as well have been cut down like a flower. But there's nothing wrong with our drinking to high hopes." He carried the paper sack into an adjoining kitchen, where he rattled glasses. "But a very weak one for you, Edwin, in view of all this excitement."

Nancy was spreading a handful of loose photographs across the coffee table. "That's Mother," said Edwin as she chose one of a woman holding a baby by a wrought-iron gate. *New Orleans,* it said on the back. When Nancy asked which baby he said, "Probably me. And here's one of Grandmother laid out in her coffin that a neighbor insisted on taking—probably wanted to be certain she was really dead. And here. One Christmas."

The two boys flanked a used bicycle. Ervin, the taller, wore a new ski cap masking his face so his hands seemed to touch Christmas while his head was in Halloween. The round eyeholes, the large false woolen teeth made her recall her own holiday face photographed beside Faye's, and she dropped the picture quickly onto the pile. Here was Edwin at high school commencement, the other twin sent to a different institution by then. She squinted over a duplicate of the fish picture she had already seen, trying to understand what was meant by the stiff, straight pose. Her voice cracked when she asked where the fish had been caught.

"It was . . . oh, no. Not in Louisiana. Here in the river."

Both boys looked harmless. "When he stole those cars, where did he go?"

"It wasn't south, Miss Finch. Give it up. You've read too much watered-down psychology."

She had been thinking, instead, of her church's teaching that evil was good gone monstrously astray. Andy served them drinks and stood looking over her shoulder. "Who in the world took this picture, Edwin?"

"Somebody who was locked up with him. He mailed it to me for my birthday without even a letter—that tells you plenty." Edwin handed her the later photograph. In the background the brick building was modern but plain, with heavy screening on the narrow window. Below it Ervin stood as if tangled in the ligustrum bush at his side, wearing a one-piece work suit with his blank face and a look that went past the lens into space. His mouth was in a narrow line. The eye was drawn to the unnatural way his hands came through leaves and twigs and were made larger by being thrust toward the camera, folded with the fingers interlaced and both thumbs erect.

"What is he doing with his hands?"

"Who knows? Who ever knew what was in Ervin's mind?" The twin leaned forward when she held the picture out. "I never noticed them. The picture came when I was sixteen."

"He was sixteen, too."

"Of course. Yes, I'll finish my drink and then rest, Andy. I promise. To wind up the story, Miss Finch, I was . . . *we* were eighteen or nineteen the summer he came home again. Grandma had just been persuaded to sell this land and Ervin naturally wanted to pretend he was due a share. He wanted half this house I was building. Wanted to live here with me."

"He wanted me not to," said Andy, moving to a chair.

"He kept asking if we were identical or not. We had to decide to be identical or not. He was incoherent. They taught him to use dope in that place. He said if we stayed together the growth on his heart would go away. We had a big fight on Grandma's porch and I pushed him into one of the posts and broke off his tooth. I was almost glad it happened because he seemed to calm down and then I said now everybody could tell which one of us was which."

"Not that there was ever any doubt," said Andy into his old-fashioned glass.

"So for one lousy tooth he almost beat me to death. When he quit I had to be taken to the hospital and he was gone."

"I don't understand," Nancy said.

"Do you think I ever did?"

Thinking aloud, she wondered whether Ervin's life might have been different, "If you'd let him stay?"

"Mine certainly would have! For one thing the bank would have turned down my loan flat and I'd have been up the hill in that old house without a dime having heart attacks with nobody—"

Andy whispered, "Hush. Don't excite yourself."

Watching them she asked, "Was Ervin much interested in women?"

Edwin's eyes were closed. "Sometimes. Not much. He thought women smelled funny."

She tried again to puzzle out the photographed boy behind the bush, one hand clinging to the other. "He used to say his car belonged to a brother and sometimes that the brother was dead."

"He'd tell *me* I was half-dead!" Edwin's eyes flew wide; they seemed more yellow. "We were maybe thirteen when he said there was only meant to be one full Childers baby boy and I got made up of all the pieces he had discarded in the womb. Can you imagine anything more disgusting? His discards explained why I was sick so much. Or maybe that last beating was enough to kill anybody so it made me dead to *him*. After that night I broke his tooth he never came home."

"So far as you know. He may have come back in secret more than the one time with me."

"That isn't cheerful," Andy said angrily. "That's not what a sick man needs to hear."

Indeed Edwin was looking sicker. "Maybe in Ervin's mind I should have been bones at the bottom of the lake. He could never decide if he wanted me alive or dead, if I was supposed to be like him or not. You're like all the others, Miss Finch. Nobody ever blamed Ervin; they just kept coming to see Grandma and me and filling out papers about what people had done or failed to do. All the time he was just crazy."

"I'm putting a stop to this distressing conversation." Andy got to his feet. "While we thank you for bringing the news of Ervin's death, in view of the recent surgery I must ask you to excuse us now."

Nancy sent her fingers skittering through the heap of photographs. It must be here. Surely there was one. Why couldn't she find it?

"He hated to look like me and then he wanted to, on and off, yes and no, but did he ever change himself? No, never that, just me!" Edwin's voice had risen again. "I was six when he cut off all my hair while I was asleep. That way we went to the first grade with me looking the worst. Other times we would dress just alike and stand in the mirror and move our hands"—he demonstrated with both his—"in unison. The very next day he would lose me in some public place so he would be the only one there looking like that, or he'd give me a bruise or a scratch. Or I'd have to dress like a girl even to play with him; that's the part"—he said loudly—"you've been waiting for, isn't it? But I broke off his tooth for him!"

Andy had reached out, not to take hold of Nancy's elbow but to tap it staccato with his fingertips and urge her from the room. "That's enough unless you want to kill him."

She spilled photographs rushing away to the hall. "I don't, no. Goodbye, Mr. Childers."

To their backs Edwin was saying, "It's ironic if they never got my parents out of the lake and they never found Ervin's body, either. Land and water. Death doesn't count when there's no body."

She said to Andy, "Yes, it does."

In the doorway he recoiled when she tried to hand him Ervin's picture with the hands that now seemed locked in some unspeakable prayer. "Keep it, take it away, anything," he breathed, and closed the door so quickly she could feel the peephole pressing her shoulder.

She walked toward the rented car, trying to make out somebody holding an umbrella for shade who was standing in the farthest front yard. As Nancy drew closer she recognized the woman with the lavender sheets, who began calling from two houses away, "You see exactly how it is, don't you? You've been around; you know! What could I tell you about those people that you wouldn't figure out yourself?" Hurrying toward her, the neighbor could not be avoided. "He claims to be a florist but you didn't see a green plant in that house, did you? Flowers won't live in that atmosphere."

Nancy tipped back the woman's umbrella to see her face and hand her the photograph. "Did you know this one, too? Ervin?"

"Mrs. Apple herself never lived long. And after she went, the cats that lived under her house died off one by one, went barren, that's what. Who? Ervin Childers? Is he out of the penitentiary?"

"He got out."

"This hardly looks like him. He had such a hard mean face. Every one of them was sick in some way, that old lady stealing us all blind for years and now the boy with his rents and mortgages for years to come. She lost her mind in the end and laid there without eating a bite because it would have to come out of her own provisions and she wanted us all to bring casseroles instead. Dried up in the bed and starved herself to death till she got down to sixty pounds and then *went*. And you know about the mama."

"She must have had cancer."

"The mama jumped right into Lake Pontchartrain."

"Jumped? I understood there was a boating accident."

"Not the way I heard it. I heard she had this bad disease."

"She had cancer, too?"

"I said a *bad* disease."

Nancy took back the photograph and dropped it into her purse. "If you know what penitentiary Ervin was in, I'd like—"

The woman broke in, "He was in all of them and he didn't have a single thing you'd like. Him and his brother, two of a kind. Anyway, he was a good bit younger. You've got a mile or two on you."

"You're right," said Nancy, snapping her pocketbook, "and I'm going home."

PART

4

19

So seldom had Nancy driven through Greenway at night that the town looked foreign, its tree-lined streets for the first time quaint. Like a stranger she noticed which mercantile buildings carried a waste of decorative stone vases or sunbursts of brick. Beside City Hall the bronze replica of the Iwo Jima flag raising ringed by fountains made her feel temporarily tender toward the bad taste she was most accustomed to.

She drove between older houses where aging black maids still walked to work daily wearing fresh uniforms, past the dark library, and home. Every downstairs room was ablaze, even the carriage lights by the entrance bright for her return. How many nights had she groped across that unlit porch, then slid fingernails along the wainscoting down the dark hall. This time the front door was flung wide. Apprehensive as Jephthah she waited on the steps while her mother's bulk filled the doorway.

Nancy hurried forward with both arms out to be instantly crushed, her embrace only plastered against such amplitude. Surprised, she whispered, "Don't cry, Mama."

"I'm not; I've got a cold." Mama pushed back, using Nancy's chin like a handle to turn the face left and right. "How are you? Yes. You were always the strong one." Her headshake trembled the flabby ovals of her face. "Faye wouldn't have lived through it."

"It's the truth!" cried Faye, coming next for a hug. Faye's rouged cheeks felt drier than usual beside curls so stiff they might be detachable for storage. "He scarred you!"

"That little thing?" Mama's cool fat finger measured the gap in Nancy's eyebrow. "You're lucky if that's the worst."

"I would be, yes," said Nancy without being heard, for Faye had pushed her until she was able at last even to hug Eddie, whose shaving lotion still smelled of fermented fruit.

His new watch ground hard into her ribs. "If I'd fought back, he'd have killed us all."

"What I meant," Faye exclaimed, "was that from all the talk about heat and sun we expected scars everywhere. I thought your skin had all—I was looking for a burn victim."

"In fact you look better than you did before." Eddie drew back, puzzled.

He had seldom looked at her before. But last of all Beckham waited behind the front screen, lightly stroking its mesh. Nancy had to pull back the door to reach him, to catch his hands. He leaned forward like a boy, and they rubbed their cheeks together, back and forth on each side. Maybe she loved Beckham because he was weak and set by nature at a disadvantage he didn't resent, or because he was innocent. Probably she loved the affliction of his innocence. He said, "I liked your letter about horseback riding."

"Sometime we'll go." Once more Nancy touched her face to his. As if he ate only grass and meadow flowers, his breath was very sweet.

"This night air will give me bronchitis," Mama grumbled.

Nancy's old irritation did not come. "Let's get Mama inside." Eddie asked if she felt like Patty Hearst. Shaking her head, she followed the group as it homed in on the sound of television. Beckham was telling her over one shoulder how large his gourds had grown, how many martin houses he could make and sell; he seemed to be mentioning a new job. Before she could ask, something odd in the rhythm ahead made Nancy watch Mama's even progress, her cane barely touching the floor. "It's been a long time since you've walked that well."

"Remissions never last." Mama gave a thin cough lest she seem too well.

"This one was well timed," said Faye, "because I can't do things as well as Nancy. Now what about a late supper? What? I can't even heat up the canned corn?" There was potato salad, too, and lemonade. Mama said everybody would take some lemonade for the vitamin C.

In the parlor Eddie went straight to the television set and lowered the sound to nothing, all of them turning to Nancy as if for a speech. But she, too, waited. Once, in the library, she had counted up the more than five thousand meals she had cooked for these people. In her absence nobody had lost a pound.

"Ah! Now look at her! In this light, Faye. There's new skin almost everywhere!" With her cane Mama tipped up the lampshade until a shaft of light fell across Nancy's face and made a path toward a row of sequined blue dancers tapping silently on the TV screen. Blue?

"When," said Nancy, "did we get a color television set?"

"We couldn't even keep up with the news the way that old picture was flipping."

"Mama? While I was kidnapped you bought a color television set?"

It wasn't, Eddie said, as if there was any connection. "And with you missing, Beckham was about to go into a serious decline. Thank you, Faye."

Mama said, "You, too, Nancy, drink Faye's lemonade now. She's been cooking all day long."

Now the old anger rose. "Mama, I've been cooking here fourteen years!"

"Mama doesn't mean anything." Faye pushed the cold glass into Nancy's hand anyway. "We're just glad you're safe. That man was made for violence; Eddie said he was built for violence."

"Wait." Nancy fished in her pocketbook. "Here he is."

"Oh no," Eddie said instantly of the photograph. "This can't be him, not even ten years ago when he just got out of a TB sanitorium. Take a look, Faye." She shook her head. "What's this secret hand sign mean?"

"He was sixteen then."

Eddie kept shaking his head while he carried the picture to Beckham, then to Mama, then to the floor lamp so she could tip the shade again while he turned the print's surface several ways against the light. "Even so, this is not the one. Oh no."

"Sixteen—there was still time, then."

Eddie told Nancy that wasn't the way life worked, while Faye pushed on her a little potato salad no matter what, and lemonade just to wash it down, insisting that none of it was as good as Nancy could fix. "But it takes me longer!" said Faye. "I've been in that kitchen day and night."

"It's definitely not him. Where'd you get this?"

Nancy took the picture from Eddie. "I was almost twenty-one. I could have married the coach."

"What?" said Eddie. "Who?" Faye said she had started peeling those potatoes at noon so everybody should let Nancy eat now. They let her. They watched her. Beckham put a cushion behind her back and then watched to see if she was comfortable.

"You put sugar in it?"

"I always do. Oh, Nancy, don't you? Well, why didn't somebody say something!"

While she ate and everyone stared at her as if her eating had become distinctive, Nancy examined the room to test whether it had improved as much as Greenway. The parlor was still Victorian, tall, dark. Across the carpets their paths were worn in paler colors. Mama said, "I hear nobody under eighty gets rheumatism in Arizona."

Already Nancy was able to carry on conversations in a murmur, without thought, while with furtive glances she continued reviewing the marble surfaces, the wing chairs with splotched armrests, the mirror over the mantel that made them all look yellowed by memory in its gilt frame. "You bought me flowers!"

Mama said no, the library board did. "Give her some corn, Faye. You know they'll make you head librarian if Miss Boykin ever dies."

While Nancy was mumbling that she had plenty, plenty, Eddie slid past Faye saying, "Well, *I* don't think it's a bit too soon. They'll never catch the kidnapper with that picture, Nancy, but I can see its use for before-and-after; let me explain." He slid a stool close to sit by Nancy's knee. "I've got this letter from *Startling Crime Magazine,*

Nancy, and we can make a thousand dollars giving them an exclusive. Of course they want pictures. I am *not* rushing her, Faye!" Nancy had recoiled from her plate in time for Faye to take it and refill her glass. Eddie unfolded a paper he had removed from his pocket. When Esau the castrated cat jumped into Nancy's lap and spread himself there, Eddie made a tent over fur and talked louder. "Not now, Beckham. I've developed the shots we took at the Linville overlook—wasn't it lucky we did? The editors can draw in arrows that say, uh, minutes after this shot was taken the kidnapper stepped from, so on; thus began the terrifying so on, so on—how does all this sound, Nancy?" He paid no attention to the way she was shaking her head but told Beckham to turn up the TV then, only not much. "Faye and I got together some old pictures we want to check with you; where's that envelope, Faye? Thanks, honey. For instance this one in the bathing suit for a teaser, they'd call it. Now wait, Nancy! People read these stories in hopes they'll be juicier than what the newspapers printed. I've made a shot of Patrick the boyfriend reading headlines, worried sick, you know. In fact I brought my camera tonight but—tell the truth—you're a disappointment. I needed some shots of the full extent of your injuries. Waited too long, I guess."

Her mouth crammed full of a chunk of cake Faye had made from scratch, Nancy squawked NO five or six times.

"Watch the crumbs. If she put on a bandage?" suggested Faye.

"There's a thought." Eddie let Nancy snatch her picture from him.

"You've been into my room!"

"Just to get the photograph album, honey, you don't know how those reporters insisted." From Faye's smile Nancy knew she and Eddie had searched through everything: souvenirs, letters. The brass cigarette box in which condoms in a plain wrapper were stored, more from wishful thinking than anything else. They had read her journal! But Faye wouldn't know who Heloise and Abelard had been, much less that they stood for Nancy and Oliver. Well. Well, who the hell cared? As if he had bellowed in her ear across the miles she could hear Hunt Thatcher's laughter roll and echo through her head and she savored the recollection while Eddie whispered, "What's she smiling at?"

With her cane Mama tapped Nancy's knee. "After we got your let-ter that you might move out and that we might rent your room—what difference does it make if your own family goes in?"

"Nancy didn't really mean she would move out," Faye said.

"I did," Nancy began, but Mama overrode her. "We'd need new rugs before anybody would even look at it. I had to walk up the stairs hurting all the way to see that black floor for myself or I never would have believed it. But don't let's argue. I want to hear all about what has happened to you."

Nancy got ready to describe each day she had spent in captivity. Mama said, "What has bothered Eddie is why you tied him so tight."

"Why didn't you try," said Eddie, "to get the keys back to me some-how?"

"He's already took a picture of me tied at the steering wheel and all—simulated, Eddie calls it. If I can pose in a halter, why would you mind the bathing suit? That wasn't even simulated. Stimulated?"

"I won't allow Eddie to publish a trash story about me, Faye. And as to why I didn't run the kidnapping to suit you better, I remind you he had a loaded gun!"

"Allow? Allow?" Eddie got off the stool, turned his back, and dropped onto the stool again.

"She's tense," Mama said. "It's understandable."

After Faye by touching his shoulders had presumably pressed down sets of hackles whose location she knew, Eddie was able to speak with his indignation under control. "I don't write it, Nancy; we just get in-terviewed. I've got an investment already. Look—this one took flash-bulbs." From the envelope he passed her a color pose of Beckham, eyes rolled up, face particularly empty, listening to what must be an obscene telephone call.

"My God!" Nancy tore it in half. The motion drove the cat toward Beckham, who stroked him, looking hurt.

"Can't I be in the magazine? I did what the man said on the tele-phone. What was I supposed to do? Something else?"

While Nancy was talking softly to him, Eddie said to Faye, "She has not changed one bit. Some people never do learn how to turn an experience to their advantage." He collected the halves of the photograph. ."There's a negative. The man can write the story without laying eyes on you if that's what you want."

"Hush, Eddie, can't you see Nancy's feelings are just hurt? She's hardly been able to say a word since she got here. Go ahead, Nancy." Mama put down her lemonade so even the tinkle of ice would not intrude and Faye, pulling a chair closer, said avidly, "Tell us, for instance, where did you spend the nights?"

"Eddie's tent." Immediately he interrupted to report that insurance was replacing everything. Nancy said, "A few times there were motels—Eddie? Put away the notebook!" She became angrier. "It's all television to you, isn't it!"

"There's a thought," said Eddie after a pause. "With that canyon scenery!"

Mama decided she understood the struggle on Nancy's face. "I know," she said sympathetically. "We seem just the same to you. But you've changed."

Is she looking at my crotch? Nancy said loudly, "If I'd had a gun I'd have shot him. I'd have knifed him. I'd have pushed him off a cliff!"

"Naturally." Eddie picked up his letter, which the leaping cat had carried aside. "It would be a better story if there were more crises of that sort, near-escapes, more struggles on the edge of cliffs. The editor says, here it is." He read aloud. "Our preferred format is the mystery which can be revealed by mounting climaxes." At this word choice, Faye giggled and goosed his armpit.

"It could have been worse; he could have been a sex maniac," Mama said with emphasis.

Yes. At my crotch.

Having waited for an opportunity that would interrupt neither the talk nor the late movie, Beckham put in, "I hope it's not my fault he hasn't been caught. I tried to do everything right."

"Nothing is your fault. He's probably dead somewhere," said Nancy quickly.

"He's probably *not*. These magazines help police catch criminals, Nancy, did you ever think of that? They alert the public. They offer rewards. They save other women in advance." Eddie grinned. "Since that picture you've got is bound to be somebody else, I think it would create more interest if we did a composite drawing."

"Did they get his fingerprints off the car?" asked Beckham.

Neither Eddie nor Nancy had thought of that. Surely Ervin Childers' could be traced. "By the time this man is found he may be bones," she said; "we may all be bones."

Faye drew back. "You've become morbid."

Shaking her head, Nancy was instead becoming tight throated and tight chested from the pressure of their overlapping voices, their incessant movements, from too much food too fast in this room full of knickknacks and Boston ferns and sconces with every color in the spectrum overrunning the next. She saw that beyond the long narrow windows shrubbery was trying to crowd through the glass to get its leaves inside but the interlaced bushes were already overwhelmed by thick yard trees which shut every star from view and cupped the house in black, humid air.

Somebody was saying, "I need . . . " and "one of the first things Nancy must do" and "we haven't been able to find" and "move away over my dead body," in such a jumble that Nancy felt her lungs work desperately before all her oxygen could be used up by the others talking and wanting everything at once: She leaped up and blew out one gust that surprised the whole family by turning into a shout: *"Beckham!"*

Instantly he left the television. "I gave you too big a cushion."

"It was fine." From the silent air she drew several slow, sweet breaths. "Come help carry in my bags, will you?"

Faye exclaimed, "Goodness! He even bought her clothes!"

She grabbed Beckham's arm and pulled him out, then stopped in the hall before the silent clock. As he waited obediently he asked, "You want me to wind it?" but Nancy led him along the dark passage to the cool porch, where a few moths were crashing softly into the lights by each door, and still there was a roar of noise even here. At last she identified steady crickets and rasping locusts with a whippoorwill breaking in. She had forgotten how many leaves and insects grew here, how crowded Nature was. Because of the oak and a dense magnolia she could still see no stars, so she tugged Beckham down the steps to her rented car and walked beyond him to the center of Crosby Street to throw back her head. Clouds. Tatters and wisps and wads and bundles of rain due to fall into each life. As far west as Nancy could see there was only a flare of lightning, which subsided against a wall of clouds and lit again with a low flourish of thunder, crowded thunder, muffled by many impediments. She felt homesick.

By the car Beckham waited with his usual smile. She could see how much she had always depended on Beckham's respite of cheerful silence, had pillowed herself on it. "Someday I'm taking you to see the west, Beck."

"I saw it on the National Geographic special," he offered agreeably. "We don't get 'Bonanza' reruns anymore."

"No, look." In midair Nancy drew a square with both hands, moved a step and redrew it suspended there, turned and blocked it in space a third time. "You can get North Carolina to fit into a television screen because it's all foreground—see? That house on the corner squares right up; you see it, Beckham? But you can't get the west into twenty-four inches, or the desert, or the mountains; you can't make the ocean look any bigger than a bathtub." Nancy dropped her arms, imagining how Eddie and Faye must be watching her curiously out the front window through a crowd of leaves.

"We can go to Grand Canyon."

"Well, maybe not there." Nancy came slowly out of the empty street to unlock the trunk and help lift out boxes and suitcases. "Wait a minute; let me, because things are arranged not to crush what's in the very back." She shifted the awkward bundle of taped newspaper aside.

Beck waited with his usual patience. "The woman we hired can't even make nut bread by your recipe."

Nancy laughed politely, but with her head inside the trunk, it sounded hollow. "How often did I suggest Faye and I share the cost of hiring somebody!" She eased out Beckham's swaddled present. "Does this woman also fill prescriptions and go to the bank and buy groceries and take the dry cleaning and give Mama her bath and—"

"Mama and I run the errands in that." He pointed over her head before taking the package.

"It's a present for you, Beckham." She straightened. "Whose car is that?"

"It's a green Buick," he said, rustling paper.

"I see that much."

"With automatic drive Mama found she could change gears after all." He tore papers open while Nancy gaped at the new car parked beyond Eddie's—crying, "You brought me a bird!" in wonderment—though she had meant him to wait until they were inside. Then he unfurled a tumble of feathers on a headdress that probably no real Indian chief had ever worn. She helped him lift and settle it, adjust the band. "Faye! Look at me! Mama!"

"They can't see and anyway you'll wake the neighborhood."

Now it was Beckham's turn to sweep grandly into the street, where the high corner light tinged him with blue and threw his long curving shadow across the pavement. He tried to whoop in whispers as he danced with irregular bounces and dips in an uneven circle. To Nancy the jerking shadow of his bobbing feathered head suggested not a chief but a giant pterodactyl, shortening as it lit jerkily on curb and sidewalk, then shrinking further as it went twanging up the dim path to the house, calling, "Eddie, come out here!" The shadow sprang up huge and black against the Finch house. By herself Nancy had to carry the rest of her things inside and down the hall (she could hear Beckham talking to the others about his display), and on upstairs to her black-floored bedroom, where everything looked slightly off-center and hastily replaced.

Nancy took the brass cigarette box off her bookcase, dumped the sealed Trojans into a waste can, and replaced them with Enovid and the compact. On its lid she noticed for the first time a twined wreath of tiny flowers—forget-me-nots. On the wrong shelf sat the bundle of Oliver's letters explaining Brunner and Mauriac and Boethius and Duns Scotus—impatiently she swept them into the trash as well and then fished them out, frowning, to save for one rereading in case Augustine could somehow still move the Grand Canyon adjacent to *De Civitate Dei*.

"Nancy? You coming down?" She could hear Mama calling. Only in July had Mama taken off her copper bracelet because it weighed too much for the wrist joint to support. She now sounded as if she could bend steel.

But at the foot of the stairs Eddie was the one waiting to have a few words in private with Nancy because it was getting late, Mama needed her rest, all Nancy had to do was relieve Mama's mind before bedtime that there'd be none of this moving out into an apartment. "You and me and Faye can talk later in more detail."

"But I do plan to move out."

A conspirator, Eddie shook his head and mumbled. "As the years pass, ahem. Eventually things here have to. Medicare. Too soon. Valuable property someday."

"Now that they've got a maid and a car there'll be no better time." Nancy pushed past, intending to announce right away that she might even move into Grandfather's old farmhouse until winter and that there was a man in Arizona—a healthy man—waiting for news; but somewhere, anywhere, out! She could no longer trust herself to hand-wash Mama's elastic stockings without complaint or sand gourds or bake nut bread calmly because—

Mama prevented Nancy saying anything by asking as she entered the parlor, "Who is this Mr. Thatcher that writes such long letters?"

Nancy rushed to the mantelpiece and the three large alabaster monkeys behind which incoming mail was routinely stacked, their magic perhaps guaranteeing that the envelopes would contain no evil. Behind their tiny digits carved over eyes, ears, and mouth, she saw her postcard with Point Sublime and then the thick envelope from Hunt. She tore it open, forgetting everything else. A packet of pages. Her body, she noticed, had filled up with interesting sensations. She skimmed topic sentences; horse, a search of Pipe Canyon, where they found her pack cached by some vandal, her note from Los Alamos; telephone him when she arrived. She said to the three monkeys, "I've got to make a private phone call."

"We've never been private in this house before." Mama stood up with her cane, making great whuffling and wheezing noises in her sudden reawakened pain. "Have you got something to hide? Is that really why you want to leave home after all these years, with some shame you're not telling?"

"She's not going far," said Beckham. "You're not going far, are you, Nancy?" His feathers were rippling.

"Everybody's too tired to talk anymore, I keep telling you!" said
Eddie in a loud voice.

"He's right. Go to bed while I make my call and we'll talk tomorrow." She stood immovable while the talk and arguing streamed
around her and past, and Faye, seeing that Nancy had not offered, finally helped Mama up the long stairs hissing, "Of *course* the remis-
sion will be back tomorrow, of course it will!" Beckham turned off
the television as he went, a few of his colorful pinions catching on
fern fronds and drifting to the rug. Eddie asked if she'd lock up; could
she do that much? She nodded and the last noise went down the hall
and outside to blend with the insects' singing.

Then she was left in the blessed silence with Hunt's long letter. She
picked up Beckham's blue stray feathers from the floor. Better one
bluebird of happiness in the hand than two in the bush? No, better
the two or a dozen. Better a flock. She sat down smiling to read
Hunt's letter.

In the morning the new housemaid stared at her all during breakfast and finally blurted in amazement when Nancy had carried her
plate to the kitchen, "So you're the perfect one!"

No one had said so in the days she was starved for praise. Upstairs
Nancy closed her bedroom door in a clatter made by the judge's
heavy cross hanging from a coat hook there. She spent the morning
going through and discarding possessions, skirts now a size too large,
shoes that had become too sensible. One hasty reading was enough to
show that, once all hidden meanings were expunged, Oliver's letters
became more ordinary than the two she had from Hunt. Sometimes
while she was picking through mementos colors would burst into
bloom below and from her high window she could look down on
Chief Beckham Finch tending his vines, though he left his headdress
at home when he rode off in the new jerky Buick with Mama on
household business. So with one thing and another the whole day
passed and it was the next afternoon before Mama cornered Nancy
for a serious talk.

Mama arranged herself on one hard Windsor chair and banged on
another until Nancy sat down opposite and watched her mother finger

the cane Beckham had made for her, formerly a green dogwood wound with live honeysuckle. She spun it between her palms like a drill. "Come closer. That woman eavesdrops and is not like flesh and blood."

Feeling herself like poor flesh and low blood, Nancy scraped forward. "I'll only be moving out of the house, not out of the family."

"Whatever has happened," Mama said with a wave of the hand on which rings were as deeply imbedded as the stem twirled into the walking cane, "whatever has happened we are your kinfolk and we won't reject you from your own home."

"Mama, I told you he didn't lay a hand on me."

"Look somewhere else but not straight at me, please. Better. What I want to say is even if he did, I only say *if,* it doesn't matter because the men have never been able to tell if women are virgins or not unless the women help them so most women don't help them." Her exhausted face grew pink, pinker, and red. "You may wonder how I know this? I just know." Even her neck was mottled now.

"Stop this, Mama. Even before the kidnapping I was not—"

"Oh, I know you weren't likely to marry that Patrick Glenn Allen, no, though he's polite enough, but somebody may come along yet that you'll want." Mama reached up to touch the gap in Nancy's healed eyebrow. "I've never had to worry about you like I did Faye because she was the pretty one."

"And I was the strong one." Acid got into her voice. "If any man had wanted my virginity, I could arm-wrestle him out of it."

"Don't turn bitter." Nancy thought the hopeless distance between them might turn anyone bitter but Mama was wearing her most understanding look. "The minute I laid eyes on you, I knew you'd lost your maidenhood. Only to a mother does it show, and except for that"—more cane-twirling—"well, extremity, and my own knowledge of how you must feel, I never would have spoken. God knows I never told Faye."

"Wait a minute. I'm no longer certain what you're telling me."

"Look someplace else, I said. I'm telling you I speak from experience and the loss is not worth worrying about."

Nancy went on looking someplace else, at the self-protected monkeys sitting on the mantelpiece, while the words sunk in. She had not been virginal for so long that the term even sounded abstract, worse than an a priori truth long since disproved. As she had once had a hymen, she had also once been three feet tall with baby teeth. But even harder than trying to recapture that former state was the mental effort required to make her mother thinner, younger, and with a hymen of her own. Against Nancy's will she was deeply moved by the intent of the confessional. Worse, she was curious.

"Was it Papa? No? Before Papa? You do astonish me!"

Her mother stood up so easily that she must have forgotten her age and arthritis. "The tears I wasted! Don't you waste one, that's all I'm saying." Shaking her head caused a bobbling that ran down her neck and quivered underneath the flowered dress. "Now you'll probably get married. I was married in six months once the mystery was gone."

Confessionals: quid pro quo. Nancy allowed herself to look shy and wistful as she showed Hunt's letter and tried to tell Mama about him. "That's good, so far so good," said Mama vaguely. "But don't you tell your sister, Faye, what has happened, either. Married women tell husbands and men tell other men. First time you introduce Mr. Thatcher to Eddie, Eddie will tell him the weather report and then that." She was walking away.

Nancy caught on to her belt. "I want you to know I'll always appreciate your talking to me, Mama, and revealing, uh, everything."

"One fact," Mama said, "is not everything." She called to Beckham that it was time for the afternoon stories. It was like watching the surface of a pond close up again while the last ripple ran off the edge—by the time Mama reached the TV set she was unaltered and nothing had happened. Beckham came in to fine-tune the color and was pleased to hear her announce, "Now your sister understands she doesn't have to move away from home."

"That wasn't the reason, Mama, I tried to tell you."

"There's no need anymore. That's too yellow, Beck."

When she moved out it would be a test of independence for all three of them, Nancy explained, but she had already lost them to real problems—an actress whose invented baby had ended in a bloodless abortion offscreen and who now was suffering from exactly the degree of moral guilt statistics would predict.

• • •

She'd been home three days before Beckham remembered that he, too, had a present for her. For two weeks he'd been working for Colonel Moffatt, local auctioneer, holding up items at the Horse-trader's Barn while people offered bids, "and I bought you something there."

"You've got a real job! Beck, that's wonderful!"

On Monday and Saturday nights his job was to keep displaying each item until a sale was made, then to scrawl in chalk the buyer's number. "Mama won't let me take the Buick by myself so Faye drives me out so she can bid on the glassware."

Nancy tried not to sound disappointed. "You bought me glassware."

He said no, it was inside this hassock somewhere, and continued to look. "What does Doctor Preslar say about you having this job?"

"He says fine if I'm careful with the Dilantin. I haven't had one in a long time, Nancy." As always, Beck looked as prim as if epilepsy were a toilet subject. "Sometimes the colonel lets me call out things." Like what? "I call the crowd's attention to the beveled mirror or maybe the dovetailing in a drawer. I run up and down the aisle to show where something is signed or dated. You can't believe what people will buy or sell, either. Did you know you can get false antiques to sell? They make them in a factory in Minnesota. They beat furniture with chains."

"I'd have bet you couldn't survive two nights a week without television."

He said seriously, "I do miss it. Here." He handed her a book in a protective paper cover with "12" scrawled across it—the shill's number, Beckham said. "The shill buys for the employees by bidding high, or for the colonel if the crowd is down too low; mostly he runs up the price. This one's old but it's not a first edition."

She slipped the cover off *Canyons of the Colorado*, by J. W. Powell.

"It's not as good as the Indian headdress, of course," he said, watching closely lest she be disappointed. But she hugged him and opened to a photo of the bearded Powell under tissue paper; next came a gray engraving of the river seen far at the foot of receding cliffs and towers that looked ghostly, all of it like a vampire's giant land-scape in a werewolf's Transylvania. He said the pictures must look like black-and-white television after you'd seen color.

"Black-and-white is as much as I can take right now," she said, hoping her smile was wide enough, her appreciation hearty. Some chapters were on travels to the Uinkaret Mountains or the Rio Virgen (Oh, Mama!) but the book sprang open to a much-thumbed chapter some earlier owner had marked and underlined. "We are now ready to start on our way down the Great Unknown" was the line from Powell's journal that had first been underscored.

If things didn't work out with Hunt, if she stayed here, Nancy could picture herself stripping the library of Arizona travel books. She could pretend to be as virginal as Miss Boykin or Evaline Sample and grow older and purer in Greenway, cultivating her quiet and harmless hobby to the point that when any local club chairman ran out of program topics she could always rely on inviting Miss Nancy Finch to deliver her well-known lecture on the Grand Canyon.

"Now you can read while I look at the morning movie." Beckham found the right channel and the gunslinger, lonely in the saddle, headed somewhere to change his life against a background of shrunken papier-mâché mountains.

She could not stand that pitiful substitute for the Rockies. "No, Beckham, turn it off," she said, but did so herself. Already she could imagine them both growing old in this room with their books and re-runs. "Ask Mama if she trusts me with the new car and we'll drive out to the farm." He lingered as if trying to predict from the vacant screen whether something new might this time happen to Gary Cooper. "And don't upset her by saying I may move to the farmhouse."

Waiting, she paced the parlor from hall door to hearth and back, thinking of Hunt's last letter. Since she was back in her librarian's life, Hunt claimed he wrote to her using reference books, that he chose to sound like Montaigne and not Rousseau. The tone desired was the quiet manner of Charles Lamb, he had said, who retired from the East India Company saying he would no longer seek after pleasure but would let his years come to him "in some green desert." "Think about living here and Arizona becoming green to you," Hunt had written. Nancy thought about it as she walked the path that had worn this parlor carpet nearly through.

But unlike Hunt, when she thought of Charles Lamb she would instantly remember his mad sister Mary, who stabbed their mother in the heart, causing Lamb to tell Coleridge, "Former things are passed away and I have something more to do than feel." Remembering, as Nancy walked toward the parlor mirror her enlarging face grew more and more a librarian's; she marked how the mouth was pursing and closing up, presumably to keep titles and quotations from spilling everywhere.

"I have the keys," called Beckham from the hall.

Probably in an autopsy no one would be able to tell her lymph fluid from library paste. She hurried outside.

Nowadays she never got into a car without checking to see that the back seat was empty. It was good to drive and be relaxed, simultaneously. Smiling next to her in the front seat Beckham said, "It's been years since I was out there. Why didn't we go?"

"We had no car and Faye and Eddie were busy on weekends in theirs," said Nancy drily.

Ten miles northwest they came to where the blackened heartpine house leaned toward the highway down a hill, only a hill, not the tall Heidi's mountain Nancy had once fancied. The Buick labored up the raw wagon road scraped in the clay. Then they walked through the tall yard grass, talking. Nancy found Beckham's memories of everything fewer than hers, coarser. In the log barn, where he could not even recall wrestling, the last dry hay wisps had lost even remembered odor; lumps of manure underfoot were porous now as sponges. Nothing remained to remind one of livestock or humans except objects more durable than either—wood troughs, iron handles, mildewed harness with rusty buckles. On all sides the onslaught of fungi and bugs and vegetation rushed to reclaim even these.

When inside the smokehouse Beckham yanked a matted creeper off the wall, wasps and webs fell onto his head. They bolted into the woods, slapping air, and finally stopped so they could breathe hard and Nancy pick gray shreds from his hair. "Beck, that's poison ivy in your hand!"

"I'm not allergic." He made a sour face as he sucked one of several stings already swelling on his forearm.

"Ready to look inside the house?"

Though Beckham remembered whitewashed hearths and a closet underneath the stairs to the loft, he had not been inside since their grandfather died. He did not recall rolling a toy truck on the hospital floor while they waited. "Nobody's been inside the house."

Nancy had. She led him through rank orchard grass no longer grazed and down the hard clay path no longer swept. At first she had rented the house Grandfather willed to her, but tenants proved unreliable; now it sat empty. "You remember the house more than you do *him*," she said—accused, really—as they climbed the stone steps their grandfather had set by hand. He had nailed these resinous porch boards into place; his were the ax marks still showing on the house timbers.

The empty kitchen smelled of mouse droppings strewn like morning glory seeds on the worn linoleum. These crackled as Beck walked into the other rooms, calling back, "Wasn't there an iron bed here?" Yes, and watermelons rolled underneath to keep cool. Grandmother died in it, so Nancy had been told, of lung fever. There was a snow; he had not been able to get the wagon down that rutted hill. On the second day he wrapped her body in a quilt and laid it in the cellar and rode the mule to the preacher's house. Many years he had slept there beside one person and then slept twenty more alongside that absence. Thinking of Hunt, Nancy stood by the window where she used to eat meals and look out at ripening pears. The west side of the house, still dark at breakfast.

Suddenly Beck yelled.

Toward the crashing noise she ran, calling. Had the floor given way? As she pounded into the next room the front door slammed and someone ran heavily down the far porch.

Beck was lying with his feet inside the bedroom fireplace and his head by an open closet door whose edge he had struck going down. His head was rolling on the floorboards, the jaw in grinding motion. Though both eyes were open and his gaze fixed on some horror Nancy could not see, the sounds in his throat came from another language.

Foolishly she whispered, "Beck, don't! Oh no!" as she pressed both hands at his temples to slow the movement. He kept panting. "That's enough now, he's gone. Beck? Don't, Beck."

She could see that his tongue was free. From one corner of his mouth the narrow streak of spittle grew longer as his shoulders began to vibrate against the floor. Nancy shouted to the unknown escapee, "Come and help me!" but by now the stranger had leaped off the porch and kept running. Gently she turned Beckham's head to one side and tried to cushion it in her hand until his jerking arms and rigid legs began to slow. In midair she caught the hand steadily slapping the wooden floor and forced it still. The knuckles were scratched. Across his crotch and down one trouser leg she saw the stain of urine blotting its shape.

The nearest neighbors—Flake Woodward's surviving sons, she supposed—still lived a mile away. Nancy could only lean over him murmuring soft but meaningless phrases and stroking the welts where he had been stung, keeping dust from his mouth, hoping he would soon hear and recognize her voice. Where he had struck his head the swelling lump seemed nearly as big as a light bulb.

And as she talked, gradually his knotted body loosened and quieted, and far too soon he wanted to sit up and find where the world was. He struggled against her ministrations, even struck once at her cautionary hands. Softly Nancy called his name again and again until, at last, she could almost watch her face be seen and matched to a word far back behind his eyes. Then he closed them and fell into deep sleep on the floor.

After his first snores Nancy eased away. Sullen, even angry, grew Beckham's relaxing face as if the spikes of electrical discharge were now subsiding into damp, unpleasant dreams. When sleep had taken full hold she stepped lightly over him into the next bedroom, the one in which she had always slept.

The running stranger had been living here a week or so, sleeping on rags and heaped pine straw in one corner, drinking almost a case of Thunderbird wine. Surprised by Beck's entry, the trespasser must have made some threatening gesture which flung Beckham into seizure; or perhaps Beck had skipped his medicine and merely convulsed at a coincidental moment and thereby terrified a waking wino this hot August morning. Though Nancy searched house, woodshed, even the cellar where her grandmother's body first became accustomed to the coolness of underground, there was no intruder to be found. Indoors she knelt to take Beckham's steady, even lazy, pulse.

As he would now sleep awhile, Nancy looked through the other rooms with a realtor's eye. This hearth she had once helped whitewash would not appeal to modern tenants. There was little insulation. Atop the weakening hand-hewn oak shakes, the present roof was tin and leaked. Water had only been pumped as far as kitchen faucets, her grandfather believing the septic tank made complicated what Nature had already made easy, and that it was somehow nasty to locate toilet functions so close to where one ate. Nancy saw anew what she had seen first when fresh home from college: a housing development was the only answer. Then she had been unwilling to trade off berry thickets and old fields for rows of box houses. Now there was Hunt Thatcher.

When Beckham groaned, Nancy slowly helped him stand in the center of a room he could not recall. "What is it?" he kept asking, once as he got to his feet, several times being guided outdoors. "Tell me what it is?" She locked the house and settled him in the car. "I'm fine," he announced as she got in and buckled their safety belts, "never been better, but what is it?" He fingered his damp trouser front, then quickly crossed his legs.

"Everything's fine." She started down the rough road. "Time to go home, Beck."

Absently he rubbed elbows and knees he did not remember bruising. "That walk must have worn me out." He smiled pleasantly though his next question rang with dead earnest. "Did we do what we came for?"

By now Nancy could tell him what already he suspected. "You had one, not too bad this time." He nodded as if to a trivial remark but one eyelid began relentlessly to twitch and now he could touch the lump on his head. "Did you take your medicine? Maybe the dosage needs adjusting. How long this time, Beckham?"

"Just before Christmas. We're going to Doctor Preslar's, I guess."

"Routine." Nancy remembered. Into the decorated tree, hands

grabbing at strands of tinsel. So many broken silvery objects. "Did they increase the dose in December?"

"He said it was just excitement and the colored lights."

"Of course." She looked sideways. "It's no wonder now, either, with the kidnapping and me getting home and those wasps. Did you see anybody in the farmhouse? Just as well."

They had so often been instructed to go straight to the doctor's, not for Beckham's sake so much as to preserve the freshness of data Dr. Preslar collected for occasional papers at state seminars. From Beckham's movements, so slight that each seemed painful, Nancy knew the damp trousers embarrassed him and took him into the clinic's side door and outside the first examining room while she explained privately to the nurse. Dr. Preslar saw him immediately.

Waiting, Nancy knew part of what Beckham would be telling the doctor. Always there appeared for him, during seizure, the same two-stage aura. Visually his world became spatter-painted with white flecks on a reddening field where all the objects of reality appeared underneath as if inside a paperweight. Later, perhaps because of the redness, he could smell fire at work. Perhaps those snowflakes fell into a waiting though never clearly seen inferno. Coming second, sharp odor always proved decisive and marked the seizure as maximum; soon afterward he would fall. In milder convulsions the blizzard blew itself past and the red stain only appeared like a blush and then also blew on beyond, so that objects turned pink and then normal. These lesser attacks left Beckham with the sensation of having catnapped.

Nancy had been with him through many small seizures as well as some that carried him relentlessly through the smell of it and onward to the presence of fire into which his body threw him, writhing. In the mild beginnings, Beckham would stare around with sudden astonished joy, as if he had just recognized the true meaning of his surroundings or, perhaps having transmigrated here, had now grasped and endorsed in an instant the full cycle of metempsychosis on which he would forever spin. In such moments the visionary light on his face was almost beautiful; then his eyes closed and the white flurries curtained whatever he had almost known. Nancy doubted that, in the canyon, her face had ever looked that way. She believed Beckham had experienced those smaller seizures even as a child and that, as he grew older, each one threatened to become grand mal, and the pink grew redder and crackled like fire. She could remember Beck screaming to their mother, perhaps from sensations in his nerve endings he could not describe. In what the Finches mistook for ordinary bad dreams, he flung himself nights across the mattress and thrashed against the wall behind which Nancy tried to sleep. At a church picnic he once became unreasonably frightened and asked details about hellfire before disappearing; deacons and elders searched everywhere before finding him asleep in a car and dazed—from summer heat.

Nancy rose. Dr. Preslar emerged from the office behind Beckham, already looking for her over his patient's shoulder, already translating his prognosis into grimace. For much of Beckham's life people with twitching faces had been communicating past or over him. Beckham was looking ahead to read hers.

With a thrust of a prescription into her hand Dr. Preslar said, "Very slight increase," while one eyebrow rendered nuances. "Especially with his new employment. I expect the wasp stings didn't help." He shook Nancy's other hand. "Nancy, we're all grateful you're safe; a terrible experience, terrible." Through bifocals he let his higher scientific eye bounce from one of her crucial areas to the next until Nancy felt like a pinball machine showing bells and lights as he rang up an unknown score. "Your mother thought you might require Valium," he said slowly as his gaze thumped from weight to color, clarity of eye, hand movements, "but I'm conservative about tranquilizers." Now that its clamminess had been recorded he released her right hand. "I waited for you to call but you don't look much like a case of nerves to me."

She had always liked Dr. Preslar. For all Mama's prodding, he had been willing to wait and hear from Nancy firsthand, year after year, injury after illness. Just before her menarche he had drawn four objects on his notepad to demonstrate, straight-faced, that *these* two were her *mother's* ovaries but *these,* which they would shortly discuss, were entirely Nancy's.

He said now, "You're sensible. You'll say so if you feel sick or need help."

"I need a piece of advice." She sent Beck ahead before showing the doctor her purse compact of Enovid. "I know of no reason I shouldn't take these, do you?"

His voice was firm and the smile wide. "Neither medical, legal, nor moral. Unless it's Patrick Allen—then I might void the prescription on grounds of bad taste. Hmmn, how is your mother? Most of the recent trauma must be hers."

"She's rarely looked better, with so few signs of pain or stiffness, but then I've never known which symptoms come from pure arthritis and which are psychological."

"Pure," he repeated as they walked down the hall. "Which eye at the moment are you using most? We've discussed her before, Nancy. Whether or not she ever gains insight into her martyrdom is her problem. She has a real arthritis and also a real martyrdom."

"Self-inflicted. Did you know she's had money squirreled away all these years? She's bought a television set! She's bought a new car!"

"That's not your own martyrdom I hear, is it?" He patted her absently with the file folder he was carrying. "I'm more optimistic that you'll gain your own insights. Naturally with you gone she had to stand up and walk and quit feeling so sorry for herself." Outside the waiting room Dr. Preslar gazed at her thoughtfully, then began turning through her file. "I'm sure any intelligent woman," he said in a monotone as if reading an eye chart, "who thought she might need a D and C or who wanted a frog test or any other diagnostic blood test would say so, wouldn't she?"

"This one would." She turned in the doorway, her laughter dwindling. "If I should ever leave Greenway," she began, "I mean permanently—"

"You'd be ten years overdue." He counted off on his fingers. "Faye lives here. Eddie. Your Aunt Aileen. There's a little money and social security and medicare. There's the house and farm. When your mother dies, of course, there'll be decisions to make about Beckham but that may be twenty years off. You could be a grandmother by then."

Her anger must have been stored under pressure. "You were never so clear before!"

"Neither were you." Dr. Preslar squeezed her shoulder. "I've tried, Nancy, many times, but you couldn't hear me then."

Beckham dozed all the way home, turned on the TV set, and then fell asleep in the recliner. From his damp clothes Mama knew instantly he'd had a seizure. They talked about it softly in the hall.

"I guess you'll be living out there by yourself in the farmhouse when he has the next one on a day I can't even bend over—and then what?"

Nancy said in a furious whisper, "He hardly ever convulses now and at this dosage may not again, but if he does, you'll telephone someone for help. Am I to sit here in this house, Mama, just waiting for Beckham's annual fit in case one of them might, just *might*, happen on a day your joints are swollen?"

"You're cold and hard now. That can happen, too, once the mystery's gone. He left you cold and hard." Discouraged, Mama sank against the coat tree and rubbed one hip.

On the contrary, Nancy felt more tender toward her family than in years, being now more certain that as they were no better than she, they were also no worse.

Mama persisted, "Once you realize that behind every valentine is nothing but the flesh, it changes you. You're ready to reject us all now."

Thinking of her mother's earlier and unexpected confidence and wishing to return the gift in some way, Nancy stepped forward to touch her, but Mama shook free with such an elaborate wince that it seemed Nancy had hurt her deliberately. "Cold, yes! Hard! You who claimed to love your grandfather—when you know how he'd feel about ever selling that farm!" Like acid drops she let each memory fall and etch. "Remember how he'd blow smoke into your earache? The time you got lost in the far field and he didn't find you till after dark? The Easter chickens and ducks he took over and raised for you, and the stray dogs and cats? Remember when you dropped his watch that you had no business playing with down the well?" Now she made the deepest cut. "And the night you let him hang sick on the fence for so long and he never regained consciousness after that?"

In June such a remark might have made Nancy cry, but every tear of that sort had dried up in the canyon, so she simply shook her head and stepped back.

Mama said, "Now everything he worked for is going to disappear under streets and fire hydrants."

"It's disappearing anyway. You tell me what's so much better about termites and honeysuckle."

"Oh cold, yes, and hard. Yes." In the silence they could hear Beckham's snores.

All right. Once more. She would try in spirit at least to match her mother's confidence. "At the farm this morning when I first heard the bobwhites I almost thought—you know—that they were even the same quail. They sound just the same as when he and I sat on the porch to hear their calls, yet the old ones must die off every few years. He'd whistle back and fool them into answering. There have been quails by the multitudes since then." ("It's people not birds I mean," her mother mumbled, but Nancy kept on.) "If I was your age, Mama, I could go live on that farm and keep hearing those birds and watching the same trees put out new leaves every season. I could do just what Grandfather did, wind down there and get ready to die by training for it. He slept on in that iron bed. He retired the mules. He made smaller and smaller crops every year, and over and over he saw the same leaves grow and fall off and then rot during winter—they must have seemed to be the same." She took a long breath. "When I was out west, Mama . . ." Silence—while she tried without success to bring the two thoughts together in the way she knew they fit, though unclearly. Out west with less rotting and blooming Nature's ponderous mass altered as slow as eroding stone, but rate was the only difference. In Arizona Nancy had looked far back at rumors of spring and winter that had left signatures in rock every million years, and none of those seasons had been tamed to human need; none of those cycles was the size to domesticate. No, the thoughts would not come together. She felt if she could say "forever" often enough and loud enough and steadily enough, that might suffice. "Oh, I'll never explain! There's rural life and it's human, human. And then there's a countryside that's inhuman. I may go live there." This time her mother paid attention. "If I marry Hunt Thatcher, Mama, I'll be moving to Arizona."

"You don't know him at all yet." Mama's head kept shaking. "What makes you think he'll make you happy?" Nancy was smiling. "Usually husbands don't."

"Don't say that, Mama. Say if you must, 'Mine didn't,' then stop." Mama stood up and turned away. "Maybe nothing has changed you, maybe I just never realized before that you had a cold hard nature."

"Why don't you ask if I love him? Yes. I do."

"That passes," Mama said, and walked into the parlor. Beckham slept there with his mouth open while on the screen two well-dressed women spoke of juvenile crime and drug abuse.

Mama sat on a chair, already caught by the conversation on the screen, while Nancy tiptoed to get her purse. "I'll fill his prescription and I'm going to talk to a real estate agent while I'm uptown. Mama? You hear?"

"There's not a one will drive a harder bargain than you yourself."

"Do you want anything?"

Mama's face struggled between anger, loss, and curiosity about the TV program. "Ask me twenty years ago."

From the parlor door Nancy turned back to see that Mama had not moved except to stretch forth her cane horizontally between both hands like a trapeze bar. "I love you, Mama."

She moved impatiently, like someone about to swing off the platform and across a crowd, someone who could not at this final moment be distracted. "Children want to have it all," she complained softly to herself. "Not only to do exactly what they please all the time but to have it approved besides. If you have any children, you'll see." She held the cane tightly as if she might push off and fly through the parlor window glass to anyplace.

Stubbornly Nancy said, "And I know you love me and Faye and Beckham. We'll work things out."

The smile as she lowered the cane was hard to analyze. "Yes, I do love you, Nancy. But we won't."

• • •

Nancy had given up her plan to camp at the farmhouse, since it had become known to winos and tramps. She was certain, now, that if she heard a nighttime footstep she would shoot at it with no compunction; that didn't mean she wanted to.

Back at work at the library, on lunch hours she examined rental apartments and with a realtor appraised the farm. As they walked the bounds together he verbally erased all buildings and fences and with fingers undulating in midair expanded the branch with its fallen footbridge into a lake. His chopping hand made building lots. He thought the project had promise because of all the new factories west of Greenway. Yes, it would be a while before she made any profit. First they would incorporate, get a loan. Money would be going out for some time on surveying, streets and gutters, provisions for water and sewer, and so forth.

She wrote to Hunt: "I need more time to settle things here and provide funds for Mama." She wrote, "Not pragmatism; I meant *The Varieties of Religious Experience.*" She sent him the photograph Eddie had been forbidden to send the magazine. She wrote: "Thank you for the roses. I've had a fear we were degenerating into a rational transaction and I cherish your note. I love you irrationally; don't you forget it. The rest is justifying." Then she wrote him a long and rational letter on the statistical chances that her children would inherit a predisposition to epilepsy.

Saturday night she and Faye went to the auction, where Beckham, a bit more sluggish on the new medication, held aloft objects and called with languid volume: *Solid brass! Two for one money! Depression glass! Ball and claw!*

These automatic phrases at too slow a speed made Faye squirm in her chair.

Beveled mirror! You're not looking, folks! Solid walnut! Made in France!

Nancy said to her, "Anybody would look foolish bawling out stuff like that for hours." *Hobnail! Sterling silver! Hand-painted!*

Faye bought a satin glass vase, perhaps to stop Beckham from carrying it through the audience a minute longer. "These people trade with Rayburn's Clothiers and they're staring at me!" she hissed. They weren't.

So why, asked Nancy, hadn't Rayburn's Clothiers given Beck a job all these years? "He could unpack stock or take inventory and you know it. It's done wonders for him to work, so if this is the wrong job, offer him another."

Faye showed lipstick on her bared teeth. "You want to give us the whole thing now, don't you?"

"I've always accepted my share of the responsibilities, Faye."

The sisters had to wait until the last item had been auctioned and the stragglers had gone and Beckham, tired and satisfied, sat between them on the front seat.

Faye sent words past his face in a breeze. "Sure, you stayed home and it made you mealymouthed. Now what you've got is just a new kind of self-righteousness."

Ouch. "I'm trying not to have any."

"I always felt guilty that you had the worst of things, Eddie too, but you're as big a martyr as Mama."

Beckham's face turned from Faye to Nancy.

"Almost as big. Can't I change?"

"Change and live happily ever after with a man who's already failed in one marriage? Oh, Nancy, a man you saw maybe one week when you were hurt and sick. What do you really know about Hunt Thatcher?"

From several answers she chose, "That I won't have to pretend with him."

"Oh wow, oh my goodness!" Faye hooted with laughter. "Oh, poor Nancy, poor big sister." So loud did she laugh and so long that Beckham thought he had missed something and released a chuckle or so himself. "You've waited so long you expect miracles."

"I didn't wait."

"Waited for marriage, I mean. Oh, Nancy, the things I could tell you!" Nancy sat very still, expectant, while the laughter stopped, Beckham looking left and then right. Faye said, "Mama thinks you're just covering up one man with another, that you had this—uh, unpleasant experience, as she puts it, and that getting married is like getting cured."

"Faye, Dwight Anderson didn't rape me."

"Really? He really didn't? Of course you'd say that."

"It may take the punch out of Eddie's article but he really didn't." In the silence Nancy wondered how Beckham passed his nights, if he dreamed of women, if he masturbated. If he had ever? She touched the uneven haircut he had given himself where the hairs were blunt on the nape of his neck. Who had advised him on sexual desire? Perhaps Ben Preslar. She smiled, imagining the doctor's possible sketches (your mother's balls, yours) on the doctor's desk.

Days passed. Because of those "things" Faye could have told her— and then had not—Nancy decided to give Eddie a small share of the development in the hope he could oversee its affairs once she was gone. With Mama and Beck and Faye they became Blue Bird Incorporated. The realtor thought it a very nice name, "very ecological these days and I'm sure you've got plenty of bluebirds on the property." She had named it for Maeterlinck.

She wrote Hunt, "At least he has given up writing the article as a business favor to me." She wrote: "When can you come? I'm beginning to hate the telephone. It changes your voice and then my picture of you becomes distorted and on my end I feel myself changing back into a toad or a toady or Little Miss Orphan Annie come to this house to stay. Don't let me stay, Hunt."

One day in the library Miss Boykin said, "Things have changed with you being a businesswoman all the time and Evaline in Salisbury."

"I thought she must be in the hospital." No, Evaline Sample was not ill this time but was exhibiting her art at a neighboring technical institute.

"Exhibiting it to whom?"

"An art teacher there claims to have discovered her." Miss Boykin pressed her sinuses with two fingers. "All those years Evaline did those perfectly beautiful drawings—Duke Chapel, the Katsewa River Bridge? You could hang them anywhere! Now all of a sudden she's taking appliances apart and drawing *that*."

"Drawing what?"

"Oh, wiring diagrams, circuits, whatever you call them. Solid-state things. Evaline stripped the back off her mother's TV and I don't know what all and just copied the pattern." Aside Miss Boykin made hasty use of a nasal inhaler. "See for yourself, here."

Nancy took the mimeographed sheet, "Aesthetics of Technology," subtitled "Beauty and the Beast-Machine." The program listed Evaline as one of seventeen area artists. While she specialized in electricity, the show would also include specialists in gears and plastic containers. The show was funded by the National Endowment for the Arts. Evaline's short biography began, "Ohm is her mantra."

She wrote Hunt, "I am reading about dry-weather gardening and high-altitude cooking." She wrote: "My grandfather's ghost is nowhere on that farm though I've had plenty of opportunity to search for it. I see now that in all those scenes he was only a supporting actor; the subject is me, me, me!" She wrote, "The corporation is buying up all Beckham's gourds for bluebird houses."

When on the next Sunday Nancy went curiously to the Presbyterian Church she expected its liturgy would now seem inconsequential. Members would buzz about the kidnapping; above the gossip the organ would sound reedy considering the heights and depths she now knew. And if you set on a scale a thimble's worth of grape juice on one side and in the balance the death of Ervin Childers and her joyful rage resulting? Except that Beck, having funds of his own, was so looking forward to the offertory, Nancy probably wouldn't have gone at all.

Before she had even climbed the church stairs the choir director spotted her. "Oh good, we're short an alto!" Matter-of-factly she was hurried into the annex and zipped into the robe she used to wear. "Glad you're back," said the bass, getting in line, and the soloist held out her open book, "Number one hundred and two; you know it."

Indeed she did know and sang the hymn easily in harmony with the rest. Never had she sung so well nor surveyed the congregation with quite so much unforced affection; they were unchanged, but they were simultaneously new to her. The sermon on Psalm 103 she only dimly apprehended—the subject was Infinite Mercy, she knew that much—but when the middle verses were read in a ringing voice she felt deeply if vaguely moved and wondered if her cycle was coming due again. Later the Gloria Patria grew so large in her throat that she ached from its fullness, or maybe from the sight of Beckham so solemnly tithing his recent income as the plate came by and then turning to watch his envelope carried on row by row until safely brought to the altar.

On the day the generous bank loan came through and the Blue Bird Corporation actually had money to expend, Nancy hurried home to tell her business partners. In the dark hall and through parted velvet hangings she could see the glow from television, hear the ethereal harp music that meant someone's constipation had been eased by modern science. It was midafternoon but the room was darkened so the colors on the screen would seem sharp and clear. When she entered the parlor saying, "Mama? Beck?" Mama flung up a spread hand as if toward an overhead fly. "Mama, we got the money!"

Without turning, Beckham, head outlined with television aura, said, "Hey, Nancy."

She picked up the cat, which set up a thrumming in its throat. "We got the full loan." She thought her mother might rise to embrace her but she was only leaning forward to point to a news bulletin on the screen.

"I heard you. Did you see that? Bing Crosby is dead. Maybe they'll name this street Boykin again."

Both swayed in their chairs to see around her, to watch the image of the dead crooner singing, "Would you like to swing on a star?" She noticed a large brown envelope propped on the mantel in the monkeys' alabaster grasp. "Is that from Hunt?"

"With this loan, will you still be moving west?"

"That's right, Mama." The letter was fat with enclosures.

"Then I'm sorry about the money."

Nancy was angry but, as usual these days, could not sustain the anger since Mama would never change.

And I already have. "You can come see us." She hurried with the letter to the kitchen while the television sang, "Carry moonbeams home in a jar / and be better off than you are."

Hunt wrote: "A weekend, halfway between? What city would you like to see under your own volition? Will your business affairs be cleared up by Christmas so we can get married?"

He wrote: "Glad you've stopped blaming your family for so much, as I have not wanted just to be your escape from them. Knowing that now you could stay on in Greenway is exactly how you know you can leave."

He wrote: "Wasn't Calvin the one whose eulogy at his wife's funeral said in its entirety, 'She never kept me from my work?' Would you consider Methodist?"

The thickest part of the letter was one of Chan's typical communications, which had been coming weekly, a tumble of scraps and notes, clippings and annotated cartoons, all crammed into a red envelope she had glued together at the last minute from construction paper. Nancy emptied fragments on the kitchen table. A recipe on a 3-by-5 card, herb tea for rheumatism. A photocopy of directions for crocheting a bedspread—in the marginal note Chan boasted that she had begun this very project "for *my* hope chest, for you and Hunt. On this end things look serious." One scrap contained a name and address in Atlanta, "He owes Lewis money; call him if your loan falls through. Lewis already has." There was a map of Globe with crayon circles around the new subdivisions where houses were for sale. Under one paper clip, obviously prompted by Hunt, last Sunday's program for eleven a.m. services at Globe's Methodist church and then, for fairness, the Presbyterian—its mimeo ink a bit smudged. On the back of one of these was Chan's answer to a remark Nancy had made on the phone. "Of course religion was never intended to provide happiness, only to mature the soul."

Then, inside still another envelope—this one used and turned wrong side out—were photographs Chan had taken: Nancy, still bruised, beside Lewis, beside Chan, with the retriever puppies. Nancy and Hunt posed stiffly against a backdrop of mountains that seemed painted in place.

Last of all was a floor plan of the Busy House, speckled with notations and advice. "This whole thing could be cleared out," said the heading, underlined twice. "Bathroom plumbing but no kitchen. See chimney, lower left. 1800 square feet." In a later hand, in green ink, the afterthought, "I wouldn't intrude." And upside down, an arrow pointing to "because I might get married myself, who knows?"

When the thick leaves that pressed upon the house were turning yellow and red, Mama fell in the bathtub. One elbow was broken. The left knee swelled to the size of a melon. Dr. Preslar put her on heavy cortisone. Her face broke out in rashes and the wheelchair had to be unfolded so all day, complaining, she could sit in it combing out wads of hair.

The maid was rehired; Nancy billed the Rayburns for half the cost. Still she was rushed and tired, running errands, driving Beck to the auction house, having less time to write letters to Hunt.

She did write: "Every day is as frustrating as it used to be, yet I'm less frustrated. But please come Thanksgiving."

And Chan wrote, "Oh well, what does a denomination matter? They were good workers, those Presbyterians."

During one of their telephone talks from Globe, Hunt put his mother on so she could ask, "Nancy? Are you happy?" She had started to answer *yes* when Chan corrected herself. "Or cheerful? That's surely better." Then Nancy was uncertain which to choose.

As November grew closer, the Finches finally made themselves accept that Hunt was coming for a visit, that perhaps even by the new year Nancy would marry him and go away. "Now don't expect too much, Nancy; promise me that!" cried Faye. "And if he isn't what you remember, don't let pride hold you to any promises. You'll always have a home here."

"I'm sure."

"Where will the man sleep?" Mama was trying to get both the TV and her heating pad at the right setting. "Economy Motel? That's the only one."

Nancy had been there with Joel; she said in a rush, "He'll stay in this house where he belongs. You're nearly well."

"He can have my room," offered Beckham. "I'll use the couch in here. I can look at movies all night."

"This is *my* house," Mama said. "People will sleep separate in *my* house, Nancy Finch. And with me crippled down here? Maybe Faye ought to stay overnight to chaperone."

By then, with Thanksgiving near, Nancy could pass easily through the long silver beam from the television set that pinned them both in place, could cross the parlor now without announcing that TV would rot the brain.

On the day Hunt was flying into Charlotte, Nancy—wearing her new tailored suit—walked across the video beam, barely noticing the teenager onscreen in her tutu, doing her tap routine while the frantic orchestra played "Get Happy," but examining the sight on her own face enlarging in the mantel mirror, less tan now and with one permanent notch cut through her quizzical eyebrow. She slid away the alabaster monkeys, who could neither see nor speak nor hear evil, in order to have a fuller view of the last monkey—herself—who could do evil and know it. But her chin was up, her mouth had lifted; all the old bruises had been absorbed from within.

Patting her hair, Nancy said, "I'm leaving for the airport now." In the mirror she could see that Mama and Beck were concentrating on how the young dancer clattered and spun in place. Though the blue light of television flung them into the looking glass like phantoms, it also lit on their faces an identical expression of what Nancy would have called happiness. Her face was only cheerful. They did not notice the smile she gave them, but she did not mind.